C000155206

BITE ME, ROYCE TASLIM

BITE ME, ROYCE TASLIM

LAUREN HO

HYPERION

Los Angeles   New York

Copyright © 2024 by Lauren Ho

All rights reserved. Published by Hyperion, an imprint of Buena Vista Books, Inc. No part of this book may be reproduced or transmitted in any form or by any means, electronic or mechanical, including photocopying, recording, or by any information storage or retrieval system, without written permission from the publisher. For information address Hyperion, 77 West 66th Street, New York, New York 10023.

First Edition, May 2024
1 3 5 7 9 10 8 6 4 2
FAC-004510-24053

Printed in the United States of America

This book is set in Berkeley Pro/ITC
Designed by Zareen Johnson

Library of Congress Cataloging-in-Publication Data

Names: Ho, Lauren, author.
Title: Bite me, Royce Taslim / by Lauren Ho.
Description: First edition. • Los Angeles : Hyperion, 2024. • Audience:
    Ages 12–18. • Audience: Grades 7–9. • Summary: A career-ending injury
    destroys track star Agnes Chan's hopes of a college scholarship, putting
    her on a journey through the underbelly of Malaysian stand-up comedy,
    and directly into the path of her archnemesis, the ridiculously wealthy
    and disgustingly handsome Royce Taslim.
Identifiers: LCCN 2023029365 • ISBN 9781368095358 (hardcover) •
    ISBN 9781368095648 (ebook)
Subjects: CYAC: Interpersonal relations—Fiction. • Contests—Fiction. •
    Stand-up comedy—Fiction. • Malaysia—Fiction. • LCGFT:
    Romance fiction. • Novels.
Classification: LCC PZ7.1.H5964 Bi 2024 • DDC [Fic]—dc23
LC record available at https://lccn.loc.gov/2023029365

Reinforced binding

Visit www.HyperionTeens.com

Logo Applies to Text Stock Only

To Sophie and Henry

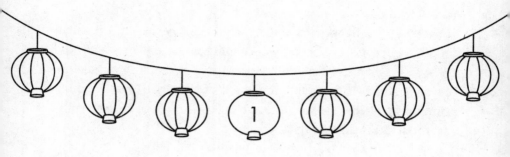

FRIENDS, EVERYONE SHOULD OWN A PAIR OF LUCKY UNDERWEAR.
Everyone.

Now, I'm not superstitious per se, but it's probably not a coincidence that in the two weeks since senior year started, every time I wore this exact pair of gray *Rick and Morty* briefs I've equaled or broken my personal best at the hundred-meter dash, my pet event. Sure, I did spend all summer training with the national sprint team, but I suspect the new breakthroughs I'm seeing have been aided by Messrs. Rick and Morty.

Too bad it wasn't another pair, though. This pair's a little old; they haven't always been gray.

Okay, fine, maybe I am a *little* superstitious. But only because I'm a prudent person and want to cover all my bases. It pays to be lucky; I should know. Going to my current school has taught me that luck is indispensable in life. For instance, if you are lucky enough to be born rich, you can have zero personality and still rise to the top of everything like fresh soap scum on water. The rest of us with just rich inner lives have to content ourselves with making it the old-fashioned way—with lots of effort and charm.

I sigh, plucking at the fraying hem of my shorts. Sometimes it's hard to be so rich in inner life; after all, it's impossible to rub your inner life in other people's faces.

There is a jolt of color darting across the adjacent field. I home in on the wearer, Royce Taslim, working out in the distance, the only one wearing neon-orange-and-black running tights. Why would anyone own, and wear, such bright-colored running gear? Flash, I think grimly, is an offense against taste and is possibly a sign of deep spiritual rot, if not malignant deviancy.

Royce Taslim is clearly rotten, despite that glossy-haired, tan-skinned facade. Deep inside, where it truly matters.

"Chan, are you tracking their times or daydreaming?" Coach Everett—the girls' coach—barks. Tall, lean, and in his fifties, Coach Everett was a former national junior title holder in the hundred meter in his youth and now, as he likes to remind us from time to time, one of the best coaches around, although we are not sure what *around* means, geographically and otherwise.

"Yes, Coach!" I say, holding up the iPad. As team captain, I am in charge of charting the team's and individual best times per practice session. I also have the "honor" of handling various routine tasks that Coach Everett has delegated to me, such as ordering sports equipment and team uniforms, mundane administrative work that brings no glory. Somehow, despite being a top-three nationally ranked junior sprinter with NCAA aspirations—every promising young Malaysian athlete knows that to bring their game to the next level, they have to be in the US collegiate system—I'm doing grunt work. I hear that my esteemed cocaptain of track-and-field, Mr. Neon-Pants Royce, does nothing of this sort. I guess the Taslim name shields you from drudgery.

"Good," Coach Everett says, marching past me to get to his seat by the track, already drenched in sweat. It's our lovely tropical weather here in Kuala Lumpur; even though the state-of-the-art running track in the Dunia American International School is partially covered, the temperature hovers around thirty-two Celsius in the shade and even higher on the adjacent field. Coach's temper is shorter on days like this. I make a note to kick extra butt in the hundred-meter dash, which is next.

I line up the track with my teammates Tavleen Kaur, Tan Qiu Lin, Lina Nguyen, and Suraya Ismail; get into the starting position; and wait for Coach Everett's signal. I turn to my teammates and give them what I hope is a smile. I've been told I'm not much of a smiler by my younger sister, Rosie, but you can't trust anyone under the age of twelve.

"On your marks!" Coach Everett shouts.

I slip into runner mode, a state of mind where I become hyper-focused and aspects of me are dialed up to eleven out of ten while other senses are muted. Anything that isn't running related fades into the background.

The electronic starting pistol fires and we take off. I take off. I transform.

I am not *just* Agnes Chan, wearer of *Rick and Morty* underpants, mediocre student, and largely unremarkable—even forgettable.

I am *the* Agnes Chan, track superstar, captain. Confident and well-liked, someone who has earned every right—if not more—to be where she is.

I cross the finish line ahead of my teammates, of course, and every-one on the girls' track team whoops and cheers—"Agnes! Agnes!" The electronic scoreboard tells me my time: 11.81 seconds on the hundred-meter dash—a new personal best. The high of my win mixes with a warm sense of camaraderie as the girls boost me onto Tavleen's shoulders. Yes, in spite of everything that's happened in my past, I can be a little lucky sometimes.

~

After track, I walk across the immaculate emerald lawn of the seventy acre campus of Dunia American International School, whose imposing buildings combine traditional Malaysian architecture with modern, state-of-the-art facilities, to the bus stop outside the school, earbuds in place. I thumb through my favorite post-workout track list of pop music, trying to find a song that matches my mood. The Hot Flashes—incidentally, my tongue-in-cheek nickname for the sprint team—are on a streak. We are going to crush the other teams in the upcoming interschool meet. Then my Malaysian teammates and I have the state championships followed by the biennial Southeast Asian Games in early February, where I aim to beat the times that won me last year's silver and bronze medals in the hundred meter and relay respectively at a recent national meet.

"I'm calling it now," I say out loud in defiance of my cultural upbringing and inherent superstition. "This is the Year of The Chan." If my senior year continues on the same trajectory as my junior year, then there is no stopping me.

I change my mind on music and instead select one of my favorite stand-up specials by the meteoric Canadian comic, Amina Kaur, to help me unwind during my long commute to the Ampang suburb where one of the unofficial Koreatowns of the city is located. *100% Kaur-nadian* is a searing one-hour set just burning with brilliant observations on everything from cultural imperialism to making and trying maple taffy on what must have been dirty ice for the first time to bond with her cute crush and shitting herself for hours afterward. My four-hour shift at Seoul Hot—the Korean BBQ restaurant at which I have been working off the books for the past ten months—starts in an hour. I'll need the laughs to get me through what will be a brutal shift. My muscles are jittery with fatigue, so much so that I don't have the energy to avoid my nemesis, Royce Taslim, who is cutting across the lawn toward the school gates, smiling from the good fortune of being born Royce Taslim.

You know how some people walk like they have a spotlight on them, and they never, ever have dandruff or trip over their shoelaces? That's Taslim. Mr. Benignly Perfect. Wearing a black Supreme hoodie, jeans, white Onitsuka Tigers, and the smile of a guy who knows that at the end of the day, somebody other than him will be washing the underwear that I hope, hope right now is sticking stickily to his sweaty butt. It's not jeans weather, my friends, but trust Taslim not to have gotten the memo.

Taslim falls into step beside me, and we do that chin-jerk thing at each other. We cross the lawn and filter out of the imposing gates to where the car pickup area is in silence. I try not to blink excessively at the sight of him, because I read somewhere that blinking can be construed as a sign of anxiety—or was it attraction? And there is absolutely no reason Taslim can cause me anxiety, or attraction, none at all. Sure, he has raven-black hair that offsets his large almost-amber eyes, and I *suppose* he's tall and muscular, but take that all away and what do you have? A skeleton; yes, we're all just walking skeletons under all that skin and hair. Besides, winning the genetic lottery isn't something to admire in a person, and neither is generational wealth, although some may beg to differ.

But the thing that really puts me on guard when it comes to Royce is his unbearable polish. Everything about him is so on point, from the way he speaks to his outfits. Yawn, but also—ick. You never know where you stand with people like that. Still waters run deep, etc., etc. Unlike Royce Taslim, with Agnes Chan, what you see is what you get.

"Chan," he says pleasantly.

"Taslim," I say, a dismissive beat later and two decibels louder. Because anything he can do, I can do better.

He raises an eyebrow and mimes the removal of my earbuds, even though I'd discreetly put the special on pause the moment I saw him out of the corner of my eye. I sigh and remove them. We come to a stop beside the pickup lane.

"Good practice?"

"Phenomenal," I say. I'm on a personal quest to improve my vocabulary and have taken to using a thesaurus for fun. "I've just had the most marvelous session. Yourself?"

"It went well," Taslim, who is Indonesian and speaks with a hybrid Indon-British accent, thanks to years of private tutoring, international schooling, and breathing in the fortifying fumes of money, says. "I broke a state record, unofficially, of course." He is the school javelin throw champion—but last I heard, he's not headed to the NCAA because he doesn't qualify, despite his being an interschool champion in Malaysia. Only the truly gifted get to compete at NCAA level. This knowledge keeps me warm at night—well, figuratively. It's always hot in Kuala Lumpur, it being an equatorial city.

"I, uh, br—shattered"—I scrabble for some kind of new personal achievement and come up with nothing—"the national record for the hundred-meter dash today, unofficially, of course," I lie smoothly. I was still three-tenths a second off the national record, but hey.

Taslim nods. I decide I dislike how his thick, gleaming brows resemble furred em dashes. "I guess that means we're on track to lead track and field together again?" he says. We'd been cocaptains at school for two years now.

Did—did he just pun at me? Surely not dull-as-dishwater Taslim. Anyway, even if he did, puns are wasted on him, because he makes everything—what's the antonym of *cute*?

Unappealing. Unattractive. Especially unattractive. Dassit.

"Mayhap we are," I say coolly.

"Pardon?"

"Possibly," I snap, coloring.

"Nice," he says.

We stare at each other, me predatorily, him bushy browly. There is no love lost between us—well, on my side at least. Taslim probably isn't even too bothered by the fact that we're one of three shortlisted athletes competing for the title of Student Athlete of the Year, an award set up by our school's alumni organization for graduating seniors that comes with a cool scholarship prize of RM20,000 and a lifetime membership to a popular gym franchise here. It's prestigious, and I could use that money for college and other things. Taslim doesn't need that money, and I hate that Taslim is in the running for the title and my only realistic competition for it—the other kid doesn't count because she's barely district-level, a token nominee, really.

It's been this way ever since I transferred to Dunia four years ago: Taslim and me, duking it out for sporting supremacy.

At the corner of my eye, I see his ride: a black Rolls-Royce Cullinan rolling up to the pickup point, the windows tinted for ultimate privacy. Even in a school filled with expat children—of diplomats, politicians, chief this-and-that, medical and legal professionals—that have drivers picking them up, the SUV is flashier than most, attracting stares from the jaded rich kids. When it arrives at the pickup point, a bodyguard jumps out and opens the door for Royce, in case, you know, he hurts his wrist doing that.

"Wow," I mutter, not entirely under my breath.

"Is something wrong?"

"I'm allergic to show-offs," I reply, giving him a pointed look.

He nods, a sympathetic expression on his face. "Must be tough, in this school."

"Oh my God, stop it!" I say, stamping my foot on the ground.

"Stop what?" Royce says, glancing around.

"This! Whatever this faux-nice persona is. I'm your only competition for Student Athlete of the Year, so treat me with the distaste I deserve and reserve for you," I say to Royce impatiently.

Royce stands stock-still. He'd probably never been called out in his life. I steel myself for the explosion that must come. There's a long silence, almost as loud as the roar of blood rushing through my head. "I don't see you as competition, Chan," he says at last. Something in his voice flattens out. "I'll see you around."

Not his competition? How absolutely insulting, as though I am beneath his consideration. "Wh-what?" I sputter in rage. "How dare you! Don't you walk away from me, Taslim," I sputter, running after him. "Don't you—"

He turns, and his eyes widen. "Agnes! Watch out!" he shouts, lunging toward me.

But it's too late.

I feel it before I know what has hit me, literally—my luck, finally running out.

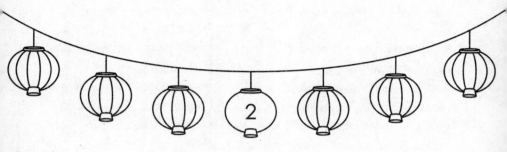

2

THERE IS A KNOCK ON THE DOOR. THREE STACCATO TAPS AND A clearing of throat. Even without speaking, I know who it is.

"Agnes, dear, I bought you food. Can I come in?"

"Berghhhh," I say in reply, which every mother understands as "Yes, please enter at your own risk." I can smell what she has brought, and it is not food. It is punishment.

The door opens and my posture automatically rights itself. From the mirror I'd fixed on my desk I watch as my mother enters head-first, eyes wary, before the rest of her appears, clutching a tray of something that smells so foul I know it has to be expensive traditional Chinese herbs of some kind. She blinks a little as her eyes adjust to the dark, pierced only by the light from the laptop screen; then her lips curl when she smells me. My room has not been aired since I was discharged from the hospital two weeks ago; that, and the fact I have been marinating in my despair and rage at the hit-and-run driver and barely showering, must have been a potent mix.

She approaches me gingerly with the tray as I continue to ignore her. Her body language is that of someone approaching an area dotted with land mines. She's trying to ignore the bestial howls coming from the speakers, thinking it's coming from the computer game I'm playing, but it's actually an experimental emo band I found on Spotify called Holy Yeast.

"You look well," she says in her sunny, Encouraging Mom voice.

I don't look up from my killing of insurgent militia in *Counter-Flash: HardBoiled*. I'm in the same sweats I've been wearing for the past few—days. "Mmfffph." I probably should change, but inertia tells me why bother. Come to think of it, I've not moved from my chair, much less my room, since I got back from the hospital, aside for toilet breaks and my twice-weekly physiotherapy sessions. It's possible that the gaming chair and I are one now. I am Chairperson.

"So, Agnes, how are you feeling today?"

One of the enemy soldiers I'm grappling with shakes me off and tries to shank me and I dodge. I drive my Superior Huntsman Knife into his body, aiming, as all experts know, for the mid left of the abdomen, around the one or two o'clock position from the umbilicus, where the abdominal aorta lies. *Die. Die. Die.* Blood fountains. He dies. I grunt, satisfied. "'Kay, I guess."

"So, tomorrow you start school again, isn't that fun?"

Grunt.

"You must miss school so much after two weeks of resting at home."

"Uh-huh," I say, which is a neutral way of responding to this question.

Because the truth is I'm afraid.

Come tomorrow, I'll know for sure what will happen to my track career, the one thing I'd been building with intention since I was eleven; it's also the one thing that really gave my mother motivation to lift herself out of the mist that engulfed her for so many years, leading her to seek the professional help she needed, and—by fate, chance, whatever you believe guides our paths—to Stanley. To our fragile new life.

My phone screen pings with a notification, and I ignore it after a quick check. It's Zalifah "Zee" Bakri, my closest friend from school. REUNITING & IT FEELS SO GOOD! 🏝

Which is all great and everything, but I wish the other Hot Flashes would show more concern. After the accident, the texts from my teammates quickly tailed off—I'm hoping they'll pick up again once I get back in school.

My mother perches on the bed. "Do you . . . do you want to talk about your meeting with Coach Everett and Coach Mellon tomorrow?"

"What's there to talk about?" I say as I hack another soldier's arm off on-screen with a Dirty Bone Cleaver. Mirror Mom cringes, so I stop playing and save the game. I keep my face impassive as I turn to face her.

"Agnes, you can tell me anything."

I take a deep breath. "There's nothing to tell. I feel fine."

"But Dr. Koh says"—she stops when she sees me blanch at the name of the surgeon—"things might not . . . be the same with—"

"Shhhhhh!" I say, bringing my hands to my ears. "Choi, choi, choi! Mom! We don't talk about the Bad Thing unless it's come to pass. I told you!" I cross my toes under the chair.

"Okay, okay," she says, alarmed at the high-pitched note in my voice. "We won't speak about it until your next review."

I calm down. "Thank you," I say, regretting my outburst at the pinched look on her face. I force myself to smile, painfully. It does not reassure her at all. Strange.

"There's, erm, something else you should know before you go to school tomorrow," Mom says, looking a little discomfited.

"What is it?"

My mother has on her faux-casual voice. "The Taslims kind of offered to pay for your surgery and physiotherapy."

I tighten my grip around the arm rest of my chair. "What?" Then, hiss-ily—as far as it is possible to hiss when a word has no S. "When?"

"Coach Everett told me this when he called me to check on you last week. Said Ming Taslim, who's on the board of that sport charity of theirs, Rebuilding Champions, the one similar to the Make-A-Wish

Foundation but for sick or hurt athletes from . . . well, disadvantaged backgrounds—says all you have to do is officially submit a request for assistance."

I'd rather crawl through a field of glass, I don't say out loud.

"And what did you say?" I ask, deadly calm.

"I told Coach Everett our insurance is taking care of it."

Bullshit. Or, well, half bullshit.

I exhale in relief, not bothering to counter her white lies. "Good. Don't ever take her money," I say. "It's blood money, siphoned from the veins of orangutans." I wrinkle my nose. "Also, come to think of it, I'm not exactly the neediest person she could throw money at, so there's probably an ulterior motive." I snap my fingers as epiphany strikes. "Aha! She's probably worried I'll say something in the press and implicate Taslim, who was talking to me when I crossed the road. Sure, I literally walked in front of traffic and forgot to, like, look for traffic, but Taslim was still somewhat involved. The whole world knows she's launching her Modern Asian Parent platform and app next month and it would be bad press to have her son linked to this, so she's trying to *buy my silence*."

"Agnes," my mother says.

My phone pings again. I glance at the screen: Coach Everett. Speak of the devil.

Hey, Chan, hope all is well. Looking forward to our meeting on Monday.

We are supposed to have a video call with Coach Mellon, my recruiter at the University of Maryland, to receive the verdict of what would happen to my place on the team in light of my latest checkup a few days ago with Dr. Koh, my orthopedic surgeon. Given that Coach Everett needed to plan for the upcoming meets during my absence, both my mother and I had given Dr. Koh permission to brief Coach Everett over a call last weekend on my condition, as far as it related to my ability to participate competitively. Now, I'd encouraged Dr. Koh not to panic Coach Everett—I believe my exact words were "Let's gently massage the truth and present the bestest-case scenario, how-about-it"—but who knows what the stupid Hippocratic oath requires physicians to do, urgh.

Yup, see you, I reply. I'm worried. If Coach Mellon rescinds my offer—

I shake my head, trying to stay positive, or at least look positive in front of my mother, who is hovering. I need to be on the team, otherwise all my college plans would have to be reset. I'd been recruited by University of Maryland early in junior year, and everyone knew that meant I was a star. If that is taken away, I'd have to scramble and apply to schools just like everyone else, based on my grades, which is not ideal. I'm just good at running. I'm not an all-rounder like Tavleen, who's a flautist and a mathlete, or Suraya, who is a concert pianist. I'm a B+-student at best. It's my fault—I don't apply myself the way I do to sports. When it comes to sports, I've always been all in, tunnel-vision style. And now I have nothing else.

Nothing.

The soup smells sour and earthy; bone, crushed root, and what looks like slivers of keratin swirling in the liquid. I wince and push the concoction away from me on the tabletop. "Yuck. Do you even know what this soup does?"

Her smile wobbles on its axis. "I think the man in the medicine hall said it'll help with the muscles, increase qi and blood flow."

"It's not my muscles that need help." I throw this sentence out like a gauntlet. Her face, always an open book, flutters shut.

I close my eyes and take a beat. It's not my mother's fault that I fractured my fibula like a jackass. It's not her fault my career in senior year is possibly over—and that probably means any collegiate running career is jeopardized, too. By one stupid mistake. *Just like when Mom*— I shake my head to clear it. "It's cool. I'll drink it." Then, with my eyes still closed, add, "Sorry." I'm usually very careful with Mom, controlled.

"It's okay," she says quietly. Seems like being a parent is 90 percent eating the shit your kid doles out and saying it's fine, at least in my case.

She reaches out and musses my long, greasy hair, something she hasn't done in ages. I don't protest. Then she leaves. I sigh and contemplate the soup, knowing my mom probably went out of her way to find the best medicine hall, the most reputed herbalist. I take the spoon and let the steam waft off the bark-brown liquid in the porcelain spoon. The first sip of the soup hits my senses, hot and bitter, as love does.

~

On an overcast Monday morning, Stanley fires up the family minivan—his words, not mine—and begins the arduous rush-hour drive to school, with me riding shotgun and Rosie, my eleven-year-old stepsister, at the back.

"Agnes, you look like poop," Rosie tells me cheerfully, pushing her dark bronze ringlets out of her eyes as she meets my gaze in the rearview mirror. I have not made any effort with my appearance on my first day back to school. It's not as though someone's going to comment on how shiny my hair is in its regulation ponytail—it's still not—when my right lower leg is in a bulky gray splint and I'm hobbling around on forearm crutches that my doctor insisted I use for at least a month, with two more weeks to go.

"Language," Stanley says mildly.

"Rosie, what have I been saying? If you want to hurt someone, you have to be more specific. Details matter. Don't shy away from being descriptive. For example, instead of saying *The sight of you annoys me* you got to say something like *That nose of yours belongs on a butt, it should be kept out of my sight.*"

Rosie giggles. "Butt. Ha-ha-ha."

"Originality would get you more points," I continue with the full wisdom of my years. "Maybe instead of just *butt*, say, a *yeti's butt* or—"

"Enough butt talk," Stanley says crisply. "Rosie, that wasn't nice. Don't be a bully."

"We're just kidding ar—"

"Words cut deep, girls, deeper than flesh wounds, sometimes; remember that a pen is mightier than a sword?" Stanley says. We roll our eyes at him in response but stop. My stepdad has a way of commanding obedience that, to me, is way more effective than my mother's anger. It's probably because he's been a teacher for almost two decades, to teenagers to boot.

"Whoever said that obviously never bled out from a swordfight," Rosie whispers. Her father ignores her.

"I agree," I stage-whisper to Rosie. She grins.

On the road the traffic starts getting dense. I sigh. When my mom drives us, we always get to school in twenty minutes, avoiding the jam and speeding tickets, all at once.

"Dad, can you hurry up," Rosie whines. "I want to get to school before Jasmine does."

"Slow and steady does the trick," Stanley says. We roll our eyes again—he and his Stanley Sayings. At the rate Stanley is driving—a snail's pace in moving traffic—I almost wish my mother was at the driver's helm. Almost. But Stanley more than makes up for it in other ways. He lets Rosie and me choose the music for the drive, and we can sing along as loud as we want. If you see a beige Nissan Serena—with one adult wincing while two adolescent girls howl, wolflike, to Taylor Swift and BlackPink—crawling through the streets of Kuala Lumpur—that's us, although at first glance you might not have guessed that we're a family. Stanley and Rosie are biracial white Haitian American, while I'm Chinese Malaysian, but spend two minutes with us in the minivan and it's clear that we know far more about each other's toileting habits than we care to admit. Besides, the fact is Rosie and I are far too blasé about Stanley's off-key singing for us not to be a family. We also know that every Thursday night is Date Night and to never, ever, walk down the landing in front of their bedroom after ten p.m., for various reasons.

"Agnes, you have your meeting with Coach Mellon and Coach Everett later to discuss your spot, correct?"

I nod. A slim flame of hope rises in my chest. Maybe, notwithstanding the scans, he thinks—I give my head a shake, unable to even hope against hope that I could still run for the interschool meet, not after what I'd heard the surgeon say. But in five months—three, if I have my way—could they wait for me to heal, field me for the state championship and nationals at least?

The minivan slows to a stop at the traffic light, almost imperceptibly. Stanley turns around and looks me in the eye. "Hey, Agnes?" Stanley has on his Stern Face, although the effect is ruined by his kind eyes and ready-to-smile lips. Stanley once tried to call me sweetie when he first met me four years ago, but my growl dissuaded him from trying ever again.

"Yeah, Stanley?" Rosie calls my mother Mom, but I call Stanley Stanley, which he's fine with. I've never had a dad growing up and the word *Dad* fills me with a dread I don't quite comprehend. I suspect my mother would prefer I call him Dad, though.

"Even if you aren't a runner, you're still special," he says, fibbing with the conviction of an educator.

My eyes blur with tears and I have to look away. Family will tell you lies to keep you.

We stop in front of the drop-off point for high schoolers first. I get out with Stanley's and a traffic warden's help, wincing but stable. "I'll pick you up after school, so just text me when you're ready to go, okay?" he says.

I nod and start my careful way to the gates.

Just then, a scream rends the air. I close my eyes and wait for the torrent of energy that is Zee as she flings her arms around me in a squeal of delight. "Agnes!" she sings. "Welcome back!"

"Zee," I say, laughing, swaying a little on my crutches. She makes a big show of sniffing my face and hair and saying how she misses the stink of me. In spite of my current doom-and-gloom mode, seeing her immediately cheers me up; I can't help it. I'd describe it as being hit by a Care Bear Stare in the gut—my shoulders loosen and a smile involuntarily etches across my grump face.

"Baby dear," she says, drawing back from me gently. She steadies me by my shoulders, then turns and lightly nudges my hip with hers and takes my school bag after some resistance from my part. It crosses my mind that this might be the first time Zee has ever carried someone else's literal burden on their behalf—as a child of a chief minister and one of the great-grandchildren of one of the founding fathers of Malaysia, she is always hemmed in by help, even the unhired kind, at school. Sucky-phants, as she calls them.

We're an odd pair, if you examine us individually. Aside from going to the same classes, we don't have much else in common, in terms of background, class, family, interests, music, etc. We don't even like the same food (I'm not a bread person, and she is, for example). But we do share a hate of sycophants, ball polishers (her words), and people who think *woof* is a good response to anything.

Zee and I met when I first arrived at Dunia four years ago, after Stanley and my mother got married and I transferred to this school. We happened to sit next to each other in my first class, and the teacher assigned her as my orienteering buddy. After class ended, she introduced herself and waited for the calculative light of recognition to flare in my eyes, but it never came. I didn't know what her name meant, didn't recognize her from the society mags her family appears in, and even after I knew who she was, I didn't change how I interacted with her, that is to say with polite disinterest, until she made an offhand comment on our fourth day together that made me snort-choke so hard I almost peed, and I responded with a quip that made her eyes bulge, and a friendship was cemented. She comes from old money, from a political dynasty, and my genuine disinterest in all that came as a relief to her. Four years later we're still great friends, which is a miracle when you understand how big the power imbalance—if you're one who thinks in such terms when it comes to relationships—between us is: She has all the networks, power, money, and I have nothing to offer her in return. Yet she knows that if her connections and money were the only way to get me out of a situation, or to improve my lot, I'd be too proud to use them. In fact, I'd once joked that I would rather show my junk on OnlyFans. "Though," she had conceded the first time I said that, "one has to have something worth showing in order to make any money on OnlyFans, *n'est pas*?" She is not wrong. Anyway, it has become kind of our running joke.

There's still another hour before school starts, so we cut across the quad—the "scenic route" according to Zee—to get to the auditorium for a special morning assembly, Zee in her dark green hijab and long mint-green baju kurung–style uniform, me in my knee-length, dark green skirt and mint-green polo shirt.

"I can't believe I haven't seen you in over two weeks! That's a life-time!" Zee is complaining. "And you didn't even let me visit you at yours."

"It's complicated. Termites," I say evasively. The last couple of times she asked to drop by, I had the entire global pandemic as an excuse, and then I said we were renovating the place and sawdust, etc. "Maybe during Christmas break."

"Oh-kay," Zee says, raising an eyebrow but deciding not to pursue it, not least because I faked a stumble.

There are a couple of reasons why I don't let anyone visit me at mine, and I can't deny it's because I don't want my closest friend in Dunia to see how modest and unremarkable my place is compared to her home, which I've been to a few times, even for the occasional sleepover. I'm not trying to put on airs at all—everyone knows I'm Stanley Morissette's kid and I go to school almost for free unlike the exorbitant fees the others pay, but there's a difference letting them guess how big that gulf is and actually showing them.

We stroll past the immaculate athletics field under the morning sun, where a few diehards are performing drills before class. I spy Royce Taslim, alone (surprisingly) by the field, stretched out on the ground doing one-handed push-ups in a black-and-gray camo print running vest and tights that are an approximation of clothes, all clingy and filmy. Urgh, show-off.

I might have said this last sentence out loud, but Zee doesn't notice, because—following her gaze—Royce Taslim has started doing jumping jacks. My so-called friend is staring at Royce's pulsing . . . thighs.

"Zee!" I snap my fingers in front of her face, and she comes to herself with a start. Honestly, does she have no taste in boys at all?

"Sorry," she apologizes, the tips of her ears reddening.

"God is watching," I remind her.

"Says the infidel who is thinking of getting an OnlyFans account," she mutters.

She grins, and I grin back. We link hands and walk toward the auditorium, Zee gossiping at breakneck speed while I try not to think about my meeting with Coach Everett in three hours, just before lunch break.

~

Coach Everett's office is on the second floor of the glass-steel-and-concrete admin center, and I have to take the elevator. I arrive a little earlier so that I would have time to compose myself and to check for evidence of panic sweats. I knock, entering when he tells me to. Coach Mellon is already on the screen, dialing in from Maryland. I give my best smile and practically shout my greetings.

"Agnes, please sit," Coach Everett says neutrally.

I sit in the uncomfortable wooden chair before him, trying not to bounce my left leg as I'm apt to do when I'm excited and/or nervous.

"So," Coach Mellon says, "how are you feeling?"

Like crap, I say archly in my head. "Just fine, Coach," I say, straightening up and adopting my favorite expression: resting winner face. Even if I were in pain at that moment, you'd never guess. I am the picture of health—from above my waist.

"When will you make a full recovery?" he asks.

"The surgeon says it's a mild fracture, so probably in three months I can start training again." It was five or six months, minimum, but like I said, I'm feeling optimistic.

And it isn't really a *mild* fracture—it's more complicated than that, and we'd have to monitor my progress over the next few months to know if I'd be able to run competitively again. I'm trying not to let my thoughts stray down that path. If I don't think about the worst-case scenario, it might not happen.

I *need* to get to the NCAA and run. My glorious future depends upon it.

Coach Mellon sighs. "That's almost half the season, Chan. You won't be able to participate in all the big meets and we won't be able to track your performance from over here. And we're not even sure you'll be performing at optimal level when you're back."

"All I need is some time, really, I'm c-confident—"

He shakes his head and drops his eyes to his lap when he says, "I'm sorry, Chan, but we'll have to rescind our offer."

An icy numbness spreads across my face, my body. "B-but . . . but, *Coach*," I say. It is all I can say when I feel like screaming.

"I'm really sorry, Agnes," Coach Mellon says in a gentler voice, "but I can't change the rules. You knew your spot was contingent upon your meeting those requirements. I wish you the best of luck with your recovery and your career." He nods at Coach Everett. "Tom, I wish I had better news. We really wanted Agnes here."

Coach Everett sighs. "Sure, Chris."

He signs off. I sit there, wrestling with shock at the turn of events.

Coach Everett rubs his eyes with a large, calloused hand, before fixing them on me. They are compassionate. "I'm sorry, Agnes." He never calls me Agnes. "You have no idea how much this hurts me, too. You're one of our best runners . . . you're *my* best runner, bar none. But if you can't run, we'll have to take you off the team here, too."

This second punch breaks me. If I'm not on the school team, I will not be eligible for Student Athlete of the Year—I wouldn't even have the consolation of that title. Nothing to mark all I'd given of my time, my effort, my joy.

A sob erupts out of me. I try to stuff it down my gullet, but it pops out of me like bubbles from a freshly opened can. I can't believe I am crying in front of this man. I mean, I used to hold in my farts in his vicinity.

Coach Everett is called Coach Everest in jest for a reason: He is a stoic mountain of a man, but at the sound of my crying he blanches, grabs a fistful of tissues, and offers them to me, which I decline with angry shakes of my hand. "Th-this was s-supposed to be *my* year," I choke out. "Now everything is ruined."

He fumbles with the box of tissues. "Well, um, Agnes, I could put you on the reserve team, but even that's not guaranteed."

"You don't need to do that," I say, standing up with difficulty—I'm no benchwarmer, and I don't need scraps of pity. He tries to help me stand, but I wave him away, wanting to preserve the last shred of my dignity. "Thank you for your time," I say, turning to go.

"Agnes . . ."

"Please, don't feel bad." I wipe my tears away and attempt to smile. "I understand, really."

"I'm here if you need to talk," Coach Everett says awkwardly. "And, Agnes?"

"Yeah?" I say, driving my fingernails into my palm. *Get ahold of yourself. Don't look weak in front of Coach.*

"If you need anything, especially help with your grades, now that . . . now that you're in this position, please don't hesitate to reach out to me . . . any member of the team . . . we're here for you, always."

Platitudes. Great. Just what I need to get through this nightmare. I nod, attempting the world's most hideous grin, before stumbling out of his office, past the door leading to the office of Coach Fauzi, assistant boy's track and field coach, half-blinded by my tears—and into a man-wall.

"Aahhh!" I squeak, thrown backward by the collision and falling with a hard bump on my butt, my crutches skidding away.

"Oof!" Royce Taslim says, tripping over my crutches and losing his balance, landing awkwardly near me and pinning my left uninjured leg with his . . . his . . .

Pulsing thighs.

I howl. The person who had caused this entire mess in the first place, by distracting me, was now trying to injure me further? "*You,*" I say, my voice thick with loathing.

"Oh shit, are you okay, Chan?" he says, horrified by either his monumental incompetence or the state of my resting winner face. He leaps up and scrabbles around, retrieving my crutches and my book bag, before offering me a hand to help me onto my feet.

"I can get up on my own," I bluster. It takes a long minute or two of awkward trying, me grappling with the floor like I'm a turtle on my back—I don't give up easily—before I sigh and signal that I would let him take my arm.

Royce bites his lip, makes a calculation, and, ignoring my proffered arm, grabs my crutches before placing my left arm around his neck while hooking an arm around my waist; then, his left arm now holding on to my crutches, he hoists me gently to my foot in a single upward swivel, whispering, "One, two, three," as he does so. He lifts me up as though I weigh nothing, and the momentum folds me to him.

For two beats I'm resting against his chest, breathing in his body scent—*odor, body odor!* I correct myself, alarmed—my forehead resting against his hard shoulders, and I am wedged against him as securely as though we'd been waltzing. I am aware that we are both breathing loudly, and that trails of my snot are dripping down my nose onto his collarbones, plain and exposed in his V-neck tank.

I lift my eyes and a shiver skates down my spine when we lock gazes, light brown on soft black. My breath hitches as I become aware of how dense and developed the muscles of his neck and shoulder feel, which is a *totally* normal reaction when one apex predator brushes up against another. It takes one to recognize another, and like me, Taslim is a wolf, albeit a cunning one who prefers to parade in sheep's clothing.

"I'm fine," I mutter, disoriented, disengaging from his half embrace while taking care not to touch his exposed, shiny skin, for hygiene reasons. My thoughts are still in disarray, which explains why I am breathing so hard.

"Can I help you get somewhere?" he says.

"No," I say, almost spitting the word out. "Why don't you watch where you're going next time?"

He frowns. "Hey, *you* ran into *me*, Chan. This is your own fault."

"How could I have run into you when I can't even *walk*?" I cry, triggered, my passions rising. "Did you know I lost my spot at Maryland and Coach Everett k-kicked me off the school team? That everything I've worked for is gone? D-do you even understand what that feels like?"

He blinks at me, stunned. Everyone knew I was the first NCAA recruit in the school's history. "Shit, Agnes," he says when he recovers. "I'm so, so sorry. I understand what it's like t-to lose something important—"

He *understands* my predicament? Hah! A snort-laugh escapes me. "Pal, please. First off, it's Chan to you, Taslim, and second of all, no, you'll never understand," I say. "You and your perfect life"—I draw two separate circles in the air and jab a point in the space between them—"and my struggles and I are not a—a *Venn diagram*." I fall silent, overcome with emotion, some of it being triumph since I am also amazed that I was capable of bringing up math at this juncture—at least, I hope it's an accurate analogy.

He flinches. "You don't even know me," he says curtly.

I shrug. "I know enough. You are the son of Peter Taslim and Malaysian ultra-celebrity, former beauty queen, and entrepreneur Ming Taslim, the scion of a palm oil dynasty that razes virgin jungles across Southeast Asia and is now diversifying into other less polarizing sectors like sports equipment manufacturing and real estate but is basically an attempt to clean up all that dead orangutan money. Am I wrong?"

As soon as the words leave my mouth and land on Taslim's head like a ton of dead orangutans, he blanches and I know I've hit a nerve. It is a lot, what I said. Maybe part of it was spillover from my crappy meeting with Coach Everett, and Taslim was collateral damage, but I don't regret it . . . at least, not too much. Given that his family's surrounded by people who tell them they are great because they give out a few hundred thousand ringgits in philanthropic endeavors every year—peanuts when you consider their net worth, which is in the billions of *American* dollars—and are doing their best to greenwash their way to respectability, they can afford to have a few unimpressed observers.

He doesn't reply for a while. He licks his lips, and I am curiously transfixed by this act. "I'm not my family," he says at last. He shakes his head and a bitter laugh escapes him. "To think—to think I was going to offer to personally tutor you since you missed so many weeks of class—"

"What?" I say, startled. Royce, one of the star tutors of the school's peer tutorage program, wanted to tutor me? "Me?"

"Yeah," he says, an unreadable look in his eyes.

That's so nice of him, a part of me, the formerly naive version, whispers. *Plus, I hear the snack situation for his sessions are like A+, stuff like gourmet popcorn and macarons . . . drool.*

Decadence is a sign of moral rot, I counter in my head, like a perfectly normal human. *And as for his offer, no, it's not "nice," it's guilt. Have you forgotten he literally caused your accident?*

That's an exagger— But Old Me never finishes because Mature Me has silenced her with a used gym sock.

I recover and paste on a disdainful smile. "Thanks, *pal*, but I don't need your penance."

His mouth flattens. "Whatever. Forget I tried. I'll see you around, Chan." Then, without a second look, he walks away in the exact direction I was headed. *Damn it, Taslim.* I stand there till he's gone, and then I power-crutch my way after him, but also not after him. I take out my phone and text Zee to cancel her plans and meet me for lunch. This is serious.

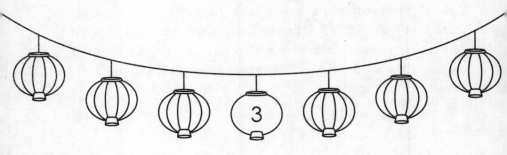

3

"THIS IS SERIOUS, ZEE," I SAY TO ZEE. **"WITHOUT MY MARYLAND OFFER,** I'll have to find some way to get to another NCAA Div One school in order to try for a walk-on. That means I've got to get better-than-good grades and find an interesting extracurricular activity to write about for my college essays!"

"Hmm?" she says, distracted. She's scanning the crowd of masticating teenagers for someone while editing a video for her social media channels under the handle @theZeeBakri, where she posts about makeup and sometimes hijabi fashion to a following of around 280K on IG and even more on TikTok.

"I'm right here!" I grumble. A couple of Flashes walk past our long table, waving but not coming over to speak. Must be busy.

"Sorry, I'm listening," she says. She reaches across the table and pats my hand. "So, what are you going to do?"

"I've no idea. I was counting on an athletic scholarship, but now it looks like I might have to pivot, capitalize on preexisting strengths, and identify new breakthrough opportunities, blergghh, something, something." We'd had some loud, very gesticulate-y unicorn startup CEO in his late twenties come in and give a talk in the first week of senior year, an alumnus of Dunia who then went to Yale or similar.

It had really annoyed me when he went on and on about how he was a self-made wizard, conveniently forgetting to mention that his dad is like some multimillionaire developer who's real chummy with politicians and who obviously could give him the seed money to fail and pivot, aka he had a Daddy Fund. "I'm supposed to meet with Ms. Tina next week to go over the options, see what I can do to improve my chances at getting into a US college, given all that's changed."

"Okay, college essays are all about growth and introspection, not really about having interesting extracurricular activities, so that's something to keep in mind."

"I think if you're good enough at something, they'll want you."

"In that case, you're good at writing, maybe we can figure out how to capitalize on that preexisting strength?" Zee's makeup tutorials feature hilarious monologues that were mostly the result of my ideation and input.

Shit. The Unicorn got us.

"I'm not awarded or anything, though," I remind her.

"We'll figure it out." Zee snaps her fingers. "Ooh, maybe you give out advice to junior sprinters and other athletes! I'll zhuzh you up, make you camera-ready. Then you can be a major TikTok influencer, like me!"

I shake my head, scoffing. "Right, like it's so easy to be a big influencer. Also, being an influencer isn't likely to get a school to scholarship-fund me, which is the actual mission, if you recall. You know I can't attend any of the schools in the US without a full or at least very generous partial ride."

She shrugs. "Hey, some TikTokkers be earning big money. At least I'm brainstorming. Seriously, though? I still don't get why competing in the NCAA is so important to you, beb."

"Sports are my best chance at being successful in life, given that I'm not a gifted student." *I'm not you*, I don't say.

"Isn't there a spectrum of possibilities between these two poles? Life isn't about achievements."

"None I will accept," I reply. If I couldn't run competitively, I'd have to find some other way to shine. I must.

Being a winner is my *identity*.

Zee chews on her lower lip as she contemplates me. As supportive as she is, she doesn't understand my yearning to distinguish myself because she has her own Family Fund. An uncomfortable silence grows between us, broken only when her phone vibrates. She drops her gaze and starts scrolling through her phone. Her tone is light as she says, "I wonder what Taslim is doing right now."

"He's right there, eating." I point to Taslim, slouched in the center of a long table filled with his usual coterie of sucky-phants/jock buddies, biting into what looks like the cafeteria's regrettable veggie burger offering. I'd clocked him as soon as I entered the cafeteria—not that I'd been searching the crowd for him, of course. He's just very hard to miss.

"Tee and Zee," she says, her eyes faraway. "Dunia's future power couple."

"You guys need to meet-cute ASAP," I say, rolling my eyes.

"Y'know, the weird thing is we kind of know each other by sight, because we grew up attending similar society events, though we've never actually talked to each other." Her expression grows dreamy. "In any case, our first meet-cute should preferably take place when I'm wearing heels, because I'm smol."

She goes back to scrolling through her social media accounts while I wonder morosely about what my options for extracurricular excellence are. We're only seven weeks in through senior year, but there's limited time left to find something extracurricular to be good enough at before college application deadlines in January; that along with my hopefully *much* improved grades should ensure that some good-enough school would give me at least a partial scholarship. If this all sounds very vague, it's because I'd never given this path a lot of thought—I'd never expected to need a plan B.

But it's time to face the truth: I am unlikely to graduate a top athlete from my high school. That's over. I need to pivot. An unfamiliar panic fizzes in my stomach as I try to figure out my next steps. What would be my next move? I'd always had a plan for my future, had always known what my next steps would be: an athletics scholarship to study at an NCAA Div I university so that I'd be able to break more sprint records, then graduate and work as a coach for the national team, win Malaysia her first Olympic gold in athletics, and be set for life, no biggie—only now I'm staring down the barrel of an ordinary, mediocre life. . . .

Going from seeking podium finishes to being an average person scares me. What's the point of doing anything in life if I'm not going to be the best? And how would my failures impact my mother?

"Ooh!" Zee squeals, jolting me out of my dour thoughts. She looks up from her phone. "I know where Taslim will be this Wednesday after school, and you're coming with me."

"Oh?" I say cautiously, remembering the time Zee suggested we camp out in the hotel lobby where an up-and-coming boy band J-qoo were filming a music video, oh, I don't know, a plane ride away in Langkawi. When we were thirteen.

Zee is unconcerned with my concern. "In the comments section of his latest post, his teammate Shyam asked if he's going to skip out on group nosh after javelin practice as usual, to which Tee said he was and he'd be doing 'the usual' with Deepak."

"So?"

"So that means, we'll know where he's going to be Wednesday after javelin practice, because we're going to follow him. See what Tee gets up to in his spare time."

"You mean stalk him."

Zee shrugs. "So, I like to do a lil' recon on my crushes before taking action, big deal."

"I'll just let you think about how creepy it is, if a guy was doing that."

"It's not stalking if he's posting about what he's doing on IG," Zee said huffily. "But I understand if you're *concerned with the law.*"

"Okay, fine, whatever. Drag me to prison with you."

"It's going to be fun, you'll see," Zee says cheerily.

I look up and see Taslim watching us, almost as though he knows something's up. I hold his gaze boldly until he flushes and drops his gaze. *I win, Taslim,* I gloat. For some reason staring him down has set my underused heart racing and my stomach flip-flopping like an electrocuted fish. I make a note to remind myself to take antacids before our proposed criminal activity.

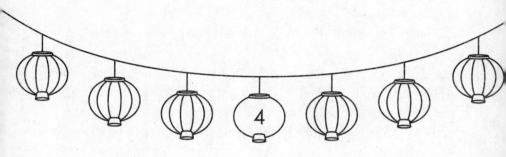

WEDNESDAY COMES. I HUNKER DOWN AT THE LIBRARY TO WAIT AS ZEE decided she needs to go home to "freshen up" for her date with destiny.

Remember, be inconspicuous, I text her as a reminder, because Zee, her survival instincts dulled by a life of luxury, has a predilection for flash and excess. We cannot stalk someone in a custom blush-pink Bentley, such as the one her mother is driven around in.

Zee's driver picks me up half an hour before I know the boy's athletics team breaks from its weekly practice session in a black Toyota Vellfire with tinted windows, i.e., her most inconspicuous family vehicle. Once I'm in, she brings up the privacy screen and I change out of my uniform into stalking-friendly attire I'd packed for this trip—a black sleeveless cotton dress for me and my white Keds. I give her a once-over: Zee is elegant in black jeans, a long-sleeved jade-green kurti, and a deep eggplant-hued headscarf, paired with seriously high black leather mules.

"Those look uncomfortable," I say.

"But my feet look amazing in them."

"I thought we were supposed to be incognito. Inconspicuous."

"Yes, that's the idea." She applies a hot-pink lipstick straight from a tube. "Just in case." She grins.

We hang out for forty minutes, playing cards and gossiping, and almost miss Taslim when he slinks out of the gate wearing a baseball cap and clear-lensed glasses, only his height and his lemon-yellow Apple watch strap giving him away, into a waiting taxi instead of his usual SUV, but not before scanning his surroundings like he's a very bad undercover agent in a hard-boiled crime novel. Interesting. It seems like Mr. Perfect might have a secret, and I am going to expose him. Not literally, of course.

~

Pak Ismail, a driver I don't recognize—Zee informs me he usually drives for her brother—obviously isn't any ordinary middle-aged man. I mean, the way he dispassionately scans me up and down, the way he sits ramrod straight despite being in his sixties, and is actually more built than most of my peers, should have alerted me to that.

The super-fluid weaving between cars as he accelerates us down the busy highway, Royce Taslim almost six cars ahead and making a turn to the right that we would have missed if Pak Ismail hadn't slalomed across two whizzing lanes of traffic to catch it, really gives it away, though.

"The trick," Pak Ismail says in Malay, not really looking at the road at all as he makes the right turn, smiling at us in the rearview mirror the whole time, "is to always keep your target in view, but not to follow too closely."

I screech when he brakes just in time to avoid flattening, I don't know, a literal *child* who decides to dart across the side road just then.

Zee is unfazed. "Pak Ismail is ex-military," she says, as though it's supposed to comfort me. *Military* means nothing to me. What he did in the military—that's more relevant. Who cares if he's the world's best sniper if he drives like a madman, which is a big part of his job?

I almost cry when Pak Ismail closes the gap between us and Taslim's cab to two cars, and then we hit rush-hour traffic on one of the highways, where, somehow, defying traffic rules and all safety precautions, a two-lane highway becomes three-lane, even four-lane at one of the exits, and we have to slow to a life-saving crawl through a classic KL traffic jam as we tail Taslim's cab into the bustling downtown. I settle down in my seat and admire the view of a metropolis dressing up for its night shift. It is almost 6:45 p.m., and the light outside the tinted windows is just starting to fade to a smoggy pink-hued extravagance, even as the army of skyscrapers flares into life. It's chaotic and beautiful and electric, but best admired from afar, not while wading through a sea of traffic.

"Where is Taslim headed?" I grumble, "Don't droids have to power down at night?"

"I'm starving," Zee complains. She has melted into a human puddle on the seat next to me and is making dramatic mewling noises.

"You're not starving; you're hungry," I say, but I root around in my bag and pass her the seaweed crackers I've been saving for pre-dinner munchies. "It's in—"

"—sulting to all the actual starving people in the world who are dying from it, I know I know, I shouldn't say that, I'm monstrous."

I shut my mouth. Zee has preempted me, word for word.

At last, Taslim's taxi slows down and takes a turn into Chow Kit, a seedy inner-city neighborhood with the largest wet market in the city and where colonial era–shophouses housing a variety of wholesalers jostle with upmarket cafés, the shop fronts burning with neon and older fluorescent signage, the creep of haphazard gentrification steadily gathering visibility, despite the area's reputation as a red-light district. I look at Zee and she looks at me. What is Taslim doing here?

Taslim's taxi turns into a side road bordered by roadside vendors in carts and food trucks selling both traditional local hawker fare like lok lok and fried carrot cake and newer, more foreign fare and edge down toward a dimly lit dead end. It stops, and Taslim hops out and, somewhat unexpectedly, heads to a roadside Ramly burger stall.

"Pull over a little farther, please," Zee tells Pak Ismail, who immediately executes a crisp left turn, narrowly avoiding knocking over a motorcyclist, and stops us in a perpendicular alley. It takes all of Zee's strength to wrench my fingers off the armrests. I stumble out with my crutches, my face ashen, hers wreathed in a placid smile. Pak Ismail speeds off to terrorize motorists anew.

We creep over to the street, poking our heads round the corner and hoping that Royce hasn't left. He hasn't. He is still waiting for his burger.

Now that we're out on the street I can smell the tantalizing aroma of bargain burger meat cooking on margarine wending its way to us. My stomach makes its plight known. "Shhh," Zee says as though that makes a difference: We're totally conspicuous as we are, waiting in the open with our backs to the building, occasionally peeking around the corner to check on Taslim, who, oblivious to his stalkers, is taking his sweet time with the street burger, probably enjoying the rare taste of trans fats.

After a while, we drop our guard and start watching TikToks, giggling. Thankfully, Taslim doesn't notice us above the general din of people and traffic. He finishes his burger at last and walks to an unmarked storefront, pauses before a scarlet door that leads to the second floor, and disappears behind it.

I turn to Zee, a finger pointed at Taslim's retreating figure, triumphant. "Did you see that?"

"Er, yes, I was right next to you."

"Rhetorical question," I say. "Going into an *unmarked* second floor of an *unmarked* shophouse in *Chow Kit*! I knew there was something seedy about Taslim. All that gel in his hair. I wonder what he's here for."

"It's seven twenty, Agnes. He's probably just here for discount electronics. This is, after all, the right place to go for that kind of stuff," Zee says, ever the generous one.

"Intellectual property infringement *is a crime.*"

Zee rolls her eyes. "Okay, let's go see what Royce is here for, then." She starts walking toward the storefront, stomping as though the pavement is a catwalk. I straggle behind, warily glancing up and down the brightly lit street, not sure what I should be wary of but sure that when it appears, I will be prepared.

"A little subterfuge maybe? Pak Ismail isn't here to protect us," I hiss.

Zee ignores me and hauls butt up the stairs; her stacked mules ring out in the stairwell, which are graffiti-laced and pocked with cigarette butts, the vermillion soles winking in the dark. I am certain they will be the last thing I see. I sigh, walking up the stairs with some difficulty; with old buildings like these, disability access is almost unheard of.

We reach the top of the staircase and find a velvet curtain, behind which a susurrus of music and low chatter drift out. I exchange glances with Zee. "Whatever is behind that curtain is not discount electronics," I mutter.

"It does look dodgy," she concedes. "Some kind of club?"

"A sex club," I say with satisfaction. My mind flashes with images, but in a detached, non-involved way. Oh boy, Taslim is going to get it now. If he isn't getting it already.

"Probably means there'll be security. We might need a password, a code."

"We can turn back," I offer.

"Are you kidding me? I didn't drive through rush-hour traffic and ruin my YSL mules to turn back now. We're going in, scaredy-cat."

"Am not!" But I still don't move.

We—well, she parts the curtain—

"Can I help you?" a man says gruffly from the shadowy alcove beside the door, nearly causing Zee and I to have a heart attack.

"Oh, sorry, Uncle! We're just a bunch of lost tourists," I squawk, clutching on to Zee's arm.

"Who are you calling uncle?" the man cries. He turns on a light switch and a desultory bulb flickers to attention. The man is in his early twenties; he is built like a mountain. There is no doubt in my mind now that this is a sex-dungeon situation.

"Maaf, maaf," Zee says. "We're, ah, looking for our friend, who just, ah, came here."

"Oh, Ray?" The man smiles.

"Ray?"

"Your friend. The performer."

"Right." Maybe everyone went by nicknames here, to keep things impersonal. "Yes, him."

"You have ID to prove you're over twenty-one?" he asks me. "If not, you won't be able to drink. We're strict here."

No alcohol to underage minors, but okay to the sex. Right. "Urm, we don't, but we'll abstain."

"Right." He nods. "Probably a good idea. Never know what happens when the crowd get drunk. They are much less forgiving of the performers. Lots of yelling, heckling. One of them even threw an empty bottle at the open miker who made fun of cricket fans."

I freeze. *Open miker* . . . Dear God, it was worse than I could imagine— Taslim was involved in amateur stand-up comedy. Taslim? Who was possibly the least spontaneous, most rigid person I knew? Who epitomized the idiom *better seen than heard*?

Also—stand-up comedy is my jam. How dare he sully it by performing. I must watch this atrocity.

"I must watch this atrocity," I say out loud.

A voice crackles over the bouncer's walkie-talkie. "Malik, we're almost full house here. Only one more seat in the house. Fire safety regulations and whatnot."

Malik makes an apologetic face "Sorry, kids, you heard the man."

"You go," Zee says generously. She isn't into stand-up comedy— she full-body cringed when she heard what was being performed. "I mean, *you're* the one who's in crutches and came all the way here and who actually likes stand-up. You can watch Taslim and let me know what you think. Then, when the show's almost over, you call me, I'll come over, smelling fresh and looking fine, and I'll pretend I saw his set." She's already calling Pak Ismail, and I hear him say he'll be around in ten minutes, which probably means three minutes. He had been eating roti canai in a nearby restaurant two streets away.

"Really? You sure?"

"Yes, I'm sure." She leans over and whispers, "Record the entire performance and send it to me." With a kiss blown in my direction, she disappears down the stairs.

Malik turns to me and says, "There's a cover charge of twenty ringgit with a drink."

Crap. I hadn't expected to pay anything; I had coins on me, nothing else. I pull out my phone to pay with an e-wallet and find my phone completely dead. Double crap. Swearing, I fish out my wallet and empty the change in one palm before laying the coins neatly on the table. "One . . . ten sen . . . oooh, fifty! Twenty sen . . . fifty . . ." I flash my most winsome smile at Malik. "Is there *any way* you can close one eye and let me in?" I push the pile of coins, which amounted to a grand sum of RM2.83, over to him. I whisper, "I won't tell anyone if you keep this."

Mailk pushes the pile of coins back at me. "Thanks, but no thanks. You either pay the full cover charge or you perform. Performers get in free."

"Well then, you should have led with that! I shall perform!" I blurt, then immediately regret it. I have never performed solo onstage in my life, ever, much less in something as dynamic as stand-up comedy. But it's that or pay, and I don't have the moolah.

He lifts an eyebrow, this talent scout. "Are you even a comic?"

"Aren't we all, when the spirit moves us?" I say mystically. "Especially gin, vodka, erm, rum." I have never drunk alcohol in my life.

He chuckles. "Okay, good one."

"So, what do I have to do to get onstage?"

"First, you need to sign up on this sheet." He hands me a clipboard and a pen, then stamps my right inner wrist with the word *comic* in blue ink. It's all very old-school. "Then you'll need a five-minute set."

Five minutes. I swallow hard. Could I really joke onstage for five whole minutes? I suppose if I speak really slowly, it will be over in a flash . . . right? I've watched so much stand-up comedy online that I must be an expert by osmosis. And some of these stand-up comedy sets I've watched were more than an hour long; I can talk onstage for five minutes, no problem. I glance at the sheet, clocking Taslim . . . *Ray's* name. Ray Lim. Who is he afraid is going to see him on a sign-in sheet of a dinky comedy club? Quel paranoia! I shake my head and scrawl *Agnes Chan* on it; I have nothing to hide.

Malik grins and opens the door to an excitable babble. "Welcome, Agnes Chan."

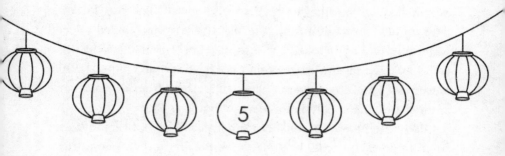

MY FIRST IMPRESSION OF THE PLACE IS, YIKES, IT'S BIGGER THAN I thought it'd be.

About thirty metal folding chairs are dotted in various configurations around tiny wooden tables in front of a small, carpeted stage with a velvet curtain backdrop, on which a banner reads KL KETAWA!: KL'S FRESHEST OPEN-MIKE NIGHT. There's a small, backlit bar bathed in neon-pink-and-white light at the end of the room with a lit sign saying COCKTAILS HERE, manned by a single faux-hawked bartender in a white sleeveless vest who's pulling a pint of beer for a customer. It doesn't look like a cocktail place, but what do I know. My only experience of nightlife before this has been twenty-four-hour mamak stalls and McDonald's. I've never stepped foot in a bar or even a comedy club until today. And now I don't know what to do with my hands and my face.

I power-crutch to the back to avoid the swiveled gazes from the full room of seated patrons. Taslim is nowhere to be seen. Presumably there's a green room or some kind of holding area for the comics? I have no idea, and no one seems inclined to brief me.

I hug the bar and ask the staff member, whose white handwritten name tag reads LAI, PRONOUNS: THEY/THEM, for a glass of water. Lai sees my cast and pulls up a folding chair for me instead of the bar stool, even as I wave their help away with mutters of "I'm fine, I'm fine, thanks," before proceeding to pour me a glass from a chilled mineral water bottle in the fridge. I offer to pay, but they decline my offer. Good, because in actual fact I could not have afforded mineral water, having just RM2.83, whereas I have just realized, from a quick glance at the menu, that a bottle of mineral water costs RM6.

"First time here?" Lai says, not exactly smiling but their eyes are friendly, soft. Up close, I estimate that they're in their late thirties, maybe forties.

I nod, glad to be acknowledged. "I'm performing, but I don't know where to go."

"The others are in the small room behind the curtain, but it's cramped, and the comics like to sneak-smoke with the window open, so with all the nervous sweats it can stink in there. Also, almost all the comics are older men, so if that's not your scene, you're welcome to hang here with me." They smile.

I accept gratefully. "Thanks, Lai."

"When they call your name, just go to the stage. It's very casual here, don't worry."

"It's my first time ever performing stand-up," I confess. I hadn't intended to say anything.

Lai winks. "Gotcha." They make a signal to Malik, who has been slouching by the other end of the bar, since he is no longer needed outside. They whisper something, and Malik nods and heads to the back of the curtain.

"Since it's your first time, you only need to do a three-minute instead of a five-minute set, and we'll put you in the second half a couple of slots before the headliner, when everyone has had a few drinks and has been warmed up by the second-half opening comic and as such, tends to be more forgiving," they say. I thank Lai profusely.

And then it's showtime. A burly, balding older white man in a black

T-shirt and jeans goes onstage. "Ladies and gents, folks, welcome to KL Ketawa, KL's Freshest Open-Mike Night! Give it up for the comics in the back!"

The crowd bursts into enthusiastic cheers and claps.

"My name is Kieren, the emcee, and tonight we have a total of nine comics in our lineup. I am excited to introduce new faces today as well as our usual pros for your enjoyment. Please be gentle—or not! We want only the best comics to come back—the rest of them can be the accountants they were meant to be, although I don't know which is worse: being an accountant or a jobless comic, I mean—comic."

A few guffaws. I wince and notice Lai doing the same. "He's done this bit so many times," they mutter under their breath.

Kieren natters on a bit about the intermission and housekeeping announcements, and I tune out. I ask Lai for a sheet of paper and a pen, wondering what I should talk about. My hands start shaking and the nervous sweats obliterate my deodorant. Despite my initial bravado, I realize that I'm in over my head. My mind is emptier than my wallet, and that's no mean feat.

The first comic, Bryan, an older man in his fifties, who I gather is a crowd favorite, comes onstage to strong applause and chants of support. In my feverish state I catch only bits of his set, which is about his work as something called a risk analyst. The next one, Kumar, who tells everyone he's twenty-three and is sweet-looking with mussed-up hair, busts out an amateur, on-the-nose set about porn and being single. The audience groans but doesn't tear into him. Lai lets me know that Kumar has been on the circuit for nine months and was one of the hardest-working new comics. "The sad thing about stand-up comedy is effort is only a small component of success. Stand-up comedy is as much about persona, stage presence, and comedic timing as it is about the strength of your written material," Lai says. "And making it big in this business also involves some luck."

I nod. I know all about Luck.

"This audience is kind to Kumar because it's still early on in the night. Last week, he was heckled to pieces for the same set."

I wince, and my sweat waterfalls down my back. Lai is encouraging and kind, but they weren't helping alleviate my anxiety at all. Why is Taslim even doing this? I toy with the idea of hightailing it out of there, but my curiosity and my competitive pride have been roused. I have to stay.

"What do you know about my friend Ray?"

"Ray? Ray Lim?" Lai says, sounding surprised. "Is he your friend?"

"Yes," I lie. "But it's my first time watching him perform." *Please tell me Golden Boy sucks, please.*

"Well then, I shall not say a single thing to color your view," Lai says to my disappointment. Lai shrugs. "None of us really know Ray very well. He's—secretive. But you know what they say about stand-up comics and their emotional baggage. We try to give everyone here the space to be whatever they want to be."

I nod. It's a nice sentiment, though I suspect that Ray's secretive for *very* different reasons, i.e., parents. What could Golden Boy possibly be working through? He's the picture of well-adjustment. His family is whole and loaded. He's the luckiest boy I know.

I try to focus on the performances in spite of my nerves. Three more people, including one woman in her thirties, perform. The woman—Gina—closes out the first half to raucous applause. I take note of her set, a sterling one that was about growing up Australian in Hong Kong. It reminds me a little of Ali Wong. If Kumar doesn't have what it takes, Gina Cheung has everything: charisma, presence, and impeccable timing; and her material was fresh.

I start hyperventilating. I'm going to bomb hard; I can feel it.

Lai lays a gentle hand on me. "It's only three minutes. Relax. Just lean into it."

I favor them with a watery smile. "Okay."

The first two comics to come on after the intermission, Hamid and Vern, are men in their early twenties, both efficient comics who get a few hearty laughs in each of their five-minute sets. I train my eyes on my watch and try to breath slowly. Thirteen minutes and seventeen seconds go by. And then it's my turn.

"And now, folks, I promised you fresh meat, and there is nothing fresher than a teenage comedy virgin." The crowd groans. Kieren leers. "Keep it PC and give it up for Agnes Chan!"

I walk with the enthusiasm of one headed for the gallows, or someone who'd picked the short straw to buy tickets for a BTS concert. My stomach gives an alarming rumble. I clench my jaw. *Please, please, please for the love of all that is good on this earth, please do not let me panic-burp.*

I climb the three steps onto the stage, sweating and itching under my cast, my arms wobbly on my crutch (I'd left the other by the bar so I could hold the mike with my free hand).

"Is the set going to start or what?" someone who was never loved as a child says snarkily.

You can do it, Agnes. If Taslim can, so can you.

And with that challenge, I start my set. "Hey, folks. I was told I had three minutes onstage. Three minutes! That's, like, ten TikTok videos! I don't have that long an attention . . . er, oh wait, um, what was I saying again?"

Silence. I swallow as the sound of my first joke falling flat rings in my ears. The crowd stares at me in silence. My throat floods with saliva, and there isn't even a pisang goreng nearby. What the heck am I on, thinking I could wing it?

I look at the people in my audience, bathed in the warm glow of the stage lights, a mixed bag of tourists and locals in their forties and fifties in varying stages of inebriation. They don't look like TikTokkers. Then and there, I decide to pivot and talk about my mother.

"My mother is not like other mothers of kids my age. She was born in the mid-eighties—basically the MySpace of millennials. She got pregnant with me when she was twenty. Apparently, Spandau Ballet was playing when it happened. For the longest time I thought she conceived me in a theater, which is semi-classy. You can imagine my disappointment when I found out Spandau Ballet was a band. And that said conception actually happened in a car." I clear my throat and say, "Which means I'm basically a bootlegged baby."

The crowd sputters. A surge of something stronger and giddying than adrenaline, a feeling that I only get whenever I win, races through me. I know what it is, of course—it's power.

"The other day we had a fight because she didn't want me to hang out late with my friends. Not like I can *get* in any trouble"—I lift up a crutch and hop, and the crowd titters sympathetically—"but she said you don't need to be able to move to get in trouble. Yeah, Mom, *you think?*" The crowd groans. "I said she's not a great example, since she got pregnant so young. She says she did it because she couldn't stand to see prime real estate"—I point in the direction of my womb—"lying vacant." Groans. "*Sure*, Mom, you were trying to prevent a subprime crisis. Just like"—I point to a man in a suit seated near the stage—"John the actual banker here." Laughter, actual laughter, rings across the room. This was the first time in my life I'd talked about the pain I carried about being an "accident"—only I'd transmuted it to comedy. To say I'm pleasantly surprised would be an understatement.

Someone flashes a blue light three times from the back of the room: I have a minute left. I throw myself in to the performance.

"I want my mom to get over her issues and be like everyone else's, so I got her to see a therapist. But we can't afford a real one, so we found a psychology student. Now every time I ask her if she's better, she says"—I pause for effect and deadpan—"'Crappy Diem.'"

The crowd screams with laughter. The same person flashes a red light three times from the back of the room and I understand that to mean my time is up. Three minutes.

I take an awkward, one-crutch bow, and the audience's applause is thunderous. I grin shakily and exit the stage, and unsure of where I should go, I head to the back of the room to join Lai once more.

"You were very good!" Lai says, grinning. "For a first-timer, count me impressed."

"Thanks." My heart is still galloping; I swallow even though my mouth is dry. "I don't know what I was saying up there."

"Your friend Ray was watching the whole time."

"Really?" This revelation triggers more flip-flopping, for some reason. They pass me another glass of cold water and I down it. Suddenly, I desperately need the washroom, so I excuse myself.

When I come out, Kieren is still doing crowd work. I crane my neck, trying to find Taslim, when I spot him, grim-lipped in the shadows by the velvet curtains, waiting to run up to the stage. At first, I don't recognize him. Taslim—*Ray*, I correct myself—has jammed all his abundant, wavy hair under a midnight-blue beanie, and he has changed into a wrinkled, faded emerald-and-navy-blue plaid shirt over black jeans—almost as though he's trying to hide his wiry, muscular frame. And then there's his posture, which is slightly hunched, unlike the way he usually holds himself, with precision and an athlete's easy grace. It's almost as though he's trying to pass as someone else.

His eyes meet mine and an emotion I can't read flashes across his face. He purses his lips. I don't think he's happy to see me.

For some reason, Golden Boy, buttoned-up, perfect Royce Taslim, whose mom regularly has high tea with a veritable Malaysian *princess*, is onstage in a seedy bar performing while pretending to *not* be a Taslim, and I am the only person who knows who he really is.

Which means I'm a threat.

"Folks, put your hands together and welcome our fresh mini headliner for tonight, who'll perform a fifteen-minute set for the very first time—Ray Lim!"

I clap along with the rest, and Ray/Taslim, his eyes trained on me, begins to speak.

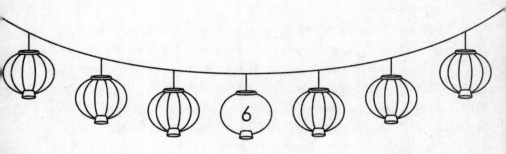

FROM THE GET-GO, TASLIM LOOKS ILL AT EASE ONSTAGE. HIS GAZE
keeps flicking over to where I sit, uncertain. I'm not sure if this is
his Ray persona, or if this nervousness is brought about by my unex-
pected presence.

And then there's the question of his set. From what I'd gathered
from Kieren's introduction, this isn't Ray's first rodeo—in fact, he
must have been coming here pretty often and doing well enough to
be promoted to a headliner, even on an open-mike night. Still, I can
tell that nothing is landing right.

To start with, he keeps saying *Er*.

"As I was saying, er."

Oh yeah, he is also saying a lot of *As I was saying*s.

And then he's swallowing. Loudly. Over the mike.

Ray/Taslim flops through a bit about schoolwork. When no one
laughs, I wait for him to switch up the material, but he belabors his
point. Nothing. And he's still doggedly going on about life as a student. And then I realize why he's sticking with his lines—he only has
that one set of jokes. And he can't think fast enough on his feet to
react to his audience.

The audience's hostility is palpable. A low hum of discontent grows. Someone boos him.

Taslim ends with a bit about TikTok and no one, absolutely no one, laughs. The booing gets louder. Taslim freezes onstage even as Lai flashes a torchlight with a red filter over its lens three times in quick succession. I see the same look of panic I felt at the beginning of my set dawn on his face, and I decide, there and then, to stop booing him. I must admit it's a little gauche of me to have done that in the first place. I don't know what it is, but competition brings out the worst in me.

Kieren hops onstage and grabs the mike from Taslim's motionless hands, breaking his spell. He shuffles offstage, ending his misery. "All right folks, that's the end of our open-mike night, give it up for our fearless performers—and someone buy Ray a diaper. Remember—every Thursday, KL laughs . . . well, most of the time. Have a good night!"

The crowd disperses, although some stay behind to order more drinks, taking advantage of the two-for-one bottled beer offer that's still running. The bar gets busy, so I shuffle off to a corner, unsure of what I should do next—hang around till someone speaks to me? Go home? I don't want to leave yet. Adrenaline's still coursing through my veins. Taslim is nowhere to be seen, not that I'm looking for him.

A few of the comics have come out of the holding room and surround me. "Hey there," Gina says, sticking her hand out. I shake it with care, balancing on my crutches. "Agnes, right? You were amazing! That was your first time? I'm so jealous. Also, I'm Gina."

"Vern, Vern Goh," says the floppy-haired, deeply tanned guy next to her. We shake hands, and I am struck by the feeling that I know him, even though I can't place him. "Good start, Ags—can I call you Ags?" I make a face and he laughs. "Noted. Anyways, took me four tries before I got a single laugh that wasn't clothes-related."

"Yeah, he relied on cheap tricks for the longest time, wearing Hawaiian shirts in clashing colors and joke socks," Hamid says.

I'm surprised that Vern has to resort to dressing in any way to command attention. He has an easy, knowing charm that must draw people to him as hummingbirds to nectar. And he's not hard on the eyes, either.

Vern sticks out his tongue. "Better than you, Hamid, you can't even write a joke," he replies in a good-natured way.

"Hey, Kumar's the weakest link: He can't even speak onstage," Hamid says between sips of his drink.

Kumar shrugs it off. "I know I'm not the best comic, but I keep coming back because I love this," he says to me shyly.

I nod. "I get it. I feel that way when I run . . . ran." I grimace. It's true that the joy I get from running is wholly distinct from the high I get from winning in a race. When I'm running, it's as though nothing can touch me. Hurt me. And then of course there's the fact that I'm—was—so good at it. Everyone at Dunia knows who I am because of my achievements, and I can't lie—it's intoxicating to be known for one's talents. I got some of that tonight while performing. That same jolt of electricity.

Like I matter.

Vern snaps his finger. "I know who you are," he says suddenly. "You're that super runner kid. I was a couple years ahead of you at SMK Taman Sentosa." That was my old school before I got transferred to Dunia.

I do a double take as a memory surfaces and clicks into place. Vern, sitting on the sun-bleached wooden tables by the football field, surrounded by his lazily confident ilk, playing hooky. The kind of guy who would make you feel like you belonged or not with a look. I remember chatting alone with him one long afternoon the week before I left my former school—when my mom, after months of progress, had gone into a dark place and I was hiding from Stanley, who'd come to pick me up from school. "Oh, er, hi?" I say, as though I wasn't sure we'd already met. "I don't go there anymore. Haven't for four years or so."

"I figured," he says, a lopsided smile creasing his face. "We stopped making those annoying announcements about your wins during morning assembly soon after that."

"Sorry," I say, shrugging. "Those *were* annoying."

"Agnes this and Agnes that," Vern says, rolling his eyes. "Man, it was like you were the entire athletics program or something. Oh, wait"— he snaps his fingers, his eyes faux surprised—"you *were*! I mean, we *did* go to an underfunded public school, after all."

We laugh till I'm gasping for air. For some reason, this observation hit me hard. Even though I've found some sense of belonging at Dunia, what with sports, the Hot Flashes, and Zee, there's still some part of me that understands, bone-deep, that I'm different.

"So, who's the best comic of the bunch?" I ask to change the topic, not wanting to exclude the others.

"Ray," Gina says. She grins. "After me, of course. I know it doesn't look like it from tonight's performance, but Ray's got serious comedic chops."

"Well, Vern's actually pretty good, too," Kumar says. "They came up around the same time, come to think of it, though personally, I prefer Vern's humor. It's darker, dryer."

Vern grins and pats Kumar's back. "You're backing the right horse, my friend."

"Ray and Vern are *so* competitive," Gina says, rolling her eyes.

"Maybe you should give us your number so we can add you to the group chat," Kumar says. "We use it for sign-ups, then leave a few slots for walk-ins and ad hoc visiting comics, etc."

"Sure," I say. I pass him my number.

"Want a drink?" Gina asks. "Lai won't serve you, but I can slip you a beer."

I shake my head. "No thanks, I'm going home soon."

"Suit yourself," she says, stretching. "Just thought part of the lure of performing for most of you teenagers is the fact you can drink and smoke joints with us oldies." Her eyes cut meaningly to the direction of the holding room. Did she mean Taslim? Golden Boy Taslim involved in underage drinking—or worse?

"I'll be back," I say. I head toward the room, the entrance that's behind the velvet curtain backdrop of the stage, my heart pounding. From the thrill of catching him doing something illicit, of course. "Hey, Roy—Ray?" I call out, tentatively, pushing open the rickety wooden door.

"What?" he croaks.

I see Taslim immediately, even in the dark. He is seated on the couch, head between his knees.

"Are you okay?"

His head jerks up with a snap. In the dark it's hard to tell if he has been crying. "You," he says hoarsely, getting to his feet.

"Sorry about the booing," I say, genuine.

He stomps up to me, and in the sliver of light from the doorway I can see his face. He has not been crying—far from it.

He glares at me, and I meet his gaze squarely. We don't say anything for some time. We are so close I can feel every exhalation of his, see every pulse of the vein of his forehead, the tension in his lips. I can almost reach out and—

Yank his beanie over his face.

"Meet me in the alley, Chan," he growls before stomping away.

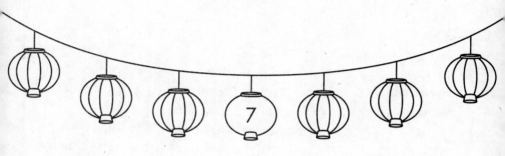

MEETING A GUY IN A DIM ALLEY OF CHOW KIT, WHERE ALL KINDS OF shady characters and rival gangs of jacked-up rats hang (sometimes together), is not ideal. But I am nothing if not a very prudent, reasonable teenager.

"Did you tell anyone who I am?" Taslim demands as soon as we're alone. His body language is jumpy, one of his feet tapping the ground in the dark.

I made a face. "What? No! I kept your secret, you weirdo."

He calms down, taking his beanie off and running his fingers through his hair. He says nothing for a while as he contemplates me, as though he's weighing the veracity of my words before he decides I'm not lying.

"Look, it's really . . . it's really important no one finds out who I am. For a whole bunch of reasons I can't get into. Do you promise me?" His voice is tight and his movements skittish; he's nothing like his usual composed, held-together self.

I shrug. "Yeah, yeah, calm yourself. I will. Geez."

"Thank you," he says very reluctantly.

"You're welcome, I guess."

He tries for banter. "Was that *really* your first time?"

"Onstage?"

"What else? Yes, duh!"

Should I tell him? Royce Taslim doesn't deserve any answers. Maybe I should let him stew or feed him with false information. But when I see his agitation, a break from his usual unflappable yeti persona, my own heart thaws. Vulnerability is contagious, which is why I avoid it like the plague.

I sigh. "Yes, it was. I mean, I've watched a lot of stand-up comedy in my down time, and once participated in an impromptu Twitch stand-up comedy rap battle, but that's it."

He doesn't say anything for a couple of beats. Then, like he's been offered to gargle glass, says, "You're good."

"Thanks," I say, gratified. I have to hold down my right hand, which is curled and ready to pump air. Immodesty is not becoming. "What about you? You been doing this for a while?"

"Yeah. A bit. This was my first fifteen-minute set, though. Urgh, what a train wreck that was."

His admission softens me. "Your set was not shit," I say, trying to be nice. "There were a couple of really acceptable punch lines. It just wasn't the right audience."

A shadow flits across his face and he grinds his jaw. "I was shit. Pro tip: The audience is never at fault for not getting your joke; the performer is. Your routine isn't supposed to be set in stone. I panicked and basically fell back on a rehearsed set, which would never have happened if I hadn't been thrown off my game when I saw you, Chan."

What? How dare he blame his incompetence on me? "Oh, so little ol' me in the audience threw you off your game? Want me to bring Mummy and Daddy next time, so they can hold your hand? Buy you an easier pass through this?"

Taslim stone-faces. "Can't do that if they don't know I'm in stand-up, Chan."

"They don't know you're in stand-up?" I say, surprised but

vindicated—my assumption had been proven right. Royce's face also broadcasts this truth: Not only do his parents not know—they would *not* approve of it. *Well, well, well*, I think. *This is an interesting opportunity.*

"What?"

"What?"

Taslim raises an eyebrow. "You said something out loud."

Dammit. I did do that sometimes. "No, I didn't."

"Yeah, you did." He smirks. "And in case you didn't know, you chirp when you're excited. It's . . ." He leans close, and I'm pinned by those eyes. Not because they're pretty—they might be, to some basic people, but not to *me*—but because they, like—the horizontal pupils of the mongoose, are intense and weird. "Weird."

"No, I'm not weird, *you're* weird," I say, the height of sophisticated debate.

He squares his shoulders in what he thinks is an intimidating way. "Chan?"

"Yeah?"

He knits his eyebrows and glares. If I chirp when I'm excited, he squints daggers. "I resent the inference that I . . . that my parents bought my way through life." He stabs a finger in his palm. "I work hard to get everything I have. I got where I got on my own merit."

Wow. Just—wow. Is he really that self-deluded? "I hate to break it to you, but you're deluded," I say, rolling my eyes. "Look, I don't doubt that you work hard, but please, please don't glibly discount the fact that you got there easier than most of us. You've *never* had to split your time between helping out at home, taking care of your sick mom, working a part-time job, and studying for some classes online instead of having fancy-schmancy Ivy League grads as personal tutors and fancy brain-food smoothies to help you as you glide your way upward through life, propelled by the farts and illusions of grandeur as your parents cheer on your every achievement." I say all this without pausing.

He is quiet for a while. "What's up with your mom?" he asks softly, seeming embarrassed.

I start. I hadn't even realized I'd said that. "Nothing. Forget I said anything," I bark. "That was a long time ago and she's fine now. Mind your own business."

A taut silence follows as we size each other up.

Finally, he says, "I don't disagree with everything you said about my privilege, but I should have clarified that I was talking about stand-up just now, nothing else. I got as far as I did as Ray with my own effort. No one knows I'm a Taslim here, and it's partly because I want to avoid everything you just alluded to. Also, only because I'm a pedant, I have to correct you on one more aspect." He pauses for effect. "I don't drink smoothies because I'm already smooth AF."

"Ha ha ha," I say dryly. "I'm dead. Never stop. All killer, no filler."

Taslim trains his gaze on the ground. "My parents don't actually care what grades I get," he says, almost to himself. "It doesn't matter in the long run. Everything is settled."

I decide not to ask him to elaborate. There is a heavy sadness in the way he says it, although he strives to be matter-of-fact. "I'm sure they care. After all, they have no choice, seeing as you're their only spawn and your mother's parenting advice platform just sold for a mountain of gold."

He raises an eyebrow. "Are you stalking me?"

"Everyone knows," I say lightly, neither confirming nor denying his question. "Your family is such annoying tabloid fodder."

"But you know," he says, quirking his lips.

"I do," I reply, looking up at him. "You have to know your enemy."

"And why am I your enemy?" he says, stepping closer to me. I sway a little at this sudden proximity and he reaches out to steady me, only he holds me by my forearm and lets his hand linger before dropping it, leaving goose bumps in its absence. I'm not used to being touched, that's all.

"Student Athlete of the Year comes with money, and you and I were in the running for it," I say.

"Did you just pun, Chan?" he says, widening his eyes for effect.

"Maybe," I say, distracted by the way his eyes reflect the gold of the streetlight. Involuntarily, my eyes drop to his mouth, which is smack dab in my sight line. His slightly parted mouth is—

Full of bacteria. Absolutely coated with *saliva.* And then I recite the facts I know about the oral cavity: *Saliva contains enzymes like amylase, lysozyme, and lipase that catalyze the breakdown of foods. Basically, digestion begins in the mouth. So, if you think about it, if Taslim's tongue enters your mouth, you're basically digesting—* Oh my God, why am I thinking about that? What the heck is wrong with me?!

Something is clearly wrong with Taslim, too. His breathing is shallow, and he looks like he's been thwacked on the head. He's watching me with a strange look, like I'm a puzzle or pizza, one of those. The air thickens with intention. He bends his head slightly and I swallow as—

"Rat!" I screech as one the size of a Pomeranian scuttles not two feet away from us, its red eyes gleaming in the streetlight. I'm gratified to see Taslim jump. We watch as it waddles into a waiting storm drain, possibly to join Pennywise the clown, its servant.

"Oh my God," Royce says shakily. I shudder, my soul slowly reentering my body.

Whatever it is, I am grateful for the interruption. Because there had been a moment when I'd actually been—

No. *No.* It must be lead paint fumes or asbestos from the building. The comedy club is, after all, in what must be a condemned building that should have been razed to the ground a long time ago, if not for someone's palm getting greased to high heaven.

Taslim also seems to have regained a grip of himself, because he was now glaring at me the way he'd been the whole night.

"What's your problem?" I snap.

"You. You're the problem," Taslim growls. He leans close to me again. Too close. I swallow, eyes fixed on anywhere but his lips. "This is my thing, Chan. Stay away."

~

"You stay away!" I counter, real sassy, ten hours later. In my head. During the first class of the day, English Literature. I usually love English Lit, but today concentrating on class is a lost cause. It's all I can do to try to keep myself awake, since I'd gotten home quite late last night.

What happened was, after our confrontation, Taslim and I had gone our separate ways (in fact, he'd offered to drop me off by taxi but I'd declined, out of principle). My phone was dead and I couldn't text anyone where I was, nor arrange for a shared ride back, so I'd taken a bus—well, three buses, paying with my concession card, and by the time I arrived home, my "good" leg numb with exhaustion, at eleven thirty, I found that my mom had fallen asleep at the kitchen table waiting for me, waking only when I shook her. She complained a little about the time but sensed a certain excitement about me that she'd not seen since my accident, which was probably why she didn't berate me about my lateness, as she knew I was with Zee; instead, she only told me off for not keeping my phone charged. I was so tired after the adrenaline had fizzed out that I flopped straight to bed, my usual nightly ablutions forsaken. And I am not one to forsake dental hygiene, especially given all I know about saliva.

So you could say I woke up this morning even more annoyed at Royce Taslim than usual. And more than a little puzzled by his reactions over the course of the night.

My English teacher, Ms. Xu, is blathering on about secondary layers and themes in poems. I zone out. I keep flashing back to Royce's expression when he warned me to stay away—he almost looked afraid of me. Vulnerable. Like I have the power to take something important away from him.

Oh my gosh, does he *value* performing in front of a crowd of strangers as Ray Lim? *That* is how he gets his kicks in life? How pathetic.

I mean, I suppose since his mom is a famous ex-model/beauty queen/serial entrepreneur and his dad belongs to an Indonesian dynasty, their family's always in the public eye and all the society and gossip mags as well as fashion blogs, so he must have gotten a taste for fame.

I frown—no, that isn't fair. Taslim's parents were the ones whose faces were everywhere, whereas Taslim was low-profile, whether it had been his or his family's choice. Plus, he'd been performing stand-up under a stage name.

And how nonplussed did he look when I brought up his parents and deduced that they didn't know he performed stand-up?

I grin, Cheshire cat–style (I never got expensive orthodontic work done, so yes, it is an apt reference). *Oh, Taslim, I've got you by the balls now*, I gloat. Metaphorically, of course. I want no part of Taslim's . . . body parts.

My phone vibrates with a series of texts. I discreetly fish it out and scroll through them.

Zee: HEY, WHAT HAPPENED YESTERDAY? I WAS WAITING FOR YOU FOR TWO HOURS
Zee: OK fine, two hours, at home
Zee: OK fine, maybe I fell asleep after an hour
Zee: Oh wait, I just got your texts, weird. So your phone died?

I type a response as discreetly as I can under my textbook.

Me: Yeah sorry beb my phone ded as soon as I got in. Yiur texts jst came in btwz
Zee: So. How was the performance? Where's the vid?

Me: No chance to get anyone to rexcord anything, I hsd to perform! Plusd my phone died! Annnnd T wore beanie onstage!

Zee: Noooooooooo! I wanted to watch your performance!

Me: You jsdt want to perve on Taslim 😀

Zee: Nah, I'm kind of over it, he was wearing a beanie. Voluntarily. Also I'm not a fan of comedians. Too needy

Me: Thanks, fam 🙄

Zee: You're the exception, of course. Anyways spill tea later

I promise to update her in the flesh after school and try to focus on class.

My phone buzzes again: I've been added to a WhatsApp group chat called Open-Mike Nights Around Town—Kumar's handiwork, no doubt. I scrutinize the list of dos and don'ts for posting on the group; then, nonchalantly, I open the participant list just to see how many comics are in the group. Electricity jolts through me when I see one particular person's name. Ray, i.e., Taslim.

I can see Taslim's phone number. The realization does strange things to my solar plexus, which appear to be seizing. I chalk it up to seasonal allergies.

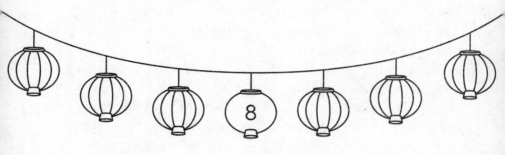

STANLEY IS ALONE IN THE KITCHEN SATURDAY MORNING WHEN I WALK in, yawning and scrolling through my notifications. The open-mike group chat is buzzing with activity: There's a gig tomorrow night in a popular Irish bar/restaurant in the city and Taslim is on the list.

I don't know why I haven't exited the group chat yet, even though it's been about two weeks since my open-mike debut. Maybe it's nice to feel like I belong to a community again. The Flashes have *obviously* been too busy with training and social stuff that they haven't had the chance to invite me to their fun hangs, but I'd also be so busy working on my college applications. On top of the D1 schools that would be "highly aspirational, given everything's that's happened"—my college counselor Ms. Tina's diplomatic words—she had advised me to target some D2 and even D3 colleges given my need for substantial financial aid. So I'd been snowed under doing all that.

"Morning, Ags," Stanley says, nodding at the oven. "Saved you some buckwheat crepes."

"Thanks, D—Stanley," I say. I scarf them down, drenched in maple syrup and extra butter. Having the freedom to eat whatever I want is the only silver lining of this tragedy.

He clears his throat and I sigh internally. "So, I notice you've not been doing much 'hanging out'"—he air-quotes this—"with your friends since you've resumed classes, though you've stopped using your crutches last Friday."

"Hmmmm," I say neutrally. He's not wrong. I wake up, go to school, stay at the library, studying, before going home, where I study some more, sometimes going over to Zee's to study with her (Mas, the super tutor she's had since junior year, doesn't mind me joining Zee), then work on my college admissions. I barely see my family these days except in the mornings. I've been busy, but I've not been social the way I used to be.

"Is everything all right?" Stanley's voice is gentle.

I nod extra hard. "One hundred percent." Sure, sometimes I'm a teensy bit lonely, and sometimes I really miss running, but only when I think about it. That's why I'm trying so hard not to think about it. "Everyone's just really busy, especially me, especially with physio and college essays and, um, life."

"Hmm," Stanley says, watching me as he sips his coffee. "Hmm."

When Stanley does this, I immediately want to tell him all my secrets. Instead, I mirror him and say, "Hmm."

"You know you can tell me anything, and I promise to listen first, above all," he says after a while. "And if it's something you can't . . . Well, y'know, I can keep a secret if it isn't dangerous or harmful." He means from my mom, obviously. In the four years or so since he's entered our lives and changed everything for us, I've grown to trust him. But not enough to tell him my secrets.

I have walls everywhere, even at home.

I have no guarantee that he'll be able to keep something like "I'm lost, I'm really sad, I don't know what my life will be like in the future and I'm worried" from my mom. I can't risk setting off her depression, even when I know she's more or less gotten it under control, through meds and counseling, for years. I've seen what she was like, and I just can't go through it again.

My arms itch and I scratch them distractedly. "It's just senior-year stress. Exams and college applications, all that."

"Right." Stanley nods. "Just let me know if you need help in any of your classes at least. I can't guarantee that I'll be much help in geography or history, but I'm good with most of the science stuff."

"Science stuff?" I tease.

"And French," he says with a poker face.

"Thanks, Stanley." I reach over and hug him. I hug him with every ounce of me, to let him know I'm okay, even though I am not.

~

Two hours later I'm seated in the bleachers of the stadium, overlooking the corner of the field where the girls' sprint team is practicing drills. There's not a lot of people here. Just some helicopter parents, helpers, friends, and stragglers who want a place to be.

I watch them run and run and run.

Just that morning I had asked them out to boba. We used to do that, have a boba after Saturday practice, but they were noncommittal. Then I found out, through some basic social media sleuthing in one of the girls' Stories, that they were planning to go to Planet Bounce, a sports café with a trampoline park, after training for some fruit shakes and trampoline time.

I love Planet Bounce. I love trampolines. I love fruit shakes. But they didn't even ask if I wanted to come, even if they thought I could only stay for fruit shakes. I'm no longer relevant to my teammates.

It's hard to be up here, on the bleachers, and not down there. Before I can stop myself, I'm crying silently while trying not to look like I'm crying, which is a skill I have never mastered. I stuff my knuckles into my mouth to stop my lips from trembling and pull the bill of my cap as far down as it can go.

"Hey," a voice says awkwardly from a few rows away.

I jump three feet into the air, squeaking, wiping my face hastily before I turn around to face the unwelcome intruder to my misery.

It is Taslim, of course. Somehow, we always catch each other at our worst, and I'm not here for it. We don't have the kind of relationship that makes being vulnerable in front of each other okay.

Do you even have anyone you can be vulnerable with? a voice says, unbidden, and I shut it down.

"Are you stalking me?" I say, even if it isn't true, but he's there looking immaculate in jeans and a polo the shade of avocados that bring out the golden sheen of his tan when I have snot in my nostrils.

"*I'm* stalking *you?*" he sputters. "Have you forgotten that you literally crashed *my* stand-up show? And you're still lurking in the group chat?"

I puff my cheeks at him. "Contrary to what you believe, you don't own comedy. It's a free country, still. Mostly. Sometimes. Anyway, why aren't you on the field practicing?"

"My coach is sick, so I went to the library to study for the first-semester exams. And then I realized I forgot something in the lockers so . . . Wait." He glares at me. "Why am I justifying myself? I have as much right to be here as you, *if not more*."

He crosses him arms and I do, too.

"Okay, I'm sorry," I mutter. "I'm just a little . . . on edge."

"You seem better," he says it like a statement, but he is watching me as though he meant it as a question.

"You mean the lack of crutches and cast?" A bark of laughter escapes me. "You of all people should know, for athletes, an injury like this goes beyond healing well enough to stand at a concert. I'm a runner, Taslim. I'm a really, really good one, too. Or rather, I was. I shouldn't be watching my teammates run—*I* should be running."

He bites his bottom lip, nods. "I've always admired your work ethic. You're a really passionate and, uh, uh, graceful athlete." His ears flame gently; maybe he's allergic to praising others.

"Thanks."

He hesitates before saying, almost to himself, "But don't you think you're more than just a runner?"

"As in, do I have other college-application-appropriate extracurricular activities? Well, I was on the choral speaking team that won district champion two years ago . . . but only because Ms. Xu was desperate when one of the girls fell sick, and she offered me extra credit for it. Oh yeah, I can cross-stitch really fast. But other than that—zero. And my grades are all right but not super, so my chances of getting an academic scholarship are slim, especially when there are so many better students than me."

"No, I meant don't you think you're so much more, as a person, than just a runner?"

I think about this but have no easy answers. My entire identity has always been wrapped up in sports. As a child, I was always the fastest in any class, and when I started winning primary school meets, the coach spoke to my mom about proper training. Running was an easy sport to get into. It didn't have much upfront costs. You just needed good shoes, and those weren't expensive if you could look beyond whether they were new or not. "I don't know who I am without *this*," I admit.

"I get it," Taslim says.

"You?" I scoff. "No, you don't, Taslim. You're one of those really annoying people who is good at everything you do, on top of your grades: javelin, chess, languages, math"—Taslim was a mathlete (not the best, but still)—"and violin. And even if you aren't especially gifted at something, if you wanted to succeed in something enough, your parents would get you the help to polish whatever kernel of talent you had. It's easy for you. Life is."

His jaw works for a while. His voice is strained, and he speaks slowly. "I don't deny that I have it easier than most. But I've had to work for things, too. Things you know nothing about."

"Sure," I say in a neutral voice.

Taslim gestures to the seat on the bleachers next to me, an

eyebrow lifted, and I shrug. "It's a free country." He moves over. I admire the ease, the athleticism of him vaulting down from his row straight into the seat next to me in one fluid move. We watch my teammates practice, not exactly side by side, but close. The fabric of his polo brushes against my arm, and a shiver runs through me. I move away surreptitiously.

He clears his throat and shifts in his seat. "Listen, I've been meaning to, uh, I want to apologize for my behavior at stand-up, actually. I don't know what came over me, I'm usually not so much of a territorial asshole. . . ."

"It's true that you're not usually territorial."

He chuckles. "Okay. I deserve that, although *usually* is probably a stretch. I'm mostly really nice to you, aren't I?"

"So you say." I turn to face him. "You're hard to read."

"What do you mean?"

"You just are," I say, very eloquently. "Meaning, I think you're like one of those career politicians. You're superficially nice to everyone and you present this really ripple-free surface to everyone, but underneath all that still water, I just know there's riptides that will drown you."

"Whoa, um, project much?" he says, staring at me. "I think I can say the same about you, Ms. I Keep My Cards Close to My Chest."

"I'm very open," I say, folding my arms and narrowing my eyes. "It's just that, unlike you, I don't try to be nice to everyone."

"You sure don't," he agrees.

"Okay, what's your point?" I say, my temper flaring.

He raises his hands up in mock surrender. "Look, straight up—I'm sorry about how I was in that comedy club. That was not . . . that was not my finest moment." He fiddles with the hem of his polo. "You caught me at a vulnerable time: my first solo fifteen, which was a total mess, and it was the first time I ever saw anyone who knew me . . . well, as Royce, it was just disorienting, and it was you, and you know, you're so, um, intimidating. Anyway, I'm not making excuses for how I acted at all, don't get me wrong, I'm just . . . This is all to say—I'm sorry."

"I'm intimidating?" I say, confused. "Why? Is it my resting winner face?" I try it out on him.

Flushing, he averts his eyes and leans back in his seat. "Never mind."

He really has amazing lashes, I note. No wonder he can throw the javelin so well; they must provide shade against glare. My gaze slides to his pecs, which are very visible under the polo shirt in his reclining position. Wow, those are really . . . visible.

I force myself to think about sea cucumbers, then panic because of their phallic shape and think instead about the spiny sea urchins. Nothing sexy about sea urchins. Nothing. Well . . . unless you get to their soft insides.

I snap to attention and realize my eyes had been glued onto Taslim's pecs the whole time. I wrench them away and look at his eyebrows, which at best, I remind myself, resemble fuzzy caterpillars. "So, what do you think about the death penalty? Is it ever justified? Discuss!"

Taslim laughs, a sunny, wheezy laugh. "Oh, Agnes Chan," he says when he's recovered. "Every day with you is a privilege."

We look at the Flashes practice without further comment for some time.

Royce rakes his nails over an invisible smudge on his jeans. "Hey, I meant what I said before. I would love to tutor you. I mean, y'know . . . not love, but, like, like. I would be very open to, um, help you polish up your grades, and help with whatever I can, schoolwork, assignment-wise. If your GPA improves for a college you're wait-listed at, it could make the difference."

"That's . . ." I hesitate, fidgeting. "I don't want to—I mean, I do but . . . but, like, only if you'll let me pay you." I finish the last bit in a rush.

"Chan, the whole point of being a peer tutor is *not* to collect payment. . . ."

"I want to . . . I *need* to."

"Okay," he says gently. "I won't accept money or anything in kind, but you can, I don't know . . ." He makes his thinking face. "You play *CounterFlash: Hardboiled*?"

"Doesn't everyone?"

He chuckles. "Definitely not. What level are you?"

"I'm level seventy-three."

He sputters, "Holy shit."

"Yeah. I didn't have much to do in the first two weeks after I got injured."

"Great. Then pay me in *CounterFlash* game loot," he says. "One item. My pick of your stash."

I mentally scan my inventory. There's a couple of things there that are worth a big bunch of money and a couple of reasonably good finds—it's a gamble, depending on how greedy he wants to be. But I don't have anything else to trade with. I nod. "Sure."

We set a date for the following Thursday after school, which, if it goes well, would be followed by a second session on the Monday after that. We'd do two three-hour sessions a week at least. End-of-semester exams are in two months or so, and if I bust my butt, I can bump up my stubborn B in AP biology and algebra to an A– at least. It could make the difference, in the off chance I got accepted at one of my second choices.

A shout from the track team interrupts our little exchange, and we check out the commotion. The girls are taking a water break, and Suraya is showing everyone a clip on her phone that makes them burst into raucous laughter.

"I miss this," I say softly.

He turns to regard me. "What?"

"I . . . I . . . It's . . ." My eyes flood again and I drop my gaze. "It's just . . . I don't . . . Well, my friends . . . I haven't seen them much s-since the accident." My teammates had sent their condolences, via texts and a group-made card, but by and large, there'd been no invitations to hang out after class or practice, like we used to. "I miss them."

Admitting this brought home the situation to me. My eyes spill over and my throat closes, swallowing the rest of my speech. I bend over to fiddle with my laces.

"Well," Taslim says after a pause, "if they're any kind of friends, they'd be making more of an effort with you. I would."

I stay bent over my laces, trying to hide my tears, when I feel a hand on my shoulder. Taslim's. Warm and firm, lingering. I freeze and something happens to my legs, which have suddenly transformed into jelly. I try to speak, to tell him to take his hand off, but I can't. I don't. We stay in this awkward position for a while, the words unsaid between us written in our locked bodies.

"Take care, Chan," he says. I grunt in what I think is a friendly kind of way. Then I see his sneakers walk their way to the exit and leave.

I sit up, still shaky, and try to marshal control over my emotions. *Breathe. Beat normally*, I tell my heart. But my body doesn't obey me. I sink on to the bleachers, staring at my teammates, trying to process the tangled web of emotions unspooling in my stomach. Swallowing the ball of hurt in my throat, while battling an unfamiliar fluttery sensation in my stomach and the heat that flames up my cheeks, my neck, my back.

Then a text from an unknown number:

Hey, if you're finding it hard to, I don't know, just this whole situation . . . I'm here. You can talk to me. Anytime. Your friend, RT.

I pocket the phone, my face tingling. *Royce Taslim*, undisputed high school king of Dunia, just proclaimed himself my friend. Why was he being so nice to me, a nobody?

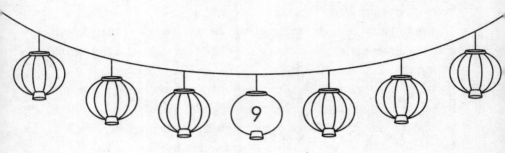

"YOU KNOW, YOU REALLY OUGHT TO GET OUT A LITTLE," ROSIE SAYS TO
me the next morning.

We are seated/sprawled in the living room on the opposite ends of
the three-seater couch. I am exhausted and twitchy—insomnia and
gaming keep me up at night. For want of a life, and to avoid thinking
about my former one, I have taken to cross-stitching. It's my mother's
thing, that her mom used to do with her back when she was a tween,
and now for whatever reason, I'm doing it.

"I go out," I say.

"You mean, you study and you game when you're not studying. I
mean hang out with people, do fun stuff. You've become *so* boring."

"Agnes doesn't exist to make your life interesting," my mother
reminds Rosie, entering the room with a load of laundry. She plunks
herself down and starts folding clothes, looking a little paler than usual.

"Yo, I'm here," I say. "I can speak for myself."

"All you do is study and work on your college applications."

"I have to do both, and I especially have to study my butt off if I
want to get as close to perfect grades as I can, otherwise I can forget
about getting even partial academic scholarships *if* I get into a college
in the States."

My mother bites her lip. "Listen . . . you don't have to worry . . . It's not . . . We can—"

I cut her off. "Don't worry, Mom. I'll find a way," I say, pasting a smile on my face. I really don't want her to feel bad about our situation.

The truth is, they can't afford to send me to the US, not even if they liquidate the house. Our family is wrapped in debt. They don't think I know it, but I've seen the bills. So long as Stanley and my mother are employed, everyone is afloat. For now. But nothing is a given.

"As I was saying, Agnes is so boring now and she sighs all the time, it's bloody annoying," Rosie says, throwing up her arms in a dead-on imitation of my mother. She has picked up *bloody* as an intensifier from her friend Jasmine, who is British. "And look how gormless she looks, splayed out on the couch like a middle-aged ancient—"

"Thanks, sis," I say while my mother says, "Thanks, Rosie," to which Rosie colors and says, "But obviously not *you,* my mother. You're barely forty-five."

"I'm thirty-seven, but I have accepted my middle-age obsolescence with grace, thank you," my mother says drily.

Rosie powers on. "And she won't even berate me anymore when I slouch, ranting about core control or whatever. It's like she's given up hope on life. I, for one, won't stand for it."

My mother pats my head. "She's just—readjusting. She'll find her old spiky self soon."

"I want my sister back," Rosie cries. "She used to be *fun.* This shell of a person sucks. Sucks hairy monkey's balls," she adds, remembering my lesson.

"Language," my mother says. "Just say, *This shell of a person is not my cup of tea.*"

"Aw, gee, thanks, both of you," I say irritably. I put my cross-stitching down. "I'm going upstairs to study, where I can be my prickly, sucky self without censure."

"Wait, Agnes, just—sit down, please." My mother stops folding clothes, puts her hands on her lap, and clears her throat. Her hands twitch in her lap. "I, uh, need to tell you girls something." She doesn't look at either of us.

"What is it?" Rosie says suspiciously.

I say nothing as I study my mother. My stomach bubbles with acid.

My mother is blushing. "I'm pregnant," she says, her voice a little unsteady. "About ten weeks, but I thought I should tell you two—"

Rosie screams and throws herself around my mother with the joy of a golden retriever getting a long-awaited treat. "Mom!" she shouts. "You've made me the happiest eleven-year-old today! I get a do-over!"

"Rosie!" my mother says, but she's grinning.

"I'm just kidding, Agnes," Rosie says, her voice muffled by my mother's hair. "I love you, still."

"Thanks, sis. And congrats, Mom," I say, trying to smile again. For some reason my voice is scratching and weak. My insides feel empty, like someone has scraped me empty. I get up and put my arms around my mother for two beats, then break apart.

"I'm so glad you girls are happy," my mother says, and I instantly feel like a shitty brat for not being 100 percent ecstatic. I pick up my cross-stitch and make nonsensical stitches, my pattern forgotten. I hear Rosie and my mother giggle about baby names, and a numbness descends until my fingers weigh like lead.

What's happening to me?

I finish a couple more rows of stitches and excuse myself. I slink upstairs, catching my reflection in the hallway as I enter my room. My posture is indeed terrible. It is the posture of a slug being propped upright on a very hot day. Everything is all wrong.

I throw myself on the bed and bury my face in my pillow. Every muscle in my body weighs like it's made of concrete. I feel friable, like I'll shatter if someone just taps me. If I'd been in a funk since the accident, then this is a new low. *I get a do-over!* Rosie's voice rings out. It had been a joke, but I felt it in my core. *Do-over! Do-over!*

I try to read one of my comfort novels, but nothing is sticking.

I launch a comedy special, hoping to take my mind off everything. I can't even do what I usually do when life gets overwhelming: go out for a run. I can't outrun this, whatever this new pit is. Even Amina Kaur's jokes fail me.

My mother and Stanley are having a kid. Together.

A tiny, unimportant thought floats to the forefront of my awareness.

Royce's words, telling me that if I ever needed to speak with someone, he'd be there for me, anytime. I flush at the memory of us on the bleachers. The way his touch had irradiated me to the core.

I dig my nails into my palm and hope that the pain drives out the sickness that has infected me, the one that makes me tingle at Royce's touch. Clearly, I had too much time on my hands. I need a distraction.

I pull up the comedy chat and idly scroll through the latest exchange, as I've been doing on the regular since I'd been added on the chat.

Gina: You guys signed up for tonight's open mike? The bar says they are running a special Sunday beer tower promotion and it's going to be a full house. And of course, I'm the headliner tonight so Please! Come! Support!

Hamid: You know it! I'm wearing orange if anyone wants to color-coordinate

Before I know what I'm doing, I have added my name to the bottom of the list and copied and pasted it back to the group.

The chat erupts:

Gina: Oh hey girl! Welcome back!

Milly: Hiiiiii! We haven't met but I've heard about you, see you tonight!

Vern: Agggggggggggggs!!!

Then a private text from Vern: We should hang out, one of these days. Catch up.

My cheeks heat up.

Me: Sure.

Hamid and Kumar text a variation of *hi* and a row of emojis. Royce is silent.

I text Zee to let her know I'm going to perform, both hoping and not hoping she will be able to join me. She replies with a row of screamy emojis that end with OF COURSE I'M IN, BRUHHHHHH!

I drop a text in the group chat for the Hot Flashes with my performance details. I've been told we should avoid inviting people we actually like to our performances in the beginning of our stand-up journey—Kumar and Hamid were especially cautionary—but there's no journey here per se, just a chance to socialize with new and old friends.

The team chat is complimentary, but no one promises to come.

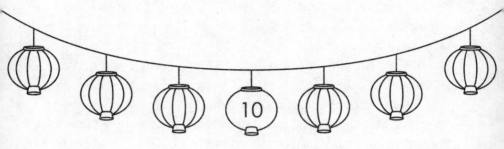

I EXCUSE MYSELF AFTER DINNER, TELL MY PARENTS I'M GOING TO SEE some friends, and make my way to the casual Lebanese fusion restaurant where the open mike Going Bananas is being held.

I quickly locate the cluster of comics. They are seated in a corner booth, close to the small, raised stage that typically houses the live band; there's no holding room here, so the comics have to go up when their turn is announced. They wave when they see me. I wave and let out a breath I didn't know I was holding when I realize Royce isn't there. I meet Milly, a British expat in her forties, who is a professor of linguistics and more of an improv comic who occasionally performs stand-up to sharpen her skills; Sai, who's another veteran comic in his late thirties, nods at me and chats only with Bryan; Kong, the first-timer, is in his early twenties and blue with nerves. He manages a feeble wave.

I slide in next to Kumar and Gina. "How are the acoustics?" I ask Gina.

"Super." She is sweating.

"Hey, you okay?"

"Yeah, nervous as heck. It's my first time doing a twenty-minute set. Most of my longer sets were ten- or fifteen-minute ones."

"It's a milestone," Bryan, who's showrunning tonight, says. He reaches out and companionably pats Gina's arm. "The first twenty-minute set is always a big deal, just like the first ten-minute set, the first fifteen . . ."

"Okay, er, break a leg? Good luck? May the Force be with you? Whatever you believe in," I say quickly when her face purples.

"Anyway, here's the set list posted on the group chat with your times," Bryan says. I scan it and see that I'm the second performer in the second half, and I'm doing a five-minute set. Ray's closing out the first half, with seven minutes.

Kong emits a barely audible squeak of thanks. Bryan says, "There, there," and pulls him out of the booth to a corner outdoors, presumably to pep-talk him. Performance nerves are contagious.

"Where's Ray?" I wonder. It's ten minutes till curtains come up.

"He told me he's a few minutes away," Gina says. "He and his dad are stuck in traffic."

I nod, vaguely clocking Royce's lie while keeping an eye on the door for Zee, who has also just texted to let me know she is on the way, which in Malaysian-speak meant she had just realized she had to leave and was going to arrive half an hour later; there's a small part of me that still hopes to see my teammates in the audience. Royce slips in a few minutes later, standing to the side of the room. Gina motions for him to join them, but he shakes his head. His eyes meet mine, cut away.

He's avoiding you, a voice pipes up.

I set my jaw. I don't know if this is true—I suspect it—but if it is . . . the idea of Royce avoiding me cuts me like backhanded slap. After our interaction on the bleachers yesterday, I was beginning to think we might be friendly, but now that I'm back in comedy he's back to treating me like I'm nobody again.

Whatever. I force myself to remember the time when this would not have bugged me, because it does, more than I care to admit.

Bryan opens the night with a strong performance, followed by

Vern, Milly, Kong (who bombs but gets raucous applause for being a sweet, bumbling comedy virgin). Kong exits the stage and runs out of the restaurant, presumably to heave the contents of his stomach onto the sidewalk.

"Another one bites the dust," Milly says.

And then it's Royce.

Royce goes onstage, licks his lips, and grips the mike so hard I can see his knuckles shining whitely. This would normally be my cue to jinx him in my head, but strangely enough, I don't, I can't.

What is happening to me?

"I—I—I . . ."

He shakes his head, then begins again, his voice firmer.

"I'm going to medical school in the UK—or so my mom tells me. She's even got my school picked out for me, can you believe it? Oxford. She wants me to go to Oxford. Kill two birds with one stone. This way, if I fail medical school, at least I'll marry someone success-ful. Preferably royalty—but *no pressure*."

The audience chuckles. Kumar leans over and whispers, "Oh cool, he's doing his pushy-mother, student-debt set. Good stuff."

Royce continues. "Anyway, medical textbooks are so expensive, so my mom says let's get your whole set now to beat inflation! I had to buy an immunobiology textbook, and the storekeeper said, 'We accept Master, Visa, and kidneys.' I told him I'm all out of spare kid-neys after my anatomy textbook, but he could have my mom's. After all, she did say, 'Anything to get you to college.'" A pause. "Bet she didn't think it meant giving up a kidney."

He gets a couple of small laughs and keeps riffing on being a stu-dent in today's inflationary world. The setup and punch lines are solid and should have gotten stronger laughs, but it's his delivery that is unconvincing. I bite my lip and cringe as the set goes on in the same vein. Why is he making these jokes? Doesn't he have other material? Royce isn't poor. He has bodyguards, for goodness' sake.

Who is Ray Lim, really?

The rest of his set goes by and ends with polite applause. Royce catches my eye and looks away almost immediately. He ambles down the stairs and hugs the side of the room, looking at his phone, while Bryan does some housekeeping announcements. There's a fifteen-minute intermission, and I wonder if he will come over when Bryan is done.

My breath catches in my throat when he approaches the comic's table and greets everyone with a *hey*. Everyone says encouraging things, but Royce doesn't seem cheered by it.

He ignores me, and I ignore him, hurt. I pull out my phone and pretend to be focused on my set. Well, if Mr. Bigshot is going to be a dick to me, for reasons I don't understand, then I'm going to forget being cordial with him. It makes no difference to me whether Royce is in my life or not.

But my fingers tremble as I run through the set.

Royce announces he's going to get a soft drink and asks if anyone needs anything from the bar. Gina goes with him; apparently the comics have an open tab for soft drinks on the house, but she needs to come with him to sign the bill.

"Is Ray the most experienced, after Gina and Bryan, at least on this list today?" I ask Vern. "Seems like he has more time than other performers."

"No, he isn't, but comedy's not about who's been at it longer, it's about who's *good* at it. Ray gets more time because he's very good, although he's only been performing stand-up for two years or so." Vern sees my befuddled expression and says, "I hate to admit it, but he's usually much, much better. He's been off his game lately, right around the time you came along." He contemplates me. "So, tell me the truth: Is there something going on between you two? There's a bit of a palpable . . . tension."

I hold myself still. "Well, we kind of know each other from school." I don't give more details, since the moment they find out which school we go to, Ray's comic persona's credibility would be shot to pieces. "Like, we're cocaptains of the track-and-field team, and, uh, we're kind of competitive."

Vern smacks his hand on the table. "Aha! So that's what it is. It all makes sense now."

"Yeah, we really don't get along because of that."

"So, you're not seeing each other?" he asks, watching me.

I shake my head, and he gives me a clouded smile. "Interesting," he says. He brushes his hair out of his face and is about to say something when Royce comes back with Gina and Zee, radiant in an emerald-green long-sleeved top, jeans, and a pink-and-white floral headscarf and rocking a dark berry lip. The three of them are carrying opened bottles of soft drinks for everyone, though Zee has one arm up taking a panning shot of the place as she narrates a reel for her socials.

"Zee!" I say, waving.

"Agnes!" she says, putting the drinks, then her phone down. "I come prepared with power banks, plural! And I bought drinks for everyone!"

"I tried to tell her soft drinks are complimentary for comics, but she basically shoved me back and told them to put all the drinks on her fancy metal credit card," Gina says.

"Oh, it's no problem, I'm happy to support," Zee says airily. "After all, Agnes is my dearest friend. Now, I know I am the odd non-comic out crashing this table, so anytime you guys need anything, just let me get it."

"Wow," Vern mutters under his breath next to me, and I feel a jolt of recognition at his tone.

"You're always welcome to hang with the cool table," Milly says, grinning, "if you're buying drinks."

Zee claps twice. "Sold. As long as it's not alcohol, for obvious reasons." She slid into the booth. "I'm sorry I'm late," she calls down the table to me.

"No worries," I say. "I'm used to it. At least you haven't missed my set."

"Yeah, though I am bummed that I missed 'Ray's' performance here," she said with a wink at Royce, who flushes. Royce must have briefed her about the situation when they ran into each other at the bar.

I introduce Zee as Zee but of course everyone recognizes her regardless—when your great-grandfather is one of the founding fathers of the oldest political party in Malaysia and your father is a chief minister, it happens.

I catch the little inhale she does when she shakes Vern's hand. Uh-oh. "Are you a model?" she asks Vern, one hand on her heart while looking deep into his eyes.

Vern scoffs, brushing his tousled hair out of his eyes. "Absolutely not." He abruptly turns to Hamid, and the two of them begin discussing Bryan's set.

Zee nods. "*So* rude," I hear her say a little dreamily.

People leave the booth, and in the reshuffle, Royce and Zee end up sitting at the other corner of the booth. I watch Royce chatting with Zee and Gina, fighting a twinge of envy as they laugh together. Royce can be very charming, although he certainly isn't trying with me. Somehow, that irks me more than it should. *Focus*, I tell myself.

Then it's my turn. I go up on the stage to whoops from the audience. There's a large table of particularly raucous diners celebrating what appears to be a birthday (the giant *30* balloon helped). Someone from that birthday table yells, "Jailbait!"

"You see, people like that"—I point to the birthday table—"is why I welcome the Purge."

They laugh good-naturedly, or drunkenly.

I segue into my set about being a teenage girl online and gaming.

"I'm in crypto," yells a man wearing a garland of fuchsia plastic flowers—presumably the birthday boy—from the boisterous table. A low chant begins among his friends, "Crypto, crypto, crypto."

"Shut up, cringe farts," I say amicably. "You speak when you have a mike, can you crypto that?"

The surrounding tables burst into applause and hearty boos, and the original heckler raises his hands up in a gesture of surrender. "I'm drunk," he says, like it's an excuse for everything.

I turn my attention away from that table. "Anyway, speaking about social media, my parents aren't on TikTok, and that's a good thing. I think they would regret having kids if they saw what we get up to. The other day I saw someone post a TikTok of zits popping in slow motion. I mean, just open the seven seals already."

I continue in this vein until Bryan signals that my time is up by making an X sign with his arms, and I finish the set with a snappy punch line. The audience claps hard, and I acknowledge them somewhat bashfully, the adrenaline leaving my system as I make my way to the comics' booth. Meanwhile, Bryan gets up and heads onstage to introduce the next comic.

I hesitate when I get to the crowded booth. There's only one spot untaken—and it's on the bench next to Royce, who's seated next to Zee.

I clench everything and force myself to slide in, like it was nothing, next to him. Because there is nothing between us that could make sitting next to him an issue, anyway. Royce is just like anybody else. Just an average human being.

Zee leans over and pinches me; her eyes are wide. "Agnes, you didn't tell me you were funny."

I smack her arm, and she sticks out her tongue.

"Scoot over," Milly says when she's back with a tower of beer and some glasses. "And this round's on me, you cheap fucks, so help yourselves."

I scoot over, wearing the expression of a slug entering a salt bath, until my body and Royce's body meet.

He and I are holding ourselves at an angle to minimize contact, but despite how we started out trying not to touch, it feels like we're not fighting it after a while. His thigh presses hard into mine with an insistence that makes my mouth go dry. Maybe he's trying to manspread, yeah, that's it. I push back, in the spirit of defending my territory on that bench and only that.

Vern reaches over to shake my hand. "Ags, you didn't prepare that set at all, did you? And I mean this in a good way."

"No. I mean yes, parts of it I freestyled because of the heckler."

"Nice job," Gina says, high-fiving me. "You're a natural. Maybe the best I've seen."

Royce says in what he thinks is a joking way, "You used to say that about me," to which Gina shrugs and says, with a conspiratorial wink at me, "一山还有一山高."

"I speak Mandarin, too," Royce grumbles. He unsticks his thigh from mine.

Vern helps himself to a mug of beer and places another before me. "Want some?" he says nonchalant.

I am about to reach for it—my first drink of alcohol, why not, it's been a whole *month* of life crapping on me—when Royce pushes the mug across the table with a flick of his wrist. "Are you trying to take out the competition, Vern?" He doesn't say this in a jokey way. In fact, his whole body is tensed. "Also, she's underage."

"Oh, don't be a buzzkill, Ray," Vern says. His voice is playful but his eyes are cold. "It's not like I haven't seen you drink, and you're her age, aren't you?"

Royce turns to me, and I can read his look. It's a "What have you told him?" flash of worry, and I shrug and give a curt shake of my head to let him know it's fine, his secret rich-boy identity is safe with me, and he relaxes a little, but not enough to move his arm out of the slide path of Vern's mug of beer.

"Cut it out, Vern," Gina says, before tensions escalate. "You don't want to get Bryan in trouble with the restaurant over underage drinking."

Vern shrugs. "I didn't think it was a big deal. She's, what, seventeen? Not a baby." He flicks his feline eyes at me and there's a dare in them.

"Yeah, *Dad*," I say flippantly to Royce, annoyed that he thought he was in any position to "protect" me.

Royce withdraws his arm and says, "Go ahead, then."

"I don't think *either* of you should be drinking," Zee says. "Especially you, Roy—*Ray*, you know. Because of who could be around." She raises her eyebrows and I know she's thinking of the tabloids. Because even with the weird hair, the rumpled clothing, and the beanie, Royce is too han—I mean he's too Royce-looking to pass as someone else, although you have to know who you're looking for beforehand. It's only because he's always kept a low profile in the media that no one's hounding him, but if anyone knew that the son of Peter and Ming Taslim was in the room—

"No one under twenty-one drinks here," Gina says, stepping in to grab the offending mug of beer and downing the contents in a few noisy glugs. "We don't need any slipups, guys." She jerks her head toward the bar, where a bespectacled man in his fifties was glaring in their direction. "See that guy in a suit? That's Nick, the new restaurant manager. I hope we don't get complaints about today's set, because he hates when we are rude to customers, even if they are hecklers. It's bad for business. We need this venue: It has a crowd that's a good mix of locals and foreigners, the stage is professional, and the setup we have here is sweet, with the free drinks and snacks during the show." She isn't finger-pointing, but I wilt a little at her words. I hadn't thought about the ramifications of my name-calling.

"Sorry," I say.

Gina waves my apology away. "Don't worry about it, it's not your fault. I'm going to check in with Nick, placate him if needed. And intimidate people into tipping."

Because there wasn't a door charge at this restaurant, the comics were passing around a tip box that was currently making its rounds among the seated diners.

"Thanks, Mama Gina," the table choruses.

To my right, in my ear, Royce mutters, "You didn't have to apologize for anything. Those bastards were rude and arrogant." He bites his lip before muttering, "And I thought your set was . . . not shit. There were some really acceptable punch lines."

A callback—*my* callback. A slow, secret glow spreads through me.

I turn to Royce to thank him just as he glances over, our gazes hook and this time we don't look away.

~

Gina goes on after Hamid and kills. Her set is polished, one bit segueing into another without hesitation. I skip along with her, barely noticing time flying by. Watching Gina at the top of a game she loves made me realize that all this, and more, is within my reach. I can be as good as I was at running, and I could enjoy myself doing this.

I have purpose again.

When her set finishes to crashing applause, she floats down the stage and joins us. A band comes onstage to set up for live music.

Nick ambles over and hands them a tip box that's been going around after the performance marked STARVING COMICS' FUND and an envelope. "The envelope's from the birthday table. Good job today, everyone." He gives an awkward salute, then leaves.

Gina's eyes widen as she checks out the amount of money in the envelope marked *Enjoy, and sorry we were dicks! –Dan.*

"Wow, guys," she says, her voice hushed, "there's *a lot* of money in here. Crypto is definitely treating Birthday Boy well." She opens the tip box and rattles the contents in there speculatively. "And there's a bunch of money in here, too."

The comics gather around Gina with reverent faces. Malaysia does not have a strong tip culture, so this is a welcome surprise. She pulls out the money from the envelope; the wad of five- and ten-ringgit notes obscene in its thickness. She counts the pile of notes slowly, as though she is savoring the experience. "Three hundred . . . four hundred . . . five hundred . . . six hundred." She licks her lips and gives a low whistle. "Holy crap. I mean, I've been a performer for a long time, and this is a huge tip. There's, like, *six hundred twenty* ringgit in here, on top of the tips we got from the other tables." She shakes her head, her eyes wide. "Usually we count ourselves lucky if we go home with five ringgit each in tips from a gig like this."

"It was all you," Kumar says. "You were the CEO of comedy."

"I don't watch stand-up, but even I could tell you were slaying. Respect!" Zee says.

Gina glows at the praise. "Thanks. You lot did well, too, especially mini Mrs. Maisel here!" She elbows me playfully. I blush.

"You were all great. Anyway, customarily, in my shows at least, headliner gets twenty-five percent of the total receipts, so—congrats, Gina!" says Bryan, who's the most experienced performer and the showrunner of today's bunch. The others murmur their assent. Sai and Milly offer to pass on their cut, and Kong is still gone, so too bad.

"I'm not going to dispute that," Gina says, grinning. She counts out her cut and divvies out the rest between the performers. I'm thrilled that my evening nets me actual money since I've been on hiatus from *Seoul Hot*. I straighten the bills and put it in my wallet, so I don't accidentally, I don't know, throw it out, although the chances of that happening is—nil.

"Here's your cut," Gina says, passing the last sixty ringgit to Royce.

"It's okay, I don't need it," he says quickly, not taking it. "It's yours."

Gina starts. "What do you mean?"

We're all watching Royce now. I know what he meant, of course, but the rest of them aren't sure. Sixty ringgit is chump change for Royce, only he's here as *Ray*, starving artist. Starving student artist.

He blinks. "I mean I don't *deserve* it, after that performance."

"Dude, just take it. Even Kumar took it, and he sucked," Gina said. She turns to him and says, "Sorry, doll. You know I love you."

Kumar nods. "I blew my five minutes."

"People were shell-shocked," Hamid said. "They regretted being born."

"Cut it out," Kumar says genially.

"I don't . . ." Royce's neck is flushing. He realizes he's made a faux pas and is wondering how to dig himself out of it. I was unnerved by the fact he thought sixty ringgit, sure, sixty Malaysian *ringgit*, wasn't a big deal to a teenager. "Um, okay, yeah, why not." He reaches out and awkwardly accepts the bills and, without even looking at them, slips them into a jean pocket in a crumpled mass. Zee raises an eyebrow at me, having clocked the entire exchange.

A hard knot forms in my stomach. I would have had to work in the Seoul Hot's kitchen for three hours for less. He's just seventeen, for crying out loud. What was his allowance like?

"I'm off," Kumar says. "Classes tomorrow, and it's almost bedtime for me. I'm a teaching assistant at a preschool," he explains to me.

"Us too, I guess," Hamid says, glancing at Vern, but Vern waves him off and says he'll stay.

"I have some stuff to clarify with Bryan about the new regional amateur stand-up comedy competition that I just found out about. Apparently, Bryan's friend is on the marketing team of JOGGCo, the cosponsor of the event, and he knows stuff," Vern says. He glances at me. "And if Ms. Chan here can linger a while, I'd like to catch up with an old friend."

I shrug. "Sure," I say. I can feel Zee's—and Royce's—eyes on me. "Erm, yeah, but you know, can Zee stay?"

Vern gives me a questioning look but nods. "Sure, why not."

"I can't, actually," Zee says, looking disappointed. "I told my parents I'd be home early."

"Next time, then," Vern says, not seeing the hope that flashes in Zee's eyes at his words. He turns to Bryan. "Okay, now spill! I want all the insider intel!"

"I don't know anything beyond what's out there, but sure, pump me for answers I don't have about the competition," Bryan says.

"What competition?" Milly says.

"That new one just for youngsters," Sai says.

"Here," Kumar says. "I've sent you a link."

The inaugural JOGGCo International Young Comedians Competition (with two legs for ASEAN and East Asia)

Calling all amateur comics from sixteen to twenty-one years old hailing from ASEAN and East Asia—the first leg of the JOGGCo International Young Comedians Competition (JIYCC) will be held for the first time ever in Kuala Lumpur; winner gets a chance to perform in legendary comedy club Comedy City in New York for five minutes opening the US tour for an exciting Netflix comedian and 10,000USD in cash!

"Holy shit, ten thousand US dollars in cash," I say as Royce says, "Comedy City, can you believe," in a tone I've never heard from him before.

"Man, what terrible acronyms," Milly says. "JIYCC, yiccck."

"I'd just call it the JOGGCo competition," Sai says.

"It's pretty exciting; I envy you guys," Gina says. "Wish I qualified."

"How old are you, Auntie?" Kumar asks.

"You bite your tongue, young man," Gina says amiably.

"It's cool that they're holding the qualifiers here instead of Bangkok. I can't wait," Vern says.

"Aren't you above the age limit?" I ask Vern.

"Are you trying, indirectly, to ask me how old I am?" he says, raising an eyebrow. He grins and leans closer. "Are you flirting with me?"

"Am not," I say hotly. Zee's face is directly in my field of vision, and she's watching this interaction like a shark.

Vern draws back, amused. "Just teasing you," he says. "I'm nineteen, Agnes. And you?"

"Seventeen," I say. Despite knowing better, I thought of him as being in his early twenties. I suppose it was his confidence, his surfer's tan, and slightly cynical air, all of which make him appear older than he is.

"Cool," he says, silkily, throwing a casual arm around my shoulders. "You should join us, compete."

Beside me, I hear, rather than see, Royce set his jaw. Urgh, he's so territorial about stand-up.

"It sounds fun," I say, "but I'm not sure if I can commit to the scene, or if I'm even good enough. . . ."

"You should, you're really talented," Bryan speaks up.

Sai nods and says, "He's right, you are a natural."

I flush, a mixture of pride and embarrassment. "Thanks, I'll consider it."

"I'll make sure she comes back," Zee says. "My girl has potential."

"Listen to your girl, Zee, she has good taste," Vern says.

Zee blushes. "Thanks." She stands up, reluctance etched in her movements. "Sorry but I've got to leave. My parents are expecting me, so I better dash. . . ."

"See you soon, love, and do come back, both of you!" Milly says. The comics nod and wave. I see Royce leaving the booth from the corner of my eye as I head to the door with Zee.

"Wow, I can see why you like this scene, there's a lot of *talent*," Zee says, waving as her ride pulls up. "Need a ride?"

"It's okay," I say. She always offers, and I usually decline. "I'll just bus back."

She blows me a kiss as she climbs into her Vellfire. I wave goodbye to her and am about to head to the bus stop when I notice Royce sitting a few steps down the curb, watching a video of a comic performing. He glances up and gives me a stiff wave, which I somehow interpret as "come over." I'm acting very weird tonight.

"Hey," he says as I approach. He puts his phone away and doesn't make a move to leave, so I wasn't reading the room wrong.

"Hey." I motion at the spot next to him. "Can I sit?"

"It's a free country," he says. I take it as a yes and sit beside him.

"So. No rats tonight," I say, because I'm clearly a conversationalist of the highest order.

"No," he says, a crinkle in his eyes. "Must be my cologne."

I snort-laugh. Who knew Taslim could banter?

"You were very good today, Chan."

"So were you."

He cocks his head at me. "Don't be polite, I was bang average."

Nothing about you is average, I think but don't say. Instead, I shrug. "It's okay. We all have off days, right?"

He gives me a small smile. "All these half compliments. It's almost as though we're getting to a stage where we can be friends."

"Yeah," I say. His eyes are very gold under the warm streetlights.

"So, are you going to join the competition?" he says after a beat where too many words were not said.

I ponder this. I've been searching for something to free myself from the dull fog of disappointment after my high school sporting career prematurely ended, and tonight's events, the natural ease of it, felt right. Maybe this was a sign. It had to be.

"Yes, yes, I am," I say, nodding. "Which means I'll have to do way more open mikes to get anywhere near polished. You'll see me all the time. Can you handle it?"

"It'll be a drag, but I *suppose* I can tolerate it," he says, and it's only because I catch the smallest quirk in his full lips that I know he's teasing me.

"I guess I'll be seeing you around, then, Lim," I say, trying to mask the hitch in my breath. *Bacteria,* I remind myself sternly.

He leans closer, so close I can smell his cologne, which smells like a distillation of Timothée Chalamet's and Timothy Olyphant's (the best Tims in Hollywood) blended essences. "Challenge accepted. By the way, um, if you're not . . . if you aren't already, um, are you sure you don't want to—"

"You need a ride, Agnes?" someone says.

It's Vern, pulling up in a vintage pale blue Volkswagen Beetle that makes dangerous guttering noises ever so often. I whip my head around. He waves. "We were supposed to catch up after drinks, but you pulled a Cinderella with your friend."

"Nice ride," I say, smiling. "Sorry, I spaced, I totally forgot. I guess I'm pretty tired after all."

"You guys know each other?" Royce says, an odd expression on his face.

"Yeah, we're old schoolmates before Dunia," I tell Royce.

"She was a superstar, everyone knew her," Vern says. "So, ride?"

"Which way you headed? I don't want to trouble you."

Vern shrugs. "No trouble at all. I enjoy driving. But if it matters, I'm headed to Damansara."

"Oh cool, I'm on the way, ish." I tell him which suburb I live in.

"Perfect. Let's go."

I slide through the door Vern opens for me, catching Royce's eye as we pull away from the curb. It's strange, but it almost looks like he's disappointed that I'm leaving.

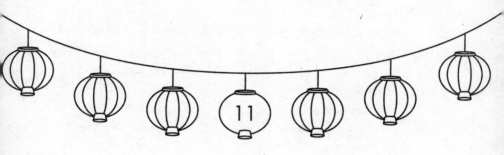

THE CAR RIDE IS QUIETER THAN I'D EXPECTED. I DRUM MY FINGERS IN
my lap and inelegantly perspire. Every possible bad outcome flashes
through my mind, no thanks to my copious consumption of true-
crime podcasts and my friendship with Zee, who believes that she
is destined to die in a dramatic (but not vehicle-related, strangely
enough) fashion. It occurs to me that aside from the fact he is a
comic and we used to go to the same school, I know next to nothing
about him.

"I know nothing about you. You could be a serial killer."

"So could you," he quips dryly. "Those pincerlike legs, inner rage—
classic early serial-killer energy."

I chuckle and settle back in my seat. We crawl to a stop at a red
light.

"You really don't remember me, huh?" he says, contemplating me.

"Nope," I say. I am allowed a white lie after the long night I've had.
I don't feel like talking, don't feel like rehashing the past.

"You find out more about your dad already?" he asks.

Zero segue. "What?" I say, startled. Vern had remembered what we
talked about four years ago. He was paying attention.

The light changes and we inch forward into a wall of traffic. A traffic jam at 9:45 p.m. in the three-lane expressway means there's been an accident. Motorists are slowing down to rubberneck, some to take down the number plates so they can buy the lottery numbers for 4D the next day. We're going to be stuck in traffic for a while.

"I guess you forgot about our chat in the cafeteria back then, before you disappeared from school?"

I shrug, feigning nonchalance. "Oh, that. My mom told me the full story about my bio dad, yeah. A couple of months after I transferred."

He nods. "How was it?"

I let out a shaky laugh. "Inspiring."

When I turned thirteen, I asked my mom for an unusual present: I asked for the entire story of my bio dad—no names, just the facts—and she complied, reluctantly. Told me how she'd had a one-night stand with an acquaintance in her sophomore year at Georgetown University and got pregnant. He came from a powerful, conservative Asian American family who would have wanted them to get married, if he had acknowledged my existence—after all, her parents had wanted that, too, on top of other things. So she kept me a secret for the longest time, even after I was born.

She did tell him about me when I was about two, she said. He was engaged to be married by then and he told her never to contact him again. He offered to pay her a large sum of money to disappear, but of course my mother couldn't bring herself to take it, although she admitted to regretting that decision in the years to come when things got tough.

She showed me a photo of him she found online. I have his large dark eyes, his expressive brows, the same quirk in his lips when he finds something privately amusing. He had been a star athlete, too, when he was young. A baseballer. That's how he'd gotten to Georgetown on scholarship. That's how he met my mom, an academic scholarship kid from Malaysia.

That's how my mother's life got derailed.

I force down the lump that always appears when I think about this and change the subject abruptly. "So, uh, how long have you been in stand-up?"

He drums his fingers against the chipped steering wheel. "I don't know. Two, maybe three years? I started after I saw Ali Wong's first Netflix special. You remember that?"

I nod reverentially. "Absolutely. My mom and I both sat down to watch it, and she doesn't even *like* stand-up."

"It was just . . . revelatory, you know? Like, damn, I can do that. I don't have to work at a desk job."

"I take it you were not a star student."

He snorts. "You wish. I got by just fine. I mean, I wasn't a star student per se, but I was a very good student. A's and B's, never struggled, just never had the extra mental sauce that made me exceptional, academic scholarship material. I could have taken the traditional path, I guess, but one day I just woke up and thought: why. Why am I doing any of it? I don't want to go to university, I don't want to have a desk job. I'm a performer. I just want to do what I want, earn enough money to live how I want."

"Oh, so you're one of those, huh," I say.

"What?"

"Family has money yet for some reason the kids go to public school?"

He is quiet for such a long time I worry I said something wrong. "Nope. Poor as a wharf rat" is all he says. "So why are *you* in comedy?"

"By accident?" I say, instead of *for company*. "Like, I, uh, literally, figuratively fell into this." I summarize the accident.

"Well, when athletics lost a star, we gained one," he says. "Lucky us."

"Thanks." My face is burning. I'd never been complimented so frankly before. "I—I don't know if I'm a star . . . Beginner's luck, I guess."

"Nope," he says with a pointed shake of his head. "You have *It*. It's a rare thing for a newcomer, to be able to hit the ground running like that. I didn't have that ease. You and Gina are naturals." He throws me a half smile. "You don't need to be a natural to be good, but talent sure as hell helps."

I'm sure my face is melting off. "I've always liked stand-up comedy. I've been listening to specials since I was twelve. There were some days"—the days I didn't like thinking about, the days I think my mother wishes she could erase from my memory—"I listened to YouTube specials for hours . . . I guess I absorbed some of it by osmosis."

"Comedy—the cheapest therapy you can get," he quips darkly.

"Not sure it's therapy so much as distraction."

We stay silent, each lost in our memories. Then he hiccups, we laugh, and the spell breaks. He fiddles with some dials on the dashboard. A catchy pop song I don't recognize plays. "What is this?"

"'Wannabe' by the Spice Girls. It's a pop song from the nineties. If you want to listen to something current, just you know, scroll though my phone and pull up Spotify." He passes me his phone, which I take without thinking. "It's unlocked."

I nod, trying to play it cool—it's not every day you get access to an older guy's entire life in one place.

He glances over and sees me staring at the phone like it's a pager, which is something Stanley once showed me, and I lost my mind over its quaintness. "Everything okay?"

"Mmfffm, yes."

He grins at me. "You haven't changed a jot. You're something else, Agnes. I like you."

His reply was so uncomplicated and easy. Very much not like the person I was not thinking about.

"Okay," I say, ever eloquent. I force myself to speak in my normal fashion and practically shout the following: "Why are you listening to nineties pop?"

"Oh, I'm getting inspiration for a bit I'm doing about old-school pop versus our pop. You know, the lyrics back then and now. I like contrasting the past with the present in my sets. It's so silly that we're always harping about learning from the past, but we're mostly just as intolerant and murderous and horrible as we were a thousand years ago." He laughs humorlessly at some private memory.

"My mom is a millennial, and she would totally laugh her butt off if she heard you refer to nineties pop as *old-school*. I mean, she probably grew up listening to even older music, like from the seventies and eighties. And then there's, like, sixties pop . . ." I was babbling.

The light turns green, and he pops the gear into drive. "So true."

We drive in companiable silence for the rest of the trip, listening to music from my mother's youth, until he breaks it with a statement. "So, I noticed the tension between you and Ray."

I nod. "A little."

"Well, you really threw Golden Ray off his game, so I'll say there's more to it than that." He chuckles at some private amusement. "You're not friends with Ray, right?"

After a slight hesitation I say, "No, but we're friendly."

A red light. We roll to a stop. Vern turns to me and says, "Well, even if he's your friend, I'll still say this: He's such a phony."

I start. "I'm sorry, what?"

"Look, I'm not stupid. Those scuffed, limited-edition sneakers? His 'brandless' designer jeans? His posh accent that he tries so hard to water down? Please. It's why his jokes about his average-Joe life never hit as hard as they should." Vern scoffs. "Especially when you're Royce Taslim."

So he knew. "When did you figure it out?"

He laughs. "Today, actually. When Zee accidentally called him Roy. I figured since she was your friend and she knew Ray—Royce, you guys had to all go to the same school. She's such a public person that it made my sleuthing easy. From there it was just a matter of a few careful search words, since you mentioned you were cocaptains of the track-and-field team before."

A cold feeling slid down my back. "You're keeping his secret, right?"

I say this matter-of-factly, so that Vern doesn't catch the worry in my voice.

Vern shrugs. "For now. But now that I know who he is, it pisses me off even more, seeing him tell those jokes of his. His whole 'struggling everyman' persona is *my* reality."

Vern was right, of course. Ray—*Royce* was a phony. I knew that. It just sounded so much starker, visceral, when it was put that way.

Phony. Phony. Phony.

"He's a good guy. He's kind."

"He can afford to be kind," Vern says. "Most people, especially the rich, are, under the right conditions. The trick is to catch them when things are inconvenient for them. Then you see their true colors."

The air-conditioning shudders and belches out hot air. He jiggles a tab and sighs when nothing happens. "Sorry."

"It's fine, let's roll down the windows."

He looks at me approvingly. He asks for my address, and we drive to mine in companionable silence.

"Here we are," he says. He checks out the modest three-bedder, double-story terrace house and says, "Nice place."

"Thanks," I say. "Also for the ride."

"You're welcome," he says. "Anytime. And, Agnes?"

I pause with my hand on the door. "Yeah?"

"I'm glad we reconnected."

I wave goodbye and bolt into the house, almost knocking into someone waiting in the living room with the TV playing: Mom. "Ten forty," she says, looking at her watch. "Not too bad."

"You should be in bed," I tell her.

"I should," she says. "But I wanted to make sure you're safe."

"I am," I say.

She nods. "I'm going to bed now."

"Mom, please don't wait up for me next time. You know I can take care of myself."

"I know." A sadness reaches her eyes. "You grew up so early."

She kisses me and heads upstairs. I wait till she's gone and head to my room. If I'm going to enter this comedy competition, there's no time to lose. I have to start practicing.

Bryan recorded the entire set on his phone—among this group of open mikers they have a tradition of having a rotating roster of comics who do this for the group, so the comics can study their and others' performances—and he'd sent out the link to the uploaded master file half an hour ago. I fast-forward to my set, noting that Royce's set was not on the recording. He must have opted out. I had seen him recording his own sets on his own phone set up on a tripod.

For whatever reason, it was important to Royce to keep his Ray persona on the down low, to hide in plain sight, to live a lie, and while I don't think his double life is sustainable in the long run—as soon as you start gaining traction as a performer, sooner or later, someone will record you and post it online, and it'll only be a matter of time before his identity is exposed—I feel compelled to respect it. It's unsporting to do otherwise, and I'm still, at the core of it, a sporting person.

I watch the video of my performance again and again, taking notes and working on my set, writing new material as I go, until I fall asleep sometime after midnight.

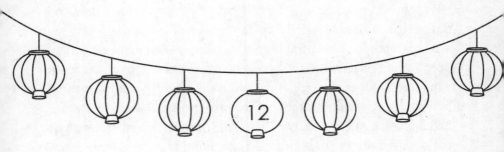

MY SLEEP IS AGITATED, COLORED BY FRENETIC BURSTS OF DREAMS. OF people laughing, of people chasing me. I wake up exhausted and disoriented the next day before my alarm even rings, so early that it's barely light outside. A quick check confirms it's 6:15 a.m., more than an hour earlier than when I need to be up by. I mutter extravagant curses at the sleep gods and gingerly make my way to the kitchen for some coffee.

There's a crack of light from the study, which is unusual—both my parents would normally be in their room at this hour. I pause a few steps outside the door, where Stanley and my mom are having a hushed, agitated discussion.

"The numbers don't work, Stan," she says. "Especially after Agnes's physio bills came in and the insurance told us they won't reimburse all of them, those . . . those—" She says something in Cantonese that makes me blush. "Urgh. We'll have to—I don't know, just . . ."

Stanley sighs. "I know, I'm trying to figure it out with the school. Maybe I can sub in when Clara Sim goes on maternity leave, teach English."

"That's a lot of prep work."

"It's fine."

"We could sell my car. . . ."

"That old clunker? It's not going to net us much and might end up costing us more if we need to take private hire cars or taxis, especially for my job." Kuala Lumpur is a sprawling city, with only certain areas being quite well-connected with public transport; it can be terribly difficult to navigate from one end to another without a car. As a litigation clerk, my mother's job involves some traveling for administrative and outreach purposes, and in her state, it didn't make sense for her to be traveling in a crowded bus or MRT.

"I could ask for overtime at the law firm," she says. "I'll speak to Khairul."

"You're already working pretty hard, Ling."

"It's a desk job, Stan."

"The doctor says your pregnancy is—"

"Stanley, I'm fine. Middle-aged geriatrics like me have babies at this age all the time these days," she says curtly.

Stanley sucks his teeth. "Ling, you know that's not it. You have underlying—"

"Mooooooommm," Rosie sobs. "Mom! Mom! I had a nightmare!"

"I'm putting a pin in this conversation," my mother says, already striding across the room.

I panic and sneak back down the landing toward my room, entering just as I hear the study door open on its creaky hinges and my mother's careful tread as she makes her way past my door to Rosie's. That was a narrow escape. Thank goodness I play enough tactical games to know how to evade capture from hostile forces.

Okay, maybe I should try to game a little less.

I text the proprietor of Seoul Hot, Mrs. Yoon, to ask her if I could come back to work, my fingers mentally crossed that she's in a good mood.

Who this? she replies almost immediately. I press my lips,

simultaneously impressed that she's up and annoyed that she hadn't saved my number. Before the accident, I'd been doing at least two four-hour shifts a week. I reply with my name.

Oh. Maybe next Friday? Usual time? Can you serve customer? Good to know my health matters only in relation to my ability to perform.

I flex my calves. I don't think it's a good idea to stand on my feet for four hours in a row, even if it's been two months since my accident.

Sure, I say.

~

"You're entering a stand-up comedy competition with Taslim? Yaasssssss!'" Zee says, gleeful.

I muster a half-hearted smile at her enthusiasm. My heart isn't in the conversation. From my vantage point by the window, the emerald lawn sparkles, freshly watered by the sprinklers. Inside the air-conditioned cafeteria where Zee and I are catching up over lunch, students are laughing and chatting as they queue up for the meal of the day (cod fish fingers—made from actual Atlantic cod and not "cod"—or veggie burger), checking out the different fresh juices lining the counter, helping themselves to premium condiments (that nobody ever steals!) and paper napkins and fresh slices of lemon and lime for their water. It's hard to reconcile that with the financial pressures at home.

"Look, if you need me to, I'm willing to take Taslim out," Zee offers gallantly.

"Like, murder?" I say, raising an eyebrow.

She sputters. "Er, what? I meant *blackmail*. We ferret out his dirty secrets and use them to get him to drop out of the competition."

"Wow, you are so much more morally superior."

"I'd do anything for you," she says. She widens her eyes. "Just like how you'd do anything for me, won't you?"

"Not murder," I say firmly. You have to draw the line with Zalifah Bakri.

She fiddles with a pin in her headscarf and looks at me coyly. "But you'd set me up with Vern, right? Isn't he your friend?"

"Zeeeeeee," I groan. "I just started stand-up. I need to be taken seriously."

"You do hear the contradiction in that statement, don't you? Anyway, dating is serious stuff, and it can be done on the down low." She flutters her lashes. "Your girl is low-key obsessed with Vee, he's so mysterious."

"I'll see what I can do," I say, refusing to commit to Zee's crush swings. Before Taslim, it was a visiting debate team champion. I'm hoping she'll drop Vern soon. "Speaking of which, I thought you didn't like stand-up comics. Too needy, your exact words."

"Nothing about Vern is needy, that's why," Zee says. She really is great at sussing people out. "So, tell me more about this competition."

I bring up the website so we can go through it together. "The competition has two legs. The qualifiers in Kuala Lumpur will be at the end of December, just before our semester exams; the semis in Singapore for contestants from Thailand, Malaysia, and Singapore will be early January; and then the finals in NYC during spring break. Winners gets ten thousand US dollars and a chance to perform at Comedy City in New York, opening for some hot new Netflix comic."

"Oooh, Netflix," Zee says, eyes wide. She looks at the sponsors and the lead judge that has been confirmed for the NYC leg. "Wow, this competition is a huge deal. Just qualifying for this would look so good on your college applications. With your improved grades—fingers crossed—you'll definitely have a higher chance of getting at least a partial scholarship somewhere in the US."

My stomach clenches; from everything I heard this morning, I'm not sure if a partial scholarship will work anymore. "There's a chance I won't be able to go to the States unless I get a full-ride scholarship," I admit.

"But isn't the NCAA your dream?" Zee says naively.

I turn away, my chest clenching with rare irritation against Zee. Of course it is. I have always wanted to play at an NCAA Div I school, to compete with the best in the world. But now that my athletics scholarship has been withdrawn, I'm constrained by my options. I need a school to give me a full ride or a *very* good partial ride. I might even have to consider a Div II school, given my current grades and the scholarship options they might offer me. I have to be practical to even have a chance to walk on, otherwise I'd have to look at options closer to home, forget the NCAA, forget the Malaysian Olympic gold—

Not everyone will achieve their dreams in life.

"You'll be able to study in the States, I'm sure of it," Zee is saying, oblivious. "And then we'll visit each other wherever we go! Road trip! We'll have so many formative experiences together—me, away from my family's influence, charting my own path to financial freedom, you, a superstar runner again and maybe a Netflix comic in the making!"

Every word she say rubs me the wrong way. "Let's change the subject."

There's a pause as Zee gathers herself. "Right, so, what do your parents think about you trying stand-up?"

"They don't know," I admit after a lengthy pause, toying with a sleeve. "And I don't plan on telling them—yet."

"But what about the open mikes? Aren't they usually in the evenings?"

"I was hoping you'd be my cover," I admit. "Pretty please?" I smile with teeth and she recoils.

"I *guess* that's fine by me," she hedges. "But how long can you keep this from your parents? What about permission to enter the actual competition itself? Flights? Don't you need a legal guardian to sign release forms?"

"I'm sure I can convince her by then," I lie. I don't want to tell her that I've been forging my mother's signature for years, starting from I was nine.

"What about your practice sets?"

"Most of the places the comics perform at are public, family-friendly places. Like restaurants and performance art places. Don't need their permission to enter such establishments."

"What if . . . what if something happens to you?"

"I'll be fine," I say. "I'll send you a pin of my every location, so you just have to send the police there if you don't hear from me after a performance. I don't want to tell my parents till I absolutely have to." Like when I reach the finals. Yeah.

She boggles at me. "But I don't get it—why *don't* you want to tell your parents?"

Zee and her parents are close, thick as thieves. She tells them everything, including her crushes. They consult her on their corporate social media strategy. She voluntarily holidays with her mom *one-on-one* and plans to do so till one of them drops dead—her words (she's not very superstitious). "Because my mom will stress out, she'll worry for my safety, and I don't want her to worry about me, so I'll have to lie to her."

"Every mom worries."

"Yes, but my mother is—" I hesitate. My mother had been through so much with me. Before I happened, she had been a star student, a perfect daughter. When she got pregnant, her conservative parents disowned her, she had to drop out of university and take care of me, and in the end, she became a clerk instead of the lawyer she should have been. It must have been tough for her as a single mom, shouldering her failed dreams. I must have caused her depression. The truth bubbles to my lips and I swallow it back down. "My mother is . . . delicate, especially now that she's pregnant. . . . I don't want her to stress out, particularly since stand-up's not the coziest place for girls." I quickly mention a couple of scandals in the light of #MeToo, and Zee winces.

"Look, I'll let her know if and when I reach the finals." I cross my fingers behind my back. "It's just the way it is, the way it has to be with my family."

She adjusts her headscarf and considers me silently. Finally, she says, "I don't understand it, but you're my friend for some reason, so I'll support you."

"Thanks, Zee," I say, grateful.

"Don't forget your promise," she says, already scrolling through her messages, muttering something about "I told them fire-eaters and velvet curtains don't mesh!" I tune out. On any given day, Zee is involved in two dozen other social things at school besides her social media obligations. This year she's been nominated as the chairperson of the school's charity gala early December. She's the most hardworking person I know.

"What promise?"

"Setting me up with Vern," she reiterates. "Don't let me wander alone in a love desert anymore."

"Oh dear God."

"Please, Ags, I want a love story for the ages—preferably something I can document for my Stories in a rose-hued reveal."

She makes pleading eyes at me and I groan; I have my suspicions about their compatibility, but try turning down manga-eyed Zee Bakri.

"Fine, but I promise nothing," I grumble. Life was already complicated enough without cross-cultural matchmaking.

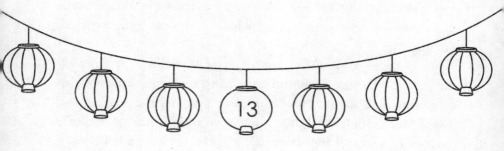

13

SO THIS IS WHERE EVIL LIVES.

I stare at the building in front of me, two stories of stone and wood that I had to walk fifteen minutes to reach from the bus stop, surrounded by carefully landscaped lawns. There's a security booth with *two* security guards by the imposing wrought-iron gate.

I clutch my backpack to me and take a deep breath: I have arrived at the Taslims' lair.

Given all that had happened between us at the last open mike on Sunday, I hadn't expected Royce to honor his offer to tutor me, but on Tuesday, he had messaged me to give me his address and ask me what subjects I needed help with, we worked out a mutually cool time slot, and now here we are. If he can be a professional, so can I.

My jaw gapes as the gate opens once the security confirms my visit is expected, revealing the sheer size of the mansion glinting in the late-afternoon sun. This isn't a house, surely. It's a resort. A sprawling urban resort in one of the most expensive neighborhoods in downtown Kuala Lumpur, Kenny Hills. I glance down at my outfit—black leggings and faded sea-green tank top—and look back at the house: I should have worn a ball gown, or at least something with feathers, surely.

I walk hesitantly up the short driveway, my mouth dry. Normally, Royce was supposed to tutor his charity cases at the library, but he must have his reasons for suggesting his home, none of them friendly, I'm guessing.

I ring the bell and a low, gravelly voice on the intercom panel asks me for my business. I identify myself and the heavy doors open; a woman wearing black linen pants and a white cotton linen long-sleeved tunic smiles and ushers me in without further comment. I am looking everywhere, at everything, transfixed, trying not to gawp. Everything in the house is dazzling. The muted brass mirrors and framed art; the floral accent walls with custom, hand-painted silk wallpaper, the vintage carpets, brocade throw pillows; the ornate lines of the dark wood furniture. The air smells of creamy flowers, and incongruously, the sea. We were right in the middle of a city, and the traffic was gone. You could even hear the susurrus of swaying palm trees, the swish of bougainvillea bushes brushing against the french doors of the living hall, overlooking a perfect lawn spilling into a view of the KL skyline. And a lapis-blue tiled pool, long enough for laps, fringed on three corners with a lotus pond. Every detail was harmonious, not an element out of place.

The maid gestures at a sunlit room to the side of the living hall, where a small rectangular black marble-topped table was flanked by two armchairs. There's a chrome multitiered stand on a side table with a plate of blush and lemon-yellow macarons almost pearlescent in their beauty, ringed with glass jars of cookies and granola bars, pitchers of mint-and-cucumber water, and a lumpy brown slab of cake. Royce is seated with his back to me, and my heart flip-flops—in disgust, of course—at the sight of his disturbingly good posture. I admire the lines the way any sportsperson would, that is to say with decided clinical detachment.

"You're on time," he says as I take a seat.

"Of course," I say. "Why wouldn't I be?" Actually, I had planned on being ten minutes late, but somehow public transport was bang on time today, thus thwarting my power play and I ended up being fifteen minutes early.

He shrugs, his lip twitching. "I thought you'd be late on purpose."

"I'm not an ingrate." He'd seen through me like I was rice paper.

He raises an eyebrow, a look which somehow only serves to underscore the resting symmetry of his face, which of course makes me even more irritated at him.

"You look nice."

I glance down at my outfit. "Right," I say. I gesture around me. "So, you trying to impress me or something?"

Now it's his turn to look uncomfortable. A light blush tints his face. "We could have stayed at the library, but I thought . . . the chairs here are more ergonomic and, uh, after your accident and all, yeah, the wooden chairs at the library . . ."

Was that the real reason, and not sheer intimidation? I wiggle around and decide he might have a point. "Thanks," I reply.

"Plus, I have way more refreshments. There's Ladurée macarons and freshly baked sugar cookies and banana cake, if you want. I, ah"— he clears his throat and brushes his hair off his forehead—"made the cake."

The ice inside me thaws. "Dude, you're the one tutoring me, *I* should be feeding *you*." I root around in my backpack. "Here, this is for you." I place the packet of melty Haribo gummy bears, which in hindsight seem inadequate. Grossly inadequate. I squelch lower in my seat, which is difficult because they really are very comfortable and ergonomic.

"Thank you," he says, accepting my paltry offering and for whatever reason blushing even deeper red. "Would you like some cake?"

"Sure," I say, giving the slab a dubious glance. He saws a piece off what should be a soft, chewy cake and puts it on a plate with an audible thunk. Golden Boy does not look like he's a baker, but who knows? Royce is a star athlete, a great student, and good-looking (objectively)—maybe he's also a clever baker.

I steel myself and take a dutiful bite. Triumph and despair fight for supremacy. The cake is hard as pavement, but I swallow it and offer a best-guest-ever smile. "Tas-tasty," I manage to say.

He drops his gaze down and says shyly, "I'd never baked before yesterday."

And it shows, I don't say. So, his modus operandi when it comes to competition is to poison them. But what he doesn't know is this—I've grown up eating my mom's home cooking, so there. I spoon another bite into my mouth and chew with enthusiastic crunches to show him I was the alpha, not him. "Mmmmmm, delicious," I say. I gesture around me. "And nice house."

"Thanks."

I look around at the walls of photos. They were mostly of Royce's parents and him, interspersed with some shots of what I presume are Royce's extended families. "Wow, is that everyone in the Taslim clan?"

There's a moment of hesitation before Royce says curtly, "No." I guess sharing time is up, so I pull out my textbook and notepad. Royce does the same.

A servant, a stern-faced woman in her sixties wearing a linen samfu in light gray, comes in with drinks. She gives me a cursory nod before reminding him, in Bahasa Melayu, that he has a session with Master Zhang.

Royce sighs and thanks her.

"Who's Master Zhang?" I ask in my casual voice, remembering Zee's quest for me, i.e., to unearth dirt on Royce.

"My chess tutor," he says.

"Yikes."

"*Yikes* is the word," he replies.

"I can't believe you have to attend chess lessons."

"Me neither. I hate chess so, so much. But apparently it's good for reasoning or whatever."

"I hate studying in general," I say. "I wish I could just sleep through the rest of school life and wake up at the good part."

He regards me with interest. "And what's that, Ms. Chan?"

"Working adulthood." Having money and freedom—win.

"What's your dream job?"

I flick imaginary lint off my T-shirt collar. "You really want to know?"

"Yes, I do, Chan," he says. "I need to, uh, know what my tutee wants in order to, uh, align my strategy with their goals."

"Unless you want me to end you, don't laugh."

His face turns serious. "I would never." He pauses, the smallest hint of a smile quirking his lips. "Especially at your sets."

I burst into hacking laughter, as does he. The tension breaks. I meet his smile with a genuine one of mine.

"Okay, seriously now, Chan."

I exhale noisily. "Sports management at the national level, and failing that, physiotherapy."

"You *want* to be a physio?"

"Don't sound so shocked! It's, like, sports adjacent, so why not?"

"Dream jobs aren't why-nots, they're supposed to be nothing-else-comes-close. So, what's your *real* dream job?"

"I don't have the money to dream," I tell him.

He laughs. He *actually* thinks I'm joking. "No seriously, what?"

I close my eyes. Maybe he put some truth serum in his cake, because I tell him about my secret, actual pipe dream. "I'd love to write for a living, y'know? I'm not really sure in what capacity, but definitely something full-time, maybe even teach a little on the side. I love how a single alternate word choice can make a sentence dance—" I close up. "I'm being silly. Forget it. It doesn't matter. I have to be practical, and physio is a safe one that's not getting replaced by robots anytime soon." I grimace. "Or AI."

"It's not silly at all, if it's what you want," Royce says. "I've watched some of Zee's makeup tutorials—you know, the ones cowritten by you. You have talent."

I redden with the warmth of his praise. "And yours? What's your dream job?"

"Stand-up comedian," he says without hesitation. He laughs, but there's no humor in it. "Now that's a dream all right."

"I'm sure if you wanted to—"

"Let's drop the subject," he says, a curt note in his voice. "What I want doesn't—" He drags a palm across his face, and when the hand is down, his game face is back on. "Just so you know, if you're thinking of becoming a physio, you're going to have to learn to love physics."

I nod, although my mind is elsewhere. It's funny to think of Royce, *the* Royce Taslim, having dreams and desires that he can't fulfill and being, well—trapped, although I might be projecting. No one is trapped in a life like Royce's.

Royce turns to his lesson plan. "BTW, I'm glad I've had a chance to be your tutor. I've always wanted to get to know you better."

I blink. "Oh really? Why?"

"I don't know. . . . You'd be walking around school with Zee, laughing and chatting, and I'd think, *There goes a girl who'd hide a body for her friend.*"

"Th-that's a really strange way to sum someone up in the first instance."

"Okay, then you look like someone who I'd want to be friends with."

My face warms. "Thank you."

He opens up the textbook, his voice all businesslike now. "We should get started."

He starts droning away on some boring equation stuff thingy, so my mind drifts. I catch myself staring at the curve of his bicep, the smooth tension of the muscle underneath the tanned expanse in a less-than-detached way, and I pinch myself so hard under the table that my eyes prickle with tears.

Royce happens to glance at me and mutters, "I hope you're not crying because of physics. Or me."

"It's cramps," I say, without thinking. Oh shit, maybe he thinks it's— "It's not *those* cramps!" I hasten to add. "Just my butt falling asleep!"

His eyes drop to my butt, and a look I can't decipher flashes across his face. I'm wearing my least-flattering running leggings, which are a little threadbare and tight.

"I should stretch!" I start stretching with great vitality. "My physio says I'm stiff."

Royce says, in a strange voice, "It's very important to stretch."

Great, he probably thinks I'm weird. Not that it matters what he thinks. I start sitting down but stop midway. In the course of my stretching, I've become uncomfortably aware that my bladder is full. "Erm, so where's, like, your, erm, powder room?" I have never used the phrase *powder room* in my life.

"Down the hallway, turn right at the third door. Do you . . . ?" He makes a show of getting up to lead me there, but I wave him down. I'm sure there will be a toilet. Somewhere.

I find it—well, one of them—and spend an inordinate amount of time testing the very luxe selection of hand creams.

"Find it?" he asks when he smells me entering the room.

I nod as I slid back into the seat. "So, why are you hiding your stand-up from your parents?"

"Because they would shut it down in a flash. It wouldn't be"—a sardonic smile—"brand appropriate."

I think about all the fancy society and business magazines, the fawning coverage in old and social media. The Taslim name is a brand that screams aspirational living. Innovation. Flair. Prestige. Those pesky rumors of illegal logging and land clearing are just rumors, and if they are ever proven to be, you can just point your finger at your third-party contractors being lax, and everything goes away if you can pay enough people to lawyer and PR the shit out of your dirty laundry.

"How are you doing all the comedy nights, then?" Royce does at least three a week. "What about your bodyguards—"

"I have my ways," he says wryly.

We pretend to concentrate on the lesson in front of us. After a while, I say, "In spite of your previous apology, you're still weird around me at comedy. Why?"

"You noticed?"

"Everyone noticed. It's impossible not to."

He tousles his hair with a rueful expression on his face. "The truth is, I'm a little . . . jealous of you."

"You're jealous of me?" I say, surprised. How? "Why?"

"Because you're naturally talented in the only thing I care about. And more importantly"—he picks an invisible crumb off the table, not looking at me—"you can be your true authentic self and talk about your everyday life onstage whereas I must invent some stupid persona just so my parents don't find out about my stage work."

Oh. That. "Yeah, your average-Joe performance stinks, but not because your lines aren't good, at least from a technical perspective, maybe."

"Mayhap," Royce says.

I grin. "I think the reason they aren't as good, especially when I'm around, is because they aren't authentic to *you.*"

"I thought so," he says, nodding. "Before you came along, I could fake it well enough because I was pretty sure no one in the audience knew me."

"But you don't have to make up an entire backstory even if you're trying not to expose the fact that you're, well, rich."

"I'm still trying to figure it out, trying to meld my humor with the topics I want to talk about but feel I have no right to talk about because of who I am," he says.

"You'll figure it out," I say. "You're not . . . unsmart."

He chuckles. "Thanks? But seriously, for the record, I like . . . I like watching you do stand-up. I think you're funny and, um, inspiring."

"What do you mean?" I say, scooting over just a little because I want to give him a chance to communicate better.

He shifts closer, too. "When you want something, you go for it. You're very direct and no-nonsense, which is so refreshing, so . . . uh . . . y'know . . ."

Our gaze meets and I am suddenly aware of how close our fingers are, practically tip to tip, and that no one is moving away despite the shamelessness of it all.

My gaze travels to his lips. *Kissssmhiiiimmmmm*, my traitorous brain opines, even as everything else in me is screaming, *Bacteria!*

I give myself a mental shake and recall the face of a soldier who'd died in the grip of tetanus in one of my history books, which works to cool down my ardor somewhat (death should). The bacteria that cause tetanus is everywhere, and for unvaccinated individuals, an unfortunate slip in attention allows the bacteria to breach the defenses, leading to a death of great agony and needless contortion. In short, tetanus, like love, takes advantage of our carelessness, and I can't afford to mess up again.

If I'm not winning, no one in my family is.

"Are you okay?" Royce asks, reaching for his cup of cucumber water. Apparently, I have not been giving myself a mental shake but a real one.

"Right as rain," I say. "Now come on, if you want to root in my box later, you better get to work first."

Royce spit-takes so hard I could see the veins in his face. "Do you hear yourself speak?" he says when he finally gathers himself.

"Yes." That was a tactical deployment of innuendo on my end.

Royce shakes his head and turns a page, smiling. "Every day, Chan. Every day."

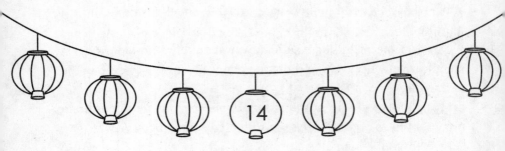

14

RTas (player ID: BashfulTactician) has accepted your invitation to join your game on CounterFlash.

~

Tavleen (facing her phone): Hi, everyone! Just wanted to let you know that the Hot Flashes and I are going to the skating rink tomorrow for some team-bonding time before the state championships! Come see us do loops.
Suraya (leaning in to kiss Tavleen's cheek): Ya habibi!
Kima: Go team!

~

"Do you have a lot of friends, Rosie?" I ask my sister on Saturday while we were watching a reality TV show called *The Sea Queen,* which follows rival Norwegian salmon farmers duking it out for—

salmon supremacy? It was that or a new reality show in a stunning Caribbean location where contestants pretended to be super horny but were rewarded for not banging each other called *Wild and Proper.*

Who the eff knows anymore.

"Yes," Rosie says without hesitation. "Droves. Sometimes, they fight to be my best friend, too, but I tell them to take turns. It's exhausting."

"Really?" I say, my stomach sinking.

"Yeah," Rosie says. "Why do you ask?"

"No reason." I ponder this. "And this has always been the case? Since like, you and Stanley moved to Malaysia from America?"

"Yeaaah," she says, "it's called having potable charm."

I don't correct her. "I seem to be going through a friendship drought."

"Oh," Rosie says. "Don't you have Zee?"

"Yes, but I meant my broader friend group."

"The Hot Flashes?" Rosie says, an admiring note creeping into her voice. "They are just so cute. Good thing you're not there to spoil things."

"Rosie!" I bark.

"Okay, okay, sorry. I'm just kidding." She makes a thinking face. "Hmm. It's true I haven't seen them around you in school since your accident." She gives me a shrewd expression. "Why do you think that is?'"

"I have no idea, because I don't think it's a me problem per se."

"Uh-huh. Are you sure?"

"Absolutely." I think hard. "You know what it is, I think with everything that's happened they're just . . . unsure of when they should reappear in my lives."

Voilà! Breakthrough! That must be the reason: I hadn't been making my availability to hang known!

So that's why I'm at the skating rink, casually hiding behind the drinks machine and peeping at my friends, who are laughing as they loop in wild circles around one another.

I really shouldn't be stalking my own friends, but in their case, how else was I supposed to meet them? I know they are really busy training, and they might have just been trying to give me space to get over my injury and all that. That's what today's about: showing them I'm able to participate again in our usual activities, even if I'm not running competitively.

This isn't the team's usual ice-skating rink; it's in a small suburban mall in a painfully chic neighborhood, brand-new and even more expensive than the last one. The price to enter, even when I bargained with the boy at the counter saying I wasn't *actually* going to skate (I wasn't cleared for skating, I don't think), was criminal, but in spite of all my debating he insisted I pay full student price, which was discounted but still painful. Apparently, rules are rules, which is what the girl behind the skates rental counter said when I told her I wasn't *actually* going to wear the skates, I just needed them for show. I was not surprised when she handed me a pair that I suspected had not been deodorized since its last user.

I duck and pretend to be lacing up when the girls, all eleven of them, tumble out of the rink in a riotous pile, squealing and chattering.

"Hey there," I say easily, not at all what someone who is stalking her friends would say.

The chatter stops and they turn as one toward me. "Oh, hi, Agnes," Kima Li says, her eyes wide. "Are . . . are you, er, going to skate in your condition?"

"Me?" I lift my right leg, the one I'd injured, and said, "Well, do you see a cast on this?"

"But Coach says—"

"Well, I'm fine," I say brightly. I stand up on my ice skates and it takes all of me not to squeak as a sharp pain shoots up from my leg. I plop back down in what I hope is a nonchalant way. "Would you guys like to go back in?"

"Er . . ." Suraya's eyes dart around. "We're headed to the movies."

A pause. "What are you seeing?" I say, not chirpily.

"*Black Ops Fifty-Five: Murder Town,*" Casey Lim says. "You know, with Charlie MacLane." Charlie MacLane is a new actor that Hollywood has cooked up in a lab, a mashup of Chris Hemsworth and one of the other Chrises.

"Ooh, that sounds fun, I haven't seen that yet," I enunciate.

No one asks if I'd like to join. A different pain shoots through my body, and my legs tremble. I'm glad I'm seated.

"Why haven't you guys reached out?" I manage to say after an uncomfortable silence stretches out between us. "I've been back for over two months. I've texted you about group hangs, even invited you all several times to see me perform stand-up comedy. Aren't we friends?"

More silence. Finally, Tavleen says, "You want the truth?"

"Yes," I say immediately. "I can take it."

The girls exchange looks that are basically musical chairs of who should speak for the group. Tavleen, who I heard had usurped me as captain of the team, takes a deep breath. "To be honest, it's kind of surprising that you think of us as your friends. I mean, we *adore* you as our captain, obviously."

"Obviously," Suraya echoed.

Tavleen nods. "The team is *the best* when you're around, but we didn't think . . . we never thought . . . well, we always thought you didn't like us."

"Didn't like you!" I bark. I recover and say, "Is . . . ? How? What?" Very eloquent.

"Yeah, I agree," Suraya says.

Holly Toi, a reserve team nobody, exchanges a glance with Tavleen before clearing her throat and saying, "To be honest, it's tough to be around you. You're kind of intense, Agnes."

"Me? Intense?" This was news!

"We like you, of course," Tavleen says, gracious in her triumph as the new queen bee. "Like, as a captain. You were just *so good* for the team's performance."

"The best," Yuna Shastri said haltingly. "But in your drive to make us the best, you were—kind of hard on us, though."

"Yeah, so scary," Captain Obvious McObvious, aka Suraya, says. "You really kept the pressure on us, all the time. And you and Coach Everest were feeding off each other's energy. Now he's kind of chiller. Still snappy, but not so uptight. Less murdery."

"You're *so* murdery on relay events. That rictus smile," Holly said.

"Those eyes," someone chimed in.

"I used to get nervous shits all the time, the night before meets, because of you," Kima volunteered squeakily.

"Those eyes!" someone else agreed.

"And whenever we were competing, individually, oh my God," Yuna said. "You are a sore loser, on the rare occasions one of us bested you."

"I don't think I've ever seen you laugh, except in triumph," Holly said.

"Yeah. And we didn't know how to respond to your texts about your comedy sets, either," Kima mumbles. She winces, not meeting my eyes. "Don't take this the wrong way"—which was a clear sign this was going to sting—"but, erm, you're not funny, Agnes."

Not funny? WTF? Kima the chatbot think I'm not funny?

"That's also why we don't want to see you perform," says Captain Obvious. Suraya polishes the hatchet before swinging it again. "Aside from . . . the lack-of-friendship thing."

I will myself not to wilt. The hits were coming from all angles. I duck my head and concentrate hard at lacing my shoes so that I won't burst into tears in front of the people I formerly considered my friends, my squad.

"Look, Agnes," Tavleen says, voice gentle. "We are the team we are because of you. We really appreciate you, honestly. We stan your captainship."

"We're just . . . not into you as a person," said Kima.

"We're sorry," Yuna says.

The silence is back, only now there's a little person in me howling and tearing things into little confetti bits, but I tamp down my emotions and look up at them. "It's okay," I say evenly.

"Well, um, see you around I guess," Cassie says.

The girls murmur their mea culpas as I concentrate on presenting a human smile, waving them off to their movies, where they will buy bucket-size popcorns and Diet Coke to snack on while they gossip about this encounter with their sad, broken ex-captain, who thought she was their friend. That she was one of *them*.

I ball my fist, alternating between rage, despair, and stomach-churning embarrassment, the kind I don't even have when I bomb onstage. Serves me right for letting my guard down. Serves me right for thinking I could be just like them. I snuffle into my palm, hoping people would think I'm snorting illegal substances instead of trying to stuff my tears out of sight.

"Hey there," a wry, friendly voice says.

I look up and gape at Vern in a cleaner's uniform, short-sleeved button-up collared shirt with matching pants in dark navy with worn patches. "What are you doing here?" I ask.

He shrugs, lifts a broom up like it's a sword and exposing a floral tattoo circling his bicep that peeked from under his right sleeve. "I work here. Well, it's one of the places where I work, anyhow." He sits down next me and fishes out what I hope is a clean tissue from the depths of a side pocket, handing it to me solemnly. "Bad fall?"

Something about the way he says it disarms me. I should have been mortified to be crying in public. Instead, I am overwhelmed with a rush of kinship. I blow my nose with a honk. "You could say that."

He doesn't speak and I don't either, and after a couple of minutes I'm almost back to normal, except the rage, the rage is still there, simmering in the background.

"Who are those girls you were with?" Vern asks.

"Schoolmates," I say.

"Oh." The disdain in that one word. "They fucking with you?" he says, picking at a loose thread, still in that throwaway tone.

I bite my lip. I don't want to talk about it, yet when I look at him, I see only sympathy radiating from his eyes. Somehow, I intuit that he would understand what I was going through, so I find myself telling him everything that's happened. Not sugarcoating it. Letting all the humiliation out.

He folds his arms, a sneer curling a corner of his lips. "Their excuse for not being there for you was—you were too good at your job?"

I gave a dry laugh. "They said they didn't call because I never let them in *here*." I point at my heart.

He makes a disbelieving face. "That the best they could do?" A snort of laughter, a look slid my way. "Don't believe their excuses. They are just a bunch of spoiled, shitty brats. And worse, they can't even be honest enough to tell the truth to your face."

I suck in a breath, mesmerized by the story he was spinning. "What do you mean?" Yes, Vern, tell me more. Help me understand.

Vern sighs and runs his hand through his dark, slightly wavy hair. "Look, I'm sorry I'm the one who has to disabuse you of the fantasy, but they didn't keep up the friendship because they didn't care enough to do so. That's all." His fingers begin an impatient drumming on his lap. "The truth is, Agnes, you're not like those girls, even if you go to school with them. They are from another world, and no matter what you do, you'll never belong. So, they don't want to make the effort."

I see myself at the track, wearing my secondhand or thrift-shopped gear; my patched-over, beaten-up backpack that I'd had for the past two years; and my "vintage" Casio watch that I pretended to love while everyone at school sported the latest smartwatches or designer watches that cost months of salary, sometimes more. My uniform, the only thing I shared with them, is an illusion. We are not cut from the same cloth, oh, no, not at all. I never fit in from the start.

He clocks every thought of mine. I never did have a poker face. His hand closes over mine and squeezes. "It's okay, forget them. You think any of those girls have half the mettle you have? That they can say the things you say onstage?"

I scoff, wiping away a stray tear. "I—I say stupid stuff onstage to make people laugh. I'm not giving a TED Talk."

"And? You think laughter isn't as hard won as any other human emotion?"

"I d-don't know."

He shakes his head, indignant. "You know that trite saying 'Laughter is the best medicine'? Even as people trivialize those who make them laugh, in their saddest moments, comedy is what most of them reach for, not the so-called deep stuff. Comedy is craft. Comedy is *power*. You're a god when you can get someone to laugh, to think, like you do. Can't you see?" He leans close, grabs my gaze with his. "And, Agnes, you're worth ten of those girls, easy. You give yourself away too easily to people who don't deserve you."

I internalized the resolute way he said this. The way he made opinion into fact. Now that I think about it, when I didn't know, didn't care what they thought about me, life was just fine. I focused on the right things. As soon as I had time to ruminate on friendships, that's when I started opening myself up to hurt, when I started wanting to be part of the gang, to force my squareness into the perfect round peg that made up their lives, when here was Vern, who didn't care about polishing himself to suit an ideal, who was authentically his own. When I look at him, I see everything I'd been trying not to see, but it's cast in a new light. My differences are my strengths—something to be proud of.

"Fuck 'em," I say. I pull off my skates and kick them aside, wincing from the force of my kick. I try to ignore the new twinge of pain in my left kneecap. "Fuck 'em." I never swear, but this feels like an incantation of power. He's right: I don't need them. I don't need any of them. They didn't deserve me, so they weren't getting any of me.

"Come on," he says, taking me by the hand. He leads me out of the rink, dropping the skates at the checkout and telling me he'll get my money back later, and past some shops to the exit leading to the parking lot.

"You see any of their cars?" he asks quietly.

I gaze around the parking lot and spot the lime-green Mini Cooper that Kima drives, which she probably got for her sixteenth birthday without needing to lift a single finger for it.

"There," I say, pointing, almost breathless with tension.

Vern quickly cases the parking lot, which has cameras near the exit, and hugs the walls, slipping down a darker stretch of the way presumably out of the camera's field of vision, his head bent low.

I see everything that happens in a daze, the quick way he darts next to Kima's car, the soft pop, and then he's headed my way, scooting with his back to the cameras as he walks quickly back to where I am.

"What happened?" I ask, even though I've guessed. I know.

He lifts up a Swiss Army knife and grins. "I brought your friends back down to earth."

"You're *unhinged*," I say, my eyes wide. I can't decide if I'm impressed or scared.

"That depends on who you ask," he says. He flicks his eyes at me. "I don't think you have anything to be afraid of, in your case. I take care of mine."

Okay, so maybe I'm . . . touched?

His voice regains its playful tone. "Now come, let's ditch the rest of my shift and to go the movies. What would you like to see?"

My answer is immediate. "How about *Black Ops Fifty-Five: Murder Town*?"

~

Vern: I had fun today. Anytime you want to hang again one-on-one, or take out some people for you, let me know

Me: 💯

Me: As soon as I get my essays done, maybe next week

Vern: K. See you at comedy. You going to tomorrow's open mike or another one?

Me: Tomorrow's. See you

Vern: 🌷

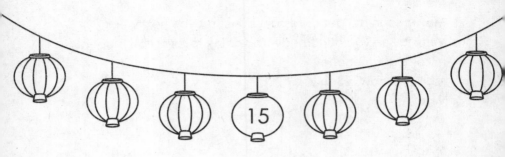

15

IT'S 9 P.M., JOHN MULANEY'S LATEST SPECIAL IS PLAYING ON MY speakers, and I'm waiting in my favorite pajamas for Royce to appear online so I can show him my box, which I have taken pains to arrange so it looks presentable when we finally play together after a hot and heavy week of studying.

And the answer is: Yes, I do hear myself. Apparently, the double entendres come faster when I'm nervous.

Okay, okay, stop it, brain.

I take a deep breath and try not to sweat or burp, which affects my playing. I need to be on form today, especially since it's our first-time gaming together. We'd been trying to sync up our packed schedules to play *CounterFlash* (no mean feat with Royce's tutoring and our open-mike commitments of two performances a week at a minimum, preferably not the same ones as each other's, plus my physio sessions); this was our first free night hanging out, just the two of us, in the week since the Saturday we spent at his home. Our last two peer tutor sessions had been held in the school library with a couple of other seniors who needed help with the same subjects, which is just as well since who needs to be alone in a beautiful mansion with Taslim, surrounded by sugary treats—not me, that's for sure.

Speaking of being alone with Taslim, my heart is doing sprints in my chest as I wait for Taslim, who's late. Gaming together is an intimate exercise. I have a bunch of people I play *CF* with online, such as NerdWolf from New York, Xilixili from China, and OldNicky from Cypress, people I've never met before but who I know intimately (where they are based, what time they sleep, how often they take toilet breaks, their favorite snacks, their go-to swear words, their strengths and weaknesses, how they deal with pain and pleasure). Some of them I've built online friendships with over the years and some relationships have even crossed over to other platforms like Twitch. The camaraderie, the bonhomie, that shared history, often translates to real life. If you gel together on multiplayer tactical games, if you have each other's backs over days, weeks, months, sometimes years of gaming together, you share LOLs, triumphs, disappointments together, and that connection is something to be cherished. And vice versa.

All to say—I'm nervous about gaming with Royce. It could get train-wrecky, fast.

Play it cool, playitcoolplayitcool.

Royce Taslim is here—or rather, his avatar is.

Cute outfit, he messages. We, or our avatars, check each other out: He's got a special edition sunset-gold Direwolf skin with a Bludgeoning Hammer, and I'm wearing a limited-edition purple-and-neon green Vampire skin with a special Soul Scythe that I found in a special loot drop, which helps you regenerate 20 percent faster.

Business first or pleasure?

Pleasure, he responds, brandishing his Hammer.

A boy after my own rotten heart, I reply, flipping my Scythe.

We turn on our gaming headsets and get to it, and it is glitchy and glorious. Royce's hammer is a new one that replaced the buggy version released a couple of months ago, and it's powerful enough that we coast through some of the wilder melees. I get to show off some of my special combo moves, and lots of brains and guts go flying. It's epic.

It's almost like a date, but better. Not that I've actually been on a one-on-one date, come to think of it. My dating experience has so far been limited to group dates with different combos of the Hot Flashes and their counterparts, and most of them were mind-numbingly boring and involved lots of flexes about vacations and fancy overseas camps that went over my head.

But Royce and I chat as we disembowel enemies, and sure, most of it is game chat ("Fray him! Fray him!" "Brain them! Harder! Watch out!" "Evacuate! Evacuate! Left! No, your other left! Aaaaaaaaaaaahhhh!") but occasionally, when we are resting in one of the Gloomy Tunnels, we exchange words of encouragement and gossip about school or the latest K-drama we're all pretending not to be into. And then back to the ending of other people's lives.

It's actually quite relaxing. And it's certainly the most fun I've had since I stopped running.

This was a pretty sick sesh, I say at the end of a three-hour marathon, and it's 1 a.m.

Yeah you were 🔥. SLAYED.

WAS THERE ANY DOUBT? I retort.

None, he responded. I knew you'd be good at anything you set your mind to

Thanks. I'm glad we mesh well together. I hurry to clarify. In the game!

Don't worry Agnes, I know what you meant 😔 God forbid IRL friendship develops!!

😊 But for real, GTG. I've got to work a shift tmw

After I have entered that into the chat field I freeze. I hadn't meant to type that. I would have normally told him I had to sleep or something.

What kind of shift? Royce asks.

It's too late to lie now.

I have a Saturday dinner shift at this Korean BBQ restaurant. Nowhere you'd know

Royce probably ate at fancier Korean places than this little hole-in-the-wall.

Which one?

He's clearly not letting this go. Seoul Hot. It's in Little Korea, Ampang

Nice! Glad you're back in action

I guess, I write, my face still burning.

I had so much fun tonight, really

Sames, I typed.

So. Now to business. He means my promise to gift him an item from my loot.

I sigh and bring him to my inventory tent. Have at it.

He barely pokes around before he clicks on an item. A Slippery Devil ring from my loot that adds some dexterity and mediocre damage to his attack. A nothing ring, really, something noobs get within the first ten levels of *CounterFlash*. I'll take this.

Oh, are you sure? I respond half-heartedly. I have way more valuable items. Like, you can get anything—except my Soul Scythe and my Hellforged Breastplate and my Invisibility ring and my—

It's OK, I only want a little more dexterity, really

Dexterity is very valuable. . . Not a +2 dexterity ring, but if he *really* wants it.

💯 Night, LilFlashes

Night, BashfulTactician

In a flurry of random emojis, he leaves, and curiously, in spite of all the disemboweling and dismembering, I'm . . . content. Somehow, despite him being my former rival, my feelings toward him had mellowed. Maybe, just maybe, we were becoming friendly, if not friends. Taslim and I are just really friendly friends.

~

Zee: Do you know any jugglers?

Zee: Never mind

Me: Er, no?

Me: Dare I ask what for?

Zee: The charity fundraiser/school ball

Me: Oh that

Zee: Any chance you can learn to juggle by December?

Me: Absolutely not

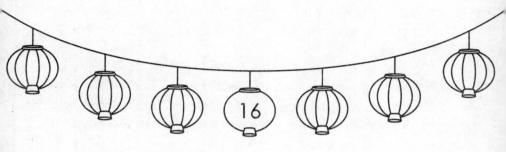

MAN, I REALLY NEED TO STOP HANGING OUT IN ALLEYS.

I'm seated on the plastic bucket in the alley behind Seoul Hot, hiding from Mrs. Yoon because my leg started to cramp up during dinnertime and I needed a break after being on my feet for little more than two hours. Turns out I was too ambitious about getting back to work. The other servers, Meriam, Zi Wei, and Samuel were understanding, but I could sense their frustration bubbling underneath. It's not fair, but life's not fair. I'll just pass them more of my tips.

"Alamak, it's *Seoul hot* out here," says Jeremiah, a bald man in his forties and one of the nicer chefs working at Seoul Hot. I had asked him for his muscle rub ointment fifteen minutes ago and he was checking on me during his break. "Get it? Seoul Hot. Ha-ha-ha."

"I don't know why you and I are friendly," I grumble.

Jeremiah cackles, then composes himself. "It's because I let you take home the leftover food."

I stick out my tongue. "It a hundred percent is the only reason, fam."

He chuckles, then fishes a cigarette from his apron pocket, which is very probably a health code violation. "Just admit you like me already, kid."

Meriam pokes her head out of the kitchen and squints at our direction. "Agnes, Mrs. Yoon is looking for you."

I groan and cross my eyes. My right leg is tingly and not in a happy way.

"She says there's a client out there asking for you, specifically."

"Oh no, is it the table with the woman who sent back the special Malaysian dakgalbi for being too spicy when she specifically requested 'deathly spicy,' despite my gentle reminders that there would be no refunds under the Seoul Hot dining policy?"

"Nah, Mrs. Yoon personally kicked that table out five minutes ago. There was a small, er, shouting match." Mrs. Yoon is known for not holding back with customers, yet her food is so good that despite a less-than-impressive Google rating, the restaurant is always Seoul full with regulars.

Good God. I need to get out of here.

Meriam shrugs. "I don't know, but she was looking for you with, let's say, some sense of urgency. Big spending table in your sector."

Jeremiah makes a shooing noise, motioning me through the door, and I sigh and make my way to where Mrs. Yoon is waiting by the service door.

"Agnes!" Mrs. Yoon says. She pronounces my name as Ack-NUS. Having moved from Busan to Kuala Lumpur two decades ago to marry a Malaysian man, she speaks Manglish with a strong Korean accent. "Haiyah, I look everywhere for you now only you here! Someone asking for you, say you must serve them. Big order. Table eleven. Be nice."

"Okay," I say, half hopping, half running out.

The restaurant's signature blend of fat, spice, and smoke hits me in the face after being outdoors, and I briefly wonder how much I must smell after marinating in this for the last two hours, and it is only 8 p.m.

"Table eleven, table eleven," I mutter, disoriented after having been away for over two months (the restaurant has two stories and twenty-three tables—thankfully, I've only been asked to wait on tables on the ground floor). I turn a corner to table 11 and the sight slaps me in the face.

"Agnes!"

It is Royce Taslim, in the flesh.

No. No. No. No. No. No.

I can't move. What is Royce Taslim doing in my restaurant? At this hour, dressed like he walked off a *Teen Vogue* editorial?

Then I recall that I had told him where I worked over *CounterFlash*.

No. No. No. No. No. No.

"Agnes?" Royce says, smiling far too widely for a smoky joint like this.

I am frozen. I don't want to go over. I don't want to go over in my meat-smelling clothes, with my wild red eyes, my oily face and hair. I don't want to. And I physically cannot.

"Agnes! Eh, what you doing just standing there? Serve!" Mrs. Yoon hisses as she rushes past me to the till. I return to my senses and compose myself, pasting a fake professional smile on my face as I gingerly make my way to his table.

"Hey, Taslim," I say. "I want to ask what are you doing here, but I did this. I told you where I'd be so you can torture me."

"Ha, you're a funny one," Royce says, blushing.

"No offense, but why are you here?" I say, cutting right to the chase.

"Well, it's, um, y'know . . ." He stumbles over his words. "I wanted to see—I mean, I had a sudden craving for Korean food, and I thought, um, hey, why not eat at my friend's joint?"

My friend. The words don't really hit the way they should because I'm swimming in a stew of conflicting emotions, the clearest one being embarrassment. Yes. I'm embarrassed he's seeing me, disheveled and smelling of BBQ sauce, here during my shift, looking as immaculate as he does in his olive-gray chambray shirt and carefully styled hair. And he's not alone.

I regard the person seated next to him, a poker-faced buff man in a tight black T-shirt who's in his late thirties. A new bodyguard. I suppose he had them on rotation.

"This is Mohan," Royce says. "He's my guest for tonight. Mohan, this is the friend I was telling you about. Agnes Chan."

Mohan gives me a steely once-over. He doesn't look impressed.

"Hi, Mohan."

"Hi. Could I have a refill of my tea, please?"

"Certainly, and what about you, Taslim?" I turn my attention to Royce, and as I do, a sharp pain shoots up my leg. I wince.

"Everything okay?" Royce asks with concern, coming over to where I stand in a flash and just stopping shy of touching me.

"Just my leg," I say, holding tight to the chair in front of me, a film of sweat already coating my upper lip. Urgh, I hate showing weakness in front of him. "Don't worry about it. Sit back down, please, or Mrs. Yoon will think you're not happy."

Royce doesn't move, his face creases in concern. "You should tell your boss you need to get off this shift."

"And lose my job?" I snap. Did he not get that I wasn't here on holiday?

"How much longer is your shift?" he asks, frowning.

"Around two hours," I say, wincing as I tried to put my weight on both feet.

"I've got an idea," Royce says. "Hold on." He turns to Mohan. "Order another round of pork cheek and some more of the mixed veg, okay? In fact, order whatever. Soju? You have my permission to drink."

"But, sir, we've already eaten—"

"It's okay, whatever we can't finish, we'll take home, because I'm going to be here for another two hours."

"Why?" we both ask at the same time in the same tone of incredulousness.

He rolls up his sleeves. "Because I'm helping you with the rest of your shift."

~

I must be dreaming. I must have hit my head on the way in from the alley, because Royce Taslim has started waiting tables under the heart eyes of Samuel and Meriam, after brokering me to help out at the till under supervision of the reluctant but somewhat charmed Mrs. Yoon, who distinctly said, "Jalsaenggyeosseoyo," when she saw Royce, and since I have watched at least a thousand hours of K-drama, I understood the compliment, even though she said it like she was calling Royce "plague bringer" or similar.

Incredible, I think as Royce ports a tray of sliced marbled meat with a dark navy Seoul Hot T-shirt, solicitous and picture-perfect. *She's letting me handle the money.* Okay, granted, she's standing right behind me, huffing and muttering when I hit the wrong buttons on the screen, but still. She's letting me touch actual cash (I mean, on the rare occasion someone hands me cash instead of paying with their cards or other online methods of payment)—she's never even let Joyce Lim, the longest serving waitstaff here run the till, ever. It's always been her or her son, Luke Chandran.

Royce passes by with a tray of beers, and my heart does a little swoosh. Of appreciation. The nonsexual kind!

The rest of the hours pass by quickly, and Royce leaves at 10:15 p.m. on the dot, because he has parents who text him if he's even one minute late past his normal curfew of eleven, and I could see Mohan doing the antsy dance at their table. When Mrs. Yoon tries to pay him as well—a sign that she is really enamored with him, because I genuinely thought she was going to split the two hours of wages between us—Royce takes the money solicitously, thanking her, and when her back was turned, he counts out and drops half of the notes in the TIP jar, instead of all as I'd expected.

"I hope you don't mind if I keep half of it; it's my first paycheck," he says apologetically, and my palms grow slick for reasons unclear to me. It happens again when he insists on his driver dropping me off, even as I claimed that I was uncomfortable showing him where I lived, a pithy comment about him being a potential stalker, so he tells the driver to drop me wherever I want after he's disembarked, and then he gives me his hand so that I can be supported as we get into his four-wheel drive. It happens again when he brushes my hand accidentally-on-purpose as he jumps out of the SUV in front of his house, and he turns to me and meets me with a gaze that's soft and open, and a moment opens between us, like a *CounterFlash* portal, before he says good night.

The back of the car smells like sweat and restaurant, and the vaguely creamy, citrusy aftershave Royce wears. I close my eyes and sniff the air, taking it all in like a total creeper.

It's just because he's been so nice to you. That's it, my mind screams.

I sniff again, for reasons that do not follow the official party line I've been telling myself all this time, since the moment I first saw Royce Taslim walking toward me to shake my hand in *hideous* neon-green tights.

Then I slump onto the seat with a heady sigh.

Good God, I have officially lost my mind.

~

Royce: You up? 🌑
Me: Nah
Royce: Liar 😊
Me: Hey, thanks
Royce: For what
Me: Everything you did today
Me: Maybe it's something you would have done for anyone because you're nice
Royce: Not just anyone
Royce: I have my own selfish reasons

I stop myself from typing, *Whatever it is, it meant a lot to me.* His coming to my workplace had thrown me in the beginning, but then he'd been so no-nonsense about the whole affair and about helping me out, that it made me wonder if I'd been overthinking things. Anyway, tonight it had shifted something for me, although I wasn't sure what, yet.

Me: Let's CF tmw 8pm? 🏹
Royce: ♟️ 🏹 😀 🏹
Me: 🗡️ 🐨
Royce: 🗡️ 💣 🏹
Royce: 🗡️ 🗡️ 🗡️

My palms get slick again and I have to lie down.

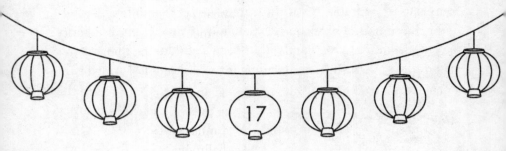

Zee: We need to talk!
Me: Why, what's up?
Zee: I've got exciting news! See you at school later

~

We meet at the library during lunch hour on a gloomy-skied Wednesday, after I'd had time to scarf down a sandwich. Zee, unusually, is on time.

"You won't believe this!" she crows. She shakes her phone at me.

I scoot over to join her on the bench so I can see what's on her screen. It's a chat between Zee and the dean of students, Dr. Maria Schloss.

Maria: OK, Zalifah, sure. Whatever. I'm tired.

This message was in response to a GIF of Puss in Boots doing its dilated pupil thing.

I look up at Zee. "Erm, what?"

"Scroll up!"

I scroll up. The chat is dense with exclamation points and lines of emojilish, all from Zee. "OMG, just summarize, puan, tolong."

"So, you know I'm in charge of entertainment for this year's charity gala, right?"

Dunia hosts an annual charity gala on the second Saturday of December, just after finals. It's a big deal and usually is held in the school assembly hall, but this year being the ball's ten-year anniversary, the school wanted to go the extra mile, and Zee's family had kindly agreed to let the school have the ballroom of one of their five-star hotels to host the event. The ball's a big deal—it typically raises a quarter of a million ringgit each year for the charity of the school's choice. This year Dunia would be supporting two mental health charities—thanks, in no small part, to my "suggestion," i.e., constant nagging.

"Yeah, I'm aware." Zee had been agonizing about acts for the past month.

"Well, the thing is, the student entertainment part of the gala usually isn't exactly great, right? I mean, I know we're obliged to showcase 'student talent'"—Zee rolls her eyes and makes air quotes, and I have to laugh—"and there's no time for an audition, so it's always a student act that's, like, a friend of someone on the committee and has no talent and we see something basic AF like amateur juggling or magic or singing, like who cares? We've seen these acts before. I mean, there was one year where they had an amateur fire-breather, and then one of the curtains caught fire—"

"Zee! Focus!"

"Oh yeah, sorry." She takes a deep breath. "What I wanted to say was—I suggested stand-up."

"Oh no," I say slowly. "You are going to be the most hated person in school by the end of the night. Everybody knows that amateur stand-up is the worst. The absolute worst! *I* should know!"

Zee's grin could power grids. "Nope, it won't be because you and Royce are going to do it. On top of all the usual acts like juggling and singing, I've set aside twenty minutes for two stand-up acts, which would be perfect for a tight ten-minute set each from both of you." She leans forward and steel enters her voice. "I know you are good enough to do ten-minute set. I saw you do a seven-minute set last week. *You can make it happen.* Plus, you need the practice in time for the qualifiers, right?"

I lean forward as well and pound my fist on the table. "Absolutely not, unless you want Royce and me to hate you by the end of this lunch break."

"I heard my name," Royce says, sliding into the seat opposite us. "What's up, folks?" He quirks his lip in a semi-smile at me, and I immediately feel like running into traffic. Theoretically, of course— once is enough, really.

"What's he doing here?" I ask Zee.

"Er, thanks," Royce says drily. "Hi to you, too."

"I asked him to meet me here to discuss entertainment for the gala. Royce and I are friends now thanks to stand-up. We're, like, mutuals on all the platforms and his family is even donating stuff to the auction. Like sports equipment from their new partnership with Frisson Cola and—"

"No! No! No!" I say, shaking my head emphatically in reference to the friendship between Zee and Taslim. Can I have one aspect of life that isn't tainted by Taslim? "No! No! No!"

"What's up with her?" Royce says to Zee.

"You mean, what's wrong? Many things, clearly," Zee replies. "But listen, we have business." She fills Royce in about her suggestion, and his eyes widen, and soon he's shaking his head going, "No, no, no, no," while I glare in triumph at him, saying "Ha! You see? Ha! Ha!" in an accusatory tone.

"Shhhhhhh!" Several students around us hiss. Royce and I scatter penitent *Sorry*s around us and shut up.

"Clearly yes, because can you imagine? Two of the most belov— well, well-known, students in school, performing stand-up? We'll fill the hall. People who had no intention of coming to the gala will come just to see you guys perform." Zee is almost purring in satisfaction.

"I can't," Royce says.

"Is it because you're performing as Ray right now? It's okay, you know, it's just Agnes and me who know about that, and we'll—"

"No," Royce says dully. "I can't perform stand-up to this audience. My parents' friends will be there, giving out the prizes, remember?"

"Oh right," Zee says, downcast. "I forgot about that familial complication."

"That's okay," he says stiffly. "But thanks for thinking of me. Although"—he is trying for levity now—"Agnes would be perfect for it."

"Would you, please?" Zee says, widening her eyes at me. "I've kind of pitched stand-up to the rest of the team and they loved it."

"Even Dr. Maria?" I say wryly.

"Yes, she came around to it, especially after I threw in a couple of free nights in Langkawi for the auction that's reserved just for bids from the faculty. Come on! It'll be great practice for you!"

"Zee," I say. "I . . . I would like to, but I'm not confident enough to be the only one doing stand-up that night."

"So, let's ask someone else from the circuit to join you as the second act."

I raise an eyebrow. "Are non-student performers allowed?"

"Yes, if at least seventy-five percent of the program is allocated to student acts."

"So, who are you thinking of besides me?" I ask, even though I already know.

"I don't know, I guess the next choice would be, well, Vern?" Her eyes widen in what she thinks is an innocent way.

"Yes!" I say just as Royce says, "No."

"Why not?" I turn to him. "Vern's the logical choice."

"Absolutely," Zee says, nodding vigorously. "He's the youngest after us."

"Plus, he's great, we've been hanging out a bit, we have a very similar sense of humor and worldview," I say brightly.

Royce's mouth flattens into a line when I say this.

"Yeah, they're tight. I don't even think she's doing it for my sake," Zee complains. "So, Agnes and Vern could be an excellent duo, don't you think? I mean, since you aren't able to perform, Royce."

Royce's smile is friendly, but it doesn't reach his eyes. "Sure. But why don't we get more women onstage? The dynamic combo of Agnes and Gina. Plus, Gina's more experienced."

"Hmm, that's actually a good idea," I say. "But if Gina comes to our school, and you're there as Royce . . ."

"Gina can keep a secret. I trust her," Royce says.

"Then sure, I'm good," I say, shrugging. "I'll do it if Gina is willing."

"I guess, yeah," Zee says with a little more reluctance than the situation warranted.

"Then it's settled, Gina and Agnes will perform!" Royce takes out his phone and excuses himself. "If you're okay with me reaching out, I'll ask Gina." We nod, and he starts tapping on his phone. "I've got to run. I'll update you all if everything goes well."

We wave goodbye to Royce. Zee looks visibly deflated by this turn of events.

"I can invite Vern, if you want," I say after a few beats of her sighing loudly.

She stops and grins. "That is exactly what I want."

"I know."

"You're the best."

"I know. How much are the tickets for outsiders?"

"Oh, don't worry about it, all performers get an extra free ticket to the gala. Free three-course meal and all that. Vern can be your plus one. I'll put you guys on the list. Provided he wants to come, of course."

In spite of my initial hesitation, excitement fizzes through me.

"Cool, cool. Although, since it's for charity, I'm happy to donate the price of his ticket."

Zee tells me the price of the tickets and I concede that my generous performance would have to suffice as an in-kind donation. We all must contribute in our own ways.

~

After school, I head to Zee's to study and scheme on how to hide my Dunia stand-up debut from my parents, for many reasons. Not least because a substantial chunk of my material was inspired by my mother and I've been withholding the fact that some of my Seoul Hot nights were actually comedy nights.

Zee figured that I could gift them a staycation, fixed dates, non-refundable. "My parents' luxury retreat in Janda Baik always has spare rooms, and as their unofficial social media adviser, I get free rooms for giveaways that they don't really monitor the use thereof, so I'm happy to get them to give you a room for a night."

"Er, is that ethical?"

"Well, I'm basically working for free, and I am a child, sooooo I don't think we need to have that whole debate."

"I can pay for it; I've been saving up some money from my part-time job." I'd never told Zee where I worked, preferring to tell her I did stuff for my mother's law firm. Working in a restaurant was so basic. I worry that she won't see me the same way if she knows—after all, she's a socialite, and most of her childhood friends are rich kids.

"No way I'm letting you pay," Zee says. "I love your dad, he's an amazing educator, and I think I should be able to treat him and your mom in a way that won't get me in trouble with some school ethics board."

"Technically—"

"Hush, Agnes. Just . . . just think of it as my belated housewarming gift or whatever. Since you know, I've never had a chance to bring them a gift at yours."

She looks at me pointedly and I stay quiet, before muttering, "It's complicated."

"Don't I know." She sighs. "Anyway, just take the spare room; it's going to waste otherwise, seriously."

"Thanks, Zee." Then I groan when I recalled a small—literally—complication. "What about Rosie, though?"

Zee puts on her thinking face. "Hmm. What do your parents think about sleepovers? At her age?"

"OMG, yes!" I say, snapping my fingers in glee. "She's had a couple with her British friend, what's her face! And I'm sure Rosie would love to help our parents have a staycation. This might actually work out!"

She pats my arm. "Imagine, ten years from now when you've got your own comedy special out on Netflix or whatever, they'll say you were discovered by Zee Bakri, the multihyphenated beauty mogul-director-humanitarian."

With friends like her believing in me . . . I shake my head, smiling. It's almost like I can do anything, be anyone.

My good mood buoys me home. I go over my latest college application essay for another school, do some schoolwork, then take out my phone, thinking of launching a *CF* offensive, so I text Royce instead of my usual *CF* buddies.

Me: Want to play CF in a bit? You're not on the stand-up rota tonight, I saw
Royce: Sorry, I'm busy. Chess lessons
Me: I thought chess lessons is on Thursday evening?
Royce: I just can't. Do I need to give you a reason for every action of mine that doesn't match your expectations?
Me: WTF?
Royce: Sorry, that's not fair. It's been a day. I'll ttyl

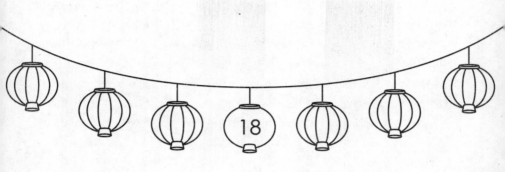

ON SATURDAY, DISTRACTED BY YET ANOTHER MUTED RESPONSE FROM Royce when I extended an invitation to game, I head with my mom to Toys for Days, a specialty toy store. It's the kind of toy store where they "rotate themes" and the lighting is gentle and pretty as moonbeams. The kind of place where motherhood is planned, celebrated, wanted.

The kind of place where you can't make a scene, and you're more likely to say yes to a free staycation in another state. The plan is to get her a present there from Rosie and me, and then surprise her with the staycation right after.

My mother glances at a display for organic bamboo cotton pajamas, picks up the paper tag on a ribbon-wrapped set, and visibly blanches, dropping the pajamas as though they burn. "Oh my God, what the heck are in these fibers?" she mutters. "Honey, we can't afford to shop here."

"Yes, we can, Mom," I say with a practiced air of unconcern. I'd saved up quite some money working at Seoul Hot, and since I don't have athletic gear and other sports-related expenditures this year, I want to treat her. I wave a gift card around. "It's too late for a refund, so you're just going to have to spend it." I've preloaded a month's worth of shifts on the card, whatever I hadn't spent on transport to comedy venues. "Anyway, it's from Rosie and me, so you can't say no."

"All right," she says, grinning. "Thank you *both*."

She winces as she makes her way down the aisle. Four months pregnant, my mother is bloated and already breathless, a combination of her genetics and the meds she's on for a variety of health reasons. Yet I haven't seen her this happy, even as she worries for me. She's radiant in spite of her pallor. I've been watching her like a hawk—her psychiatrist has changed up her prescription ever since she found out about the pregnancy—holding my breath and waiting for the cracks to appear, the signs of old distress, the vacant melancholy, the withdrawal, the crying, all of it, but thankfully, they haven't returned.

"Everything okay?" my mother asks, looking up from caressing a plush, velveteen fox with a vivid clay-red fur that a price tag reveals as costing even more than a live fox, surely.

I paste on a bright, happy expression. "I'm so good, Mom. Everything is perfect." I gesture at the fox. "Great choice for Sweet Pea." That's Stanley's placeholder nickname for the baby because my mom's too superstitious to use the name they've selected.

I've seen the cross-stich project she's made for her, though.

Yina. Yina Esther Morissette. A perfect new girl.

"Thanks, hon," she says, a tiny crease between her brows. She looks back down at the fox and picks her words. "You know, it's been a tough few months for you, since the accident."

"It's okay, Mom, I'm getting through it." I brace myself for what is coming next.

"So, lately, you've been running off with Zee and your friends"—I may have embellished this fact a little—"every other evening when you're not studying or working, which I want to emphasize I'm happy about, seeing that you're getting out of the house again. . . ." She hesitates. "Can you—can you tell me what you guys do?"

"Sure, we play board games," I say, having already planned for this. Zee was apprised of my every stand-up set so she could corroborate my plans with her. "Very safe. Very stationary. Very . . . above-the-board." I smile, pleased at this last pun.

"I see." She observes me closely. "And who's with you at these game nights? Anyone I know?"

"The Flashes, of course," I say brightly. "You know, Suraya, Qiu Lan, Tavleen . . . them lot."

"I see." She strokes the fur of the fox. "With all these changes at school and at home, if something's . . . bothering you, you can always tell me. I'm here for you."

"Likewise," I say. "Anything at all that's affecting you, y'know, with the pregnancy and how you feel on your new meds, samesies. Tell me."

She flinches. She puts down the fox and says, "I wish you wouldn't do that."

"Do what?"

"Take care of me. Like you're the mom." The words come out jagged.

I feel something in me well up. Words that I'd not said to her, ever. *If I don't watch you, who will? Stanley doesn't know you the way I do. He wasn't there.*

"Agnes, I've been well for the longest time."

"Sure," I say. It can't be a coincidence that when I started excelling in sports around the age of eleven, when I started showing her that she didn't have to worry about me, that I wasn't a mistake that couldn't be redeemed, on top of me holding us together at home, running the household when she checked out, that she started pulling out of the darkness. It could have been the new psychiatrist she started seeing, of course, the new meds, even Stanley, who she met around then by chance—but I think it really was down to me. But now that I was just—just like any other kid, would she be disappointed? Would she still be all right?

Maybe this child is what's making it all okay, a little voice said. *Maybe she's already moved on with her hopes and dreams, because now she can start over the way it should have been.*

Maybe she's fine, even with everything that's happening because this time—this time, everything was done right. This time, this . . . this pregnancy is wanted.

I swallow a lump that appears in my throat and force down the tears that threaten to erupt. No. *Stop it*, I admonish myself. She loves me, she does. I know it.

I know it.

My mother leans over and hugs me close, surprising me, and says in my hair, "I'm glad you found your new thing, Agnes. I hope . . . playing board games brings you joy."

"It has," I say, and I don't even need to fake this emotion. "It's really allowed me to channel my competitive spirit in healthy ways and to meet new people."

We break apart.

"All right," she says. "Because I'm rooting for you in everything you do."

"I know, Mom." It's now or never; I launch my offensive. "By the way, you'd never guess what Zee—and I guess her family, too, by extension—and I got for you and Stanley: a staycation in Janda Baik!"

I hurriedly tell her the details, emphasizing that it's nonrefundable, especially when she starts protesting that it's too much. "Don't worry, it's really no big deal because it's low season for Janda Baik. *Practically* a ghost village."

"But that's the weekend after Christmas. That's, like, peak season, surely?"

"Yes, but it's, like, fruit bat season, and you know, snake mating season in the forest near Janda Baik, so her family's pretty much giving away the room for free. And it's really the least fancy of their properties. It's *barely* four-star, if even."

My mother stifles a smile. "Well, I guess Stanley and I have no choice but to go to this very average retreat. This is very generous of you and Zee. I'll have to thank her personally."

"You know how these rich kids are," I say. "They've got free stuff leaking out of them. But yes, do thank her when you see her, that's all she wants."

"I'm the luckiest mom in the whole world," she says, giving me a quick kiss.

She picks up a smaller version of the fox and makes her way to the cashier, but before she can get to the counter, I'm already there with the original one and paying for it with the gift card. Being there for my mom the way she's always needed me.

~

Me: Hey, is everything OK?
Royce: What do you mean?
Me: You're acting a little weird. Like you're avoiding me
Royce: I'm just figuring out some stuff. I'll explain when I'm ready
Me: OK, see you at comedy tomorrow? I see you're doing a 15-minute set at the special comedy night at Bar BiBi
Royce: Yeah . . . See you there

~

Zee: So how?
Me: It is done

Zee sends me a GIF of Mr. Burns rubbing his hands together and saying, "Excellent."

Me: Mwuahhhahhaahahhaha slay
Zee: 🪶
Zee: I worry for our future
Me: Me too

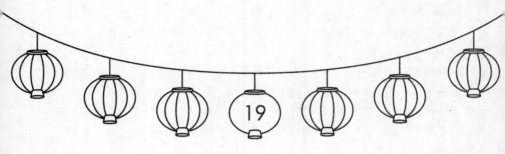

19

I STARE AT THE CROWD QUEUING TO GET INTO THE BAR, WAITING FOR
Zee to join me for this early Friday evening set, buzzing with nerves
and quite possibly the effects of my third energy drink of the evening.
In the line before me is a bachelorette party with ten very drunk
women who are being processed by the harried-looking doorman,
and my right leg is starting to get splintery, although the adrenaline
drowns out some of the pain. I'm running through the set under my
breath: qualifiers are in three and a half weeks, a couple of weeks
after the charity ball, and the young comics that are trying out for the
competition—Royce, Vern, and I—are going up at every single comedy or even variety open-mike nights now, no matter the crowd or
venue. I can get through a bachelorette party; I've done worse.

"Oh boy," Vern says, appearing with Kumar. He side-eyes the
screeching bunch. "This is going to be a wild night."

"I hope I get to do my set without interruptions," I say. "The qualifiers are less than a month away and I need all the practice I can get."

"No one's ever ready," Kumar says sagely. "For stand-up and marriage."

I chuckle. "Is that going on your dating profile?"

Kumar winks and flexes his biceps to our amusement. "No need. I
let my sticklike physique in sleeveless tops speak for me."

I giggle.

Vern shakes his head with an affectionate smile as he says, "This boy is a menace to society."

We finally make our way in. Royce is milling by the side of the stage, checking out the lighting. His body language stiffens when he sees me walk up with Vern and Kumar—or maybe it's my imagination.

"Hey," I say, trying to sound casual even as my heart picks up speed for unclear reasons.

"Hey, Agnes. Vern. Kumar." Royce peers around me. "Zee's not here yet?"

"She's on her way," I say, rolling my eyes. "Meaning she's running twenty minutes behind. She told me she wouldn't miss our sets for the world." Also, she had mentioned wanting to run into Vern. Literally.

"You excited?" Vern says to Royce. "I saw you on the list. It's your first fifteen-minute set in a while, right?"

"Yes," Royce says, setting his jaw.

"Is this going to be your set for the qualifiers?"

"I'm not sure yet," Royce says curtly.

"Whatever it is, I look forward to it," I say.

Royce smiles and the recent strangeness between us thaws a little, although it's still there, that new coolness. I don't know what put it there.

"How about you, nervous? It's your first ten-minute set closing the first half?" Royce asks. I nod. "That's an achievement."

"I'm a little nervous, yeah," I say. "Although it might be due to the three cans of dubiously named energy drinks I downed today. I've got a couple of new bits to test about celebrating Father's Day as the child of a single mom—they could swing either way."

"Ooh, I love your mom bits," Kumar says, then colors when he realizes what he's said. "Crap, I mean, sorry, although—"

"If any of you say, *That's what she said,* our friendship is over," Vern says. He turns to me. "Sorry if my boy Kumar scarred you for life. He isn't house-trained."

Kumar smacks Vern.

"It's okay, I'm already scarred for life with all my mom-related trauma," I say ruefully.

"You mine that gold," Vern says. "At least your trauma is real, not manufactured." He smirks at Royce, who frowns in response.

I flail for a distraction. "You coming to the qualifiers, Kumar? Support us?"

"Absolutely!" Kumar says. "By now I can almost recite ninety percent of your sets, but the great thing is I'm still laughing. That's how good you guys are." He shakes his head. "I really should work on my existing material that gets laughs, but I'm always tempted to try new bits."

"You can and should try new bits, but if you want to get good routines at different lengths, you have to work on building and expanding upon a set that is thematically resonant, and then every time you go onstage you're basically tweaking and refining each line till every word is killer," Royce says.

Vern turns to Royce. "Shouldn't you be preparing new material, though?" he wonders. "Since your last few sets when Agnes was around didn't . . . go down so well."

"I don't think you need to worry for me. Maybe you should focus on your own material, Goh."

"You're right. I should focus on my own set. Well then, break a leg up there, Taslim," Vern says. Then his expression changes. "Oops," he says, his voice laced with guilt as he turns to me, eyes wide. "Sorry, Agnes. I didn't . . . It just slipped out."

"Taslim?" Kumar says, mercifully dense.

"Can I speak to you in private?" Royce says in a tight voice.

I nod and follow Royce to a quiet corner in an alcove backstage, my palms slick with sweat.

"You told him?" Royce whisper-shouts. "The one person I . . ." He palms his face. "Damn it, Agnes."

"I—I didn't!" I say, annoyed that he thought I was the leak and wondering what he had meant to say. "Well, not directly. He figured it out by himself."

"How?"

"Because of our mutual connection to Zee," I mutter.

Royce's eyes flash. "Great. Now he holds this information over me and can deploy it whenever to hurt me."

"What?" My skin flushes with anger. "Vern would never use it. . . . I'll tell him not to. I trust him."

His expression darkens. "How can you be sure of that? What do you know about Vern?"

"I know enough! What do *you* know about Vern?"

He takes a step closer to me. "I'm trying to look out for you."

"For me—or your own interests?" I challenge.

He makes an exasperated sound and grabs his hair. "Agnes, oh my God, you're *killing* me."

"Why do you hate Vern so much?" I say, relentless.

"Because he's my biggest and only competition!" Royce almost shouts. "For . . . for—" He stops himself, his breath irregular and fast.

I swallow. Royce was referring to stand-up and wanted to spare my feelings. "That's good to know." My stomach twists with this new knowledge. I'm not good enough to be his competition, yet again.

Royce winces. "Oh, I didn't mean . . . Shit. Everything is coming out wrong," he says. "There's just so much . . . Vern is my . . . goddamn it." Royce takes another step toward me with a pleading expression, but all I can think about is how I'll never be good enough, even here, even at my best, for Royce to treat me as competition.

"Let's talk after our sets," I say brusquely. I whirl around and head back to where Vern and Kumar were, but only Vern is left. Now I'm fired up again. I'll show him competition.

"Here you are," Vern says. "I'm so, so sorry for my slip of tongue . . . I hope I didn't get you in too much trouble."

I shake my head. "It's fine; you didn't mean to."

"Was Royce being condescending to you?" Vern asks, his face full of concern. "He's very dismissive of me, as you've seen for yourself."

"He's nice to me. Most of the time."

"But does he treat you like an equal?"

I struggle to keep my face impassive. "He is very caring" is what I manage to say.

Vern studies me. "You *have* gotten closer to him in spite of what I said."

I look at Royce, now seated at the comics' booth near the stage and talking animatedly to Milly, who's showrunning tonight, and Zee, who had just arrived. "He's . . . he's okay once you get past the packaging."

Vern frowns. "Oh my God, Agnes—you *like* him."

"It's not like that," I say, and I'm not sure if it's in response to Vern or to my own internal debate. "We're *just* friends." I'm not so foolish, no naive, to fall for someone like Royce Taslim. We're barely friends as it is, and now that I know he doesn't even consider me a worthy adversary in comedy, the one level playing field we're on, I should be yeeted into the sun if I did fall for him. Because to Royce, I'm just a charity case he's entertaining, and that's all I'll ever be to him.

"Sure you are," Vern says lightly. *"Just friends."* He shrugs. "Look, I don't blame you, whatever your feelings. It's easy to be seduced by their lifestyles. I mean, they are spoiled rich kids, buying their way through life."

"Stop it," I say. "My friends aren't like that."

Zee chooses that moment to head to the comics' booth with what appears to be two supersize tubs of gourmet popcorn, and everyone cheers. "The manager made an exception for me regarding outside food," she can be heard saying over the general din.

"Okay, fine, they're rich. So what? That doesn't automatically make them bad."

"I never said that." Vern shakes his head, like he's disappointed in me. "I'm more concerned about *you*. It's okay to like these people, but I want you to take care of yourself, to just . . . hold some of you back. Don't forget your place. Once you start thinking you're like them, that's when you're going to be disappointed. Because when push comes to shove, they'll always look after their own."

There's a funny taste in my mouth and I swallow. "That sounds like a terrible way to see the world."

"It's the smart way to see the world, Agnes," Vern says in a low voice. "It's how you avoid getting hurt, giving yourself to the wrong people." He gestures at Zee. "You won't ever be enough for them because of what you lack, but you are—to me."

We fall silent. My heart is sick with a dull weight. I don't want Vern, who is a friend, to hate my school friends. If only he knew them like I do, like they know me, like they accept me—

I start at the realization that there were so many things about myself that I couldn't share with Zalifah and so many things about Royce's life that I couldn't even comprehend.

"Let's change the subject," Vern says. "I want you to be in the right headspace for your set. Think happy thoughts. Think of the both of us tearing through New York in March, eating street food and watching stand-up, because you know"—he winks, knowing how superstitious I am—"maybe we won the national lottery and needed to spend all our money."

I laugh. "Okay, player." The finals of the comedy, *if* we made it, would be held in March, during spring break.

"I heard from Gina a couple of days ago that both of you are performing at a school function."

I blink. "Yeah. It's a charity gala." Recalling my promise to Zee, I power on. "Wanna come as my plus one? You'll have free food, and we'll dance after. It'll be fun, I promise. We'll have to suit up, of course. It's black-tie." A little shiver of excitement courses through me: Zalifah and I have plans to wear matching tuxedoes—I found something in my size on an online thrift site in a shimmery midnight-blue fabric and bought it on a whim. We're going to look so good.

Vern shakes his head. "Nah, it's okay. I mean, I'd love to hang out with you, but I don't want to put on a penguin suit and pretend to belong."

The underlying meaning of his words cut me. "That's too bad."

"Enjoy the gala," Vern says. "Call me when you need a palate cleanse." Then someone makes a sign at Vern to get ready for his opening set and he heads off.

I ace my set and head home without staying for Royce's in a state of turmoil. Vern has a very binary way of looking at the world. Even if he doesn't intend to, he makes me feel like I'm a fraud, some kind of traitor or fool for liking Zee or Royce. Yet if Vern's the only one who truly knows me, who understands where I come from, who has demonstrated that he cares for me, maybe I *should* listen to him. Maybe Vern knows best.

A message lights up my screen. It's Royce.

Royce: You home?
Me: Yup
Royce: Your set was great 🔥
Me: Thnx

I can't help my dead-end, one-worded replies, now that I know how I feel about him—and how he feels about me. I have to hold myself back.

Royce: So I've some explaining to do about why I've been acting strangely around you and I'd rather do it in person. Are you ok to meet tomorrow afternoon?
Me: I guess
Royce: How about my place? We'll study after, if you want. Kill two birds with one stone

Smart move, mister, appealing to my deepest Chinese instincts by issuing that idiom. Against my better judgment, I agree.

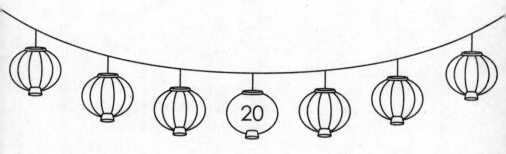

THIS TIME, I TURN UP AT THE TASLIMS' ARMED WITH PROPER FOOD—
a generous oblong slab of fruit cake that Stanley made for the family,
but I'm sure he won't miss, even if there was a sign that said DON'T
TOUCH.

Which is not the same as DON'T EAT.

The nuts in there are brain food, after all.

My phone buzzes. Stanley. Oops. I ignore the call.

Royce opens the door dressed in a white T-shirt and filmy
Lululemon joggers that I have to drag my eyes away from, because I
am morally deficient. I blame Zee and the reality shows she's watched
that I have absorbed by osmosis.

"So," he says once we are seated in the living room, "I wanted to
explain about my behavior."

I cross my arms and look at him expectantly, saying nothing.

Royce clears his throat, his face hot. "The thing is, Agnes, as you
know, we've been spending some time together, haven't we, and we're
both in comedy."

I press my lips together and give him a terse nod.

"Yes. So . . . um, and in this time, I've come to . . . I've, uh, the thing is—"A loud rumble issues from his stomach and he turns even brighter red.

"Yikes," I say.

"Sorry, I missed lunch. I came back late from violin because of the traffic, and then you arrived on time."

"No worries, please eat something, we can continue this conversation after." There's already a tray of nyonya kueh and gummy bears and various potato chips set on the table, but I cake-block him triumphantly. "Try my cake," I intone, brandishing it with a flourish. "It's *homemade*."

"Wow, a homemade cake," Royce says. He reaches for cutlery, cuts a generous chunk of my—Stanley's—cake and pops it into his mouth. His eyes widen. "Oh my God! This is amazing!"

"Thanks," I say. I try some and have to stop myself from snatching the rest of the cake for myself, it is that beautiful.

We demolish three-quarters of the cake in ten minutes.

"What's that liquid it's soaked in? Tastes a little alcoholic?" Royce says between mouthfuls.

"I'm not sure. Prob not, I mean, there's kids and a pregnant lady in my household."

"So you didn't make it," Royce teases me.

"Nah."

"I'll have more, then."

I reach over to smack him, and he grabs my wrist. And doesn't let go.

We face each other, our breaths hot and fruity.

Wow, Taslim's eyes are criminal. Like, literally, because of his family's crime against nature. I will myself to think of spiders and licorice, but his lips are there and something has loosened in my brain.

"Agnes," he whispers.

It's going to happen. The air is making humming noises and we're drawing closer to each other and—

My phone buzzes on the table like a trapped hornet. Taslim,

startled, drops my wrist and, unbalanced, I pitch forward into his lap, face-first, where his crotch is.

"Oh my gosh," I say, jerking upward. "I'm so . . . I'm so sorry!"

Royce puts a pillow over his lap, his face flaming. "Don't . . . don't apologize, it's my fault!" He is also louder than usual.

My phone continues to buzz with messages. I glance down at the screen. Wow, why are my eyes not focusing? I rub them and try to read the screen.

Stanley: Agnes, did you take the cake that I made for the faculty's End-of-School Bash?
Stanley: That cake is SOAKED in rum. Do NOT eat it!
Stanley: Where are you?

Oops.

"Oops?" Royce says, his eyebrows knitting comically.

I grin at him. "I think I just accidentally drunk you. And me."

"What?"

Stanley: Agnes, where are you??

I type confidently: Im fine, don owrry m at Royce's tuitioning at his! ya.

Royce reaches for his tea and knocks it over the table onto his white T-shirt. "Oh no," he slurs.

I hold on to his arm. "You okay? You need help getting to your room?"

"I'm fine," Royce says. "But if you really want to see my room so much, just follow me."

"I do actually want see your room," I say point-blank.

"It's upstairs," Royce says, not steadily.

We walk-wobble toward Royce's room and pass a couple of servants on the way up, which helps bring me back down to earth, somewhat. How many people work and live here?

And then I'm standing in Royce's stunning, light-flooded room. I can't believe it.

"Just hold on a sec," he says, ducking into, I don't know, the ante-chamber? A walk-in closet? I peek and confirm that it is indeed a walk-in closet. Wow.

There's a sound of a door banging open deep in the closet. "I'm going to change," Royce says. "Make yourself comfortable."

I wander around the room looking at the grays and creams of his room, broken up by the occasional splashes of color of a framed print or photos. I study his books (mangas, David Walliams books, the entire Percy Jackson series, a couple of Hanna Alkaf novels, loads of nonfiction books and textbooks). And his bed, which is neatly made and very inviting. I wander over, run my fingers across the plaid bed-spread and sit. I have to resist the urge to sink my face into his pillow and sniff the damn thing.

Snap out it, I admonish myself. I turn and check out his minimalist nightstand, with only a small dimmable round lamp, an Apple watch, and a small silver photo frame tucked between a fluffy plush mar-mot and a soft brown bear, and a tissue box printed with a dancing lemur logo.

I pick it up, curiosity getting the better of me. It's a studio photo of a young man in his twenties around a gawky, younger boy of around ten years of age, who I realize with a start is Royce.

"Hey," Royce says.

I drop the photo in a panic. "I'm sorry," I chirp, "I'm not snooping, I promise."

"It's okay." He sees the question in my eyes and sighs. "That's my brother." He takes the photo I am holding out to him. "My older half brother, actually."

I look at the way Royce is grasping the photo frame and under-stood that they had been close. "He looks much older than you," I say cautiously.

"He is. He's nine years older. When his mother died in an accident, my dad took a second wife—my mom—then they had me." A half smile curved his lips. "The spare."

There's a weight in every word he's saying. I keep quiet, willing him to keep talking.

He traces his brother's face. "This is the only photo of him left in the entire house. My mother had all his photos taken away and stored when . . . when he left. Back when we were in Jakarta."

"He left?" I say, not understanding.

"Yeah." His voice roughens. "He . . . he left home years ago."

"Shit," I say. "What—where . . ."

"I don't know. As the elder son of my dad, who himself is the only son of his generation, my brother had been primed from birth to take over from him for a specific branch of the family business. He went to the best schools in the region, then college at Stanford, then Harvard for his MBA, then straight to work. Everything was going along swimmingly, then about five years ago, out of the blue he j-just snapped." Royce's voice drops to a whisper. "He told us he wanted nothing to do with the family business, that he hated the pressure, and poof! Bye. Gone. He didn't even want to tell us where he was going. I haven't seen him since then."

He has that silver frame in a death grip, looking like he would shatter if I made the wrong move. I put my hand over his and give it a brief squeeze. His hands relax at my touch. "I'm sorry. . . . What happened then?"

Royce ducks his head. "My father was so angry, he had a stroke and was in the hospital for almost a month." He inhales and exhales with force. "Then the machinery cranked into action, hushed up my brother's disappearance and my father's stroke, because the illness alone would bring down the stock price, even crash it. And then they just—they just quietly replaced my brother in the company and stopped mentioning him in press releases. There was this vague planted story about how he joined a monastery, and maybe that's true . . . maybe that's what happened." He shuts his eyes. "And then he was cut out of the will and from our lives, as though he never existed. One day I woke up and just saying his name become anathema. His belongings were cleared away, his photos disposed of. After that, at age *twelve*, I started having to do everything he used to do. Attend these business courses, academic programs, *chess lessons*"—the frustration in his voice could cut glass—"golf lessons, and show up in the business proper, shadow my dad in meetings, conferences, all of it. The spare had to step up." He laughs, low and bitter. "All the proverbial eggs were in my basket now. But do you know why . . . why we're in Kuala Lumpur now, where my mom is from, instead of Jakarta?"

I shake my head, my stomach tensing.

"I had . . . an episode."

"Meaning?"

Royce's face twists and he drops his voice low. "It was half a year after my brother had left us . . . left me, and everyone at home was pretending he never existed, they were making me go t-to fucking *mini*— MBA courses and Mandarin and French lessons and the corporate ski trip and YPO outings. I just . . . lost it." He balled his fists, the photo frame forgotten in his lap, his breaths shallow. "They came to pick me up at school and I just . . . I just . . . I just started screaming."

My heart stopped.

"I—I just screamed and screamed and screamed in the middle of my classroom. The teachers had to drag me to the infirmary so I could be sedated by the school doctor. My parents freaked out. I didn't mean to, but I was only twelve—"

I grasped his arm, wishing I could hold him instead. "Royce, you don't have to justify what happened at all," I say, my heart squeezing so tight that tears prick my eyes. "It's not your fault. Something traumatic happened to you and nobody gave you any support. *You were only twelve.*"

I stop, hit by a stunning realization: I, too, had been though something traumatic—my mother's years of mental illness, and nobody had thought to see how I was coping with it. Not even myself. And

I couldn't blame my loved ones for missing this check-in, not when it feels like the world is only just beginning to tolerate the field of mental health.

His gaze meets mine. "Thank you," he says simply. He gathers himself before speaking again. "Anyway, that's why we left. There was no way they could save face if they lived in Jakarta. The community is so small, and with two 'crazy' kids . . ." He used air quotes on *crazy*.

I withdraw my hand and cross my arms. "I hate that word, *crazy*," I say quietly. "My mother . . . they used to call her crazy in front of me, when she used to pick me up at school in tears. The kids, even the teachers." This is the first time I'd ever told anyone about this, but why stop now? I mean, I'd already face-planted in his crotch.

Royce gives my arm a brief squeeze. "That's not right. I'm sorry you had to go through that."

"So, what did they make you do?" I ask him, almost afraid of the answer.

"My parents were so worried they tightened the network around me and sent me to a mental health professional to get assessed. Here, let me show you something." He goes to the door and points out the lock system, with a simple lever apparatus. "See that lock? I don't have the key. My doors don't lock. Not even in the bathroom." He pauses and smiles mirthlessly. "They don't trust me. They are afraid of what I might do." His eyes are glassy, unseeing.

I feel like someone had punched me in the stomach. Suddenly, the walls of his room felt too close, the cavernous space too small. My mother—I'd done the same to her, hadn't I? I'd been tiptoeing around her, treating her with kid gloves, too—even though *I'm* the kid in this equation.

I don't feel good for many reasons, and not just because I'd accidentally drunk myself. If this is what rum does to you, I'm never drinking again . . . at very least not until I turn eighteen.

"Man, this is not what I expected when I asked to see your room," I say, trying to lighten the mood.

Because I *cannot* be the girl that makes Royce Taslim cry in his own bedroom.

It works. He chuckles wryly. "Believe me, this is not how I saw this day going down. I had other plans." Royce joins me on the bed again. "Anyway, this is why I've got a finger in so many pies, why I'm involved in a bazillion after-school activities, and why I'm killing myself to excel in everything. That's the only way to get my parents to let their guard down. To them, success equals normalcy. So I show them what they want to see, and I've learned to make it work for me." He shrugs. "This way, I'll always have excuses whenever I want a night to myself at the comedy club: Peer tutoring! Russian movie marathons! Javelin practice! Marcus, Killian, Shyam, my crew—they take turns covering for me. I get dropped off at theirs, they assure my parents they'll take care of me, and then I cab off. . . ."

I see, in my mind's eye, how the people I had dismissed as his "flighty, rich jock" friends, were standing by Royce and making up excuses for him, inviting him around, doing all they could so their friend could let off some steam. No, it wasn't just letting off steam—Royce loves stand-up, the way I love running. I understand that kind of passion. If I'd been in his place, I would have done everything I could to preserve this secret garden of mine, too. I understand Ray Lim, and I think I understand Royce Taslim now.

I rest my hand on his arm. "Taslim?"

"Yeah?"

"I'm so, so sorry your family put you in this position. And for all that's happened to your brother. And you." I make myself look him in the eye, even if doing so messes with my respiration. "I really . . . I really appreciate you telling me this."

"Thank you for listening," he says. "I was afraid you'd think less of me if I told you about my past."

"Not at all," I said. "In fact, I think I like you better now."

"Great," he says. "Although—" Something shifts in his eyes. A question in them.

I blush and drop my hand. "How's your dad doing these days?" I say, trying to sound nonchalant.

"My dad, he's never been the same, physically, since the stroke. He's actually in Switzerland now, and they are doing some experimental stem cell treatment thingy on him. The results have been promising, but he had a little setback last week. Please don't tell anyone."

I nod. I would never use this personal information against him. I hesitate. "Thank you for sharing this with me, Taslim. It's . . . very, erm, personal."

I am so good at this.

He smiles at me and says, "Don't you think it's time you called me Royce?"

"Royce." I try it out and my face burns at the newness, the intimacy of his name.

"I like when you say my name," he says without irony now.

"You can call me Agnes, too."

He gives me that Taslim half smile I've come to know. "Haven't you realized I've been calling you that for some time?"

I think about it. Yes, yes he had. And I like it, more than I should.

Royce shifts closer to me and reaches over to put the frame back on the nightstand and doesn't move away. We're too close. We're not close enough. He bites his lip and I am mesmerized. He moves just that bit closer, again. I wait for the panicked warnings to start up, to tell me to move away: *Bacteria! Tetanus!* but my thoughts are conspicuously silent now even as my mind sharpens to take in every minute shift in his movements. My heart is a bird trapped in a cage, my blood is both too slow and too fast. The mattress dips and our fingers graze. When I don't pull away, he takes my hand and threads his fingers through mine, and I stare at our clasped hands, transfixed by the slightly calloused feel of his touch.

"Listen," he says, in a new voice I'd never heard before. "Before you drunk me, I'd been meaning to tell you something. It's about—"

A very loud rapping at the door jolts us apart. "Tuan! Tuan! You in there? Semua baik? Should we come in to help you in case you fainted?"

The spell breaks; Royce clears his throat. "We, ah, we should go down before my housekeeping staff calls my mom home. They've been briefed to keep an eye on us, in case we, uh, sin," he says this with a hint of amusement in his voice.

I nod, trying to act nonchalant even though my heart is still racing from what I thought was going to happen. It was probably just the alcohol, I admonish myself. *Get a grip, don't forget yourself. Even the servants have been briefed to keep you and Royce apart.* We should keep things simple, friendly—but that's it. "Let's get back downstairs to algebra, then, Royce," I say in a clipped voice, already walking toward the door.

"Sure, Agnes," Royce says, sounding a bit confused at my sudden coolness.

We finish revising and I head home to a rightfully upset Stanley, who I placate by helping him with making a substitute alcohol-free butter cake (he'd used up all the rum in the previous cake anyway).

And then, when my mother comes back from her doctor's appointment, her eyes bright with some secret joy, I go up to her and hug her.

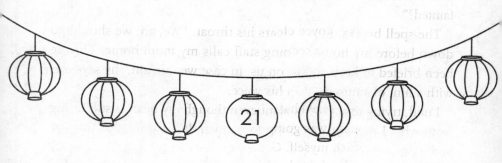

21

TONIGHT'S THE NIGHT. ZEE AND I ARE GETTING READY FOR THE CHARITY
gala. Because I don't know my foundation from primer, Zee has
offered to do my makeup and hair.

I wait patiently for some kind of cream to sink into my skin while
she livestreams her makeup routine. My shoulder-length hair has
been meticulously teased into soft waves à la Miriam Maisel from the
show *The Marvelous Mrs. Maisel* with a little online help, Zee's top-
of-the-range curler, and a brand of hairspray that Zee claims airily
"would be illegal in the European Union, where they have standards"
but is "relatively safe, I think?"

"You only live once. We should have standards!" I protested. But
Zee waves my concerns away as people who can afford black-market
lungs do.

Zee's done with her look: She's wearing creamy pastel-orange lids
paired with a darker coral lip, and the bold colors pop against her
deep golden-brown skin. She adjusts her hijab, removes the makeup
bib she is wearing to protect her white shirt, throws on her tuxedo
blazer, and does a little spin for me. Zee's gone for a classic black
tuxedo styled with a pearl-white formal shirt and a silk sunset-hued
hijab. She looks fabulous.

I wolf-whistle. "Gorgeous! You are an artist."

She beams, then sighs. "Too bad the one person I wanted to impress isn't coming."

"His loss," I say. "Anyway, we look good for ourselves, so."

"Absolutely," she says. "And of course, social media."

I snort-laugh.

Zee paints a matte, deep cherry color onto my primed lips, then proceeds to mist some kind of fixing spray over my made-up face. The look she is going for is Winter Fox—a clean, dewy base with neatened brows, a hint of white sparkle on the inner corner of my eyes, and a soft violet shimmer over my pale lids, which contrasts beautifully with the dark blue hue of my tuxedo and the beaded black bandeau top I've paired it with. Zee has loaned me a pair of sparkly crystal studs—at least, I hope they're crystal. I look so ridiculously good and yet recognizably me; I can't stop staring at my reflection.

Zee makes appreciative noises as she sprays more, well, spray into my hair. "Someone's gonna lose his mind," she sings.

"I'm not trying to impress anyone."

"Even so, he's going to be impressed anyway," she says, grinning.

My phone buzzes. I flick a glance at the screen: Agnes, would you meet me before the gala? I have something to tell you. . . .

I turn the phone over.

"Is that Royce?" Zee says shrewdly.

I make a face. "Yeah," I say, keeping my tone light. "It can wait."

"Why are you avoiding him?"

"I'm not."

"You like him?" Straight for the jugular, as always.

I turn away and busy myself looking at the mirror. "Nope, don't be silly."

"Huh." Zee eyeballs me. "So you'll be totally fine if he kisses someone else tonight?"

I blanch and Zee says, triumphantly pumping her fists in the air. "Ha! I knew it! *I knew it.* My sulky baby likes Royce!"

I play it nonchalant, even though just hearing those words out loud makes my heart race. "It's pointless being into Royce," I tell Zee. "He's going to leave in a few months, and then what?"

"It's, like, a whole half year!" Zee protests. "That's, like, forever!"

My stomach drops. In six months, I'd lose her, too—and then what?

Maybe some of that emotion telegraphs on my face despite my best efforts. "Agnes, you have to give people a chance to love you, and you have to give yourself a chance to love someone," Zee says softly.

"I love you," I say lightly. "That's enough for me."

"No, it's not," Zee says. "You deserve more than me. Truly. I wouldn't want to end up with just one love of my life, even if it is you."

I bite my lip, dangerously close to tears. "Shuudd upppp," I say, mature person that I am.

We both pretend to be busy with various nothings for some time; then, when the air lightens, Zee comes over to apply the final touches to my face with a little fluffy brush.

"And we are done!" she says, grinning. "Alexa, launch my Sexy Baby Dance Party Spotify playlist, please."

Ariana Grande booms from Zee's Bluetooth speakers as I assess myself in her full-length mirror. Zee has loaned me a pair of inch-inch (modest by her standards) gold pumps and a beautiful acrylic clutch with brass leaves as handles.

"*Girl*," Zee says emphatically, standing next to me in five-inch transparent platform heels studded with crystals.

"Girl, you too," I say, nodding at our reflection. We vogue in front of the mirror for a good minute.

Zee's phone beeps and she's suddenly all business. "Let's go! We've got to get there by four thirty." Organizing committee and student acts had to get there by that super-early call time because Malaysian traffic is unpredictable, and we aren't exactly known for being on time as a nation.

We giggle and then haul butt to the long black sedan in which Zee's mom's driver, Pak Khalid, is waiting (I say a tiny prayer of thanks when I see that it's not Pak Ismail, and then I panic when I realize Pak Khalid could be worse). And then we're off, or at least as off as one can be in snaking Saturday-shopping traffic in the city center, with Pak Khalid driving a stately, dignified pace while Zee gets increasingly agitated as the minute hand ticks closer to 5 p.m. Her phone beeps nonstop in her frantic hands, so much so that I confiscate her phone and make her take a screen break.

"How are you doing?" Zee says, popping a handful of cashews into her mouth. "Nervous?"

I search my feelings. "Just a little." Wrong. I have been in low-key panic mode since early this morning, barely managing to eat more than two slices of toast and an apple for lunch. For the first time in my life, I'm going to talk about the things that have made me *me* in front of a crowd of people who know me. "But I should be calmer once I start performing."

We arrive at the hotel on time, carrying bags of stuff Zee had ordered for decorations (the team in charge of decor had "run out of budget," and so Zee had come to the rescue, as usual). Both of us let out a gasp when we enter the ballroom. It is amazing. The already imposing space with its dramatic, twenty-foot-tall ceilings dotted with hand-cut crystal chandeliers and mirrored panels is awash in pink light, its walls having been softened with dreamy floaty draping. White silk flowers on gold branches burst out of tall vases on each table. The stage had been decorated with rose-gold and white balloons and strings of fairy light. Flanking the stage were integrated screens that would be projecting live gala feed from a dedicated social media channel during the lulls between acts—at the moment it projected all the event sponsors' logos on a black background. There's only a couple I recognize: Zee's parents consortium's abstract logo, a gyrating lemur from Frisson Cola, but they all pop on that high-definition screen. Zee's going to raise so much cash.

Zee excuses herself to handle the various mini crises that needed her attention, shooing away my attempts to help. I wander outside the ballroom aimlessly, past the photo booths, the registration table with the gift bags (free aviator glasses from a new start-up owned by someone's family, vouchers for the movie theater, skating rink passes, and exotic-flavored gourmet popcorn from another student's family). I find one of the organizing team's smaller prep rooms (Orchid) behind the photo booths, filled with bags of decorations and markers and stationery. There's no one around, most of them congregating in the larger room next door.

In spite of my best efforts, I start obsessing over Royce's message. What could he want to tell me in private?

I'm in love—with Dr. Maria.

Dr. Maria . . . is my mother.

Cut it out, I admonish my stupid imagination.

My phone buzzes; this time, it's Vern. Hey have fun up there, he says.

Me: You can still come if you want. I put you down as my plus one and never changed it. (Zee wouldn't let me.)

Vern: Really? I'm touched.

Me: Yeah.

I am distracted by a picture my parents sent of their villa in Janda Baik from earlier in the afternoon. I send them a generic smiley face, pleased at how well my sneaky plan is going.

Things are going so swimmingly that I start relaxing. I yawn as exhaustion envelops me in its furry paws—it's been a really tiring couple of months, what with my frequent nights out, the twice-weekly Seoul Hot shifts (with Mrs. Yoon consenting to let me take more frequent breaks), exam prep for our finals in ten days, then prepping all those essays hoping that I could update them come January with something like "winner of the qualifying rounds of JOGGCo regional stand-up comedy competition . . ."

Royce: Agnes, please, we really need to talk.

I should see him, right? Just to see what he's wearing tonight. Then I'll nip whatever this is in the butt . . . bud! Freudian slip!

Me: Let's meet in the organizing committee's prep room by the photo booths, Orchid I.

Royce: Sure. Btw, save the first dance of the night for me, OK?

I don't respond. I can't dance with Royce. I just can't at the rate I'm disintegrating.

I don't expect Royce for another hour as he's not performing today and has no role with the committee, so I switch the lights off and stretch out on the couch for a little nap after setting a thirty-minute alarm.

I'm woken up by a firm tap on my shoulder and I leap up from the couch with a shriek, jolted out of my dream of—well, Royce-related stuff. I land awkwardly on my bad leg and yelp. The light flips on.

"Agnes!" Tavleen and Kira exclaim in unison. They are both wearing sleek, delicately sequined dresses, very high heels and very fluffy hair, accessorized with glittery fine jewelry, and I suddenly felt very homely. My tuxedo had had to be dry-cleaned and deodorized because someone might have died in it, and my mom had had to take it in at the waist rather inexpertly. "What are you doing here in pitch-darkness?"

"Just napping before my show, I've had quite the week and the door wasn't, like, locked or whatever." I cross my arms. "Shit, I almost got a heart attack."

"Sorry" is what a normal person should say. Instead, Tavleen says, "Even if it's unlocked, this is clearly a private room. Only committee members can be in here."

"Yeah," Kira says bossily. "There's professional camera gear and auction shit in here. What if something gets stolen? You'd be, like, the prime suspect."

"Hey, you know me, I'm friends with"—I almost said *you guys* out of habit— "Zee, so maybe you can give me a pass?"

"We'd have to give everyone a pass, then," Tavleen says. There's no warmth or give in her voice. She and I could have been strangers—come to think of it, we might as well be. I leave the room before I do something that could get me arrested.

"Angry much?" a familiar voice says behind me. I turn around and squeal when I see Vern, almost unrecognizable in neatly slicked-back hair and a slightly oversize navy suit that's somehow a tad too short at the arms and legs at the same time.

"Hey there, Agnes," Vern says. "Surprise!"

I hug him like he's candy incarnate. "You came!"

"Of course I did," he says, pulling back with a smile. "Well, at least I did in the end. I thought, what kind of friend would I be if I did not come and support Agnes in her first non-comedy-club set?"

"What kind of friend, indeed," I echo. After what just transpired with the Flashes, Vern's solid, unpretentious presence reassures and centers me. I look him up and down. "Damn, boy, you scrub up well."

"So do you," he says, giving me an appraising look. "Nice outfit."

"Hey, Agnes." Royce chooses to appear at this moment, dapper in a burgundy tuxedo jacket and black trousers. He's carrying a tiny gold paper bag that he's trying to hide behind his body. I can see a small handwritten card addressed to me, or at least someone called Agn—. It's all very sweet, until he turns and sees Vern.

"Hey!" I say, faux jaunty to diffuse the glare-off that's happening before me.

Royce collects himself and turns his attention to me. "Wow, Agnes," he says. "You look"—he takes a deep breath—"so . . ."

"Isn't she a doll," Vern says, throwing his arm around me. "I mean, she's always beautiful, but today, wow. I guess she dressed up for me, since I'm her date."

The air sings with new tension. I decide to play along, maybe to prove a point to myself that what was happening between Royce and me was reversible as footprints in sand. "I—um, I, erm. Yeah. Technically, that's true." God, someone give me a prize already.

"I didn't know you were coming with a date," Royce says.

"I—I, well, yeah, I asked. And here he is." I was on a roll!

"Nice suit," Royce says flatly, his eyes fixed on Vern's arm. It's hard to tell if he's sincere or mocking, it's so emotionless. He stuffs the gift bag in an inner pocket in his tuxedo jacket. "Is it a rental?"

"Thanks, man, it's actually *not* a rental, would you believe," Vern says easily. "It's my dead uncle's one suit. Can't say he and I are the same size—or height, for that matter." He brushes imaginary lint off his shoulder. "BTW, which is it here, Ray? Royce?"

"It's Taslim to you," Royce says.

"Right," Vern says, shrugging. "It's so hard to keep track of your, ah, personas."

My stomach churns. "Guys, please—"

"Agnes!" I hear a squeal and Gina appears, dazzling in a silver sequined V-neck dress that showcases her fuller figure. We hug and the tension dissipates between the boys somewhat.

"I was hoping to speak with you alone, Agnes," Royce says.

"Later," Gina says, grabbing me. "Zee's on a warpath looking for us. We should go to the green room, stat."

"Save the first dance for me, or better yet—all of them," Vern says as I am physically hauled out of the room by Gina, who's scarily strong. The last thing I see as the door swings shut is the hurt look on Royce's face.

~

All the performers for the night are gathered in the meeting room that connects to the ballroom, which the committee has designated as the makeup room/talent holding room; no one is allowed to wander out unless they inform Yun, the talent manager of the event, the reason for leaving. "Or else," Zee says menacingly.

Fine by me. I have no desire to untangle the Ken vs. Ken battle royale out there. There's a buffet table laden with fancy finger food with nonalcoholic drinks. I am safe here.

The speeches are over and the performances are up. Our stand-up act will follow a slam poetry reading; then the student performances end and the live band will start playing.

Sometime around the interpretive dance duo that precedes us, I head to the ballroom and stand "backstage" with Gina to prepare for our performance. Yun appears and tells us, "I'm moving you two up before the slam poet, her parents want her to close out and they're a sponsor. Is that cool?"

"Yes, yes," Gina mutters absently. She is ashen-faced and sweating.

"Are you okay?" I ask her worriedly once Yun was gone. Gina was usually the paragon of calm before a performance.

"I don't think oysters and milkshakes go together," she said in a tight voice.

One of Zee's minions pokes her head behind the makeshift partition that separates the stage from the back of the hall. "You guys go onstage in five, the dance is almost over," she whispers.

Gina's stomach rumbles like an earthquake. Her eyes are glassy. "You go first, do your ten. Excuse me, I've got to, y'know."

"Now?" I squeak. She was supposed to perform her set before mine.

Gina's only response is to break into a run out back where we'd come from. Of course, as soon as Gina is gone, the minion turns up, frantic. "I got the timing wrong. Gina's on! What? She's not here?" She tears at her hair, hissing, "Fine, whatever, Agnes, you're on! You're on! *Get onstage!*"

Then I'm onstage, blinking in the bright light. I'm discombobulated by the sudden change in schedule. Dear God, the lights are hot, and there are so many adults in here.

So many *parents*.

I can't talk about my mother to this crowd. I have to pivot!

"Ahh . . . erm." I clear my throat and try again. "So the thing is, you know . . ."

Shit, shit, shit, shit, shit. Where's Gina? My mind is blank as a fresh sheet of paper. I'd never ever frozen onstage before, ever. I'd always been able to freestyle, deal with hecklers and setbacks. I've been doing this for almost four months, three to four times a week, so I'm not exactly a novice. Yet here I am, freezing like a noob.

"I—I . . ."

"Get on with it," someone shouts. Bile rises in my throat and my insides feel like they've been dipped in acid: Could I be more of a loser than I already am?

"Hey there," Royce booms as he bounds across the stage to join me. "I'm Royce."

What the . . .

"As you all know, I'm rich."

Surprised laughter.

"And that's great, most of the time. Except everywhere I go, I'm a target for kidnapping, so I'm always surrounded by bodyguards. I don't remember a time I've never been watched over by a man. Except, y'know"—he wiggles his eyebrows suggestively and the audience is rapt—"when I . . . take my exams!"

Hooting.

"So I was on a date with a girl. A real one. And at some point she was like, 'Let's go to that dark corner and make out,' and I said, 'No,' and she said, 'Why not?' And I said, 'If we do that, you will die. There's this figure in black that follows me all the time, and he doesn't like other people touching me.'"

He shrugs. "For some reason, I didn't get a second date."

The audience laughs. Royce is freestyling and looking like he's having fun. Our eyes meet and the block inside me dissolves.

"I'm sorry, Taslim, your life sounds so tough," I tease him, finding my voice all of a sudden. "What's the matter, you couldn't buy milk with a bar of gold? They didn't have spare change?"

"What, Chan, you mean they don't take gold anymore in corner stores? Do they take diamonds?" he shoots back.

We roast each other, going off on tangents, improvising, and it's not exactly stand-up, yet people are in stitches, laughing. The spotlight is intoxicating, and the enthusiastic reception from my peers is everything I've been missing. I'm home.

And then I see Gina frantically gesturing just beyond the curtain to my right, and I signal to Royce that we have to wrap up our performance.

I say, "This has been super fun, but now that you all are sufficiently warmed up, let me introduce you to our good friend and fellow comic, the real star of the night, Gina Cheung. We're Royce and Agnes, thank you!"

Gina stumbles onstage, mouthing "Sorry, the runs" to me as I hand her my microphone, and Royce and I amble off to deafening cheers.

We wait in the darkened sidelines after an assistant takes Royce's mic from him. I'm dizzy and smiling from the high of our performance. "You were amazing," I whisper to Royce.

"Thanks," he says. He leans back against the wall with a soft exhale. "Wow. That was a rush."

"Yeah, it was. Thank you for helping out onstage when I was floundering." At risk to his cover, too. I cringe when I recall that I had introduced him as a fellow comic. *I hope he doesn't get into trouble for this.*

"You've got to believe in yourself more, Chan." A wry note enters his voice. "The way a Taslim would believe in himself."

I can't help laughing. "I'll try."

We watch Gina telling her signature bit about returning to the homeland—Australia—after a decade of living in Hong Kong. "Suddenly there was just so much space around me that it felt wrong to be bulimic," she joked, owning the stage without even trying. "So I started eating as much as I could. Gave myself permission to take up space. Problem was, no matter how much I put in my mouth, people still couldn't see me, maybe because I'm four foot eleven. So really"—she sighs dramatically—"I gobbled all those penises for nothing."

There's a shocked murmuring amidst the laughter. Royce chortles. "I can see the whites of several teachers and parents' eyeballs from here, they're so offended."

"So what if they are," I say brashly. "I'm not saying we give comics carte blanche to offend, but I think it'll do all of us some good to examine what exactly about the joke offends us, and why, then take a step back to see if we should react, especially if a comic isn't punching down. Gina's joke is layered if you actually parse what she's trying to say."

"Most people don't bother looking under the hood of a joke, they just care about the aesthetics. Propriety. Saying the right thing to the right audience."

"I couldn't care less about check-the-box virtue signaling," I say.

"Most people aren't like you. You listen, you think for yourself. It's . . . it's what I like about you. Though if I'm honest, I like a lot of things."

I turn to look at him, completely floored by this turn in our conversation. "Excuse me?" I say before I could stop myself.

He clears his throat, suddenly shy. "You heard me," he says in a low voice.

"Penis! Penis!" someone—hopefully a teenager—in the audience is chanting.

"Tell me again," I say quietly.

He doesn't speak—instead he closes the distance between us with a deliberate step. I could move away but I don't. Why should I? What am I afraid of, of this attraction not making sense? To whom? In this space, we're finally equals again. I turn to him just as he does. In the dim violet light, his eyes are hopeful, questioning. I close the space between us in response. His arms encircle me, clasping me to him, and he tips my chin back, his breath quickening. He traces my face with his eyes, murmurs my name as I whisper his. Our heads lean toward each other, so slowly I can practically feel seasons change, my heart pounds with elation, with—

"Royce, are you there? The student committee wants you, they said you're going to be awarded Athlete of the Year, so you need to come with me," a very familiar voice says, and I snap apart from Royce to see two shadowy figures emerge from the connecting room. It's Zee—and Royce's mother, Ming Taslim. Her eyes narrow in suspicion at Royce and me, at our guilty postures. I back away before I realize what I'm doing, wanting to get as far as physically possible from her icy contempt. That's when I trip over a bunch of cardboard boxes holding sponsored merchandise in the corner of the room and fall—landing, once again, on my barely healed leg.

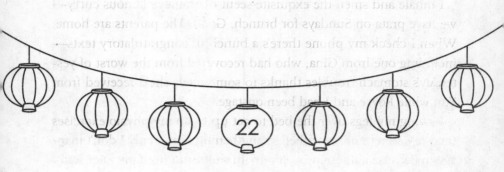

I OPEN MY EYES AND GROAN AT THE SUNLIGHT AND MEMORIES PIERC-ing through morning fog. Had it just been—I check the clock—twelve hours since Royce and I left the gala? Feels a lot more recent than that. The embarrassment is especially fresh.

Just after Royce and I had almost—my face reddens—kissed, I think, we were interrupted by Zee and Royce's mom, who happened to be done with her other thing and decided to drop in on her son's gala. I cringe at the memory of her glare and the way I'd scuttled away from her. And then I'd crashed backward into a bunch of boxes, although in the panic I was in, I hadn't felt much. Royce was then summoned by Zee to wait by the stage so that they could announce him as Student Athlete of the Year and Vern drove me home in his car.

My leg didn't stop hurting even after I got home, but I dismissed it, chalking it up to weeks of putting weight on it and not resting like my physio recommended. I was healing so fast, after all! I went to sleep after taking two painkillers, thinking it would be better the next day. Stanley and my mom are scheduled to come back this morning to pick up Rosie from her friend's, and I was planning on sleeping in as I always do every Sunday.

I inhale and smell the exquisite scent of Stanley's famous curry—we have prata on Sundays for brunch. Good. The parents are home. When I check my phone there's a bunch of congratulatory texts—including one from Gina, who had recovered from the worst of yesterday's stomach troubles thanks to some meds she'd received from Yun while Royce and I had been onstage.

I swing my legs over the bed to get up to do my physio exercises (and my secret nonprescribed strengthening ones), only I don't manage to because a lightning bolt of pain shoots up from my knee and I gasp-shout. I stumble and fall hard onto the floor, dazed, sweat running down my face. When the waves of pain subside, I crawl to the door and weakly call for help.

"Stanley," I manage to groan out, hoping that his super-sharp hearing, honed from years of teaching screamy tweens, would catch it.

Stanley hears me from the study next door and hurries over. He helps me walk to my bed, every step torturous. When I knock my shin against a post climbing into bed, red explodes in my vision and I almost scream. I fold onto the bed, breathless with pain.

Stanley grimly fishes out the crutches from under the bed and I blink back bitter tears at the sight of them, but my frustration is quickly buried by a wave of agony. I whimper.

"You need to see a doctor, now," he says, helping me to his feet. "Let's go. Ling! Ling!"

He calls for my mom, who appears at the door pale and bloated; I can tell she'd been sleeping in, and I'm ill with worry on top of everything else that I've caused her distress. I'm the worst. I'm the worst.

"What's—what's going on?" she says, disoriented.

"Mama," I cry.

The sight of me in this state galvanizes her into action. She herds me into the car with Stanley's help, the car keys already in her hand, while Stanley is on the phone with Rosie's friend's mom to ask if Rosie can stay a little longer at Jasmine's because the waits at public hospitals can take hours. He grabs some provisions for us—coffee, water, snacks—and we go. I don't even remember to take my phone.

The ER in the closest public hospital is packed with unfortunate people who chose Sunday to get sick. We get an X-ray and the results come back delivered by a young doctor who believes that I've injured my ACL—again. I would need to get checked by a specialist who can give me a further opinion after an MRI, and soon.

"It might be less severe than it feels . . ." she says.

I turn my face away to hide my tears. I am—was—an athlete, and I know the truth: The prognosis isn't good.

~

The next available appointment with an orthopedic specialist was weeks away, being that I am:

1. Not dead
2. Not walking around with a shard of bone sticking out of leg or spurting geysers of blood
3. Not otherwise important enough to be bumped up

"That's not quick enough," my mother says, noticing my distress.

"I'm sorry, her case isn't high priority," the nurse in charge of scheduling says bluntly.

As soon as we get out of there and safely installed in the minivan, Stanley and my mother start texting and calling friends to see if there's someone who could see us outside of the public healthcare system, and who could give us a discount.

"We're going to have to find a way to front the expenses, I don't think our insurance covers private healthcare that's discretionary," my mom says in a terse voice. My heart rate doubles at her tone.

"We'll find a way," Stanley says. He turns on the radio at high volume and doesn't even seem to register that it's blasting hard rock, which he dislikes. He's lowered his voice to talk with my mother and I understand it's a private conversation, so I let my mind drift.

My phone buzzes and I look down.

Zee: Any updates on the leg sitch?
Me: Not good, I have to wait a few weeks for a specialist consult and my parents are trying to find a private specialist.

A few minutes later she calls me back.

"You should see Dr. Zulkifli," she says without preamble. "He's a personal friend of the family and a premier orthopedic surgeon in the region. Super famous. Like, the national badminton team go to him, and when that celebrity influencer had that hotel bed contortion incident—"

"Thanks, Zee, I . . ." I drop my voice so my parents can't hear me over the music and their fevered discussion. "We won't be, y'know . . ." I sigh. "He sounds expensive."

"He won't charge you," she says simply.

I fall silent as a myriad of shouty, competing emotions battle for supremacy. "Zee, that's too much," I say at last.

"Say *Thank you, Supreme Light*, and we'll call it a day."

"Sounds cultish."

"OMG, just say thank you."

For some reasons the words jammed up in my throat, words that I'd never had a problem verbalizing before. "Thank you," I manage.

"Tomorrow morning, eight thirty at Murni Sports Medicine Private Clinic, okay?"

"Okay."

~

My parents were thrilled to hear about the early appointment, and the visit went well. Dr. Zulkifli saw me and told me what I already suspected: I had sprained my ACL. It wasn't *too* serious, but it had set back my recovery and it was going to take more months of physio. I would probably not be able to run competitively unless I got surgery, which was elective, of course. Another out-of-pocket expense for a dream that's surely dead by now.

My parents sat down and told me they were prepared to pay for the surgery, but I refused.

"You have a baby coming. There's going to be so much more expenses."

"Agnes—"

"It's fine, the whole point about wanting to get better was just so I could run competitively. It's not like I won't be able to participate normally in all activities without the surgery."

They exchanged looks. Stanley says, "We know how important your sports career is to you, but also—"

"Look," I say, keeping my gaze, my breath steady, "it doesn't matter anymore, because my senior year is halfway over, and my place at college and the track scholarship were already pretty much out of the question a couple of months ago when I got injured, so—I've accepted my fate!"

"You've got your creepy face on again," Rosie observed.

My mother says, "We're thinking about college, and running in college. And even beyond. Agnes—you love running. Not just competitively. We want you to be able to do what you love again."

Do what I love again . . . what a joke. In a way, I know I am privileged to be able to go to a school like Dunia, that my athletic prowess affords—afforded—me choice in terms of universities, that I could even consider university at all. I know all that. That's why I want—wanted—to make the best of my chances, convert it to a sure win in later life being the best, being able to provide my family with the best. But now—I'd be working so hard, and there would only be the quiet knowledge that even if I got a scholarship, I would still not be going to run in the NCAA. I make an excuse about needing to work on my homework before power crutching up the stairs.

In the safety of the darkness the tears fall, fast and hot. "It's no biggie, Agnes," I whisper furiously to myself, blotting my snot with toilet paper, because absorbency. "It was just a chance at a walk-on anyway, and somebody had to give you a place that came with a good scholarship before that."

That was true . . . but now the door was definitely closed for any sporting glories in senior year. I will close out senior year a nobody.

Unless—

I had a vision of myself in a lit stadium, being applauded, the next Amina Kaur, the next Ronny Chieng.

Comedy is the answer. To everything.

I glance at the JOGGCo International Young Comedians Competition schedule—I *have* to win. Otherwise, there'd be nothing to distinguish me anymore. In the drama from yesterday and this morning, I hadn't checked my phone. As soon as I turn it on it buzzes with a stream of congratulatory messages, which I ignore. There are multiple messages from Zee and Royce from last night, .

I respond with a short message to assure Zee that I'm fine and that I'll call her later; then I turn to Royce's messages.

Royce: My mom saw videos of me onstage

My heart sinks: I know how important it was for Royce to appear like the perfect, uncomplicated kid, his perfection a cover he needed, his invisibility cloak. Now he'd been caught in a lie, a shadow life to explain away. They were already worried for his mental health—what would they think now?

Royce: She's so mad. She wants a talk once we're back home
Royce: Saw you leave with Vern, hope everything's OK. Text me
Royce: She just called me downstairs. Wish me luck
Royce: We just had a chat. Text me when you get this
Me: Hey 🐨
Me: Finally have time to myself, I'm sorry I took a while
Royce: Hey! How's your leg? I've been so worried
Me: There's been some developments. . . .
Royce: I'll facetime you? I want to see your face 🫣
Me: Sure

Royce video-calls me. "Okay, tell me first, mine can wait."

I explained all that had happened that day, including my prognosis. Royce looks contrite. "Shit. I'm so sorry."

"It's okay," I lie. "I'm back on crutches for a week or so, then I'll be able to walk again. The tear is a partial one and the surgeon says its manageable without surgery."

Royce, who'd never had pro-athlete aspirations and who saw sports as just another thing he needs to be good at, does not pick up on what's unsaid. "What about the JOGGCo qualifiers next weekend? Can you perform?"

I sigh. "I don't know. I haven't told my parents about stand-up yet. I know they probably won't let me go. I'll just have to figure it out later. What about you? What happened? Your parents found out you've been going to open mikes?"

"Kind of. I had to come clean to my mom after she got videos of my set. She was the one people were texting pics and clips of us perform-ing to, telling her the jokes were offensive, et cetera."

"Yikes. What happened next?"

Royce scratches at the stubble on his jaw. "Well, actually, after she'd calmed down, I apologized for keeping them in the dark about try-ing stand-up. I showed her the video of the performance, and it was really sweet, my mom actually smiled when she saw me perform. She laughed at our jokes. She hadn't laughed in the longest time. . . . She doesn't laugh much, since my brother left. And she complimented my stage presence. Said I was a natural—like her."

I swallow. "That's great. Have you told your parents about compet-ing in the JOGGCo Competition?"

Royce's face grows animated. "Yes. I pitched it as being a really pres-tigious thing, that many famous people from various professions were in their college's improv or stand-up troupe. I told her about Comedy City and the opportunity to share the stage with a Netflix comic, that winning the competition would open up lucrative media opportu-nities for me and look good on my CV." Royce shrugs. "I spoke my parents' lingo, I guess, because I got to them: She agreed. The money would be a sweet bonus, of course. Anyway, she said that if she gives me her blessing to do this, I better make it worth her time. I have to place in the competition. Or stop."

I turn away. In spite of everything that had happened, I can't help the jealousy that wells up in me at this. Royce is one step closer to resolving his situation, whereas mine just seems unsolvable. "That's great."

"I've got to go, my mom wants me to video-call my dad with her." His voice softens, gathers meaning. I—I really enjoyed our time, y'know, before . . ."

"Sure. It was so fun being onstage together," I say, glossing over the part he's really getting at. "Good night."

I kept the tone of my reply light, but my insides are churning. I'm a fool to think that the things we said during the gala made any difference, that Royce and I have any chance of being together when our paths are already bifurcating. He is preparing to step into the light and take control of his destiny, while my future—in stand-up, in everything—is as uncertain as ever. If I'm not careful I'll mess everything up, just when I can't afford, literally or otherwise, any more slipups. I need to focus on the only thing I have a real chance at: winning the comedy competition.

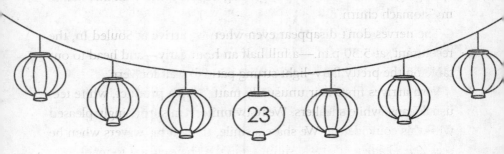

Zee: Whatcha wearing? Dress to kill, please 🌶️
Me: Only if it's to kill at comedeeeeeeeeeeeeeeee
Zee: Why. Are. You.

To be honest, I don't know either.

It's a date night for Zee (and Vern, although he doesn't know it yet) but it's another comedy night for me and, more importantly, the last open mike I would be on before the comedy qualifiers over the weekend. Since my visit with Dr. Zulkifli I'd canceled my shifts at Seoul Hot and used my time to double down on comedy, using Zee and study sessions as my cover to my parents, who said nothing. Knowing that the injury had thrown a spanner in my pro-athlete plans, they accepted my flimsy excuses, figuring I should occupy my mind with my studies instead.

I put on my usual stand-up comedy get-up: black leggings, a plain white T-shirt, and white Keds, my stomach churning with more than my usual nerves. I wish I could focus on my set, but I'm distracted. Royce will be there tonight, too—and we haven't really spoken in person since the charity gala. That knowledge, and the fact I will be springing Zee on Vern, who's expecting a quiet drink with me, makes my stomach churn.

The nerves don't disappear even when we arrive at Souled In, the restaurant, at 5:30 p.m.—a full half an hour early—and head to our table on the pretty fairy–light strung patio to wait for Vern.

Vern arrives first, hair unusually matted with product, white tee, usual jeans, white sneakers. We're twinning. I'm surprisingly pleased with this coincidence. We share a smile, though his wavers when he sees Zee. "Ladies," he says, sliding into the chair closest to me.

Zee says, "Funny we should run into you here, ha-ha." (She really did say *ha-ha*.)

Vern's smile is professional. "Zee, right?" They'd never actually spoken one-on-one before this.

"Yeah," Zee says, blushing. "That's what my parents didn't call me."

Don't ask me why Zee was; she just was.

"Hey, am I interrupting something?" says a voice I recognize. Royce comes up behind Zee, his eyes on me.

"Hey, Royce! I mean Ray!" Zee says, waving. "Right on time."

"Hey, Zee," Royce says. "And . . . Agnes and Vern." I can tell he wasn't expecting me or Vern.

"Ray and I have become quite friendly during this stand-up thing, so I figured I'd ask him to join me—well, us for a pre-stand-up hang."

Zee is trying to set me up on a double date. Crafty. I turn the full force of my glare at her, but Zee ignores it. Then again, Vern had not been expecting Zee either, so I guess both Zee and I are terrible people, and we deserve each other.

"I can spare fifteen," Royce says evenly. "Then I have to prepare for my set." His performance according to the set list is in the second half, more than two hours away.

Brr. It's cold in here.

"Aw, c'mon, Ray, surely you can spare some time for your . . . peers," Vern says, his smile perfect.

Royce looks at him. "I certainly can for Agnes and Zee," he replies. "And from now on, I'm going to perform as Royce Lim. It's a compromise with my family," he tells me.

"Oh wow, another persona," Vern says. "Gosh, it's just . . . so hard to—"

"Let's order!" I shout, desperately flagging down a server, who is not impressed with our orders of Cokes, emphasis on "full sugar, none of that diet crap" from Zee.

"This is dinner service, would you perhaps like to order some food?" she says.

"Absolutely not," Vern says at the same time as Zee says rather bossily, "Yes, let's get two orders of truffle fries and see how we feel later." The server nods and leaves.

"I don't want truffle fries. I've had dinner," Vern says.

"I don't want any, either," I say. I'd had a sandwich before I left, and also, I just saw how much those truffle fries cost.

"Maybe we should hang at the bar and leave these two," Vern says, smirking.

"I don't want food," Royce snaps.

"I'll eat all of it, then, no worries, it's on me," says Zee, both getting and not getting the subtext (as in, I'd just sneakily texted her under the table: nO mooney!).

The drinks come. "So, you guys officially registered for the JOGGCo qualifiers?" Vern asks after we've discussed what we've been watching and listening to lately.

"Yes," I say, perking up.

Royce hesitates. "Yes."

"Oh," Vern says. "Even though, I don't know, there might be some rules against . . . Especially after the new sponsors—" There's a question in his voice I don't understand.

"You're mistaken," Royce says harshly.

Vern laughs. "I figured you'd have some justification."

"Hello?" I wave my arm. "What's going on here?"

"Nothing," Vern says airily. "Just sussing out my competition. Anyway, you guys have your sets ready yet?"

"Yes, I started working on my two different sets of tight tens, with some backup replacement bits."

Vern nods and slings his arm around my chair. "Excellent. You know, we should practice with each other at mine. I can record you and give you pointers, I've made it to the semifinals for another one of the smaller regional stand-up competitions last year, and the format is the same."

"Yes, I'd love that!" I say, gratified.

Royce gets up and says, rather rudely, "Zee, I'll send you the money for my share of everything, drinks and food. I have to run."

"Yeah, sure," Zee says, her face registering surprise. "But the fries haven't even—"

He leaves without saying goodbye.

"How rude," Vern says, lifting his arm from my chair. "I guess some folks aren't raised well. Not like you, Zee."

"Er, sorry?" Zee says, an eyebrow arched in question.

The fries arrive, a fragrant basket of crispy perfection. I regret my earlier stance of not wanting to partake, but I must stay strong.

"Yeah, you know, you being Zalifah Bakri and all?" Vern says in his usual frank manner. "I mean, I know you've never really mentioned your full name or who your family is, but we all know. And we've certainly appreciated how generous you are with money, much thanks, but in spite of all your almost-suffocating displays of pocket money, I must say you're actually much more fun that I thought." He rubs his chin and gives her a thoughtful look. "Yeah, you're all right, Zee Bakri. Anyway, I gotta run, too." He gets up. "I wish I could hang, but I need to work on my set. I open tonight."

"I can't wait," I say. "Your last set was so good."

"Jinx," Vern says affectionately. Then he's gone.

I watch him go. "Well, that was . . . a short date. Zee, thoughts?"

Zee is looking at the fries with a weird expression I'd never seen. "I've been doing it, haven't I?"

"I'm sorry?" I say between a mouthful of fries.

She's doing a weird blink. "I've always said my family doesn't define me and I believe it, I really do . . . but here I am, buying people's favor like a politician on an election campaign."

"Whoa, hey, you're not that, I mean, you don't do it *consciously*."

She throws up her arms. "Isn't it worse if I'm doing that subconsciously, in spite of all my talk of being a modern, independent woman?"

"Well, technically, you're a—" I try to lighten the mood.

"You're telegraphing your punch line," Zee says sourly. "I know I'm a minor."

I sigh. "Zee, you're just being generous. There's nothing wrong with wanting to treat people," I say. "I mean, you know I'm not with you for that, at all." I push the half-empty bowl of fries away for good measure.

"If you're the exception to the rule . . ." She pauses, gathers herself, continues. "Sure, there's nothing wrong with wanting to spread some money around, but now that I think about it, 'spending to seduce' does seem to be my default mode." She swirls her Coke in her glass and gives a short laugh. "Maybe I'm insecure and I just didn't realize it. Or worse, m-maybe I don't know who I am without my family or the money. For all my talk about moving to California for college, about finding myself beyond my family's reach . . . maybe I'm just deluding myself. Maybe I'll just end up losing whatever it is that makes me, me, and then I'll find out that nobody wants to hang out with me, the *real* me, without the money filter."

"That's not true," I tell her with vehemence. "You're not defined by your family or your money. You're Zee. You're a bright, vivacious, and funny person. You're good at makeup videos and languages." I put my hand on hers. "And you're a terrific friend."

"Friend. Right." She contemplates me with that same searching expression. "If everything I said about family and money doesn't matter to friendship, then how come the inverse is true for you?"

A cold feeling spread over me. "I don't understand," I hedge.

"Tell me, Agnes, why haven't I, in the four years we've known each other, been introduced to your mother except in passing, or been invited to your home?"

"It's . . . just . . . it's just . . . I—I . . . My mom—" I swallow. "We just . . . y'know. Renovations," I finish, my face as hot as a furnace.

Zee makes an impatient noise. "God, you're doing it again. You're like a one-way mirror. Why do you hold me at arm's length, Agnes?"

"I . . . I d-don't, no, that's not what I meant to do at all!"

"Sure you don't," she says sadly. She shakes her head. "I'm done trying to convince you to let me in. I've got to go. Have a good set, Agnes."

Then she leaves without a backward glance, and for the first time since we met, she doesn't foot the bill.

~

I mess up a couple of times during my set. It's a mark of how affected by everything that's happened with Zee that I don't even obsess over my performance. All I can think about is Zee, my closest friend. Maybe my best friend. I cannot lose her.

Me: Hey, Zee, you up? Can we talk please?

Three dots appear and disappear. I don't blame her. I know more than anyone that trust is a hard commodity to come by and to give out. When I was ten and my mother's first episodes started, the kids I thought were my friends made fun of her and us, not understanding why I came to school with clothes that were wrinkled and sometimes dirty, why my lunch box was often empty or filled with torn pieces of white bread and nothing else, why she was weeping outside the school gates when she dropped me off. Before I came to Dunia, the only person who had ever helped me when he saw I needed it by sharing his food with me, who gave me a listening ear, for that one afternoon, when it would have cost him more to be associated with me, was the then fifteen-year-old Vern. Not my peers, not my teachers. Only Vern.

I'm miserly when it comes to giving out trust. To protect my family, and myself, I've stockpiled it like people hoard goodwill in a famine.

Me: You were right. About everything
Me: I'm sorry I didn't let you in, Zee
Me: I'll tell you everything you want.

The three dots appear and disappear.

I make a decision then. Sometimes, we can't wait for the other person to reach out first. We have to be vulnerable first.

I start recording my story over voice messages and sending them to her.

I just hope it's not too late.

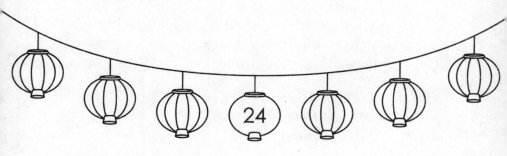

24

SHE DOESN'T TEXT BACK. I WAIT FOR HOURS BEFORE FALLING ASLEEP, and the next morning—nada. She doesn't talk to me in school either. Whenever we run into each other, she would acknowledge me but not approach. I spend a week utterly alone during lunch break. Even Royce, a friendly face, is nowhere to be seen.

At least I could distract myself with finals and then Christmas break.

I eat lunch in a corner of the field, like I used to in my old school, and for company I video-call Vern. Whatever he's doing, at work or otherwise, he'd pick up. He'd find a way.

> **Vern:** Chin up. She's not worth it if she doesn't come around.
> You don't need her. You're stronger without dead weight.
> Anyway, with these people, it was bound to happen sooner
> or later
> **Me:** What do you mean? She's my best friend, Vern
> **Vern:** They are not like us, Agnes. Trust me. They only look out
> for their kind
> **Vern:** Where's Royce in all of this?
> **Me:** He's busy with peer tutoring and classes, I guess

Vern: Too busy to realize you're in pain?

He has a point: Where is Royce? Is he avoiding me? He'd been acting weird since our double date that wasn't a double date—heck, he'd been acting weird since the morning after our charity gala thing.

Vern: Forget them. Focus on the qualifiers this Friday and let me look out for you. Focus on us. Focus on winning.

~

Mrs. Yoon: Agnus, you coming back to work this week
Me: Hi, Mrs. Yoon, sorry I don't think I can wait tables anymore, because I reinjured my leg, do you need someone to work at the till?
Mrs. Yoon: No need is OK you don't come back
Mrs. Yoon: Bye
Mrs. Yoon: Also tell your friend Royce he has work with me if he want anytime

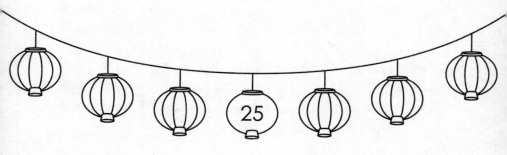

25

AND THEN THE QUALIFIER FOR THE JOGGCO REGIONALS ARRIVE ON THE Friday before Christmas weekend, held in a small theater in the city. I arrive early and see the place is packed, a long queue snaking out of it. I duck in the much-shorter queue for comics and production crew. I wonder if Zee remembers the date. I miss her terribly.

I follow the signs to the holding room next to the stage and find it packed with new and familiar faces, and my pulse starts racing. I look for Vern, who's supposed to meet me here, and find Royce practicing in a corner, his face pale. He doesn't see me, and I don't go over to him. Instead, I find my own quiet space to practice behind the heavy velvet curtains, going over my set list, which I have scrawled key words of on my wrist in Sharpie, in case I blank onstage and need a prompt.

While it hadn't happened before, this week, during other open mikes, I've blanked onstage. Twice. Each time because I thought I saw Zee in the audience, but it was just another hijabi girl that the dim light and my longing have transmuted into Zee.

About thirty minutes before go time, Evans does a roll call of all the performers, noting Vern's absence (I say he's on the way and apologize on his behalf), and gives us the rundown of what to expect.

Then there's a dimming of lights on the stage and an assistant tells us to wait in the holding room, where there's a screen for us to see what's happening on the stage and folding chairs have been set up in haphazard bunches. I take a seat and Vern bustles in, arresting in an all-black ensemble, and throws himself into a seat beside me.

"Hey, good-looking," he says, uncharacteristically grabbing my hand and giving it a squeeze in front of the twenty or so other comics. "You ready?"

"Yeah," I say. "You?"

"As ready as can be."

"I thought we were meeting half an hour before call time?"

"Yeah, sorry I'm late." He nods toward the direction of the curtains. "I had to guide my aunt to her seat, she's small and there's so many people I was worried she'd be hurt. There's, like, only one usher on duty, and she's overwhelmed. Looks like the marketing for this event is really reaching the masses. It's a full house."

"Your aunt's here?" I say. Vern's aunt is his closest living relative—she raised him alone when his uncle died.

"Yeah, I try to include her in these things when I can. Even if she doesn't really understand English."

Evans bounds on the stage to get things started. He breaks the ice with a couple of formulaic jokes and does some crowd work to warm up the audience, before launching into a spiel about the rules, the format of the competition (ten minutes per contestant, eight semi-finalists progressing out of this round), and lays out the housekeeping rules before announcing, "Now let's get this party started with Nassir from Thailand!"

My phone buzzes.

Zee: Break a leg, Chan
Zee: But not the same one
Zee: 🦴

My heart explodes wide open. My lower lip trembles.

Me: Zee! I missed you so much
Zee: Me too
Zee: But I'm hurt. I'm still hurting. You've been holding back so much from me, when you know everything there is to know about me
Me: I know and I'm sorry. I wish I could redo everything. Please give me a chance
Zee: I want to, but I need time. I have my own stuff to process on top of your revelations
Me: Absolutely. Take your time
Zee: Let's talk later, OK? Now go kick some butt 🖤

I'm smiling. Suddenly, I know that everything will be all right. I would remember my sets. And I would have my friend back.

Royce catches me smiling. He gives me a hesitant thumbs-up, and I give him one, too.

Vern leans over and say, "How are you guys these days, you and Royce?"

"We're okay, I guess?" I say. "We're going through a weird patch, but I think it's fine."

"Interesting," Vern says, considering me.

Four more contestants blaze through their sets, then Vern goes on. I cheer and whoop, as do many of the Malaysian comics who know him. But not Royce.

I slip into the audience, taking a seat in the first two rows reserved for the comics. Nothing beats being in the audience for a live comedy set, and I wanted to be there for Vern's set. All the comics who have gone before Vern are scattered through the two rows, decompressing and supporting their fellow nationals.

Vern's set was new, a blistering, darkly comic one about his life. "These muscles, you like?" he says, striking a pose. The crowd cheers. "I'll tell you how to get them"—his voice turns jovial—"child labor!" He drops a weighted pause, peppered by the nervous laughter of the audience, then says, "Or as I was told, joining the family business."

He tells a story of how he started working as an electrician at age fourteen for his uncle's business after his aunt took him in when his parents passed—"By which I mean, they passed on me! Got up and left me one day!"—but at least he knew where he stood with his uncle and aunt. "Working with my uncle, there was less of that feel-good shit about being proud of you when you do well, and more of that do well, so we can feel good about having a place to shit tonight!"

Shocked laughter. Even though it was painful, the audience is lapping it up. I am lapping it up. His authenticity is inspiring on so many levels.

He finished to thunderous applause. Vern exits the stage and comes toward me, grinning. I hear Royce's name—well, Royce *Lim*—being announced as the next contender and as I lift my hand to give Vern a high five. Out of the corner of my eye, I see Royce waiting in the sidelines, watching us as he waits for his turn.

"You were brilliant," I say, buzzing with excitement as he takes his seat beside me, and Evans announces Royce as the next performer. "I was hanging on every word!"

"I'm glad," Vern says, brushing his hair off his forehead. "You're the only one in here that matters to me."

Then he says the strangest thing: "You trust me, right?"

"Yes, of course," I say.

"I'm testing out a theory," he says.

And then he kisses me.

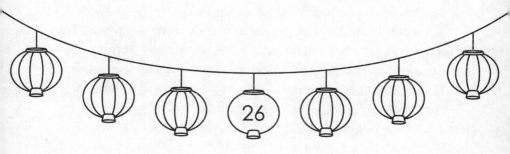

26

THE AUDIENCE AROUND US EXPLODES IN ENTHUSIASTIC CRIES AND wolf whistles. It's a peck on the cheek, but the way they were going on, you'd think he'd just pulled a rom-com move and got down on one knee and proposed using a bottle cap for a ring or whatever.

Although, for a friendly peck, it had lingered a beat, two beats longer than appropriate . . . and it landed closer to my lips than I'd like.

When he pulls back, I distractedly rub at the spot and glance toward Royce, wondering what he'd seen from his vantage point. If the kiss looked as innocuous as it had been, from Royce's elevated angle.

Royce is frozen on the side of the stage, his face twisted as he stares at Vern and me, and I realize it's exactly as I feared—the kiss looked more than platonic. An unfamiliar anxiety overcomes me, even as I tell myself it doesn't matter, Royce and I are just friends and could never be more.

Evans, who's on the sidelines, clears his throat, and says, "Ray, Royce, whatever you are called now, stop rubbernecking like a pervert, and, Vern, stop necking and get a room with your girlie. Goddamn teenagers," he says to laughter.

Girlie. Anger surges through me: Evans had seen me a couple of times before, once at the briefing earlier today, but he'd already forgotten me or chosen to dismiss me as *just a girl*.

Royce comes to the center of stage, nonplussed. He speaks. The mike makes a serious of alarming beeps, then stops working. He's flustered now. The assistant calls for a new mike and Evans calls a time-out. Royce heads backstage and the audience starts murmuring.

"You shouldn't have done that, Vern," I say. "What were you trying to prove? It totally looked like you were kissing me to Royce."

"And that's exactly what I was going for," Vern says in a conspiratorial tone. "I'm trying to help you and Royce realize you guys have feelings for each other. It's just a peck on the cheek, you know how Europeans sometime kiss in greeting. Sorry if my methods aren't traditional."

"That's not why it bothered me," I say, my voice strained from trying to keep it low. The kiss itself wasn't the issue, but the intention, and the feelings it invoked in me, jumbled and confused, was. "Just—just don't do anything like that again, even if you wanted to 'help'. . . I—I want my first kiss to be special."

The air between us chills noticeably.

"Okay, got it," Vern says coolly. "Loud and clear."

"Don't take it the wrong way—"

"I need the washroom and a beer," Vern cuts me off. "Need anything?"

"N-no thanks."

He nods, avoiding my eyes. "If I don't see you before, good luck." Then he disappears.

No, you should have said "Break a leg!" Everyone knows that! On top of that, he *knows* I'm superstitious. But before I can fret further, Hettie, one of the visiting comics from Singapore who I'd met a couple of times, turns around and pokes my arm. "What was that all about?" she whispers, grinning. "Are you and Vern a Thing?"

"No," I say. "That was just a joke." My thoughts had scattered to four corners of my hitherto perfectly mapped world.

"Sure," Hettie says, grinning. She whispers to her friends. I realize that a lot of the other comics are whispering and glancing my way. I sink down in my seat, my emotions all over the place.

Onstage, Royce finally gets a mike. I wonder if the various interruptions would throw him off as they had in the past. It's a sign of how far we'd come that I'm not wishing the worst on him.

Until he speaks.

He gestures at me. "Is this a competition or junior camp?" he says. "I mean, I know this is a teen competition—"

He lifts an eyebrow. The audience laughs. I stare at Royce through smarting eyes, my stomach clenched as though I'd been sucker-punched.

"I come from money," Royce says, giving the audience a confident grin. Money's great . . ." He pauses, frowns, the audience hanging on every word, waiting for the twist. "That's it. That's the punch line."

The joke shouldn't land as well as it does in this crowd, but Royce somehow pulls it off. Because they believe in the truth of his words, and Royce is playing into the stereotype with everything he's got.

"I'm single and on the apps. My friends tell me I need to be relatable, so for my hobbies I put things like hiking, reading, traveling, instead of running through my money vault naked. What—doesn't everyone have a vault? Where will you stay when the apocalypse comes? And more importantly—where do you hide the gold bars from the tax men?"

Under the cover of a fake cough, he says, audibly, "One-MDB."

The audience, mostly Malaysians, shrieks-laughs. Even if the scandal is no longer in vogue with other comedians—Hasan Minhaj did a great bit on this in 2019—we will probably never get over it. We laugh because we can do nothing else.

"I've been going on some dates. . . ."

He launches into a modified bodyguard/bogeyman bit he did at our charity gala, and then joke after joke in the same vein, growing more and more confident with every laugh he gets. He's killing it—and it's all thanks to me.

Royce finishes to thunderous applause as people chant, "Royce! Royce!" and he saunters off the stage, smooth as you wish. Royce, who thought that $10,000 US was a nice "bonus" to have. Royce, who won Student Athlete of the Year when he wasn't enthusiastic or didn't even care that much about sports. Royce, who never needed to worry about anything. People like him always win. Always. Why should I make it easy for him?

Vern returns with a beer. I hand him my phone so he could record me for my socials and walk up on to the stage, almost shaking with self-righteous anger.

"Wow, new persona much, Royce? Couldn't hack the pretend-poor-boy persona anymore, so you're reverting to type?" I taunt before I can stop myself. The words are gushing out me in a torrent. "Man, I guess being rich really can't buy you a personality. But I guess you wouldn't know what a personality is even if it hit you."

As soon as the words leave me, I know I've made a mistake, and a sick feeling churns in my belly as I meet Royce's shocked gaze. The crowd titters nervously, unsure if this was part of the act. But Vern whoops and cheers, the tension in the air breaks a little, and I grin in reaction, until my eyes catch a face in the audience I never expected to see.

Oh my God.

My heart nosedives into the pit of my stomach: It's Stanley.

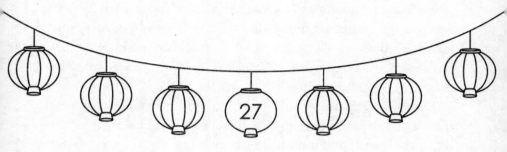

27

STANLEY IS SEATED FIVE ROWS FROM THE STAGE WITH TWO TEACHERS I recognize from Dunia. He catches my eye and gives me a quick, terse nod that says *Later.*

As a recipient of multiple Later awards, I know what's coming.

I manage to finish my set (a reworked set about conditional and unconditional love vis-à-vis Asian parents and being an average student that sticks the landing) and slink off the stage to wild clapping that barely registers, that's how nervous I was in the face of Later.

When I get back to my seat, the comics who know me and Ray— Royce—observe me with expressions of pinched disappointment. I tense, waiting for their admonishment, waiting for punishment, maybe. But they don't say anything—I have shocked the words out of them.

I have shocked the words out of myself.

In my head I hear every single word I said onstage in a reverberation chamber, and I cringe. I could see my face, hideous with greed, like those motivated demons depicted in Chinese hells. Twisted. Possessed.

The results come, and from Malaysia, Vern, Royce, and I make it through along with another girl Natalia who had flown in from

Penang, but I feel hollow. Hollow and nauseous. So much so that when Evans comes over to the bar to hand me the consent form to go to Singapore and says I don't half suck for a female comic, I don't take my pen and slot it up one of his nostrils. Because I don't advocate violence in any situation, but also, I'm slower than I used to be on my feet.

Stanley and I do not say much in the car ride home. I can tell from the way he grips the steering wheel and how fast he's driving (still under the speed limit, incredibly) that he's upset—but I don't detect anger.

After ten minutes of utter silence, he breaks it. "How long?"

"Four months or so since my first appearance onstage," I mutter, shamefaced.

"So all those nights studying with Zalifah or working at Seoul Hot?"

I keep my gaze trained at my lap. "Some of them didn't happen," I admit.

"Your mother is going to be so disappointed," he says, shaking his head. "Why didn't you just tell her you were performing stand-up?"

I bit my lip. He doesn't get it. In our culture, sometimes we have to hide the best parts of ourselves from the people who love us most, just so they can continue to love us the way we want to be loved. I want my mother to look at me the way she does when I'm winning. When I'm not messing up or in danger of messing up. For my sake— and hers.

"You know why," I mutter, hunching away from him to lean against the car door.

He sighs. "Your mother is stronger than you think."

"I've known her for longer," I counter before I can stop myself.

He doesn't reply, but the car speeds up just a little. We spend the rest of the ride silent. My heart pounds and my blood whooshes in my head; it is difficult to breathe. The stress of having to come clean to my mother drains me.

My phone chirps, and I glance down.

Epic burn, Vern says, a row of fire emojis following this. Way to show that 0.001 percenter about authenticity and our truth as comics! That was so brave of you, Agnes.

He thinks I'm some kind of rebel. It makes me feel like it hadn't been a sloppy kneejerk reaction, but something I'd planned in furtherance of a Greater Goal. It makes me feel good.

When we near our neighborhood, I muster whatever courage I had left to ask, "Could you . . . could you please keep this secret for a while longer? I just . . . I need to find the right way and time to tell her."

He doesn't reply as we turn into the driveway. He parks carefully, then turns off the engine. At this point, I'm practically hyperventilating from nerves. My mother is an unpredictable element to introduce this late in the qualifiers—I can't risk it now. I can't. There's a big chance she'll just pull me out.

Finally, he says, "I'm not going to be the one to tell her. No more non-work or school-related nights out until you do."

I had till the new year to hand in my consent form that would allow me to perform in Singapore in the semifinals, which is happening on the second weekend of the new year.

"I'll tell her soon," I say, trying to convince myself.

A drumming on the steering wheel. That's Stanley's cue for I Have More Words, Wait for It. So I wait. "By the way . . . at your show, I saw the way you were acting with Royce—I just wanted to say it's not cool. I'm really disappointed in you. That's not the way your mother and I raised you. We don't put other people down to raise ourselves up."

Tears sting my eyes. I'd never heard Stanley say he was disappointed in me, ever. It hurts almost as bad as my leg does.

"I'm going to make supper," Stanley says, reaching for the car door handle. "And Agnes?"

"Yeah?"

"Apologize to Royce. He didn't deserve any of that."

I know he's right. Part of me knows I went too far at the scene, that Royce didn't deserve that. I had been so remorseful at first.

But didn't Royce belittle me first, onstage? I flash back on his snide comment and the rage comes roaring back. Why should I apologize to him when he's got everything I've ever wanted?

And then there's this other part of me, a part that has tasted a new kind of drug, the surety of Vern's approval, the thrill of putting someone in their place, that whispers, *So what if they don't approve?*

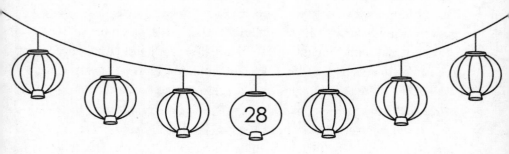

MONDAY COMES AND I'M WAITING IN THE LIBRARY FOR ROYCE TO appear for a peer-mentored college-application-essay writing session, my heart swooping about in my chest, hawklike. I have an unpleasant mission today: apologize in person. Stanley made me promise to do so today, and much as I don't feel like it, now that more time had passed, I have reverted to my original feeling of shame over my actions at the qualifiers this past Friday.

Zoltan Pali, a classmate, lounges next to me, all tousled brown hair and sullen eyes. He keeps glancing at his watch because Royce is almost twenty minutes late.

"Your boy is very tarty."

I do a double take. "I'm sorry?"

"Tarty. You know, when someone is coming late. I'm not saying it right?"

I bit my lip. "Yes, Zoltan, that's exactly right."

Zoltan nods. "Thought so. English is so idiotic."

"You mean, idiosyncratic," I correct him gently.

"No, idiotic." He lifts an eyebrow at me. "You know I speak and write six languages, including world's hardest language, Polish?"

I am about to point out that I speak three myself—well two and a half languages, really—but Royce comes at this point in a clatter of files, Zoltan not-so-softly whispering "Tarty" at me and winks, and this time I'm not sure he's referring to Royce's lateness.

"Sorry I was late," Royce says, still a little breathless. "I, uh, my mom came to school with some, er, correspondence for me."

"Not cool," Zoltan says. "Our time is precious, too."

"I know," Royce says, a bit snappish. "I said I'm sorry." He is flustered, his hair mussed, and I resist the urge to slick a strand of sweaty hair away from his forehead. He riffles through his backpack before taking out some books. "Let's get started."

"You two go ahead setting up, now Zoltan's turn to excuse himself, go do big boy things," Zoltan says. "Toilet," he clarifies when Royce starts to protest. He slouches off.

"Right," Royce says, opening a reference book on the essentials of college application essays. His tone is cool. "So, Agnes, what help do you need with essay writing?"

I shake my head. "I've actually completed most of my essays and sent them out yesterday." With my qualifying win included as part of my credentials, as planned.

"Well, I guess you could have skipped today's session, then," he says tersely.

"Perhaps," I agree, in a tone of voice one could say was only Slightly Disagreeable.

We both fall silent. The air between us crackles with big, unsaid words.

"Where the hell is Zoltan?" Royce asks after a few minutes of intense avoidance of eye contact had passed.

I say in a small voice, "Look, I'm . . . er, well, yeah, y'know, sorry about the whole thing."

He turns to me. "Oh, at last she deigns to apologize," he says sarcastically. He crosses his arms across his chest. "If only I knew what for."

Spots of heat rise to my cheeks. "Okay, fine, I deserve that. I'm really, really sorry about how I acted at the comedy show. For calling you out like that. For acting like a class-A jerk. I mean it. No excuses."

The sincerity thaws his stance. He unfolds his arms and nods. "It was a really crap move, but let's move on. I have exactly forty-seven minutes until my driver comes for me."

"What do you have next?" I noted that *he* hadn't apologized for the things he'd said at the qualifiers. It leaves a bitter taste in my mouth and my guard goes up.

"Tennis lesson, then chess." He pauses. "Then Russian." He rubs his eyes. "What are you doing tonight? Maybe we can *CounterFlash* after Russian, say around nine."

I *did* have plans to play *CounterFlash* in fifteen minutes with my usual hangs like NerdWolf and Z-Flash, but I couldn't go on to game now. Urgh. Now I'll have to cancel.

"I'm going to run lines with Rosie for her drama class, and then I'm watching this reality show that Zee has been on my back to watch called *Marriage Truth Bomb Trial*, so I guess I can't." I hate lies, but what else can I say? *I don't want to hang, I'm mad at you.* Where was my apology? Didn't he realize he'd hurt me, too?

"What's wrong?"

"I want an apology for how you acted, too. When you made fun of me when Vern kissed me."

Royce flushes. He hesitates, as though he's wrestling with something. Maybe indigestion from being called out. "I'm sorry I did that. I don't know what came over me," he says in a formal way. "Are you and Vern—"

"No," I say, hating myself for how quickly I gave him my reassurances. "I don't know, maybe in the future," I add.

A sticky silence spreads between us.

Royce clears his throat, "I guess I can thank you for the advice. I think it really helped me unlock my performance, just leaning into the stupid-rich-kid stereotype and being self-deprecatory. The audience lapped it right up. I guess that's my shtick now: Annoying Rich Jock."

"How terrible," I say sarcastically. "If only the rest of us could have such problems."

"Please, Agnes, I don't want to fight, not today." He rubs at his eyes. "I've got enough on my plate as it is."

"What do you mean?" I ask, curious despite myself.

"This," Royce says, putting down a crumpled piece of paper on the table and smoothing it out. "Something my mom found in the trash. She had enough feelings about it that she got her driver to bring her over to school and yelled at me by the gates as soon as she called me out." He gives a bitter laugh. "But not after making sure no one of importance was around."

I stare at the Harvard insignia. *Dear Mr. Taslim, I am delighted to inform you* . . .

So, Royce got in to Harvard. A lump forms in my throat. There he goes, moving on to bigger, better things that are out of my reach. "Congratulations," I manage to say.

"I don't want to go there," he mumbles, his voice thick. "I only applied because my dad went there. I was secretly hoping . . . But my parents . . . when they hadn't heard from Harvard, they were already calling the office of admissions, preparing to donate all this money, and then when they—well, one of the housekeeping staff—found the admissions letter in my trash. . . ."

I double-take. "Wait, your housekeeping goes through your trash?"

His face is reddening. "No, I mean, they don't usua— I mean, this was just sitting there and I don't have much trash since they empty it every half day. But I guess my parents must have . . . enlisted their help."

What the eff.

"Amateur mistake," I say, attempting to lighten the mood. "Next time, I recommend shredding or burning the letter."

"Yeah," he says moodily, twisting his fingers in his lap.

"Was that your only acceptance letter?" It couldn't be, but I had to ask.

He shakes his head. "No, I got three more. Two other Ivy Leagues."

And here I am, praying for a response from any school, even the Div II ones.

"Where do you want to go?"

"Here." He puts down another perfectly folded paper and says, a little unsteadily, "Open it."

I swallow and reach for the letter.

"Toilets are so far," Zoltan says before I can unfold the paper. "I had to stop for snack." He spies the paper and grabs it. "Oh, what's this? Test?" He opens it, ignoring Royce's protests, reads it quickly, and claps Royce on the back. "Congratulations for your Columbia offer. Theater? Wow, friend, who thought?" Zoltan chuckles as he gives Royce a flirtatious once-over. "Hot and artistic, my favorite type."

I look at Royce and he looks at me. "I haven't accepted anything yet," he says. "I also got accepted at NYU and Dartmouth in similar programs, so it's a bit premature."

My temples throb with a looming headache. "Fancy," I say dully.

"Where are you going?" Zoltan asks me.

"Nowhere in the States, unless I get a scholarship," I say, dropping my gaze on the textbook and keeping my voice level. "Without financial assistance, the best I can do is a public university in Malaysia."

"And there are great public universities. . . ." Royce trails off at my glare. Whether or not great public universities exist in Malaysia is beside the point. Studying, or rather being successful in the NCAA was *my* dream. Other options can exist, but they will never be an adequate substitute for what I'd trained for almost half my life to achieve.

It's okay, Vern says in my head. *You're still a star in comedy. Maybe that can be your new way to shine.*

I try to rally myself: I could leverage a star turn in this competition into a comedy career in America, like my comedy heroes. That is still possible, and that's what I must focus all my energy in pursuing. Then everyone would be proud of me.

Zoltan claps my back, hard. "Or be like Zoltan! My parents want me to go to Oxford for Philosophy, Politics, and Economics, but I'm thinking of self-sabotaging, just fail everything and retake the year, drop out of high school and to ultimately graduate from school of life." This was a joke, of course. Zoltan's parents are diplomats and they come from a family of doctors and scientists; there is no way this is even an option. He tips me a wink. "You are welcome to join me in this very free school. Want to join me and surf Bali? We can stay indefinitely in my parents' investment villa."

Vern's voice in my head says: *Only the strong flourish. Use everything you have to get where you need to go.*

I decide to take a leaf out of Vern's playbook.

"Thanks, Zoltan," I say, smiling sweetly at Zoltan; I can feel Royce's eyes boring into the side of my head. "I guess at this rate, since I'm thinking of taking a gap year, anything is possible. I do need to explore my—creative side. You may have heard that I'm an amateur stand-up comic."

"Sexy." Zoltan leans forward and winks. "I can promise you *a lot* of sexy creative space." He offers his hand to me.

"Perfect," I say, slipping my hand in his with an exaggerated giggle. "I love surfers."

Royce gets up abruptly. "If you're going to paw each other, I'll leave you two to it. I'm out."

I flash back to his comment about me before his set at the qualifiers and my blood boils over. "Jealousy is a terrible look on you."

"What makes you think I give a damn what you do with your affections? You're so fickle-minded anyway," he shoots back.

Oh my God. I could tear his face off his . . . face.

"You guys are turning me on," Zoltan purrs.

"Come on, Zoltan, let's get out of here and get some *action*," I say. I grab a grinning Zoltan and practically drag him out of the library to a chorus of hissing and shushing, even as Royce shouts that he was leaving first. I don't think either of us won today.

~

I lose interest in maintaining the flirtation once Royce is gone and swiftly make my excuses to leave, citing plans with Zee—it would be our first meet-up since our big fight. Not that Zoltan was too shredded by my about-face—he was already making eyes with a passing junior.

My heart lifts as soon as I see Zee at the school gate. We give each other our most solemn hug, but midway she starts squealing and laughing. "Baby dear," she says. "Oh, I've missed you! I think stand-up has rubbed off on me, my high-tea gang is *just* so tediously boring in comparison."

I rub my nose into the side of her hijab. "I didn't have any gangs to compare you with, but I missed you."

We board my usual bus home. "You ready?" I ask her.

"Are you?" she asks me back.

We squeeze each other's hands.

The bus drops Zee and me roughly a mile from the terrace house where I live.

"How was it?" I ask her, thinking it was the first time she'd ever taken a public bus.

"Exciting," Zee says, rolling her eyes. "You know, I've taken the MRT before. Many times."

We walk in silence, sweating, to my house. Even the voluminous Zee is silent by the time we arrive, her magenta-and-silver backpack hanging limply on her back.

"Well, here it is," I mumble, gesturing at it.

Zee stares at my house. "Haiyahhhh, this is where you live?" she says. "This?"

"What?" I retort a little snappishly.

"I was expecting a tent with a colony of rats the way you hid it from me. Geez, it's like any other house. Look," she says, rapping at the door. "It even has a door! Made of . . . wood!"

"Get in," I say sulkily as I start unlocking my front door.

"I just want to say before we get in," Zee says, taking my hands and facing me solemnly. "Even if you did live in a tent with a colony of ants, I'd still love you. I'd never change the way I think about you. You're Agnes, my sulky, bossy, sometimes funny, but always bestest friend. ILYSM."

"Shaddduuuuuuuuuuup," I say, gagging to hide the fact that my eyes were on the verge of the waa-wahs, as Mom likes to say.

"Masuk masuk," she says, shooing me into my own house. Who's the bossy one in this relationship?

"Anyone else home?" she says, looking around. "I'd love to meet the whole family."

"Stanley's got something on at school, it's just Mom, us girls, and Rosie. Hold on, let me call Rosie down."

Rosie is enamored with Zee. "I love your hooded cat eye tutorial and the one where you lip-glossed your lids for the holidays."

"Thanks, I love those, too. You should check out the one where I use a wet brush and setting spray to transform eyeshadow into eyeliner."

"Epic," Rosie says.

I bring Zee into my living room. Rosie excuses herself to do her homework. My mother brings a tray of keropok and some iced tea and leaves us to chat.

"What are you going to do about Singapore?" Zee says in a low voice.

"I'm going for it." That conversation with Royce had cemented that resolve. "What about Vern? Do you still want me to . . . ?" For some reason, I made a weird fist-to-fist smushing action.

"Nah," she says. "I don't think Vern is into me at all. When I ran into him on the way out of the restaurant, he basically gave me a wave and looked back down at his phone. I lingered and tried to chat, but he wouldn't engage."

"Oh," I say. "Maybe it's because it's before the set. I could—"

"Agnes," Zee says. "Drop it. It's not happening between Vern and me, and that's fine. Even I can't always have what I want in the world." She says this in a jokey way, but there's an edge in her words. A silence falls between us, staticky with unsaid words. The tension between us from our fight is still there.

"There's—there's something else I wanted to discuss," Zee said after a while. "It's about your contribution to my videos. Your script."

"What about it?"

Zee takes a deep breath. "I'd like to start paying you for the work."

I stare at her. "Why? I'm doing it as a friend."

"Yes, and that's exactly why I should start valuing your contribution as a friend. This has gone on long enough, and if it goes on any longer, I'd be taking advantage of you. Your time and effort deserve to be compensated. "

She's right, of course. It just felt strange in the context of everything that had recently happened between us. "I like working on those videos with you."

"I know. This is about compensation. If I'd hired a freelancer or an agency to come up with prompts, I'd be paying them. Why shouldn't I pay my best friend?" Her smile brightens. "This is the right thing to do. You know I'm making mad money off those videos, with the sponsorships in kind and in cash."

I nod, embarrassed. "Okay, whatever. Sure."

"Cool." She claps her hands in excitement. "I have a totally different direction for next season. I'm thinking of changing my social media handles, dropping my dad's name, Bakri, so I'm just a mononym. Just focusing on me and what I do best. And not working with or promoting the businesses of family friends, et cetera, unless the products or services are genuinely worth my followers' hard-earned cash."

"Th-that's a big step," I say, taken aback.

She shrugs, reddening. "Like, I know realistically that I'm never going to be completely rid of the family influence, but at least I'll know that if I want to rep something, it's purely because I believe in it . . . and I believe in myself."

I hug her. "I'm so proud of you," I say sincerely.

Zee smiles. Then her eyes sharpen, "How are things with Royce? After your apology?"

"It's weird," I admit. It was weighing on me, and only Vern's encouragement for me to put distance between Royce and me, since Royce was leaving anyway after senior year ended for the States, helped me put things in perspective. I need to keep Royce at arm's length for my own sake. "Anyway, it's not like we're, like, dating or anything."

"Girl, I saw you two backstage after the gala. There was some serious chemistry. And I know chemistry—I got an A in AP Chem!" Zee always makes sure she reads the ingredients in her makeup and skincare before recommending them.

I make a dismissive sound. "It's a lost cause, so let's move on."

Zee presses her lips together and says nothing.

We enter the nursery. The bones of the room were done: I'd bought the specialty, child-safe paint—a lovely buttery-yellow that Stanley and Rosie had spent last weekend painting the walls with; the white crib is one we'd bought from IKEA. The sturdy wooden chest of drawers (white, scuffed), the nightstand (pale gray) and changing table (beige wood) had been sourced secondhand from the school's staff network, and the fantastic old-fashioned rocking chair in natural blond wood were gifted from the partners at my mother's law firm. The mismatched furniture was eclectic and cozy—us.

I side-eye to see what Zee thought. "Very pretty," she pronounces, and I relax.

Zee and I are here to bedazzle the room with some decor. Zee unpacks her large bag of stuff, which I am sure contains gifts for my mom. Since she's on a mission to be more careful about how she "spreads her influence," I told her she absolutely did not need to spend a lot of money. We had everything we could need, including essentials, gifted or sourced from the school and law firm: bags of new and secondhand baby clothing and toys, and a veritable pyramid of diapers.

"I couldn't help myself," she says, taking her first gift out sheepishly. It's a boxed-up, high-tech something that looks, naturally, expensive. "It's a top-of-the-line breast pump," Zee explains. "Like, the Maserati of breast pumps."

I groan. "Zee," I say. "I love you, but this is too much. Honestly, you can just go with a Perodua of breast pumps if you had to, and it would already be enough. On top of the first babymoon room that we didn't—"

"Shhh, ma biche, shhhh," she replies, putting a finger to my burbling lips. "It's okay. Let it happen. Let it happen."

She spreads out her other goodies on the parquet floor of the nursery: a bunch of newborn toys with fancy Scandinavian brand names and some nondescript newborn baby clothes from a local department store. I made little noises of protest, which she waved away. "These are from my parents, so you can't give them back."

"Thank you," I say, defeated. I hug her, my sweet, kind friend.

"Nice paintings," she says, eyeing the lightweight white wooden frames in which I'd stuck the best photos of the family and a trio of sweet, monochromatic prints of kids holding balloons and one of a llama, just because.

"We're going to stick those up with these specialty tapes and hang these old cloth buntings Rosie and I made. And then we're gonna sort all the clothes and put them in drawers and keep the diapers away."

"Ah, good, honest work," Zee says, and I roll my eyes at her rolling her eyes at me, having predicted that that would be my exact response. I don't mind. At the end of the day, that's what true friendship is: getting the core of a person and cherishing it for all its beauty and flaws.

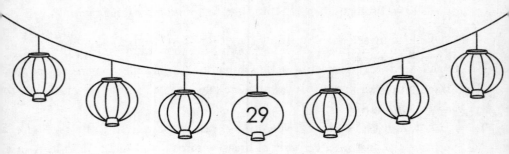

29

Royce: Agnes, I don't know why we keep clashing when all
I want is the opposite. Can we meet up, please?
Royce: I miss you
Royce: Agnes, please text me back

~

Vern: You up?
Me: Yeah. Gaming
Vern: All right. Not practicing for your semis in Singapore?
Me: I was, but I'm having trouble concentrating
Vern: What? Why?
Me: Ever since Stanley caught me, I still haven't come clean
to my mom about comedy, and until I do, I'm not allowed to
perform stand-up. Stanley's starting to lose his patience, and
I'm distracted by all of it. I'm almost tempted not to go. Almost

There's also Royce, but I sense that I shouldn't bring him up, not
to Vern.

Vern: You have to go, c'mon. Don't tell your mom and just do what you need to do. It won't be half as fun without you

I smile to myself; I'd been planning on forging my mom's signature and making my way to Singapore no matter what.

Me: One less person to beat, right?
Vern: You're my friend, I want you there . . . In fact, we should really work on all our sets together. Let me help you. That's what a friend would do
Me: Sure
Me: I don't know what I would do without you
Vern: 🔥 Good, keep it that way

~

On Thursday, Vern and I meet for bubble tea after his work and my school at the same mall where I stalked—yes, I'll admit it now, I stalked them—my faux friends. We sit by the dead fountain in the open-air park that no one uses, because the equatorial humidity is no joke, and he runs his semifinal stand-up set with me.

"It's really good," I tell him after giving him a couple of minor notes.

"And now it's your turn," he says.

"Aw, I don't know." It hits a little differently when you're performing for just one person.

He nudges me. "Come on. It's only me."

I steel myself and deliver the set that I'd been working on.

He is really helpful with mine, taking notes and giving good feedback.

"Don't cross your eyes."

"Really enunciate your words, you mumble sometimes."

"Simplify the language there, it'll get you to the punch line faster."

"Oh my God!" I say, but only half in annoyance. "Were you actually taking notes?"

"Yes, the whole time, and I've been recording you, too." He gestures at a second phone that has been filming me beside his backpack. I shriek and try to dive at him, but he's much taller than me and holds the phone out of my reach to my great annoyance. I try to be strategic and wait for his energy to flag, but he doesn't drop an inch. "This is why I wasn't going to tell you until you were done. Trust me, you need to see yourself on video to improve. You know I record all my performances, even the practice sessions."

"Ew, I hate recording myself."

"Why?"

"I'm so gangly. Like a large spider."

"Do you want to improve or not?"

"Yeah," I grunt. "Send them to me, I guess."

"Excellent. Now I'm going to lower my arm, and you're going to promise me you'll refrain from snatching my phone, yes?"

"Yes," I say sulkily.

He cautiously drops his phone arm, but I don't attack. I keep my word. He makes approving noises as he goes through my set. "You know, if you want, you should write bits about the money sponges at your school—and the kids they send there."

I giggle. "I'm not a mean comic, though."

"Maybe you should be. Self-deprecating doesn't work for everyone in comedy. You're allowed to explore the darker side of comedy, too, you know." He points at a particular bit. "Like this. The punch line would land so much harder if you go low, out of nowhere. I mean, you have such a nice, sunshiny personality, and sweet, pretty face, that if you contrast that with a hard-hitting no-holds-barred material—" He mimics an explosion.

I bite my lip, flushing at his wedged-in compliment. "I don't know, it feels . . . not me."

"Don't knock it till you've tried it," Vern says. "Anyway, you feeling better about your friend situation?"

I bite my lip. "What do you mean?"

"I meant how you shed what I like to call Baggage Friends. Your so-called track teamsters? Hot Flushes? Flashers?"

"Flashes," I correct automatically. I thought about this. On the one hand, I did think what they said about me held some water. I'd expected them to be friends with me when I never opened up about myself. Clearly, I wanted connection with them. On the other hand, I don't think they ever extended a real attempt at friendship at me either. Vern had helped me see that. That I'm not one of them, and it's okay—and what's more, I don't need them.

"It hurt at first," I admit. "I did think we were friends and not just teammates. But I'm better off without faux friends."

"Be like me, Ags. I'm focused on the goal, and I keep my support systems lean," Vern says. "I have people in my life who I can support and who support me." He grins. "My clan. My people. My wolf pack."

"You mean, friends?"

His eyes are mocking. "*Friends*. That word means nothing to some people. What's a friend to girls like your Flashes? The people they *hang* with? Party and trade gossip? I don't need 'friends' like those."

It didn't sound too bad, what he was talking about. Belonging. "So, what do you need, then, Vern?"

"I'll put it simply: Anyone who can't enrich my experience here on Earth, anyone who doesn't have the potential to make a real difference, is not worth me opening up to or having in my life."

"Seems a bit . . . transactional."

He scoffs. "All relationships have a transactional element to them. As you grow up, you'll see that. We all give and we all take from the people in our lives. The difference is some people take more than they give. I believe in giving as much as I'm taking. Quid pro quo."

I keep quiet. I don't disagree, I suppose, but it sounds so bleak when you put it that way. But he's older, so he must know what he's talking about.

"So what happens when you don't see utility in a pack member?"

"We part ways, no harm, no foul."

I shrug. "I don't think . . . Well, that sounds so cold."

He laughs. "It's not. If I've admitted you into my pack, it's because I know we won't easily part ways. It would be for life."

"So, am I in your pack?"

He squints at me and I squint back. "What do you think?"

"I hope so." I really do. I've come to value Vern's friendship, whatchamacallit.

"Of course you are, then," he says, a small smile on his lips.

"Cool, cool. You and Zee are part of the Chan pack."

Vern turns to me, something I couldn't decipher in his face. "Do you think Zee's really someone you want as a pack member?"

I flinch, sensing the undercurrents of hostility in his question. "Absolutely. She's great." I say this with a bite of vehemence.

Vern regards me. "She's very different from you."

"What's wrong with having friends who are different from you? Doesn't it enrich your life?"

"What are Zee's hobbies and interests? Her goals or"—his voice takes on a sarcastic inflection—"ambition?"

"Zee loves reality TV and makeup and making makeup tutorials. I think she wants to go to USC for film studies."

"Film studies? Is she planning to make that her career? Why California?"

I laugh. "I think she just wants to be in California."

"There you go. She's going to distract you from your goals. People like her, and Royce, they're made no matter what they do or don't. You and I, we need hungry people to help motivate us, keep our eyes on the prize. Zee is a liability."

I instinctively want to protest this matter-of-fact statement, but then I run through the times Zee distracts me during classes with whispered gossip, at our study sessions, disrupts our study sessions by asking me to be her model or enticing me to watch TV. She can afford to goof off. "She's not," I say with less conviction,

Vern shrugs. "Look, I'm trying to help you succeed in life. Do what you want with my advice."

We sit at the fountain without speaking for a few tense beats. "I have to get back to work," Vern says after a while. "BTW, how are you doing with money? All that travel across town to the stand-up comedy sets, and the fact that you no longer have a part-time job. And how about your future expenses when you make it all the way to the finals?"

I rap on a twig I find in a panic, Vern watching me with a knowing gleam. "I guess . . ." I hesitate, and swallow. "I guess I'm a little low on resources."

"I can get you a job at the skating rink."

"You would?"

"Yeah. They always need people at the skate counter."

The idea of seeing my teammates, handing them their skates and deodorizing the used ones after all that had happened—

Vern nods. "Okay, gotcha, no skates. You good with working at the Grub Hub? They are looking for someone to start right away, evening shifts."

The Grub Hub was a tiny refreshments corner in the skating rink's space, selling ancient hot dogs, greasy, floury burgers, and soft drinks. No one from my squad would ever eat there, even on their cheat days. I square my shoulders. "Yeah, I guess."

"Great. You could sit down all shift, rest your leg. Work on your sets. Easy-peasy, plus you'll get paid." He winks. "We'll have more time to brainstorm on bits."

And it'll be the perfect cover. . . . I could tell Stanley I'm done with stand-up and use my Grub Hub shifts as a deflection. I'd never have to come clean to my mother, saving her all the grief of finding out about my double life.

I break into a sly grin. "You are the best."

"Listen," Vern says, looking hesitant. "You know how we've been friends for such a long while? And we're always meeting at this shitty, hot fountain park?"

"Yeahhhh, I know it sucks, but it's free and quiet."

"Well, I was wondering, if"—his face flushes—"you know, to save money and stuff, but not like, die in the heat, you'd like to have lunch at my aunt's place, this Saturday, to work on our semifinals set? A late tropical Christmas lunch, if you wish. No big deal."

"I get to see where you live?" I say, touched.

"I mean, it's a casual hang, don't get excited," he mumbles.

I put a hand on his. "Vern," I say, "this is an effing big deal to me. Before last week I'd never even invited Zee over to mine. I know how sacred it is to invite someone into your sanctum." The other thing that was unsaid—Vern had always been up front about how he'd grown up in poverty, and as someone who'd been through that, I understand how hard it is to show a person who'd never experienced it the limits of your existence. It takes guts, a lot of guts.

"You'll come over, then?" he asks.

"Yes," I say gently. "Yes, of course."

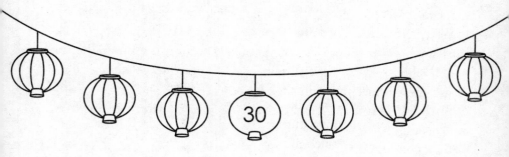

30

ZEE'S FACE, WHEN SHE HEARS THAT I'M GOING TO VERN'S PLACE TO hang, is a picture. "You are killing me." She sighs. "Are you sure I'm the flighty one?"

"I never said that."

"I know. I said it."

She insists on dropping me in front of his aunt's place, for recon purposes, and tells me to text her if I run into any trouble. I roll my eyes. It was ridiculous how little faith Zee has in Vern. Somewhat uncharitably, I wonder how much of it is tied to his socioeconomic status.

Vern lives in a single-story terrace house in an unglamorous part of Shah Alam, "where the annual floods dump their shit"—his words.

His aunt opens the door when I knock; she's dressed in an old T-shirt and a muddy-red sarong that's cinched tight around her waist, and her undyed gray hair makes her appear older than she should be. "Oh," she says in Cantonese. "You're here." She turns away and leaves the door open without another word; I take this as an invitation to enter, which I do gingerly. I take in the small, sparse living room, with its cheap curtains in a flowery print, a two-seater sofa in black faux leather, a rattan recliner, and a tiny brown dining table with two metal stools pushed against a wall. A few framed photos, mostly of Vern, perch on top of a low bookshelf next to a boxy TV, which flickers with a silent film. The living room is sectioned off from the rest of the house with a bead curtain, which parts to reveal Vern, smiling and dressed in T-shirt and shorts, like I am.

"Hi," he says, the bead curtains clattering shut behind him. "This way."

I follow him through the beaded divider with some hesitation. Vern chuckles, "Don't worry, we're just headed to the kitchen so my aunt can watch TV without disturbing us. I'm not bringing you to my room; that's only for romantic liaisons."

"Oh, I . . . I . . . didn't assume . . ." My face is burning.

Vern laughs. There's an edge I don't understand in his voice. "I know, Agnes, stop hyperventilating and come to the kitchen. I'm not interested in you that way, believe me."

I follow him, cheeks flaming, into the clean, bare kitchen with its beige Formica countertops and off-white everything else; only a small pot of plastic yellow flowers lend any color to the space. He gestures for us to sit at a narrow wooden table covered with a white vinyl lace tablecloth with two padded stools in the corner, next to a listing stack of newspapers.

Vern catches my questioning gaze and says, "Those are good for cleaning the windows with. What would you like to drink? I have room-temperature boiled tap water and"—he gestures expansively at the fridge—"chilled boiled tap water."

"Chilled, please."

He comes back with two glass tumblers and a plate of mixed fruit. I thank him and bite into a star fruit, my favorite.

Vern opens his laptop and brings up his set. I eye a stack of mismatched cooking pots and pans on a counter. "Do you cook?"

"Yeah, nothing fancy, though. Mostly one-pot dishes like noodles or rice." He shrugs. "Someone has to make sure we eat right. My aunt would happily eat instant noodles with an egg for every meal if I don't intervene."

His aunt raises the volume of the TV. I hear a man and a woman chatting animatedly in Cantonese. His aunt grunts at the dialogue. A memory flickers to life and tugs at me. Of my mom and me in a similar kitchen, with a similar plastic table covering, eating soft-boiled eggs, toast, and baked beans for dinner, her taking small bites while I scarf down most of mine.

"My mom and I did that for a time, maybe when I was eight or nine, way before Stanley and Rosie came into our lives," I say, unprompted. I don't know why I am sharing this. "She would never let me go hungry, even when she did." I hesitate, then ask, "Was everything in your set true? About working since age fourteen?"

"Thirteen," he corrects. "Don't look so shocked. I basically helped my uncle with wiring and minor construction work; it wasn't like I was abused. I had a very early growth spurt and I was bigger than most kids my age. My aunt and uncle loved me in their own fashion. I was always given all the support I needed."

I nod. That was mostly true for my mom, except for that one year when she lost her job and fell into a depression. That had been hard to be around, knowing that her breakdown was due to her feeling inadequate as a parent and some bills she couldn't starve herself to get us out of. It spun her out. It was only thanks to the timely help from a charity that focused on mental illnesses that she got the support and meds she needed to turn her life around. It's why I will never let my mother worry for me again. She can only see me succeed.

"My aunt has had a hard life. She didn't have to take me in, but she did. She's not even a blood relation. My uncle was the one related to me."

"Where's he now?" I ask tentatively.

"Dead," Vern replies. "Lung cancer. Five years ago."

"I'm sorry," I say softly. I thought he'd been joking, at the gala, about the suit.

"Me too," Vern says, glancing down at his lap for a while.

My phone buzzes with a text. It's Royce, again: Agnes, will you be performing at Saloma's tomorrow? Can we talk, please?

I place the phone facedown. *No, Royce, I don't want to.* Being with Royce was hard—and it didn't make sense. I focus on Vern. "What does your aunt do now? Does she still work?"

"Yup, she's part of a janitorial team in one of those new coworking spaces. Real fancy, an up-and-coming regional one." He twitches his lip and I think he's smiling, but it doesn't reach his eyes. "She says they don't look at her when they pass her in the space, but they certainly greet each other. Real *community* spirit they have. And they often make the janitorial team do nonjanitorial stuff, too, like moving stock furniture back into a space when a tenant leaves." His eyes narrow. "I don't like her working there, but we don't have a choice. She has diabetes and she has all these problems with her vision and her feet, and even with the wonderful public healthcare system we have in Malaysia, we have other expenses, and we have to think about her future when she's no longer able to work. . . ."

So that's why he works so hard.

I hear the clicking of the bead curtains parting, and his aunt comes in. "Eat, eat," she says in Cantonese. I nod and say I've eaten in Mandarin, and she smiles, a real one. "Bagus," she replies in Bahasa, making a thumbs-up sign, and retreats with a hot cup of water.

We work on our sets for hours, drinking hot Chinese tea and eating cut fruit and prawn crackers. Lunch is a mess of flat rice noodles stir-fried with egg and bok choy and lap cheong, his aunt eating in front of the TV watching a classic '80s Jackie Chan comedy with us seated at the dining table. I laugh at what the characters are saying, even though I don't understand some of it. It occurs to me, as I banter with him and sometimes his aunt in an implausible mixture of Bahasa, English, Cantonese, and Mandarin, not code-switching like I do in school, that I feel at home here.

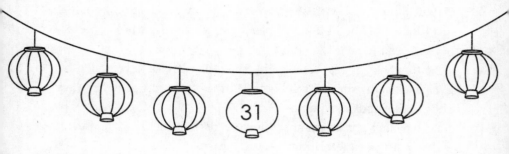

NEW YEAR'S COMES AND GOES IN A BLUR OF MUTED CELEBRATIONS.
I get the part-time job, which is a relief. It's just as Vern said—there are so few customers that I have time to work on my set, and they pay me in cash with a little slip at the end of the day, which I can wave in front of a visibly suspicious Stanley and my mother.

About a week into the job, Stanley corners me before I leave for my fourth "evening shift" in a row, which was in actuality another comedy open-mike night. "Have you told your mother about the gigs?" he asks without segue.

I can see Vern's car waiting in the shadow of the neighbor's mango tree. He'd offered to drive me to our gig, and I'm anxious to leave—it will be our last chance to finesse our sets before the qualifiers.

"Why?" I say, shrugging. "I have no intention of heading to the semi-finals in Singapore this weekend." That was a lie: I had already handed in my permission slip, my mom's signature carefully forged, over the new year. But, like Vern always said, sometimes the ends justify the means.

Stanley looks taken aback. "Why not? Don't you think she might support you?"

"It's okay. It was a stupid hobby; I need to focus on senior year. I'm over it," I say dismissively.

Stanley's eyes cloud over and he bites his lip. "Agnes, I don't think—"

I cut Stanley off with a sharp shake of my head. "Look, just . . . just please don't tell Mom I've been lying to her the whole time. She doesn't need to hear how I've failed her."

He flinches. "Agnes, you haven't failed her. You've never failed her. Ever. That's why she *needs* to know. Why don't we just go to her, now? She's in the study, reading—"

I catch sight of the time—at this rate, we're going to be late. I panic. "Please, just don't tell her yet—Dad. Please."

It slipped out. How much of it is calculated, I don't know. We look at each other, and to my great horror, Stanley's eyes are tearing up. "Agnes, I—I . . . You don't know how much . . ."

"It's no big deal, I'm going to be late, bye!" I say; then I'm moving as fast as I can without hurting myself out the door to Vern's car, willing myself not to think about how I've just manipulated Stanley. *I had a good reason*, I remind myself. Vern was always telling me I needed to be more strategic—well, I did that. I got myself out of telling my mother and out of Stanley's lecture. I'm evolving.

Vern's car rattles all the way to the venue, but he cranks up his sound system and we sing along to our favorite pregame Spotify mix. I tumble out before he leaves to park behind the restaurant we'd be performing at, grinning from the endorphins of yelling out lyrics at the top of my lungs with the windows rolled down, people staring. It felt so freeing to be so authentically me while not caring how I appeared to others.

And standing there on the hot curb, still giggling as I watch Vern nose his car into an empty spot down the street, I realize that was probably what I like about stand-up. Sure, I like the craft, always have, the competition. I like the scene, with its oddball crew of misfits. Even at the most conventional end of the spectrum of comics, these are people who don't really fit square in square pegs. But really, I guess what I like most is how onstage, I have the freedom to be absolutely, imperfectly me.

I turn around and see Royce, standing by the entrance, watching me, fresh as a pop star in his red plaid shirt and dark blue jeans. My stomach nosedives when I realize he saw me with Vern. I lift my chin at him. "Royce."

A pause. "Chan."

He opens his mouth as if to say something but changes his mind in the end. He turns away and walks into the café. I wait on the curb till he disappears, and Vern joins me, fluid as a shadow. We go in together.

~

That night, whatever destabilizing effect I ever had on Royce is gone. He does his set and kills it, and I understood why he was called Golden Ray before. Conversely, I was starting to struggle. The direction that Vern had given me over the last few sessions pressed on my delivery, making it less natural than it was before. Or maybe—

I shake my head. It wasn't because Royce barely looked at me. Not at all.

Vern came up to me after my shaky set. "You okay?"

"Great," I say hollowly.

"I felt your new direction was so exciting."

I start. "Really?"

"Absolutely. The delivery was edgier and I like your new eyeliner look, too. And I liked that new bit you threw into the mix about how hard it is to be a girl even in the gaming space."

"I don't know. . . ."

"You just need to work on the setup a bit more and I'm sure it'll work out."

"Okay." I nod. Vern had more experience, after all.

"That's the spirit." Vern claps me on my back. "Now let me give you a ride home. I have to protect my fam from the likes of him." He jerks his head at Royce, who's looking our way from the other side of the restaurant. Vern leans close and says, "You just can't trust people like Taslim. They have nothing *real* to lose."

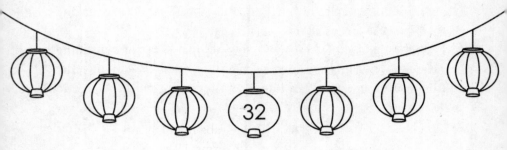

Zee: BREAK A LEG TOMORROW

Me: 🪨

Zee: Metaphorically speaking to be clear

Me: Remember, I'm supposed to be with you the whole day studying and sleeping over at yours tomorrow night, OK. Don't go wandering in a mall and post it live on Stories or whatever. ROSIE IS FOLLOWING YOU on socials.

Zee: Urgh YES naggy bench

Zee: Oh, btw, don't be mad, but I told Taslim how you were getting to Singapore. He said you were still ignoring his texts and he wants to clear the air.

Me: !!!

Zee: Sorry beb trust Z OK

I groan and palm my face. I trust Zee with my life, but she wasn't the problem—the combination of Royce and Vern was.

~

I try to relax while I wait for Vern to arrive at the bus depot bright and early Saturday morning, hoping for a fun, peaceful six-hour ride

230

into Singapore. Despite it being 8 a.m., the large, double-storied air-conditioned complex teemed with travelers, many of them making long-distance journeys all over West Malaysia.

I head to the right terminal and find Vern already there, smiling and waving, a backpack slung over his shoulders. "Hey, partner," he calls out. We bump fists. "Right on time, too."

"Hey, partner," I say.

Our bus noses into the bay, and he grabs my luggage. "We better get these stowed away before the queue forms. I'll see you in the bus?"

I nod. Royce turns up then, flushing, rolling a flashy jade-green carry-on. He gives me a stiff nod. I realize he is accompanied by someone—his bodyguard, who also ambles up with a muted gray rolling suitcase.

"I'll bring the luggage to the back of the bus," the bodyguard tells Royce, who nods. Then Royce and I are alone—or as alone as we can be surrounded by twenty other passengers waiting to board the bus.

He gently guides me by the elbow a little way from the others.

"I really wanted to clear the air before the competition, or it would mess with my head," he says softly. "You matter so much to me, Agnes, and I hate that we're in this situation." His expression clouds with pain. "Ever since the gala, things have changed between us. . . . I thought telling you I liked you, a-and you saying it back, would bring us closer together, but it hasn't. It's driven us further apart. Maybe it was just too much pressure on us, maybe my feelings weren't recip- rocated, and you felt somehow obligated . . ." He closes his eyes and speaks before I can say anything to disabuse him of that notion. "If my confession has ruined our friendship, then it's not worth it. I'd rather have you in my life, one way or another, than nothing at all."

My heart twists. He saw the impossible truth of the matter and wanted to rescind his confession. "It's fine," I say with nonchalance. "Let's forget we ever went there."

Something flickers and dies in his expression. He nods. "I'm sorry for my behavior at the qualifiers and after. I was hurt and lashed out."

"I'm sorry, too. I wasn't a saint either."

He laughs wryly. "Friends?"

"Friends," I say. He hasn't released my elbow still, and it's both wonderful and too much at this moment.

A tapping from the window above us. Vern. He waved at me and indicated he'd saved me a seat.

"I should—" I gesture at Vern.

"Yeah, sure," he says. "I'll sit with Jit. My bodyguard." He catches my expression and says, "Yes, I know. Another one."

I grimace-chuckle and the energy between us warms, just a little.

We queue up with the rest of the passengers. When it's my turn to go up, he lets my elbow go without another word. The finality of that gesture feels like a farewell.

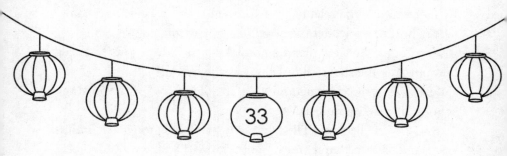

WE ARRIVE AND CLEAR CUSTOMS WITH LITTLE ISSUE BY 2 P.M. MY stomach hasn't stop churning since Royce and I spoke, and Rosie's cheerful texts telling me during the bus ride that I had just received "some kind of crest-y college letter" didn't help. And now we've arrived at our destination—a run-down mall with a large parking lot that serves as a bus terminal—and we have four hours to kill before showtime.

"Where should we go?" Vern says as we collect our bags from the bus conductor, who's offloading them from the belly of the bus. "We have time. We can sightsee, visit a museum, watch a movie . . ."

"You decide," I say to Vern. "I don't know Singapore at all." Vern had already done the Singapore comedy scene twice last year.

"Cool, I'll show you around," Vern says, grinning.

"Royce?" I venture tentatively, since he's also waiting for his luggage and within hearing distance.

"Why don't I meet you all at the comedy club?" Royce says curtly.

"Where are you going?" I ask.

"To my hotel, which is just across the street where our competition will be. Where are you guys staying?"

I blush. Because I hadn't planned on staying overnight in Singapore

(#Skint); Vern and I had decided we'd take the midnight bus back to Kuala Lumpur, where I'd crash at Zee's and Vern would head home. "We're headed back after the event," I say.

Vern nods. "We were planning on taking the last bus out to Kuala Lumpur after the show. Did Agnes not tell you that?"

Royce keeps his voice neutral. "No, she didn't. Well, see you at the venue." He walks away.

"Bye, Royce!" Vern says cheerily, waving with a bit too much enthusiasm and slinging another arm around me. "I'll take *very* good care of Agnes, don't you worry."

Royce doesn't respond. My insides contract with pain—maybe I'm more hungry than I thought. "Let's find somewhere to eat," I say roughly.

We grab a quick lunch of chicken rice and walk around the National Gallery to pass time checking out the permanent exhibition (and taking advantage of the air-conditioning) before getting to Capitol Theatre, a white, four-story neoclassical building where the competition is being held. That's when the nervous sweats really start.

More than ever, winning is important. I can feel like myself again. I won't feel so lost, like I don't have a purpose in life. I'll feel like I matter.

I enter and see Lai milling about at the reception, checking tickets and laughing with a burly man. I run to hug them. "Hey! What are you doing here?"

"The organizer is my best friend," they say, breaking apart with a grin. They introduce me to the burly man, whose name is Nigel. "Nigel here owns a big events company, and they bring in many of the touring big-name comics. I'm just here to support him."

"I'm glad." The way Lai and Nigel are making eyes indicate there's more to the story. I grin. "So, where do I go?"

"The holding room is beside the stage. Royce is already there."

They bring us to the comic green room, which is basically a sort of storeroom/dressing room hybrid, where I counted eight other comics, pacing and muttering lines, standing alone in corners going through their set and scribbling in notepads, or chatting with other comics in English, with a smattering of other languages and dialects.

Royce, predictably, is alone.

"Hey, Ray, where's Shadow Man?" Vern calls out to Royce. I realize he's referring to the bodyguard.

Royce presses his lips together before replying, "It's Royce. Anyway, run out of easy targets to kick, Vern?"

Vern laughs. "Always a pleasure, Ray—I mean, Royce." He winks and walks to the other end of the room. "Hey, Ags, come here, we can practice here."

I hesitate. I don't want to go to Vern with Royce staring at me like this, but I also don't want Vern to think I'm going to ditch him to be with Royce, which is a lousy friend move, so I say, "I think I'm just going to go over my lines over—" I glance around the room. The only empty spot was by a pile of moldy costumes in a box in a cobwebby corner. "There." A good spot, in case I faint.

A showrunner comes to the room and gives us the rundown—Vern's fifth in the first half, with a fifteen-minute intermission, and I'm opening the second half, followed by Royce. My heart beats so fast I feel light-headed, but the adrenaline is exhilarating. It's a similar rush to how I feel before I run competitively, only with lashings of dread, because with comedy, so many more things can go wrong.

I wish Zee could be here. And my parents.

We can hear everyone that goes onstage, and the energy is electric. The first half goes quickly. I'm too nervous to pay much attention to the other contestants' sets, even Vern's, immersed as I am in rehearsing my lines. I'm so distracted that I barely noticed when he's back in the holding room until he taps me on the shoulder and I turn to see his smiling face.

"How was it?" I ask him. Royce looks up from his perch on a seat nearby, his eyes following our interaction.

"Magical," Vern says, his eyes blazing. "I hit every note." Then he pulls me into a hug. "And I owe it all to you, Agnes. Your support means everything to me."

It's just like any other time we've hugged, but also not. He holds me closer, longer, possessively. It doesn't feel platonic.

"Stop," I say weakly, trying to wriggle free, but Vern's hold only tightens.

"Let her go," Royce growls from behind me. I feel Royce wrench Vern's arms off me and give him a shove. Vern wheels back, a look of surprise in his face. I stand there, shell-shocked at the turn of events. Royce steps between me and Vern, shielding me.

"What's your problem, Royce?" Vern drawls. "Jealous?"

"She told you to *back the hell off*," Royce says in a voice so low, I almost can't hear him over the comic performing onstage; my eyes drop to his fists, balled so tight I can see the veins pulsing.

Vern looks at me, his eyes now full of concern, and says, "I'm sorry, Agnes, but what's wrong?"

"I—I . . ." I say, still shivering. I'm not sure why my body is having this reaction. He hasn't done anything wrong—has he?

Royce takes a step in Vern's direction. "Touch her again and I'll tear you apart."

"A direct threat! I should call security," Vern says, smiling, although his eyes are hard. "I should call security and get them to throw you out of the competition."

The other comics are whispering behind us, and I hear, "Yeah, get security." I take a deep breath and say, in a false cheery voice, "Guys, honestly, please, let's all tone down on the toxic masculinity, okay? Geez." I didn't want either of them getting into trouble.

A couple of guys chuckle and the situation diffuses. One of the organizing crew pokes their head around and calls to Vern, needing his details. Vern leaves with a casual nod at me, as though nothing had happened. As though it had all been in my head.

My head is throbbing. I sit down on one of the boxes of costumes, Royce next to me, not touching, an intense energy radiating off him as he scrutinizes me, asking me what I need, and I keep shaking my head that's filled with cotton.

I hear my name being called from a distance to get ready to go onstage. I blink and take the cup of water that Royce is handing me.

His eyes meet mine and my fugue state breaks. "I don't know what that was about, but Agnes, it's going to be your turn in five minutes. I need you to go out there and crush the competition."

I shake my head, hugging myself. "I—I don't know if I'm in the right headspace . . . if I can even perform . . . "

"Yes, you can, Agnes. You're the strongest, bravest person I know. You can do anything. Just shut all the noise out, Agnes. Close your eyes."

"I—I—"

"Look, I'll do it." He closes his eyes, and after some hesitation I follow suit. "Go into your pregame headspace."

I close my eyes. My ritual of visualizing the things that give me strength, power, hope. I picture myself running, I picture my parents, Rosie. I picture Zee.

I picture Royce.

Royce places his hand on mine and squeezes. "I'm here for you whenever you need me," he says. "Always."

My throat tightens with emotion. I open my eyes and look into his hazel eyes, brimming with tenderness, not pity, as I'd always assumed. My head is clear. "I'm ready."

Then, finally, it's my turn. I go onstage ready to show the world who I am.

I talk about my mother. I talk about my blended family. I talk about my school, and what success looks like to me versus my classmates. About losing and making new identities as a chronic overachiever.

Every line flies off me like it's nothing, like arrows from a bow. The audience laps them up. When I'm done with my set, the applause is thunderous.

I walk off the set and see Royce, who's clapping so hard, smiling so brightly for me, and my insides twist, my knees wobble. Big Bird himself could have been in the room and I wouldn't have noticed; all I see is Royce, who's wrapped in sunlight.

Royce has always been there for me—I just hadn't seen it because I'd been afraid of what that could mean. But now I do.

I see the truth: Royce likes me for who I am.

I don't care about our differences anymore. Not after tonight. Not if he'll have me the way I want him to.

I want to—

My face flushes. Nah, I should calm down. Jit, his bodyguard, will no doubt be there to, as they say, cockblock. He'd probably be there, watching. Disapprovingly. Not a bogeyman as in Royce's bit, but some kind of weird custodial/guardian hybrid who knows Krav Maga and defensive CSI, aka the art of hiding bodies.

The last comic performs, and the judges go to a room to deliberate on the two comics who will go to the finals in New York.

I close my eyes and try to calmly take breaths. Beside me, Royce is doing some kind of breathing exercise, saying, under his breath, "You've got this, Agnes. No matter what, you're already a winner. You were fire."

I don't know how it happens, but suddenly we're holding hands—and I'm having an out-of-body experience, every cell in me is in first place, doing laps around the freaking moon.

The judging takes longer than the allotted half hour. By now, it's almost nine thirty, and despite the adrenaline, the early day and the stressful competition quietens the holding room. Then a crew member calls us to the stage, and we file quietly to the stage before a full house of people. I see Vern slip out of a dark nook backstage just outside our holding room and join the comics onstage. At first it looks as though he's heading toward me, but when he sees me standing next to Royce, holding hands, he scoffs quietly and walks to the other end of the lineup.

I blink under the hard lights and stare unseeingly at the crowded room.

The head judge, Lola Hashim, a well-known comic in her fifties from Malaysia, goes onstage at last, clears her throat and gives the standard spiel about the quality of the contestants. Then she says, "We have ourselves the first person through to the finals, and this was a unanimous decision, and our first pick is—"

Royce's hand tightens around mine. I know that this is the culmination of two years of stand-up for him, and all he has ever wanted.

"Vern Goh!"

I gasp. Vern steps into the limelight, smiling beatifically. Vern, the so-called underdog, is the best one tonight. I don't know how I feel about this, about Vern, even. I still haven't properly processed everything that happened earlier.

Lola looks a little discomfited. "We do have a slight situation—"

Both Royce and I are gripping each other's hands tightly now. A thought enters my hear, unbidden: *If I win, will Royce still like me?* We are both competitive people.

"We have a tie between two comics, and we're going to do something unusual."

I look at Royce, whose face is ashen. My heart thuds.

The judge hesitates before saying, "Royce Taslim—and Agnes Chan!"

The room around us erupts in a spectrum of responses, ranging from dismay to congratulations. Next to me, Royce is silent, and I don't know how to construe his response. Every muscle in my gut knots.

The judge says, "We're going to need the audience to decide for us tonight. Royce and Agnes, please come to the front of the stage."

We do that and the judge says to the crowd, "Now, you're going to decide who goes with a final clap-out! The performer with the loudest clap goes through."

My stomach drops and I freeze. A popularity contest. I'm a goner.

The judge waves at Royce. "Let's hear it for Royce!"

The audience shouts and screams so loud it is like we're swimming in it. My heart lifts for him.

Then at me. "Let's hear it for Agnes!"

I am overwhelmed by the sheer force of the noise. Next to me, Royce is clapping and cheering for me.

"Great! Great! Wonderful!" She frowns. The other judges, who are facing the stage, shrug. "Er. Let's do the exercise again!"

They go through three rounds without a clear winner. People are filming us with their phones now. It's a tie. Lola excuses herself and joins the judges offstage. They consult among themselves, looking unsure.

There's a break in the noise when Vern waves at the audience and flashes that lopsided, disarming grin of his. He raises his arm to signal he needs to speak, and a hush descends.

Vern starts pacing onstage.

"Now, folks, we know that a female comic is a minority in this business, right? How many of such comics did you see onstage today, including Agnes? Three out of ten?"

The audience murmurs.

He stops. "That's right, it's tough being a woman in this space. They have to deal with so much more crap as performers. So how about we give Agnes Chan a little more support? Come on, she deserves it. Let's do this again, Royce versus Agnes, tiebreaker! For Royce!"

The clapping dims a little.

"For Agnes!"

This time, there is a clear winner.

Lola trots up stage, relief visible on her face. "All right, everyone, it seems we do have our second winner. Let's give it up for Agnes Chan! The crowd has spoken. Agnes Chan wins second place!"

The applause crashes on us again.

I fall to my knees onstage, tears in my eyes. I can't believe it: I am going to New York.

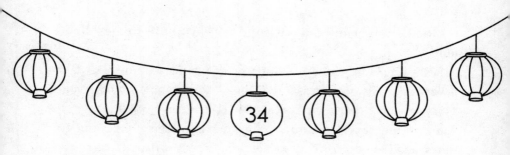

"CONGRATULATIONS," ROYCE SAYS.

I get up shakily and see that he's smiling, a pained smile that is nevertheless genuine. He pulls me to him and hugs me tightly, whispering his congratulations. "I always knew you could do it."

I stare at him wildly. "But . . . but it's . . . You're not . . ."

He shrugs. "That's life, isn't it? Nobody is owed success at all."

Then Lola taps me on the shoulder and asks me to follow her. "You and Vern have to provide some sound bites for the press."

I follow her through a fog of elation.

The next hour passes in a blur. Vern and I are paraded across the stage, there's a ceremony and the judges shake our hands, photos are taken, and then the audience starts to file out, and I look around for Royce, who is no longer there.

Vern taps me on the shoulder and asks for a moment. Lola murmurs an excuse and leaves us to chat.

"We did it. So, how does it feel to be a finalist in the most prestigious under-twenty-five international comedy competition?" Vern says quietly.

"I didn't need your help," I say. I flash back on the lingering hug and shivered. "Any of it."

Vern clears his throat. "Agnes, I'm sorry about what happened with Royce."

I look straight in his eyes. "And what you did to me," I add quietly.

"That hug? Oh, come on, don't be dramatic. It's not like we've never hugged before. It was a *hug*, Agnes. I don't know why everyone always assumes that any physical contact between a boy and a girl is automatically sexual in nature. You and I have been alone countless times, and I've never, ever done anything inappropriate to you."

"That didn't come off as appropriate."

Vern throws his arms up. "I'm sorry you feel that way. You're completely miscasting my actions. I can't help how Royce feels about you—or you about Royce, it seems."

I bite my lip. When he puts it this way . . . "What about that clap-off? Everything you said?"

"I didn't help you. I merely clarified things, sped the decision-making up. You deserved that spot."

"Did I?" I counter.

He scoffs. "Oh, Agnes, grow up. You can't win without hurting people. Only winners get far in life. I thought you got that. You and I, we're cut from the same cloth. We both want to win."

"We're not the same," I say slowly.

"I had your best interests at heart," Vern insists. "I promise you. Think about it. Who's been helping you this entire time, with no expectations? And more importantly, haven't I always acted correctly when we're alone?"

I think about our time together and have to concede that he's right. He'd never ever behaved inappropriately with me.

"You may not agree with my methods and ways, but I've always looked out for you, you know that. I'm sorry, really, if I crossed a line."

He sounds sincere, and I thaw. "Okay," I mumble.

He clasps my hands briefly and then releases them. "I've got you, Agnes. Don't you forget that." He nods at me. "I'll see you on the bus."

"I need some space," I say.

"That's fine," he says. "I'll give you all the space and time you need. Just remember that I'm on your side."

As I leave the theater I see Royce, waiting for me. His eyes are red but he's smiling. Jit is lurking a few meters away, pretending to study the stage.

"I wish we could have gone to the finals together."

"It's okay," he says, shaking his head. "We don't all— We don't always get what we want . . . and that's okay. That's life."

That's what a loser would say to comfort himself, Vern says in my head.

"But this was so important for you."

Royce places a hand on my face and strokes it. "Agnes, I'm so happy for you, really. I don't have to get everything I want, but I'd like to think . . . I'd like to think I won something more important today, something I've always wanted." He steps closer to me, and behind him, Jit mutters that he's going out to smoke, and he'd be back in a few minutes.

"And what would that be?" I whisper, my blood crashing in my ears. Even though I know what will happen next, what must happen, what we've been drawing toward since that day in his room, I need him to say it first. I need him to tell me what I've been wanting to hear from him clearly, irrevocably, so I can leap into the dark with my eyes wide open, so I can believe.

"You," he says, his eyes pinning me to him as he envelops me in his arms, tips my chin up, and finally, finally, we kiss.

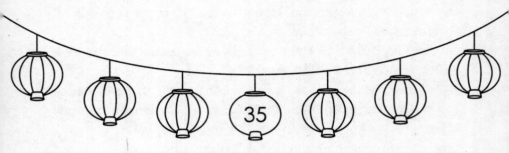

Me: Scream!!!
Zee: SCREAM!
Me: I KNOW! I can't believe I'm going to New York
Zee: Oh, I thought you were talking about Royce and you, K-I-S-S-I-N-G in the freaking Capitol Theatre!

Obviously, I told Zee literally seconds after I unlocked lips from Royce.

Me: That too! SCREAM!

"Shhhhh!" someone in the row in front of me hisses.

I am on the bus back to Malaysia with Vern, although we are seated three rows apart. It was a mutual decision, although there have been moments in the almost-six-hour journey that I missed having him next to me, and I think he did, too. I caught him checking up on me.

Royce: Have a safe journey home 🌀 🖤 🌀
Me (screenshots): Oh my gaaaaaaaawd Z look what he just texted me
Zee: OMG BOY HAS THE HOTS FOR YOU
Me: HE SO TOTALLY DOES!!

Zee: SQQQQQUUUEEEEEEEEEEE SO TELL ME, WAS THERE
TOUNNG?

Me: what?

Zee: 👅 I didn't know how to spell 👅

Me: NOT GOING TO TELL

Me: 👅

Me: Aha ha. Ahahahahah! So much tongue. A tongue tsunami!

Zee: Ewww Agnes GROSS stop TMI I used to LIKE ROYCE

Me: !!! You're right, oh my gosh, that is so INAPPROPRIATE of me

Me: Apologies

Zee: Ahhaahahaha, as if! This barely registers on my gross-o-
meter! Give me all the deets and GET IN THERE! 👅 🦉

Me: 🍆

Zee: I love you

Me: You too

Up front, three rows away, I hear Vern say, "Agnes, please. I can hear
you texting from over here."

"Shut up, Vern," I say.

I'm absolutely wired, and it's not just because I'm going to New
York, it's because—it's because I can't stop replaying the moment of
Royce's kiss.

The way his eyelashes fluttered down. The way every second grew
taut with longing until our lips met at last, and then every fiber of my
being flooded with light even as my eyes closed, as we met again and
again, each kiss a caress. And as his kisses grew surer, he pulled me
to him, deepening the pressure until our lips parted and—

I give out the world's tiniest, most silent squee.

~

The reckoning comes as soon as I arrive home late the next morning
after a short nap at Zee's.

After I get home, I find my mother is waiting for me in the living room, Stanley having left for some conference. She holds up her phone, where an announcement of the winners of the semifinals have been announced in the local daily. I'm there, front and center onstage, with Vern next to me.

"Oh shit," I say. "I didn't know that old media could be so fast." I give her my best resting winner face even though I'm feeling anything but winnerly.

"Get some breakfast and we'll talk," she says.

After breakfast, she sits me down.

"So you weren't with Zee yesterday."

"No. And I'm sorry you found out this way." My poor heart has been through a lot these past twenty-four hours. I try to keep my answers light even as I scan her for signs of distress.

She purses her lips but seems remarkably calm. "Was this your first time? Using Zee as an excuse?"

I avert my eyes. "Urms . . . mayhap?"

She shakes her head, disappointment lacing her words. "I didn't like finding out you were in Singapore from the freaking *national papers,* and I certainly don't appreciate finding out about the times you lied to us about hanging out with her when you were performing stand-up. Why couldn't you tell me?"

I hesitate. This would be a good opportunity to tell my mother that I'd been keeping all kinds of things from her my entire adolescence, to preserve her sanity. It would be a good time to come clean, since she appears calm. But I have firsthand experience seeing her being calm and fine, until she wasn't. And with her on pregnancy meds, which I'd read online meant adjusted or lower doses of what she usually consumed or different drugs altogether, I just can't risk it.

I say, "I didn't want to jinx it by saying something—I wanted it to be a nice surprise when I won." I didn't tell her how stressed I had been. A few years ago, I'd made the decision to keep my mom out, to show her only the happy, thriving part of me, and now I find it hard to change the settings, to be vulnerable, unsure in front of her. I do this to preserve her. I find myself thinking of Vern in spite of all the messy things that have happened between us—he'd understand. He does this for his aunt. "I didn't want to tell you until I was sure."

My mother's eyes grow sad. "I would have liked to share in the journey with you, honey."

"What's my punishment?" I ask, eager to end the conversation. We just don't have that relationship.

"You're grounded for a week," she says. "I know what a social butterfly you are."

She really doesn't know me.

She hands me an envelope. "This came for you."

My stomach drops; I had forgotten about the letter that Rosie had been talking about.

"Do you need some privacy?" she asks.

I nod and she heads to the dining room.

The envelope is stamped with the blue logo of Rhode Island College of the Arts. I open it slowly and read the words with disbelief.

Rhode Island College of the Arts—one of the backup options Ms. Tina had asked me to consider—is offering me a generous partial scholarship covering more than half my college fees, a scholarship reserved for international students in leadership positions. I can't believe it. My emotions are jumbled, the news bittersweet. Rhode Island isn't a fancy Ivy League school or even a top state school like what I'd been set up to go to, but it's an NCAA Division II school in women's track, it's in New England, and they have a very highly regarded creative writing program, should I want to major in that one day.

It's perfect.

I sit down on the floor with a loud thud that brings everyone in.

"Are you okay?" Mom asks.

I wordlessly hand her the letter.

"Oh wow," she says, sitting down slowly with an even louder thud on the floor. Rosie flops down next to her theatrically. "Et tu, Agnes?" she says. "Will you betray me so?"

"*Oh wow* is right," I say.

"Creative writing?" my mother says.

"Drama queen," Rosie says.

"We can't afford to help out with the fees and living costs," my mother says, looking pained.

"I know," I say hurriedly. "I don't expect you to. I can always defer a year, start working toward the goal of saving enough for school."

"A whole year?"

"Makes sense—maybe my leg will miraculously revert to its original state and I can use that time to earn enough money to go to college. It's absolutely fine," I say. And should I place in the JOGGCo competition . . .

A small flame of hope kindles in my chest.

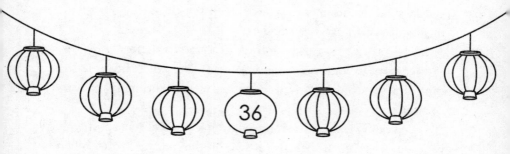

36

A FEW DAYS AFTER THE RHODE ISLAND OFFER ARRIVES, VERN COMES TO my shift at the Grub Hub with a candy bouquet and more apologies. His sincerity thaws the last of my anger, and I decide to give him another chance. I can't discount the many times he'd come to my aid when no one did, so I tell myself that sometimes things aren't always so black and white—I should know.

I don't expect anyone to care about my win, but I'm swamped by well-wishers at school, in person, and over social media. I get DMs from everyone, from the Flashes—Suraya and Tavleen going as far as to post a flashback reel of us, laughing, arm in arm after a meet. Everyone just loves a winner, especially one that's going places, by which I mean places that matter to my generation—the internet. When TentPole Productions posted one of my bits on a reel, and Taylor Addison, one of the hottest zillennial stand-up comics, liked it and commented as much, the numbers of my social media followers ballooned overnight. What's more, the JOGGCo competition has become a legit mainstream hit beyond the region, thanks in part to many of the bits that have gone viral on TikTok, so much so that TentPole Productions posted that exciting new developments are in the works.

Not everyone is impressed by my new celebrity fandom, though. Vern sees the reel from Suraya and screenshots it, saying, Faker.

I know, I type. But what can I do?

Call her out, he says. Expose that fake little ass kisser.

I don't want to, and he needles me. Says I'm too nice. But what's the point? I'm back on top, and it feels good, and this time I won't have a shelf life.

I'd been doing things all wrong, chasing top scores in a sport where everybody has a shelf life. In comedy, on the internet, you—by and more importantly, your money-generating content—can live as long as you want, if you play it right.

I try to catch up with Royce, but he seems preoccupied. Every time he sees me, he smiles, waves, and ducks into the nearest open door, which I'm sure has nothing to do with me. It must be the upcoming exams in a month—the last ones for seniors—which finish about two weeks before we fly to New York during spring break. I hold back from telling him about Rhode Island, not just because it is a pipe dream still, but also because every fleeting encounter we have in person feels like he's radiating stress.

Yet on texts—he's the same Royce, only more affectionate than ever.

Royce: Sorry I'm a bit absent. It's not a good time, we'll connect after the exams . . . but I can't stop thinking of you xoxo

Royce: I love that you're taking off xx

Royce: You make my whole being light up, I can't wait to be with you once this madness is over xx

Royce: Dreamed of you last night, wish I had you here for real in my arms . . . xo

~

I'm so distracted by everything that's going on with my upcoming exams and shifts and stand-up that I almost miss the update on the

Instagram account of TentPole Productions, Lai's "friend" Nigel's events company.

The post says: Following the overwhelming interest in the competition, the organizers have discussed with all relevant parties, including the event sponsors Frisson Cola and Swoosh Airlines, and have come to the decision that we will allow 3 contestants from both legs of the competition to go through, instead of 2. The prizes also been adjusted upward to USD25,000 , USD15,000, and USD10,000 for first, second, and third prize respectively. May the best comic win.

TentPole explains in the post's comments that the organizers had officially changed the format of the competition so that the finals would have six contestants, instead of four, thanks to the expanded budget approved by its original sponsors and the production company that would allow more broadcast time for the finale.

I almost drop my phone in surprise and happiness—what a miracle! That means Royce will be coming with me to New York! His journey isn't over yet. And that prize money is mind-boggling. I'm even more determined to win.

I message Zee with the update.

Zee: Er, sign from the heavens that you guys are meant to be? Woo-hoo!
Zee: 😊
Zee: Oh wait, sorry that was meant for someone else.
Me: Ew?

Then I text Royce: HAVE YOU HEARD? ON THE COMIC COMPETITION? CONGRATS??! Xoxo

Royce reads the text—I see the green ticks. He doesn't reply.

I send him two more gentle nudges after a couple of hours. He doesn't reply.

I drop a kiss emoji. Nothing. It's now been eighteen hours.

Give him another day, my inner voice urges.

Burn him! another voice that sounds strangely like Rosie says cheerfully.

I go to sleep, uneasy.

The next day, TentPole Productions releases another post on IG: The secret is out! We've been teasing the identity of the comic the winner of this inaugural JOGGCo Young Comedian Competition will open for, and here it is at last!

The lucky winner will have five minutes to open for red-hot Canadian comedian Amina Kaur on the first night of the New York leg of her nationwide tour at the Comedy City!

Vern texts me: AMINA KAUR! Opening for her 🫠

Me: I KNOW!

I try once more to reach out to Royce.

Me: Have you heard? We have a chance to perform for our favorite comic!

Thirty-eight minutes later—

Royce: 👍

THUMBS-UP? What am I, his grandmother?

What's going on? I type, dread settling over me. Tell me the truth.

Royce: I'm sorry. . . . It's . . . it's complicated.

Royce is typing. He stays typing for the longest time.

And then, for whatever reason, he goes dark.

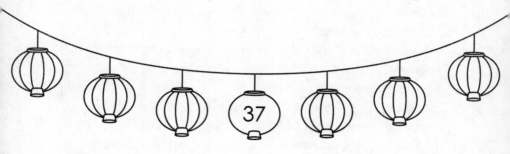

A WEEK PASSES. I GO TO SCHOOL. I GO HOME. I PLAY VIDEO GAMES.

I rage at Zee, who is surprised and sad by Royce's ghosting. I rage at Vern, who stopped by to see me at Grub Hub after a shift and says, "Maybe he doesn't want to be involved with the competition."

I balk when I realize he means me. "I—I don't . . . it can't be."

Vern flicks a speck of dust off his uniform. "Who knows. He's so used to getting what he wants in life, he probably doesn't know how to deal with you being in his way."

A dead weight settles in my stomach. My mouth is dry, unpleasant.

"Watch out for speeding Vellfires if you're alone in a dark alley," Vern says. He's joking, but I see it in my mind's eye: one of Royce's drivers/backup bodyguard, eyes narrowed, driving his Vellfire at me, who is somehow cornered in a dead end with nowhere to run from my impending doom. The face shimmers and changes, and then it becomes Royce.

Insomnia, something I haven't had a problem with since I was twelve, returns to haunt me. I head down one evening to fix myself a hot Milo when I see someone in the living room watching the news on silent. It's my mom.

"Hey," I say, joining her. "Can't sleep?"

"I should ask the same," she replies, arching an eyebrow. "Isn't it a bit late for you to be up."

"I was practicing for my set," I say, glossing over my heartbreak.

She gestures at her stomach. "Well, kiddo is practicing martial arts in there, and I figured I'd wait till she's calmed down before going back up."

We sit and watch, not watch, the news in silence.

"How are you feeling?" I ask.

"I'm good. I'm really enjoying being pregnant again. I didn't think I would, at my age, with all the things I've got going on."

An unexplained emotion rises in my chest.

My mother grins and musses my hair. "I remember when I had you, things were simpler. All I had to focus on was you."

I look at her. "But you were a student. And then you weren't. Things were . . . different. You had no choice but to focus on me."

The things that aren't said descend around us.

"I *had* a choice," my mother says after a silence so loud my ears ring at it. "I chose you."

"You say that."

Her voice hitches. "Agnes, it's true."

Maybe because it's dark and it's late, the words that I've been keeping in since she first told me about my bio dad tumble out easier. "Maybe you couldn't *not* have me, because of your parents." My mother's parents are Catholic, very, very religious and very conservative. They'd done their duty when she was pregnant to make sure she had me, and then they cut off all ties with us when it was clear my mother wouldn't be marrying anytime soon.

My mother flinches, and her face in the blue light of the TV is even paler than it normally is. "Th-that's not what happened! Of course I had a choice when it came to you. I *chose* to have you."

I get up. "Mom, it's fine. It's in the past. I know you love me now." I'd earned her love after all, bit by bit. And for everything I had cost her, I would repay her one day. "I'm going to bed."

"You've got everything wrong," she says quietly. "You are my pride and joy, from day one."

I stand in the landing and look down at her. "That's not how I remember it," I say; then I enter my room and shut the door.

~

The strange thing is Royce's weird radio silence is actually good for my concentration. Now that I know Rhode Island is an option, I've redoubled my efforts to boost my grades.

With my stand-up finals in place, I put my head down and study with Zee, who's morphed, overnight, into a bit of a scary taskmaster. Zee's drawn up spreadsheets on what we need to do to punch up our "problem subjects" and found a TikTok on how to biohack our brains and our bodies so we can absorb more knowledge on less sleep—she is generally experimenting on us. Her cooks whip up nutrient dense foods with ingredients like wild salmon, kale, goji berries, and macadamias, while she screams "Hydrate!" every thirty minutes like some scary, water-obsessed version of Coach Everett.

And because her tutor, Mas, had given good feedback to my parents, I'm allowed to attend a rare stopover gig from eminent Swedish comedian Lars Peterson in Kuala Lumpur, who was heading to China for a tour. Lai has a spare ticket, so I am kind of their date. Given the past few weeks and how wound up I've been, I was so grateful for their generosity that I practically prostrated myself before them when they asked me at the last open-mike gig.

We're midway through the opening act, an up-and-coming local comic named Jeff See, when I see Royce a few rows ahead of me with someone I recognize from school, one of his teammates, and everything turns on a dime. My cheerful mood evaporates. "That asshole is here?"

Lai sighs. "What happened?"

"Royce. We *kissed* in Singapore, and I thought maybe . . . I don't know . . . that he was my . . . that he cared for me?" I can't bring myself to say the word *boyfriend*. "And now he's ghosting me, and I don't know why!"

Lai raises their eyes to the ceiling. "Oh boy," they mutter.

I shake my head. "And now, of all the things he could be doing, he chooses to come to my show. The nerve!"

Several people whip around and shush me, and Royce, perhaps noticing the disturbance in the Force, turns and sees me. He has the good grace to look embarrassed as his teammate, Han or something, elbows him with a grin. "Can we talk outside?" he whispers.

"No!" I whisper back. "It's too late now."

"Get out," the people around us hiss.

Lai palms their face. "This is the last time I'm asking a teenager to join me for a show."

Royce heads to the exit, and Jit, who'd been sitting a few rows back, slips out to follow him.

Once outside, Royce turns toward me with the stoic expression of someone who knows he has it coming, only he isn't sure how he will be ended. Even Jit looks afraid of my expression.

"Go on," Royce says.

"Me? You tell me what's going on," I say, getting angrier by the moment.

He shakes his head. "I don't know where to even begin."

Royce's SUV pulls up just then, presumably because the driver thinks he's leaving the venue. The door opens, and I notice something on the floor of the vehicle.

A lime-green paper bag bearing a dancing lemur logo and that of TentPole Productions and the streaming company's logo.

Something clicks in my brain.

The dancing lemur. The same insignia that I'd seen on the screens at the charity ball. On his polos and tissue box in his room.

Frisson Cola's logo.

"What is that?" I say, pointing at the paper bag with those two logos side by side, my mouth dry.

Royce blanches. "It's . . . it's . . ." He swallows. "It's not what you think."

A fury I'd never experienced before engulfs me. I hiss, "I think it's exactly what I think it is."

It all seems pretty clear to me now. It wasn't hard to put two and two together. When Royce shed his Ray person and competed under his name—well, half of his real name anyway—Frisson Cola, which was probably part of the F&B conglomerate held by Royce's family, decided to increase the sponsorship so that their precious son could scrape through. That's why he was acting so shifty over the past few weeks, literally right after we'd kissed.

Maybe he'd kissed me because he wanted a backup plan, as a way to manipulate my feelings, and I'd let him. Why else would he have done it? He could have had anyone he wanted. It had to have been some kind of power play.

Vern had been right all along.

A surge of humiliation as thick as bile rises through me. "You pulled strings to get to the finals, didn't you? Frisson Cola's sudden generosity?"

Royce starts shaking his head. "No. I did no such thing. Frisson Cola is not a company controlled in any way by my family."

"Oh please," I scoff. "It's what, one of your dad's golf buddies' companies, then? That's how it works, right?"

Royce stills. "Agnes, I had nothing to do with this. Neither did my father. I asked. This was his business partner's decision."

"Sure," I sneer. "Sure. Zero conflict of interest here. Poor, innocent Royce!" I turn away and start jogging to the street, while trying to hail a cab through a maelstrom of competing emotions. *It's not an act,* I think to myself, desperately blinking back tears. *I am a fool. A naive, silly fool of a girl.* But I'm not going to cry in front of him.

Royce catches up to me and tries to grab my wrist. Jit trails us uncertainly, his expression one of deep unhappiness. "Please, Agnes, I had nothing to do with this. Nothing."

"Just because you weren't the one to pull the trigger doesn't mean you didn't supply the ammo, that you didn't sanction it."

"What can I do to make this better?"

"You can drop out of the competition."

"What?" Royce looks genuinely riled now. "That's ridiculous. I did not influence the judging at all. The judges are independent, selected by TentPole! I got third place, fair and square."

"And you wouldn't have made it to the finals if your daddy's friend hadn't paid your way in."

"He acted on his own, and neither me nor my dad did anything to encourage this decision. We didn't even know until it had been decided."

"So what? You still benefitted from it."

"Like you benefitted from Vern's intervention at the clap-off?" he says softly.

I reel as though I'd been slapped. A twist of guilt flares in my gut. "I had nothing to do with *that*," I snarl.

"Same as I had nothing to do with this," he insists. He reaches out for me again. "Look, Agnes, let's work together to fix this. I only found out after the extra slots had been announced, and I wanted to tell you. I had a huge argument with my dad asking him to ask his friend to rescind it, because I know how it will look if anyone finds out about their link, but I was prevented from doing so because it wasn't just his friend, the other sponsor also agreed to do it and it had been announced. . . . Look, we're in the same boat. I didn't ask for any of this."

I recoil. It's true that Vern's offhand comments had swayed the judging, I couldn't deny that. But having Daddy's friends pay your way to a competition—how is that even in the same league as what happened with Vern?

"I've been thinking about this for ages, and there's no way I can resolve this fairly," he says.

"Declare a conflict of interest to the judges and see what they say."

He throws his arms up. "But why? There *was* no conflict of interest at the judging. And there won't be at the finals either." The judging is supposed to be done by a panel of stand-up comics, whose identities were still unknown. "But if you make me declare this, then my reputation will very likely be ruined, Agnes. Forever."

"If you're not declaring a conflict of interest at very least, save whatever you want to say for the next fool," I say, pushing his arm away. "Touch me again and I'll start to scream."

Royce drops his hand. I hail a cab I can't afford and jump in, just before the tears come for real.

~

I text Zee, asking her to call me. When she does, the words spill out of me, hot and furious, and for once she is speechless.

After a while, she ventures to say, "Look, I think it's not necessarily so black and white."

Of course she would say that, Vern's voice speaks up. *Her family is an old politically connected dynasty, they probably deal in gray areas like this all the time. Wink, wink, nudge, nudge, eh?*

"I disagree," I say to Zee. "Some things are pretty black and white, to me at least. I just think that sometimes an omission can be just as bad as an action. Also, I've never been comfortable with these types of string pulling." I make my voice high-pitched and grating, "Oh please, I'll donate a hospital wing if you allow me to be a patient in your drug trial! Please, let my son get into Harvard, I'll donate a quarter million! It's a competitive tender and your offer isn't, but because you and I are university mates, I'll accept your bid!"

There's a sharp intake of breath and I realize, too late, that there's been a recent case in Zee's extended family that mirrors the last scenario. "I'll respect your decision," Zee says curtly, "but in this instance at least, I don't think this case is as clear-cut as that."

"Vern says—"

Zee interrupts, "I don't put much stock in anything that boy says."

I stare at the phone, stung. Why is Zee reacting so badly to Vern? Why does she hate him so much?

"Are you jealous of Vern?"

"Urgh, absolutely not. He's got nothing I want."

Zee didn't mean it that way, but all of a sudden I hear Vern's voice in my head: *For people like Zee, it's all about what you have to offer to them. For now, she's interested in you because you're different. She and Royce exist in a cocoon, in their own hermetically sealed world. You are interesting to her because you are everything she isn't, and she's a voyeur, isn't she? With her fascination with reality TV, the hoi polloi. When she graduates, she's going to a non-Ivy college, right? Berkeley, was it? Film and media undergrad? Wow. Once she's there in California and finds herself surrounded by cooler versions of you, you'll no longer be special. She'll drop you like a stone. You'll lose her.*

My eyes blur. "Just because Vern isn't like you, you look down on him," I say. "You don't see what I see because he has nothing to offer you."

"TF? What the hell are you even on? Have you completely lost it?"

Dump her first, Vern's voice advises.

"Now that senior year is almost over, we're no longer going to have anything in common."

That's not true, another voice, possibly mine, squeaks. I think about our inside jokes about other Dunians, our love for what we called non-rom K-dramedies, our little textual shorthands. *Abort mission! Abort mission!*

But I can't stop. Vern is right. She's not from my world—she never was. She's already a star, and I'm a speck of stardust.

"Maybe this is the end of the road for our friendship, Zee."

A jagged intake of breath issues from my phone. It only took five minutes to undo four years of friendship. My lips tremble and I have to jam my fist in my mouth to prevent myself from howling.

"Agnes, wh-what . . . n-no, don't."

I hang up on her and block her number before my resolve breaks down.

My phone buzzes.

Royce: Agnes, please
Royce: What can I do?

My fingers quake as I type out: You can stop contacting me and drop out of the competition

Royce: I deserve to be in this competition. I got where I did, fair and square. We were tied at no. 2 on points! And no one knew who I was. I went onstage officially as Royce Lim in the semis, you know that
Me: I don't know what you're capable of anymore tbh
Royce: Winning at all costs isn't my thing. But I'm starting to think it's yours
Me: Don't insult me. I'm a fair competitor
Royce: So when Vern helps you, that's fair?
Me: Low jab for the person who pulls strings to get where he wants to go
Royce: For the last time, I had nothing . . . my family had nothing to do with that. I thought you knew me better than that
Me: So did I

~

It's midnight. My heart hurts. My head however is clear as day.

I don't want Royce to drop out. I don't want him to go through, either. Not until it is objectively determined that there isn't a conflict of interest.

I need to talk to someone. Someone who understands.

I video-call Vern and tell him everything.

"I can't say I'm surprised," Vern says, making a face. "Another rich boy manipulates the situation to get what he wants."

"Zee . . . Zee doesn't think he did anything wrong."

Vern's laughter has a cruel, mocking ring to it. "Of course she'd take his side! I *warned* you this would happen. They always look out for their own." He sighs. "Agnes, you really are too nice. Anyway, what do you think we should do?"

"We?"

"Sure," Vern says. "We have to do something. It's only fair if we expose him."

"I . . . I don't know."

"I don't know why you are always looking out for Royce. He certainly wasn't looking out for you throughout this competition."

"What do you mean?"

"Well, how much help was he, tutoring you? Didn't he *refuse* to be your peer tutor?"

"It's . . . er, I mean . . ." I hesitate. Actually, I had been the one who decided to stop getting tutored by Royce sometime after our third or fourth session (Mas was more than enough help, plus I caught myself staring at Royce when I thought he wasn't looking, even when we were in a group) but he could have fought harder to help me, right? Like Vern had been doing. Fighting for me.

"And super-convenient timing of how he kissed you, only when he thought he had no chance of progressing in the competition. And didn't he just *avoid* you as soon as you officially become competition again? Not exactly someone who puts you first."

It's hard not to find Royce's behavior damning when it's cast that way.

"I can't—I don't have the headspace for this now. My final exams start tomorrow."

"I understand," Vern says. "And I wish with all my heart the timing was better. But this is important. The finals for the competition are in two weeks. We should strike when the iron is hot."

"What are you planning on doing, then?" I ask, uneasy all of a sudden remembering Kima's slashed tires. "I don't want to hurt him."

Vern's face breaks into an easy-going smile. "Leave it to me, then."

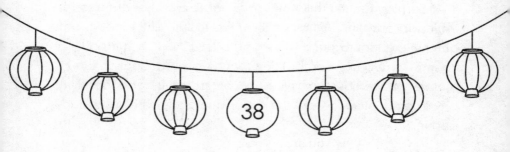

38

AsiaOnlyNews.com

Breaking news! Gossip has it that billionaire Peter Taslim's scion Royce Taslim is in the finals of the inaugural JOGGCo International Young Comedians Competition—and he has his daddy to thank for it.

According to an inside source, Frisson Cola offered to sponsor Taslim Junior's spot in the competition when the CEO, a friend of Taslim Senior, was prompted to do so by Taslim Senior. How cheeky! Wonder what else Royce has had help from Senior with?

HotGossipLah.com

What would you do if you missed out on a spot in an international competition?

If you're Royce Taslim, apparently, all you have to do is run to Daddy and ask him to get his friends to pump money into the event. This is allegedly the reason why the sponsors for JOGGCo International Young Comedians Competition suddenly decided to let Taslim, who was ousted in the semis, enter the finals. Talk about privilege!

The Singaporean Times

According to the family, which released a statement through their publicist Nina Bell, nobody in the Taslim family induced or otherwise encouraged the co-sponsor of JOGGCo International Young Comedians Competition to increase the pool of finalists therein. Ms. Bell insists that Frisson Cola acted independently of any external influence, but the social media backlash has already begun.

@TentPoleProductions TentPole Productions would like to assure everyone that the competition was judged fairly and at no point in time did the judges receive any monetary compensation or otherwise to let Royce Taslim compete in the finals. In fact, up till the semis, Royce Taslim used a pseudonym to compete and was careful to keep his real identity secret.

The judges, event organizers, and the production house stand by Royce Taslim, who is an outstanding young talent.

@sassybrekkie21: #IStandByRoyce And @HeyRoyceTaslim, please feel free to slide into my DMs or more 😊

@BoyWandering097: Rite? Isn't he luscious? RoyceT is my jam! I want to slurp that yummy treat rite up. No way he could be a cheat with a face like an angel.

@danyulbebe: Rich Good 4Nothing dickhole #FuckTheTaslims

@you_turn_here: I'll bet his family sacrifices virgins to get where they got. Watch my YT expose on the Taslims here#DirtyBillions

@neitherhill: Innocent until proven dirty #IStandByRoyce

@BetchesBeKillin: Typical of the patriarchy

@GIRLCOMEDIAN00: Honestly, poor @VernChaz and @ReallyAgnes, way to have the rich worm their way in #TrueWinners

@Thedukeofalltruths: He definitely cheated! It's a fact that he cheats for everything, even in sports! I saw it!

@badbabybunh: The School @DuniaIntSchool should expel R*yce T*slim immediately! We have receipts of him cheating in a MAJOR COMPETITION and they stay silent! SILENCE IS COMPLICITY!

~

Me: Royce, please pick up the phone
Me: I'm so, so sorry
Me: I had nothing to do with this
Me: It wasn't me, I swear
Me: Please

I see Royce typing, but nothing comes through.
What have I done?

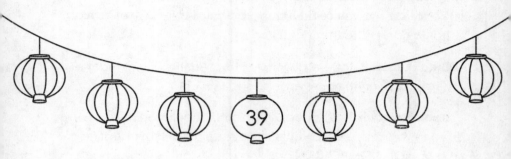

WITH EVERY DM, EVERY MESSAGE, EVERY NEWS STORY, POST, MY WORLD
shrinks and presses down on me till I can barely breathe. Although
it's only been three days since Vern leaked this story online, it feels
like an eternity has passed. I can't imagine how bad it must be for
Royce.

Thinking about Royce and Vern and Zee, about the whole fiasco,
incapacitates me. I can't even pretend I'm okay in front of my parents,
my mom.

I have locked myself in the room, dazed and nauseous. It doesn't
matter that I have two more weeks of school after this, or the Young
Comedians Competition, I decide. I will never leave my room again.

Vern calls me and I ignore it, but after a dozen more tries, I shakily
pick up.

"Hey, are you okay? I've been trying to reach you for ages," he says,
sounding concerned.

"Why?" I choke out. "Why did you leak it?"

There's a silence, a silence so long and profound, I worry I might
have lost my mind and had imagined him calling me, when I hear a
soft chuckle.

"Because you wanted me to."

My stomach bottoms out. "I wanted *no such thing*."

"Well, Agnes, you could have fooled me. Anyway, if you're record-ing this, I am admitting nothing, and if any texts were exchanged between us on the subject matter, they've been erased."

Fool. I've been a fool.

"I thought you'd be happy with the fact that the expose happened when all your exams were done with, at least."

"I didn't ask for this," I say shakily, as though I could undo every-thing, turn back time. "I didn't."

He actually laughs out loud. "You asked for it in everything but name."

I'm shaking my head. "No. No I did not. I thought . . . I thought you had something less—less life-wrecking!"

"God, Agnes, face it, stop being a faux innocent. You *knew* this is what I was going to do. The fact is, Agnes—you want to win as much as I do. We're winners. This is what we *do*."

Is he right? Could I be as heartless and vile as Vern? Because that is what he is, I realize now. Cold and manipulative. "No. This was disproportionate, what you did."

"It did spin a little out of control, I'll admit," he says. "But you know how these things go. They always go away for guys like Royce. Don't you worry about it. But at least we—we'll get a chance at the fair competition we were supposed to have."

"I don't want anything to do with you, ever again," I say.

A note of uncertainty cracks his bravado. "Y-you don't mean that."

"I'm not kidding, Vern. You're not a good influence on me. I'm done."

He scoffs, "You say that now, but when you're all alone, when all your popular friends have dumped you—again I might add—you'll come back. And guess what? I'll be here for you when no one is. Where's Zee in all of this?"

"She's—she's standing by me," I lie.

"Uh-huh." His voice smooths again. "Don't you see? You can't rely on any of those flaky fakes. I'm your best friend. Your only friend. Your *true* friend."

He made it sound so . . . so . . . true. Panic rises in my throat. The only constant in these bewildering months has been Vern—I can't deny it. But why does being his friend come with so much toxicity? I shake my head to clear it. "No. No more of your bullshit, Vern. Th-this isn't what friendship is supposed to be like. . . . I don't even think you see me as a friend.

He raises his voice. "Agnes, I told you—you're more than that. You're family. That means I'll be here waiting for you until you realize how much you *need* me. I—"

I hang up, trembling. If Vern is right, then I'm all alone now. I wrap my arms around my body and wait for the shivers to leave. They don't.

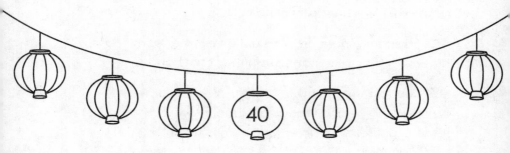

40

@**VernChaz** Justice @TentPoleProductions @FrissonCola @SwooshAirlines #IDontStandWithRoyce

@**TentPoleProductions** Update: We are still in discussions with our sponsors. We urge to everyone address their concerns in a civil manner and to not dox or send death threats. We will be involving the police should we feel that our contestants and our crew are unsafe.

StraitsNews.com

In a rare interview with the media, former beauty queen Ming Taslim speaks to our reporter Alisha Carter about a conspiracy to target her son and their family, by extension. Here are some key moments as transcribed:

> **MT:** "I want to state unequivocally that my family had nothing to do with this sponsorship. My son has been through a lot this past week. He's had death threats! He wanted to drop out to spare our family further controversy, and at first my husband and I were on board, but after much discussion, we decided

that it wouldn't fix the problem. It would look like we were guilty when we are guilty of nothing."

AC:. "Certainly there are trolls out there who seem determined to take matters into their own hands—"

MT: "I've told my son many times that some sectors of entertainment—and I speak as someone who's had some experience as an entertainer, Alisha, mind you— is just brimming with toxicity, and stand-up is one of them. Let's talk about #MeToo and how we still haven't resolved some of allegations brought up against famous comics. . . ."

@TentPoleProductions We have received official notice of a contestant dropping out due to the media scrutiny. We are unable to release their name for now. Thank you for your understanding.

@FrissonCola We would like to state unequivocally that our decision to increase the sponsorship amount was agreed independently with the co-sponsor in light of the overwhelming interest in the competition even before the finals and was not intended to benefit Royce Taslim.

In light of the controversy, we are in discussions with another sponsor to take over our amount, so that there is no longer any contention about the independence of the competition.

If no sponsor can be found in time for the finals in four days, it is likely that the event will be canceled.

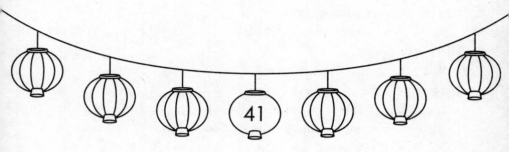

41

THERE'S NO LIGHT.

There's no hope.

It's over. I'd ruined my life and Royce's. And I don't know how to fix things.

After three tumultuous days of refusing to go to school, of refusing to leave my room and only eating whatever was left outside my door on a tray, of not telling them what was going on beyond pleading that I was sick, I finally open the door and knock on my parents' door, even if it is Thursday night, aka date night. When they open the door, their faces are wan but hopeful.

"I need to speak to the Taslims," I say.

My mother makes a sound. Stanley makes me sit down and run them through the entire chain of events. I do so in a monotone. When I'm done, both of them are stunned silent.

"Oh, Agnes," my mother says. "How did it come to this?"

"I'm so sorry, Mom," I say. I hear my voice as though it's filtering through some kind of dense fog. "I didn't mean for it to blow up like this. But I have to take responsibility for it. I have to save Royce."

"You can't take the fall for this," Stanley says urgently. "It's not your fault. It's this Vern's fault!"

"He'll never come forth with this. He's too smart. He's already taken care of whatever trail he left."

Stanley puts a hand on my shoulder. "Agnes, if you do this, it could affect your future."

"And what about Royce's future?" I respond quietly, pulling out of his grasp.

Then I start to sob. Now I've done it. I've tried all my life, all my life, to be the best version of myself so that I could have the best future I could have. To deserve my mother's love, her sacrifices. In the end, I'm just a good-for-nothing, throwaway *mistake*.

No wonder my father left.

No wonder Zee left.

No wonder the only kind of friends I make are bottom-feeding scum like Vern.

I am worthless.

"You don't deserve a child like me," I say through sobs.

My mother throws her arms around me and crushes me with the force of her hug. "Don't you say that," she says, her voice low and urgent. "I don't ever want to hear you say something like that. You're the best thing that ever happened to me." She turns to Stanley and offers a weak grin. "Sorry, Stanley. No offense."

"None taken," he says, kissing the top of her head tenderly.

"Gross," I mutter, swiping my eyes, which cracks a smile from my parents, even though nothing has changed and I believe every word I said just now. In that moment, I realize that I have been using comedy as a shield for my real emotions. And I still didn't believe my mother: She had to say these things. Wait till she has Yina. Wait till she has her do-over.

The idea of saying all that I had said in front of the Taslims made me sick. I can't believe that Royce hadn't said anything to anyone thus far. He might not want anything to do with me, but he's still protecting me. What did that say about me?

"Let's just go to the Taslims," I croak. Not that I could lose Royce any more than I'd already lost him, anyway.

~

At the Taslims, both Peter and Ming Taslim sit before me and Stanley (Mom had to stay behind for Rosie), a tray of warm water and tea on the table, as I explain everything. Royce doesn't make an appearance, which I guess is a small kindness. Ming's face telegraphs such alarming feelings for me that I shrink behind Stanley, who places his arm around me. "I'm truly sorry for my part in this," I say in a small voice. "I didn't know Vern would . . . would run with things the way he did, and then the internet mob . . . just twisted everything, amplified it, and made things so much worse. Please tell Royce I'm sorry for the damage I've done to his reputation, and I'll do everything, *everything*, I can to resolve this, explain to TentPole, go public with my involvement, whatever. I just want to make things okay for him again. I am also sorry your family got caught up in this."

Peter's face softens. "Thank you for coming forward with this, Agnes, even though you aren't the true culprit. I can't speak on behalf of my son, but for my part I forgive you. You are very brave." Ming's face twists, but she does not contradict him.

"So, how should we resolve this?" Stanley says.

"Of course we'll need to discuss this with TentPole and give them any evidence Agnes might have to support that Vern started these baseless rumors. This will help exonerate Royce, above all, and me, though I was never really worried about the outcome of the investigation, since I'm not invested in Frisson at all, plus I have a friendly"— he slides a look at me—"but utterly professional relationship with the CEO and his team. Also, Ulrich—the CEO—tells me that his team already has the emails in which they had discussed the raising of the sponsorship amount to back up the independence of this decision— in fact, the genesis of the whole discussion came from a suggestion of their marketing intern, who saw the potential of bigging up this competition in light of the interest from social media, early on, so that's helpful."

He takes a sip of water and continues. "And just yesterday, Ulrich also mentioned that they managed to secure a third-party sponsor that is interested in taking over their commitment, and everyone is coming out of this without too much reputational damage. In fact, Frisson is probably going to get a lot of good PR out of this once it's made clear that they did nothing wrong." His eyes are kind. "Look, just give us another day to sort things out without you needing to make any kind of public statement, okay? We will regroup in a day or two."

I swallow. My eyes well with tears. "Thank you."

"Do you have something that can prove this Vern guy master-minded this?" Ming snaps.

I open my mouth, then shut it before shaking my head.

"Well then, you are dismissed," Ming says.

Suddenly, her phone vibrates and she takes it out, making a face as she does. I start when I recognize the phone case—it's a sleek brushed metal case with the initials RT embossed on the bottom left and the Dunia crest.

It's Royce's phone.

Ming taps in a passcode and taps quickly on the screen. A moue of distaste twists her perfect features. "Another DM with a girl offering to flash her tits at my barely legal son. Wonderful, just wonderful. Thank God for Nina's quick thinking and that sensible suggestion to screen his messages and social media accounts! God knows what other PR mistakes he was going to make in the name of—"

She breaks off and gazes at me curiously. "What's your social media handle?"

"Why?" I ask.

"Just tell me"—a sickly sweet smile spreads across her face—"please."

"It's . . . it's ReallyAgnes."

"Do you have any other handles on other apps?" she says softly.

"Er . . . n-no?" I have one handle across all the apps.

"What's this about?" Stanley interrupts, his patience fraying.

"I'm just trying to figure out the identity of the person who messaged Royce on the day the news broke. All I saw were the messages that popped up in the notifications, since he's been chatting with this person on a locked chat app and I can't seem to compel him to show the entire history to me"—she waves her arm around, like what she's confessing to is normal and not a total breach of trust—"but I think that person and my son was in some kind of age-inappropriate relationship, because she kept asking how he was doing and begging him to call her. Only, of course, Royce saved this person under some kind of code name."

"Oh?" I say casually, my palm sweating. As she was speaking, I'd slipped my hand into my bag to turn my phone off, just in case she decided to call it. "What was it?"

"It's LilHotFlashes."

Stanley makes a little noise next to me again, composes himself, and says jokily, "Are you sure you know your son as well as your spying suggests?"

Ming's glare could slice steel. "I'm going to assume you were joking, Mr. Morissette."

"I wouldn't dare," he says, poker-faced. "Anyway, it's late and we don't want to take up any more of your time, so I suggest you let me liaise with the school to get this cleared up as much as we can?"

After we have bid farewell to the Taslims, Stanley waits till we're in the car before he turns to me and says, "This does not mean you're off the hook at all, *LilHotFlashes*."

Then he sort of shudders a little and a wave of belly laughs roll over him. I've never actually thought a human being could hoot in laughter but there he is, educating me. I guess when you come this close to a catastrophe as a parent, you kind of have to see the funny side of things or you might genuinely—forgive *my* French—lose your shit and run screaming into the proverbial dessert, never to return again.

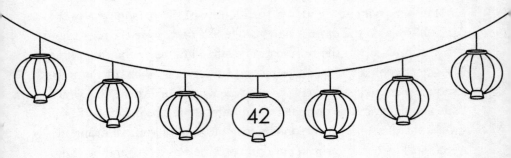

42

WHEN I GET HOME, MY MOTHER IS STILL UP, AND WE DEBRIEF HER. "LET'S
hope the situation is contained in the coming days."

My chest tightens with the disappointment in her voice. I drop
my gaze.

"Maybe . . . maybe I should withdraw from the competition—"

"Nonsense," Stanley says firmly. "You worked hard to get here,
and we don't think taking the chance to compete away from you is
an appropriate punishment." I wish it had been my mother
who'd said that. I wonder if she felt the same as Stanley, even as
she nods.

"Also, they canceled our family vacation to Langkawi next month
so you can have money to enjoy yourself in New York, because it's
expensive and they don't want you couch surfing," Rosie added. That
had indeed been my plan, because even with all the money I'd saved
and the basic travel expenses covered by the sponsorship, four days
in New York was going to be expensive, especially at the ringgit's
crappy exchange rate. I'd to pay for all kinds of insurance and our
own accommodation.

"We'll deposit the money in your bank account next Monday," my
mother says, then weakly, "Surprise!"

I groan, feeling guiltier and guiltier. "Mom! Dad! That was the babymoon!"

"We'll figure something out later," Stanley says, kissing the top of my head. "Now go and rest. You've been under a tremendous amount of stress over the past week."

I drift upstairs to my room, where I slide into my bed and burrow under the covers, preparing myself for the worst, mentally.

Could they charge me for anything I'd done? As an accessory, as they say on legal shows. Which one would I be guilty of: Libel? Slander? Defamation? All of them?

I imagine myself splayed desultorily on the floor of a lone prison cell, rats circling my rotting flesh (from the wounds of my self-flagellation), taking random chunks out of my flesh, as the jailor(?), a pockmarked woman who with yellowing, bitter eyes, encourages them. "This one is the worst," she would say, pointing a pustule-laden finger in my direction. "She brought down an entire family, just because she wanted to win."

I hear Vern in my head: *Or maybe the real problem is you got soft, you had to say something when you could have kept your head down, kept your eyes on the prize. They would never have charged Royce's dad. You don't have what it takes to be a winner. You're not a winner.*

If I don't have what it takes to be the kind of winner that Vern—who'd certainly seen himself through hardships with a blend of tenacity, charm, and wiliness—is, what does that mean for my future? If I don't become a success, what do I have to offer anyone? Who would care about me if I'm a nobody? Out of all the people I know, Vern is the only one who'd seen the worst of me, and still wanted anything to do with me.

Maybe I need to speak to Vern. . . .

No. I shake my head. Vern was not the solution to this problem. Catching myself automatically reaching out to Vern was sobering. Wow, he really got his hooks into me.

No, I *let* him get his hooks into me. Sometimes, inaction can be just as bad as action.

I miss Zee with the sum of all my parts. I'd tried to send her texts several times over the past few days, ultimately chickening out each time. I try texting her again, an apology at hand, and erase the whole thing. She doesn't deserve me—she deserves much better.

I fire up *Revenge of the Soul Flayer: Hellfire* and start hacking enthusiastically away at a Blood Binder, the minions from hell out to get the hero, Flayer the Bastard. As predicted, my blood pressure starts dropping with each kill.

My phone vibrates. I let out an elated-terrified squee when I see who it is.

Zee: I saw you writing and erasing so many texts over the past few days, I decided to give you an opportunity to explain yourself.
Zee: So explain. And how are you? How is Royce? I can't get through to him.

I drop Zee several long voice notes to explain all that had happened and Vern's involvement in all of this.

Me: I'm so, so, so sorry, Zee. I was a shit friend to you and to Royce
Zee: Yup, I know. As your friend, I love you, but what you did still stinks
Agnes: 💯 owning it 😓 I am not worthy of your forgiveness.
Zee: Good that you know
Zee: But I'm giving it to you anyway

Tears flood my eyeholes. On-screen, Flayer the Bastard is being eaten by giant fire ants, because I cleverly forgot to pause the game.

Zee: Also—I TOLD YOU SO! THAT VERN IS SKETCH!
Zee: Aaahhhh it feels SO GOOD TO SAY I TOLD YOU SO!
Zee: Like pricking a boil
Zee: If only I could boil Vern

I send her a flurry of what I call kowtow face emojis. Zee has earned herself a lifetime right to tell me she told me so, because she's endured so much of my nonsense.

My phone pings again.

Unknown: Hey Agnes, Royce here.

I squeak and almost drop my phone, my heart pounding like a timpani. I felt nervous and elated. After almost five days of not hearing from him, why is he reaching out now?

Me: How do I know this is really you? ARE YOU A BOT?
Unknown: I can prove it. Call now?

My fingers trembled as I type, Sure.

I pick up on the second ring. Royce's lovely, deep voice flooded the speaker. "Hey, LilHotFlashes."

I smile. "Royce, I'm so, so sorry about this. This is my fault."

"And I don't deny you had a part to play in this mess," Royce says wryly. "I was very pissed, to be honest. I'm not a saint."

"I get it," I say in a small voice. "I would have been furious if I were in your shoes."

"Sorry I didn't come down the other day when you and Stanley came over. One of my mom's bodyguards, Uwe, had been stationed outside my door, with strict orders not to let me out. I've not been allowed to leave the compound since the news broke."

I swallowed, feeling sicker and sicker to my stomach. "Shit, that's . . . that's extreme."

He sighs. "Ordinarily, I would agree, but there's been some death threats sent to me and my family, so my parents are rightly very worried for me, and I feel bad enough about everything to try to fight it. My father has"—his voice grows gruff—"some nasty competitors, and they were waiting for an opportunity like this to bring him down."

I cover my eyes with trembling palms. I hate that Vern's and my actions have led to this.

He clears his throat. "To be honest, there was a part of me that didn't want to see you until I knew what the meeting was about, either. I told you, I'm no saint. I was mad at you, and worried for you, not sure if you'd been implicated in this in anyway, especially since I didn't know what Vern would do to you if you retaliated." My heart flutters at his concern. "I had no idea what was happening on social media, the internet, what people were saying. I've just been banned from going online, and my mom . . ."

"She has your phone. I saw it tonight." I swallow.

"Yes, she swiped it pretty much as soon as the first few stories broke. Our publicist recommended that they craft any social media responses from my accounts, since I couldn't be trusted to 'keep to the narrative.'"

"How are you even on the phone with me now?"

I can hear the grin in his voice. "This is Jit's phone. And I'm in my walk-in closet."

"Royce—" My voice hitches.

"Yeah?"

"I didn't want him to do any of this. I swear."

"I believe you. And I've forgiven you."

"You shouldn't."

"How could I not?" His voice is gruff. The line crackles. "When the girl of my dreams was willing to confess to a crime she didn't commit, just so I can leave my house without being accosted by internet haters?"

The hairs on my arms raise. *Girl of my dreams.* Maybe the acoustics in his walk-in closet had distorted what he said. Maybe he'd actually said *girl from my team* or *girl who makes schemes*, or maybe he said *the former girl of my dreams*.

Or maybe he did mean to say exactly *that.* "Well," I say, aiming for levity, "I wasn't actually going to take all of the blame. I did state that Vern was the perpetrator. I'm silly, but I'm not stupid."

"Agnes?"

"Yeah?"

"Just take the compliment. Just . . . just take what I said. I don't know when I'll have a chance to speak with you again . . . Jit isn't even supposed to see me, much less hand me his phone. My mom switched him with a bodyguard she trusts. Jit's supposed to be on a shift with my dad. Any minute now someone will be looking for him."

"Okay, okay." I let my air out in a whooshing breath. "I can't. I can't accept it. I'm not worthy."

He chuckles. "Most of the time, you are."

We stay on the call for a bit, saying nothing. Finally, I whisper, "Okay. I accept. Are you going to New York next week?"

"Do you want me to?" he asks.

"If I say no, would you cancel your spot?" I challenge him rhetorically because I already know the answer.

"No," he concedes. "But I also know you'd never ask that of me."

"You're right, I wouldn't. It's not in your best interest to retreat now."

Vern spoke of me and him being in a wolf pack, but he looks out more for his own interests than others. I thought I'd met the one person who got what it was to be me, an outsider, an outlier, who had spent her life trying to fit in, smoothing out all the jagged little pieces of herself, but actually Royce has been the one who sees me for who I am—the good, the bad, and the gray—and he accepts all of it. And if there's anything he draws out of me, it's my better self. I know that now.

"You wouldn't want me to give you an easy win," he says.

"That's true. And neither would you." Vern would have taken the win.

"I wouldn't," he concurs. "I respect you too much for that."

Words are forming in my heart and crawling out of my mouth before I could parse or stop them: "And that's why you're the guy of my dreams."

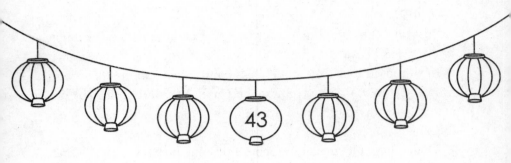

43

VERN WAS RIGHT—AFTER A FEW DAYS, THE ISSUE DIED DOWN ONLINE.
Frisson Cola found a sponsor to take over its obligations (MAXJ
Soundsystems), so Royce is officially 100 percent back in the com-
petition.

And then it's the day of my flight to New York. The qualifying par-
ticipants from Asia would land a day before the preliminary round,
which made up 25 percent of the judges', scores for all the finalists.
I suspect they set this up to mitigate the jet lag for the contestants
flying in for this. It is, after all, almost a full day of travel in a plane,
with a connection in Japan.

I wander the departure hall of KLIA, my heart flip-flopping between
the excitement of finally seeing Royce again and a deep unease at seeing Vern.

I see Vern first, just as I'm about to join the queue to clear security,
wearing dark jeans and a hoodie and rolling a small, battered navy-
blue suitcase and a camo backpack.

He stops when he clocks me, and a smile brightens his face, throwing me off guard. "Agnes," he says, like we hadn't spent the last week
and half not-talking.

Seeing him again is like a punch in the gut. Once I'd really cared for

Vern. I thought we were chums. The long nights texting and chatting, of online watch parties, of comedy together, and the undercurrent of some kind of tension I could feel building between us, not exactly platonic in the physicality of its pull—it all comes crashing around us, and I can't breathe from a combination of pain and sadness. It is a loss, a loss of any friend you hold dear. As though someone has burnt a hole out of the fabric of your soul.

He takes a step in my direction, and I bring my palms up. "I don't want to talk to you," I say.

"Agnes." Vern's brow furrows. "I didn't mean for it to spin out of control. And as I said, the Taslims would get through this unscathed, which they did."

"You didn't know that."

"I did. And I was right."

He reaches out as if to hold me and I step back quickly.

"Enough," I say.

I turn away before he spins new half-truths to bring me back into his sticky web. I brisk-walk to the gate and look around for Royce, who'd texted me a few hours ago to tell me he'd be on the same flight as me—only in business class with Jit, who was back in rotation now that the PR crisis was over.

Since Nina Bell had assessed the PR situation and found it sufficiently low risk, Royce's cell phone has been restored to him literally on the day of our flight, although she did make him sit through another lecture about what he was and wasn't allowed to do or say on the matter. ("Saying and posting nothing is best!" Royce told me one night after he stole Jit's phone again, imitating Nina's stern voice. "Lay low online until the storm passes and the controversy is over. At least in your case you did nothing wrong, so it should blow over quickly. Don't screw up in New York, though!" Her exact words, apparently.)

Anyways, here I am, in the queue, waiting for Royce to turn up and wondering if he might feel differently about me when he sees me again today.

I'm just an ordinary girl crushing on an extraordinary person, and what's more I've really hurt him in this process. He shouldn't be into me at all.

Yet here he is, smiling like I'm a ten when he sees me.

Also, here's Jit.

"Hi," I say, smiling at Royce (and Jit).

"Hello, LilFlashes," he says, using my online gamer handle. Such a metaverse stalker.

Jit announces, "I've been tasked to frisk anyone not on the Taslim's approved list before they can approach Royce, for safety reasons, but I'll give you a pass."

"You might want to rethink that since I have already tried murdering his reputation," I joke with Jit.

"Do you want to get frisked, at least by me?" Royce teases me, and all the bones in my body turn to liquid.

"Stop trying to get an upper hand in this competition," I growl.

"I'm right here, within hearing and visual distance," Jit says, just the tiniest sigh escaping him.

"We should really focus," I say, our eyes never leaving each other.

"Then I'll need to keep my distance," Royce says.

"Only for three more days, one of which you'll spend very comfortably on your flight snoring on a flatbed next to Jit," I say.

"Dreaming of you, naturally," Royce says, and I can see Jit's eyes clawing the ceiling.

"I won't be, because my seat will be so uncomfortable."

"Do try to get some rest"—Royce's fingers graze my cheek—"because I will end you onstage."

"In your dreams, Taslim," I say, hackles rising.

"That's exactly where I was talking about," he says, his voice husky. Jit's eyes twitch, because he is that good at giving poker face, but it's enough to tell me that at this moment, he is regretting all his life choices.

The announcement comes for first-class and business to board, and Royce gives me a wink; then Jit practically marches him to the gate, while I fight to marshal all Royce-related thoughts as much as I can.

Royce was joking, but I wasn't. I do want to win. More than anything. It's the only way I can salvage anything out of the trouble I've caused my parents.

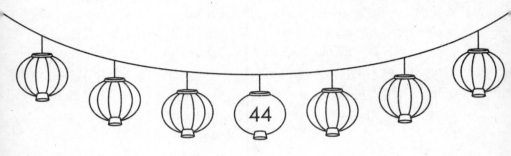

44

I CHECK IN MY ROOM IN A ONE-STAR ESTABLISHMENT THAT'S PLAYING loose and fast with the label "hotel" (it's called the Standard American Hotel). Originally, Vern and I had picked it because it would be within walking distance of the competition (and by within walking distance we meant half an hour on foot, but hey, we have limited funds).

I take a quick nap (by which I mean three hours), wake up refreshed, and then realize it's almost midnight, local time.

You up? I text Royce. No response. He was probably still asleep, because obviously traveling business class was very tough on a teenager's health.

I leave my room, dressed in a puffy jacket, jeans, and boots, ready to start exploring NYC like a true tourist, which is to say with my fully charged phone, which has the cheapest roaming data plan; my house key jammed like a claw between my index and middle finger; and a backup map in my jeans pocket, the fear leaking from every pore of my body (because of all the media set in NYC, including true-crime podcasts, I'd consumed).

Of course, I bump into Vern, shivering slightly in the cold marble lobby in spite of his winter clothing.

"Going somewhere?" he says.

"Just exploring."

"You shouldn't go alone," he says lightly. "It's not safe. We're not exactly in a nice neighborhood, if you realize."

I weigh my options. Outside, there is a literal boulder of a man in a ratty parka, the hood up, his hands in his bulging pockets, staring at the entrance of the hotel, like a vampire waiting for a victim to cross the threshold. Every so often, he stopped muttering to laugh maniacally before lapsing back into a low mutter. He seemed to be in discussion with someone we can't see.

Vern catches my eye and raises an eyebrow.

"He's just . . . chilling."

"He sure looks harmless," Vern says mildly.

"*Not* a vampire," I added, à propos de rien.

"So why don't you go out there on your own, then?"

I take a deep breath and mutter, "Okay, fine I need company, *but I'm not talking to you.*"

We walk in silence down a random street, dazzled by the lights and grime and noise, the streams of people, until I locate a hot-dog cart with a surly, half-asleep hot-dog vendor. Stars in my eyes, I buy one from the man (despite Vern opining that it looked like we'd been the only customer in hours) and gobble it up, sauerkraut, mustard, and rubbery frankfurter sliding down my throat in a woeful mass, but my pride is too strong and I refuse to admit Vern is right, so I gamely chow down the entire dog.

"So, you basically paid New York prices to eat skate-rink food," Vern says.

"Shut up, don't ruin my buzz," I say. The onion clings to my throat like it's alive (and maybe it is). No matter how much I swallow, I can't get it down the hatch. "Y-yummmm," I choke out.

Vern sighs and passes me his water bottle. "Please, Chan."

I take it with ill-disguised relief.

We walk around the block till I start to wind down around

2:30 a.m., taking in the bars, the clubs, the eateries, and the unidenti-
fiable shop fronts without speaking, as poor tourists do, just walking,
the silence between us strange but not hostile, and finally, hearing me
yawn, he suggests that we head back and I don't protest.

There's a finality to our hanging out that filters through the head
fog of my jetlag, a kind of low-grade sorrow. We'd been each other's
confidant for almost seven months, and now we'd never be anything
more than a footnote in each other's histories.

We stop in front of the lobby. The man from before is still there,
leaning against a graffitied wall with his head tilted to the sky now,
still muttering and laughing. It occurs to me that it sounds as though
he's conversing with someone he likes.

Vern faces me. "I wish"—he clears his throat and swallows
audibly—"I wish things had turned out differently."

"Me too," I say, meeting his gaze.

It's not an apology. It's not nearly enough. I take it anyway.

He presses his lips together and the smile slips back on, askew. "See
you tomorrow, Chan."

"See you tomorrow," I echo.

He nods and waits for me to enter the lobby first and take the lone
elevator, the half smile on his face the last thing I see as the doors
close and I rise.

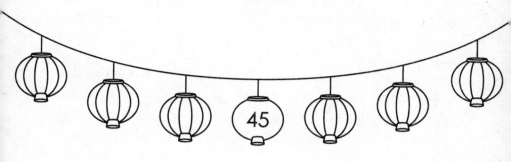

45

OUR PRELIMINARY ROUND IS SUPPOSED TO BE A CASUAL THING, NOT televised but judged in front of a live audience, as in the previous rounds, so I was expecting to perform before, like, twenty, maybe thirty people.

Imagine my horror when I saw the queue stretched around the block and being told the "smaller lounge" in Comedy City, where our prelims would be judged, could hold a hundred people. Apparently, watching young, newish comics is considered a fun outing for New Yorkers?

What's more: Our main event the next day, which will be held in the main showroom, can hold *three hundred nine people*! (A very specific number.)

I meet Vern, Royce (both of them ignoring each other), and the other finalists milling about the front of the stage. The showrunner, a lanky man in his thirties, introduces himself as Andy, and gives us a briefing on the proceedings to come. I glance out at the empty lounge and swallow, thinking about the crowd outside waiting to be let in, and my anxiety shoots through the roof in spite of my efforts to control my breathing.

After we're dismissed from the briefing and directed to head to the holding room, I spy Andy staying back to converse with Vern offstage. Maybe Vern had very specific lighting instructions or whatever. Under the harsh stage lights, I realize he looks unwell, like he hasn't slept in days.

"Hey you," a voice says, and I spin around to find Royce smiling at me.

"Royce!" I hug him, breathing in the warm, soapy clean scent that's his. I think it helps, although I'm not sure it's done anything to calm my galloping heart.

"I thought you might need some coffee, if you've had a night like mine." He hands me a coffee in one of his collapsible coffee cups. "I got you a flat white on the way here, not sure if it's still hot."

"Fancy," I murmur before downing the coffee in three gulps. Bad idea, since I've already had two energy drinks so far today. My stomach clenches and I start to sweat even more. Everything becomes hyper sharp and saturated.

"Whoa, your pupils are dilated," Royce observes. "Would you like a banana?"

I wave his concern away. "I'm good," I insist, blinking to moisturize my suddenly dry eyeballs.

Andy comes to check attendance and give us our order of appearance. A comic named Satoshi will open. I'm last.

Last is good. Last is especially good if you end strong.

"Erm, good luck and/or break a leg, and may the wind under your wings bear you and all that," Royce says.

"Likewise," I reply.

I head to a secluded corner and avoid everyone else, muttering calming chants like "YOU CAN DO THIS! YOU'RE NUMBER ONE! BE, BE AGGRESSIVE!" the way I do before I run. On the underside of my left hand's wrist, I have written keys words from my different sets in black marker, with words like *Asian parents*, *Asian kid priorities vs. desires*, and *gaming/perverts*.

I am so wired, I barely follow what's happening onstage, only vaguely aware when Satoshi is done, then Kitty, whose set I had meant to pay attention to (as Vern kept saying she would be my biggest competitor, being a similar comic to me), then Vern, then Alaia, then Royce, who brings the house down, then my name is called.

I go onstage, ready to crack into things. This is what I have been working toward for most of senior year.

The audience is packed into the lounge at capacity in tight, watchful rows.

I open my mouth, ready to do a quick bit of crowd work before starting on my time-tested bit on how "Asian parents love their kids unconditionally—until." I'd even prepared my opener—"Anyone here have Asian parents?" to which I would respond with a sympathetic "Let's talk" to any answers to the affirmative, or "Well, then this is going to go *really* well" if no one says anything (unlikely, since we're in NYC).

Instead, nothing comes out of my mouth. In front of the crowd of a hundred people, I go blank.

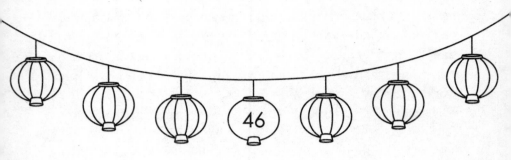

I STAND ON THE STAGE AND SAY NOTHING FOR TWO MINUTES BEFORE
walking offstage to a shocked audience. Royce tries to talk to me but I
shake my head, whisper that I'm fine, I just need to clear my head; Jit
calls out to Royce to wait for him, which distracts him, and I take the
opportunity to run out of a side entrance and melt into the throngs of
people out on a Saturday night in Chelsea.

Twenty-five percent of my total score, gone.

Gone before I even tried.

I'd put all my hopes, all my energy into this. All my dreams. And
now it's over. I don't know what I have left to offer. I'm going to dis-
appoint everyone who ever believed in me, who sacrificed so much
to let me come to this stupid pipe dream. At least with sports there's a
scientific approach to it. You train and you calibrate and you take the
data and work toward a goal. You know exactly where you are, where
you're going, what you're capable of. Stand-up, and by extension, my
wild ideas about having a career in writing . . . these are all shots at
the moving target. I'm reaching for a pie in the sky.

I'd exposed myself to the world and pretended to be worthy. Now
I'm just another loser. A fake. How am I supposed to do this tomorrow, in front of an even larger crowd, with a camera recording my

performance? The mere thought of it makes me sick. I run into an alley and heave acrid liquid onto the street behind a dumpster. I'm lucky the alley is empty, but I don't take any chances and quickly rejoin the people on the street.

I walk for hours. Well, forty minutes. Finally, the hunger and fatigue get me, and I stop for a hot dog (a better-looking and better-tasting one, thank God) and start heading back to the hotel, dispirited.

A vague idea is forming in my head: I don't have to show up tomorrow. What would be the point, anyway? I have no shot realistically to win.

I get to the lobby, and Royce is there with Jit, chatting softly. When he sees me, he walks over without another word and folds me into his arms. "I was worried, you didn't respond to my texts."

"I'm sorry," I say thickly. "I think my phone died. I had to use my gaming-honed orientation skills to get back."

"I got a surprise for you."

"I hate surprises."

"Well, I think this one is going to be quite nice. Come with me."

We walk down a couple of blocks and stop in front of a striking, Gothic-looking hotel with those intricate wrought-iron balconies on its red-bricked facade. The people swanning in and out of the premises look fancy. I swallow. "Look, Royce, I don't know if I'm dressed—"

"You're fine," he says. He leads me through the doors, Jit trailing a few lengths behind us, and we come to the elevator banks. My heart is pounding so hard it is threatening to explode. Did he think— Was this surprise . . . attached to his body? In which case, it would be extremely bad timing. Right?

I walk down the hallway with him, warily.

He sighs. "Agnes, whatever you're thinking, I guarantee you're wrong."

He knocks at a door and then it swings open. "Voilà," Royce says, practically dragging me into the room.

It's my mom.

"Surprise!" Royce says happily.

"Hi, hon!" my mom says, grinning at my gaping face. "Imagine running into you here!"

I laugh and hug my mom, then turn to Royce. "You—you did this?" I say, my voice quavering.

"Yes," he says, beaming. "I brought your whole family here. I thought you'd appreciate some support for the main event tomorrow."

Great, now my family is going to see me fail—in person.

It's not his fault, I know he meant well, but my anxiety levels shoot through the roof.

"Er, well, I'll leave now. Bye, Mrs. Morrissette!"

My mother thanks him, and he gives an embarrassed little wave before ducking out.

"Mom, are you supposed to be flying in your condition? Is it safe?"

She grins. "I'm just seven months pregnant, my dear, plus I was cleared by my ob-gyn and the airlines for travel, so I think I'm good. This is my babymoon."

"Stanley, Rosie where now?" I blurt eloquently.

"Went for a walk down the block to get some snacks, we landed, like, five hours ago."

She pats the space on the bed next to her and I sit down cautiously.

"So, let's talk," she says, and my throat tenses and I see my back hunching in the mirror beside me. I realize I haven't actually spoken to my mom one-on-one for the longest time about anything serious or even personal, not even the everyday disappointments of life like losing money to a faulty vending machine or forgetting my completed homework at home and getting reprimanded for it, not because I don't trust her with the information, but rather, in my desire to protect her, not telling her about the minor and major disappointments I face has become second nature.

"How were prelims? Did you record yourself as we asked?"

All the stress of that moment boils to the surface. "Yes, but . . ." I swallow, my voice drops to a whisper. "I froze onstage; I didn't say a thing."

I recount what happened and she hugs me in sympathy. "Oh, Agnes, what a pity. But you're still going to go up tomorrow, right?"

"No." My eyes prick with tears. "Let's go home."

"But you worked so hard on your set. You should at least try, you never know."

"There's no point in doing something if it has no chance of success."

She squints at me, confused. "But you *like* stand-up comedy. That should be enough."

I draw away from her. "I should be spending my time better instead of frittering it on things that won't bear fruit."

Mom says, "You're only seventeen! You have so much time!"

"You were twenty when you had me, and everything was ruined."

It slips out. I didn't meant to say it that way, but my mother's face blanches, a hand goes around her throat and circles it, and she just stares at me. My mother's a naturally chatty, sociable person, someone who instinctively knows what to say in every situation, but now she's at a loss for words.

I swallow and continue. "I've made everything difficult for you at a time when you should have been . . . thinking about, I don't know, your first internship, your first impulsive trip with a bunch of people you met in a dive bar . . . okay, fine not a dive bar, but at this internship, and these people become your lifelong friends, and you make bad decisions together, maybe accidentally kill someone on a road trip, and then you cover it up together, and then you get your first—I don't know, whatever adults think are important milestones in your twenties. But I took that away from you."

She makes a pained noise. "Why—why would you even *think* that?"

"I don't know. . . ." Some words someone said on TV about a person in the similar situation, words that had lodged in my young, impressionable brain and rooted darkly.

She drags a palm across her face. "Look, the year that I fell into depression . . . when you were ten—that had nothing to you or our life together. Things happened. It was just a bad year, Agnes. I sought help, and I got better because of therapy and my meds. And I'm good now because I'm still on therapy and meds, Agnes."

I take a deep breath and turn to my mom. "That was just one part of it. I think I just . . . felt like, if I lived out the life you wanted for yourself, you'd be happy. I just wanted you to be happy. You sacrificed everything for me. . . . I just . . . I just wanted you to feel like you had made the right choice, back then. That if I had everything sorted out, and never worried you, an-and that if I were successful and had a great stable job, then one day I—I can take care of you, the way you did, the way you always do. I just want to deserve your love."

"Oh, Agnes," my mother says, tearing up. "I'm so sorry you thought . . ." She is weeping softly, and my heart shatters. She gathers me in her arms. "I'm sorry you felt that you had to be a certain way to be loved. That's absolutely *ridiculous*, because I would love you no matter how you turned out."

"Even if I become the leader of a cult?" I whisper, unable to help myself.

"Honey, please. I'm trying to tell you something."

"Sorry."

"Look, I only want you to be happy, and I'm sorry I never made that clear enough." She tightens her arms around me. "You are *not* a mistake. You were a *choice*. My choice, and I knew, even back then, that you would be the best decision I ever made. You are more than enough, Agnes—you are my perfection. Do you understand?"

"Okay," I say, muffled against her shoulder and trying not to cry but failing. "When you put it that way."

She lets out a bark of laughter and we pull apart and grin, embarrassed, stuffing tissues at various leaking face organs. She bops my nose. "I don't need you to take care of me. I just need you to be happy, and to love me. Chat with me like we used to, y'know? Tell me what's going on in that big, wonderful head of yours that actually writes jokes? What?" She shakes her head, awed. "I'm going to need you to send me clips of all your stand-up sets, okay? Even the ones you bomb. And all the wonderful things you will dream of and write in Rhode Island, or any other college you want to go to, and I'm stuck with a screaming, pooping kid—and baby Yina, okay? You promise?"

I chuckle. "Promise."

She kisses me on the top of my head. "My baby," she says. "My first baby."

The door beeps.

"Oh my God, I leave for one minute and you guys start crying?" Rosie says, running over to throw her arms around us, while Stanley, struggling with a bag of groceries, says tiredly, "Surprise!"

"Zee says to break all the legs," Rosie chimes in, holding the phone up. "I don't think she means it metaphorically, since she clarifies in another text, 'Not yours, Agnes. You've done enough to yourself.'"

She isn't wrong. I have done a lot to myself, and I'm going to stop holding myself back. "You tell Zee that I will," I say, laughing and wiping my eyes, "break a leg. Metaphorically speaking."

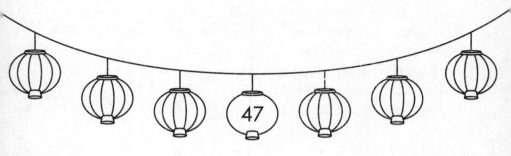

I GO ONSTAGE THE NEXT DAY, THE OPENING ACT AFTER THE EMCEE
announces the lineup—the hardest spot, to be honest, but I grin and
bear it, no worries, what's the worst that can happen, I break my
other leg? ha-ha!—and do my set with gusto. With passion. Giving it
my all even if I don't expect to be able to win.

I even switch up one of the bits and do a really random one about
what makes people choose a specific medical specialization, especially proctology, and how even an Asian parent, when asked if their
child was a proctologist, might just say no, they are just a regular
doctor, and oh my lord, is that or is that not Chow Yun Fat walking
through the door of *this very dim sum palace*?

A very, very risky joke, but I don't care. I love it, and I want to share
it with the one person in the audience who gets it.

Because life isn't about that. I mean, yes, winning is important.
It feels good. But it shouldn't be the only thing that makes you
feel good.

Life's too big for that.

I do my set just for me (and maybe the three hundred people
watching me, and the people who might one day watch this . . .
yikes).

It feels great to make people laugh, all these people older than me. What I'd gleaned about life from older people is how we get so bogged down with figuring out the day-to-day stuff of existence that we forget to laugh at the small things, like—

Pufferfish after a fright.

A toddler thinking it's walking.

The word *poot*, which is a Scrabble word. And onomatopoeias in general.

And maybe when you forget to laugh at the small things, you stop experiencing all the wonders around you after a while. You don't wake up and think to yourself: *Damn, who's the genius who taught to pair peanut butter and jelly? Or soy sauce and sesame oil? Or fish sauce with sugar?*

Okay, so maybe I'm a little hungry.

All to say that I go up there, and I slay. I slay as hard as Vern and Royce. And the other three finalists.

And then the judges go into deliberations, and I sink into a seat back in the holding room next to the stage, sandwiched between Royce and Satoshi. Vern sits at the far end of the room in a single folding chair, occasionally our gazes would meet and break apart. I wish him well, I do.

I wish all these people well.

When it comes to announcing the results, I'm calm. I've done all I can, and I had a great time doing it.

That's more important than winning.

The chief judge is Margaret Zhou, the legendary badass Asian American comic herself. She flounces onstage, all sequins and rage and Dr. Martens, and thanks everyone for supporting new comics. "Now let's break some of these fragile little Gen Z hearts!"

"In third place—Kitty Graham!"

My heart thuds. Okay, maybe I had harbored a secret hope that I could still place third, if not second.

"In second place—Vern Goh!"

I clap. I do.

Beside me, Royce is breathing hard. I cross my fingers for him. Margaret Zhou wiggles her eyebrows.

"And this is the big one. Drumroll, please: The first prize goes to— ROYCE TASLIM!"

I whoop. I scream. I cry.

Royce staggers onto the stage, and from the holding room we see him go onstage, smiling and waving at people. He stares at the audience, where my parents and Rosie sit in the second row, and Jit in the third, and I know he's looking for his own miracle but doesn't see it. They aren't there of course, his family. A hobby is not important enough when you have empires to maintain, territories to expand into.

I wonder if, by now, Royce understands that even if the people he cares for most do not take his passion seriously, what matters is how he feels about it, not others.

In the end, the only person who can decide what pieces make up your identity is you.

A shadow passes across Royce's face. Then he composes himself and says, "Ladies and gentlemen, folks, I am pleased to be your winner tonight—"

The crowd starts chanting, "Royce! Royce! Royce!"

"But sadly. I won't be accepting this award. I forfeit." Without another word he walks off the stage toward the holding room.

The audience gasps. There is a swell of shocked silence; then the noise breaks upon us in a crash of chatter.

"Hey! You're supposed to be out there! There's a prize-giving ceremony after," one of the miked assistants says as Royce sweeps back in. He's trailed by the three judges, who do not look pleased.

"Someone please explain what he just did?" says Libby Kelk, one of the judges.

"I'm bowing out," Royce says calmly. "I'm sorry for any inconvenience caused."

"What's going on, Taslim?" asks Mike D'Arcy, another one of the judges. "You won."

"And I don't want it," Royce says. He addresses the judges, but I know he's really speaking to me. "My whole life has been about what other people want for me. This was the first thing I ever wanted for myself, the only thing I did solely on my own merit, and I just needed to know if I was good enough to fight for it. The money and the title, it can go to someone else. . . ."

He glances at Vern and says to him quietly, "It can go to the second-place winner."

Vern's eyes flash. "I don't want your pity money, Taslim."

"Vern, it's not. I'm forfeiting. Under the rules, the second-place winner should be promoted. You all get promoted a rank."

"So I'm second?" Kitty says. "Great!"

"Who's fourth? Don't they get promoted to third?" Satoshi says.

Margaret says, "Satoshi was fourth."

"Woo-hoo," he says, pumping his fist. "Excite!"

Royce is close enough to me that I hear him when he whispers to Vern, "You got here, fair and square. I'm merely leveling the playing field. Just take the money and use it for your aunt."

There's a stare-off as I watch Vern debate this turn of events. For as long as I've known Vern, he'd always placed winning as his ultimate goal, yet I don't think even he could have envisaged coming up tops this way, even if ironically this had been as clean a win as it could be. Vern's face clouds over and he gives Royce a terse nod, which the judges take as acquiescence.

Libby rolls her eyes, sighs, and says, "Okay, well, we'll announce the winners again with the corrected lineup and make a note to production to cut out the entire part about Royce forfeiting." Then, not entirely under her breath, she says, "Kids."

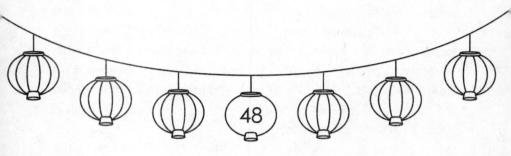

48

THE VIP AFTER-PARTY HAS BEEN DECORATED WITH SILVER AND GOLD streamers and strings of fairy lights, with tall tables with mason jars holding candles and flowers. Servers circulated bearing silver trays of canapés and incredible-looking cocktails, which would have been tempting if my family wasn't around.

Here they are, crowding around me to hug me, as my mom proclaims that "I'm the funniest person onstage, ever," which is statistically improbable, but I accept it. Humor has a subjective element, after all.

"Is it too soon to call you loser when I see you?" Rosie quips.

I flick a finger at her forearm and miss.

They hang around for half an hour, Rosie name-checking every remotely famous person she could identify and posting a stream of TikToks. Then they take their leave, a combination of jet lag and my mother's pregnancy fatigue claiming them.

"Stay out as long as you want," my mother says. She gives me a hug. "I trust you."

As soon as they are gone, I wave Kitty over. "Please get me a beer, I think I deserve one."

"Right on," she says. She comes back with a bottle, and we clink ours together. I chug mine. It's both delicious and disgusting. I love it.

Suddenly, Royce is in front of me. He's backlit by this weird, angelic light, and I can't wait till this thing is over, or maybe during this party we'll be able to sneak away, because I have things to say to him.

"Hey," he says. "Come with me. There's someone who'd like to meet you."

He leads me by the hand to a corner, and there she is, in the flesh, smiling at me. Amina Kaur.

"Ahh!" I say, very eloquently.

"Yes, so I've been called," she says with a twinkle in her eye.

After I gibber my admiration to her, Amina asks me how I'm doing and tells me that she'd just asked Royce if he'd like to open for her in Singapore, to which he has tentatively agreed, pending clearance from his parents.

"What?!" I say. Obviously, it's too late to impress Amina with my wordsmithery. "Royce! I'm so happy for you," I say, throwing my arms around him and hugging him with all my unresolved ardor.

Royce smiles. "Thanks. I've decided I will talk to my parents about taking a year off as a gap year, defer my entry into Harvard, and hope to God in the meantime that my dad will find someone better than me to groom to be group CEO, and then maybe he'll agree that I can just be an SVP or something."

"Wow, that's a change."

"It's worth a shot. I always thought I'd stop here, but then I thought, *Why should I?* I deserve a gap year before I'm chained to my father's empire, right?"

Amina turns to me and says, "What about you, Agnes? Would you like to join me and Royce?"

I stare. "I'm sorry, what?"

She grins. "Onstage in Singapore, when I go on my Asia tour. I saw your other performances. You have that special something I like."

My mind is spinning. I had come last in the competition. Everyone had *killed* at the televised finals. There is no reason why Amina should pick me. "Wh-where did you . . . ? When . . . ?"

"Vern. Vern showed me."

Turns out that after the award ceremony, Vern had cornered Amina and showed her the clip of my performance at the qualifiers that he had recorded on his phone—and a bunch of other clips, too, apparently—and Amina had been blown away. He'd convinced Amina to give me a chance, since Amina had always said that she would love to support more female comics.

Vern . . .

"There is something in the air between all three of you," Amina comments. "The showrunner, who also works with me on other projects, told me that just before the prelims, Vern was asking him if he could drop out, too. He had to talk him out of it."

This revelation socks me in the gut. I look around the room and there Vern is surrounded by a gaggle of admirers, a small smile on his face. He flashes me a thumbs-up and I mirror him. He mouths something I don't catch, or maybe I don't want to.

Oh, Vern.

"Honestly, I don't know what's going on between you three, but hug it out."

My eyes dart at Royce. I really doubt we'd be hugging it out with Vern. Still . . . this is a start.

"So, do you accept? Performing with Mama Amina in Singapore? It's going to be fun!" Amina winks at me. "That is, if you don't mind working with your boy, Royce."

"Oh," I say, coloring. "Royce and I aren't together."

"And that's the other question: Would you like to be?" She leans over and says, sotto voce, to Royce, "All right, champ, I delivered the message, now you have to do the rest."

"Thanks, boss."

"My pleasure," she says. We watch as she sashays into the crowd of adoring fans.

Royce turns to me. "So, tell me, after everything that's happened— do you want to be with me, Agnes Chan?"

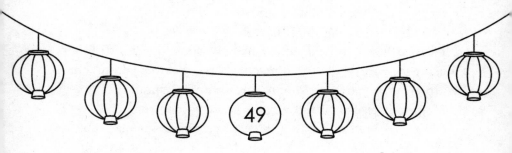

49

MY MIND GOES BLANK AGAIN FOR THE SECOND TIME THIS WEEKEND.

"Hellooo. Earth to Agnes Chan," Royce says, smiling down at me.

I blink and snap to attention. "Erm, so, when you say 'be with me,' do you mean, like, go onstage with you and Amina, or . . . ?"

He laughs huskily, and my innards turn to jelly. "Girlfriend-boyfriend business, Agnes. And to the performing-as-an-opening-act part."

"Oh, in that case, yes. Yes! Yes to both!"

Royce's eyes sparkle. "I was a little worried you'd say no to one or both options. That all the plans I had for our hot couple summer together before college starts would be over before they even began." He makes a face. "Well, hot throuple summer, I guess. Since I'm stuck with Jit."

"I'm right here," Jit mutters suddenly from the shadows, making me jump. Man, he's good at his job.

"Jit, you know what I mean," Royce says with a playful jab.

"But how will this work?" I wonder.

"We can get into the specifics later," he says in a low voice, pulling me close to him. Jit sighs and mutters that he has to go outside and check the weather or traffic, something, something.

I wriggle free. "Before we do this, I should . . . I should thank Vern for, you know, what he did for me, vis-à-vis Amina."

"Yeah, sure. Do what you need to."

I leave to speak to Vern and am halfway across the crowded room when I see a scruffy bearded man walk up to Royce with intent. I whip around, paranoia shoots through me. I shoulder my way through a protesting crowd. Where's Jit when you need him?

"Royce," I shout in warning, a few steps behind the man. But the closer I get, the more I realize I've seen his face before. Wait, is that—

"Royce," the man says just as Royce utters a strangled cry of recognition and embraces him: "Rayford!"

It's Rayford Taslim.

It falls into place then. *Ray* Lim. I'd never asked Royce why he'd chosen that particular moniker. Royce had been trying to honor his brother, to keep his memory close.

The brothers are hugging so tight they have collapsed into each other, tearful and laughing.

"I'm proud of you," Ray says. "You were so good out there."

"Thank you," Royce is saying in a muffled voice. "I wasn't expecting you to . . . I mean I had a feeling you might be in New York, but . . ."

Someone walks up to the brothers and taps Ray on the shoulder. The brothers break apart with shy smiles.

"Royce, this is Alexis," Ray says, wiping his eyes. "My . . . friend."

Royce is beaming so hard. "Hi, Alexis."

"Hi," Alexis says. "Your brother has been following your career this whole time, and he wouldn't shut up about you. I'm so glad we managed to catch you in town. He rescheduled, like, five private life coaching sessions to be in New York."

"When the Google Alert came in, I acted fast," Ray says.

Royce motions me over. "This is Agnes. My, erm, friend, too." He leans over and whispers at length in Ray's ear, to which Ray says, "Nice."

I'm still staring at Ray because something still isn't quite adding up. "I *know* you, though."

He cocks his head as he contemplates me. "You do?"

"Yeah. Do you play *CF*?"

"Doesn't everyone," Ray says.

"You're NerdWolf," I say with satisfaction. "I knew I'd seen your face before. You look just like your profile pic. I'm LilFlashes!"

He snaps his fingers. "The LilFlashes? What? That's mind-blowing, what are the odds?" We shake hands, grinning. "Although I do have a confession to make: There's a selfish reason why I hung around on the same team for so long—even if you're an absolute terror in the game."

"Oh yeah?"

"I figured out somewhere along the way that you were Royce's schoolmate. You would go on and on about this poncy, jock-face, obnoxious bag of air." He turns to Royce, apologetic. "She even had a special nickname for you on the days you particularly annoyed her, just after her accident."

"What was it?" Royce asks casually and I have to avert my eyes.

"Roycey the Poncy." Ray clears his throat. "And I figured it had to be you, since there aren't exactly many rich teenage athletes named Royce running around in your part of the world."

"That was before I got to know you," I assure Royce through a strangled voice. "Only some of those nicknames apply now. When you're chatting in game, emotions tend to run wilder, you understand."

Ray is smiling, but his eyes grow serious. "I'm glad you were so vocal. It was the only way I could get news about my pompous, snooty brother."

"Er, thanks?" Royce says.

Ray slings his arm around me and tells Royce, "Anyway, I wouldn't get on this one's bad side, ever. Now, what should we all do tonight?"

Royce glances at Ray. "The thing is, well . . . Agnes and I kind of . . . have plans for tonight." Royce gives me a meaningful look and I burn red. The memory of our first kiss is a core memory.

"Oh . . . right!" Ray says, quickly catching on. "Of course—no problem! How about tomorrow, instead?"

Royce nods. "Done. But there are some, um, logistics we'll need to maneuver around before that happens. Like an NDA." He nods at Jit, who has just returned from giving me and Royce privacy and is now glaring at Ray as though Ray's Pennywise the clown's ugly twin. Royce stage-whispers, "The thing is, Jit has never seen Ray Taslim in the flesh before."

We all laugh as Jit's face blanches. Poor guy, how much more could he take?

"So, we're on for tomorrow afternoon?" Alexis says. Everyone nods. "What shall we do?"

"If nobody has better plans, I'd very much like to have a brunch bagel at Russ and Daughters, then Nathan's Famous hot dogs, then Sugar Sweet Sunshine Bakery for dessert, followed by a visit to the Frick Collection, please," I chime in brightly, having recovered from the embarrassment just in time.

"But Nathan's is over in Brooklyn—" begins Alexis.

"Well then, I'll settle for just the bagel and the cupcakes please, and maybe the Frick." In this respect, nobody could argue that I didn't know my priorities. Then Royce excuses us and pulls me to a quiet corner of the room.

Neither of us break eye contact.

"So, Agnes Chan."

"So, Royce Taslim."

He encircles his arms around my waist. "I'm going to kiss you now, if that's fine by you?"

"You better," I whisper.

He bends his head and presses the lightest kiss on my forehead, then the tip of my nose, and I think he's trying to do some butterfly kiss bullcrap on my chin, but I don't let him. I waylay the trajectory of his mouth by putting both hands on his face and bringing it down to mine, hungrily, and then I kiss him like I'm claiming him, which in a way I guess I am.

~

Okay, I'm not going to go into details about what happens next.

Okay, fine, I'm going to give you some details. It goes *bow-chicka-WOWWOW.* 🏔 ✳ 🏔

We give Jit the slip and run to his hotel, hand in hand, laughing, skipping up the stairs because the elevator was busy, three floors like it was nothing, our hearts beating in our throats. He stops in front of his room door, suddenly shy, and I urge him to hurry. He wraps his arms around my waist and brings me close and shuts the door to our room, our kisses frantic and electric, our breaths hot with whispers and need, and he says, "Agnes, Agnes," like it's a mantra, and then I pull him close on top of me and forget about anything else.

I wake up next to him the next morning, my hair tousled, smiling. I'm wearing his shirt and my jean shorts. He's bare-chested and very much a distraction.

"Hey, you," he says.

"Hey, you," I say, faux serious.

He traces my face and my heart. "Hey, you," he says again, bending to drop another kiss on my lips.

We go back and forth like that for a bit.

"Look, we really should brush our teeth and get some breakfast," he says at last, when my stomach growls. He runs his fingers through my hair, and I almost stop him and say, *Let's stay,* but given that we'd been offline and unreachable for over twelve hours, I guess Jit has to be debriefed, or bribed, or killed.

Just kidding. He's loyal to Royce.

"Let's go," I say, pulling him out of the bed. We dress quickly and head into the chilly sunshine. March in New York is bracing. We grab some takeaway coffee and croissants from a nearby bakery and head back to the hotel.

"I hope Jit isn't too mad," I say.

Unbeknownst to Jit, Royce had taken the opportunity to covertly switch rooms when he'd checked my family in yesterday, so Jit was probably a teensy bit worried by now if he'd heard nothing from Royce and nothing from the connecting room door.

"I told him we needed some alone time and that he shouldn't worry, but yeah, he's probably somewhat pissed."

Royce knocks on the door, and predictably, Jit is in the doorway. He does not look pleased to see us, even though we bear coffee and croissants. Maybe he hates gluten. Or caffeine. Or me.

"Sorry, Jit," Royce says. He points at Jit's mobile phone, which looks crushingly fragile in Jit's muscular hand. "Did you see the texts I sent when we switched rooms? Hope you didn't freak out when you lost us."

Jit's lip twitches and he says, "Well, I tailed you two when you left the venue, all the way back to your room. You two weren't exactly keeping a low profile the entire time, so it was quite easy to follow you. You were in room three-thirteen last night."

Royce grins. "You should get a promotion."

Jit says, "And a raise."

Royce says, "I'll speak to management."

Jit says, "If you go to New York, your parents will probably not send me along. They want someone who's one hundred percent theirs."

"I know," Royce says. "Thanks for yesterday."

Jit nods. "Tell me if you need to . . . hang . . . in room three-thirteen a bit. I'll wait in mine."

Royce turns to me and I, him; we're at the stage where a single look is all we need to communicate—and if that failed, he could always read that I was mouthing to him, not very subtly. "I think Agnes is hungry, so we're going to head out. We're probably going to explore the city, see the Statue of Liberty, Times Square, eat some local food—"

"Kimchi tacos! Absolute Bagels! Levain Bakery!" I blurt; I'd been making a list for some time now.

"And watch some comedy later at the Comedy Cellar. And maybe some jazz after that."

"Wanna come?" I say to Jit.

Something like a smile creases Jit's face. "Okay." He doesn't really have a choice, but I know, as well as anyone else, that it's nice to feel wanted.

~

So here's what will happen, if all goes well:

July is when Amina starts touring, which means Royce and I will have a few months to polish up our half-hour sets in time for our official debut in Singapore. We'll hang with our families and plan our next moves for September, when Royce will move to New York City and I'll go to Rhode Island on scholarship, while (hopefully) working part-time on campus and online (somehow, I've become a legit micro influencer on social media, thanks to the JOGGCo exposure).

Amina has promised me and Royce that if we do well on her Singapore show, there might be future opportunities to open for her when she performs in smaller venues in New York City later this fall, when she'll try out new material in preparation for her tour next year. Royce and I will visit each other (or rather, he'll do most of the visiting, because he can afford it) as much as we can, and I'll learn to be comfortable being tailed by a skulking figure in black.

I'll start trying to run again, non-competitively.

I'll learn to ~~appreciate~~ tolerate the cold.

My mom, dad, Rosie, and my little sister Yina (who'll be a real brat, for sure) will come visit me over winter break, hopefully, and we'll all take a family trip to New Orleans, where Stanley is from. Zee and I have plans to visit each other on each coast.

There are a lot of contingencies in this scenario. A lot of maybes, ifs, and whens. So much can happen between now and September, or after I've gone to college this fall—for example, the purveyor of the fine cartoon undergarments I favor may stop making them in the regulation white I prefer; Royce might develop a habit of interjecting *woof* or similar or start wearing beanies in earnest—even in summer; I might tire of performing stand-up and stick to writing short stories and novels about the hidden lives of people who look and sound like me. I might start running competitively again, even without surgery, who knows. Or the zombie apocalypse might come in a sudden, sweeping wave of destruction and end us all.

Anything can happen, and that's . . . perfectly acceptable.

This is The Era of Agnes Chan, and I want to live so much: I want to live so well.

ACKNOWLEDGMENTS

BEFORE THE BIRTH OF MY FIRST CHILD, I WAS AN AMATEUR STAND-UP comic for two years in Singapore. I say *amateur* because I got into the scene with little ambition to progress as a stand-up but rather to dabble in it as a dilettante: I loved the art form, the people, and the bars I could legitimately hang out in afterward "to network" (plus it was also an excellent [free . . . ish] place for me to work out my issues). For two years I terrorized audiences in Singapore (and eventually in open mikes in Hong Kong and Australia) with my random bits on everything from proctology (a joke that ended up in my debut novel, *Last Tang Standing*, and here) to Asian parenting. The scene never recovered, but at least I got some books (and friends) out of the experience—and this is one of them, directly inspired by my time onstage. I hope you'll have as much fun reading this as I did writing it.

I wanted to thank the following individuals who helped with this book, in one way or another:

U. K. Shyam, current national 100m record holder of Singapore, who patiently gave of his time when I consulted him on his experiences with the US college athletic recruitment process and sprinting.

Ying Wei Lum, still the best doctor in Baltimore, and Ian Matthews, still the best ER doctor in Singapore (and sometimes funny 😊).

Tina Forbush, college counselor, who talked me through the US college admissions process for overseas students and answered many, many panicked messages. Any errors are mine entirely.

Prescott, Jon, Kenneth, who also helped me re-create an authentic American international school experience.

Sam See, one of Singapore's best comics, and a friend.

Suffian Hakim, Sarah Bagharib, and Sarita Singh, who gave me some useful feedback during the writing of this book.

Writing this book was a riot and a half, and I had a wonderful time collaborating with my editor, Rebecca Kuss, assisted by Ashley I. Fields. I also wanted to thank everyone who worked on my book at Hyperion, even if we never officially crossed emails!

I am grateful for the support of my families, the Hos and the Wohl-Schneiders, without whom my writing career would not be possible.

I have made wonderful author friends in my career so far, but I must single out Jesse Sutanto, who is a genuine light in my life, as well as Ali Hazelwood and Hanna Alkaf, both generous and kind souls who have helped me a lot during this journey.

My agent, Katelyn, thanks for guiding me thus far, I am of course your biggest fan; I also want to thank the entire JGLM fam (Denise and Sam especially) for all your kind support.

To my loyal and new readers: Thank you for reading *Royce*. Please remember to rate and review this book when you're done; it's a massive help to authors, wherever they are in their careers.

And of course, my husband and my children, who understand that when my eyes glaze over at dinner, it's not them, it's me, and I must immediately jot down the book idea or bit that the Muse has granted me or toss and turn all night trying to recall it.

And to all the comics out there: I'm rooting for you. It's not easy being funny, and it's not easy being funny in a world where every word is weighed and dissected online for far longer than that joke was meant to run in real life. Keep on trucking.